Blaze is tu

Watch for our ne
featuring
There are six sizzling reads for you in 2014,

starting with

UNFORGETTABLE
by Samantha Hunter

CAPTIVATE ME
by Kira Sinclair

UNRATED!
Super-Sexy Reads

Don't miss your

Blaze.

March books

From 1st March 2014, Blaze paperbacks will no longer be available as we'll be producing the Blaze series exclusively in eBook format.

Look out for our **special Blaze offer** and find out how you can stay up to date with the latest news at the end of this book.

UNFORGETTABLE

BY
SAMANTHA HUNTER

MILLS & BOON

Published in Great Britain 2014
by Mills & Boon, an imprint of Harlequin (UK) Limited,
Eton House, 18-24 Paradise Road, Richmond, Surrey, TW9 1SR

© 2014 Samantha Hunter

ISBN: 978 0 263 91225 8

14-0114

Harlequin (UK) Limited's policy is to use papers that are natural, renewable and recyclable products and made from wood grown in sustainable forests. The logging and manufacturing processes conform to the legal environmental regulations of the country of origin.

Printed and bound in Spain
by Blackprint CPI, Barcelona

Samantha Hunter lives in Syracuse, New York, where she writes full-time for Mills & Boon. When she's not plotting her next story, Sam likes to work in her garden, quilt, cook, read and spend time with her husband and their dogs. You can check out what's new, enter contests or drop her a note at Sam's website, www.samanthahunter.com.

For Sandy, always a puppy in my heart.

1

"ERIN, C'MON, YOU'LL have fun, and if anyone needs to have some fun, it's you."

Erin Riley shook her head at her friend Dana Rogers, who grabbed Erin's hand and pulled.

"Come join me," Dana invited. "Let loose."

Erin let her friend drag her along, and before she knew it, strong arms were boosting them up on top of the bar. Dana was grinning like the wild woman that she was, dancing even before the music started.

They were having a fun night out, and as she looked around the bar, Erin was self-conscious at first. She seriously thought about climbing back down, but everyone was watching and chanting *dance, dance, dance*.

So she started to dance, and that's when things got better. A lot better.

Letting go, she raised her arms high and put more hip-swing into it, much to the crowd's appreciation. Dana hooted in approval and danced with her. Erin had to admit, she enjoyed how the guys were slack-jawed as they watched. She smiled at them and winked as she turned and shimmied to a blaring version of "I'm

Alright." For that one moment, she *was* all right. Perfect, in fact.

Erin felt sexy, which she hadn't in a long time.

Noting the heat in the eyes of a few men who watched, she also felt powerful. In control, for the first time in a while.

Dana was right. This was exactly what Erin needed, so she planned to enjoy herself. This was her second chance. She wasn't going to waste one single minute.

She'd almost died, after all. A former firefighter, she'd been inside a building when an explosion had knocked her down and she'd been trapped by a loose beam. After several brain surgeries and a week in an induced coma, she'd come out of it all with no memory of her life. Most of her adult past had been obliterated, though she could remember her childhood. The doctors said it was uncertain when or how much of her memory would come back.

Tastes and some emotions remained. She could like or dislike something—a place, food, etc. She could experience familiarity, without remembering something exactly. It was the same with people. For instance, the firemen she'd worked with for eight years had been her support system since she got out of the hospital. Still, they were strangers to her—mostly. When she was with them, or with Dana or her sister, she could *feel* the familiarity even when she couldn't remember their history together.

She couldn't, however, recall anything about the accident or being a firefighter. Another member of her crew had died in the same incident, and there was an ongoing investigation since the fire had been arson.

Erin couldn't remember what happened. And she

had tried. She had suffered and punished herself for not being able to remember, and she couldn't do it anymore. All she knew was what people told her.

She also couldn't remember who she was, but she finally realized that meant she could be anyone she wanted. Smiling as someone handed her a beer, she and Dana danced right into the next song.

Good thing she'd worn her new jeans and one of those tees that showed a teeny hint of belly. It was all courtesy of a recent shopping trip with Dana, who had helped Erin supplement her otherwise pitiful wardrobe. Apparently it was something Dana had wanted to do for quite some time.

When she'd gotten home from the hospital, Erin thought there must be a guy living at her house. Most of her clothes were for work or bore the insignias of her department. Not a single pair of high heels in the lot—not like the ones she was wearing now.

Even her pajamas were cotton pants and oversize fire department T-shirts.

Those days were over.

Sending a sexy smile to the cute bartender, she planned on making up for lost time. She tilted her head back and chugged her beer as the song ended, enjoying the chants that accompanied her finale.

When she was done, her head spun. Her skin was warm. She laughed, wobbling a bit as she handed her glass back to the bartender.

She and Dana finally made their way down off the bar to riotous applause. Several burly men—most of them firemen or cops—happily offered a helping hand.

Dana was a dispatcher and engaged to a firefighter

in the unit Erin had worked with. He met her back on the floor with a kiss.

"I can't leave you alone for a minute, can I?" Scott scolded, but he was grinning. His eyes were warm as he took in his fiancée. Erin averted her eyes discreetly from the deepening kiss that the two were sharing in front of everyone.

Erin cleared her throat. "Okay, well, then, I'll just go back to the table and eat all of those wings."

Dana never broke the kiss while waving her away, making Erin laugh. She suspected the lovebirds were going to find some privacy, and she left them to it.

As she walked back to their table, she figured she should have known better. She could hear the boisterous voices of the crew the minute she crossed the floor toward the tables at the back. They saw her, too. No doubt they'd seen her up on the bar, as well.

"What's up, Buttercup?" Hank shouted.

"Tulip!" Leroy followed up.

"Daisy!" Derek added with a snicker.

The last one got a round of high fives as Erin took a breath and approached the group, smirking at them for teasing her about her work at the flower shop. Her sister owned the shop and had taken her on as soon as Erin was able.

Still, it was a far cry from being a firefighter to working as a florist. Not so long ago, she'd been one of the guys, so she tried to act like it. As if nothing had changed.

"You guys calling each other pet names again?" she asked as she joined them. Giving as good as she got was par for the course with this bunch. "Leroy *must* be Daisy, since he's always fresh as one."

Another round of laughter rose and then settled down as Leroy eyed her from the other side of the long table.

"Someday, when your memory comes back, you'll pay for that one." The threat was playful and made with a glint in his eye.

"I hope that day comes," she said, more serious than she meant to be.

"We do, too," Pete said as they all became quiet.

Erin frowned. "Sorry, didn't mean to be a downer. Hand me a beer?"

"Gladly. Nice moves up there, by the way. We never knew you could dance like that."

"Yeah, me, either."

She accepted another beer and helped herself to some wings.

"Carry on, then," she said, waving them on like a queen to her subjects. That succeeded in lightening the mood again.

"Hey, we thought of something that could help with your memory," Leroy said.

"Yeah. What?"

"You said the doctors told you that things from your life before could help bring your memory back, right? We have a lot of stories we could tell."

"Those stories are probably things she'd rather leave forgotten," Pete said with a grin.

Erin smiled. It was good to be around friends who could joke with her about her memory loss. It balanced out the absolute terror and grief that had been frequent, though less so these days.

"I'm game. Take your best shot."

"Well, there was this time when Riley came running out from that fire at the old folks' home, carrying the older gentleman, buck naked and thrown over her shoulder," Pete offered with a wry smile. "They got him on the gurney and he wouldn't let the medics take him away until he asked her out on a date."

Erin's jaw dropped. "That did *not* happen."

She liked how they called her by her last name. She felt more like a "Riley" than an "Erin" anyway, in spite of her sexy clothes.

"Oh, it really did. And you said yes."

The guys made a few lewd comments and laughter picked up, and Derek put a hand on her arm.

"You were being kind. You brought him dinner a couple of nights when he was in the hospital and watched TV with him. That was your date. He passed away a few months later, and his family sent you a thank-you for your visits."

Erin swallowed hard and nodded.

"There was also the time we told you everyone was dressing up for duty on Halloween and you showed up at the station as Princess Leia. The alarm rang almost as soon as you arrived. You had to change in the truck, which you did, without batting an eye, I'll add. Though you fought the whole fire wearing the braids. I have to find the picture that made it into the paper," Pete said nostalgically.

Even Erin had to laugh at that. She lifted her hand to her hair, now boy-short as it grew in after being cut and shaved for surgeries. She couldn't remember it long, but in most of the pictures she saw, she wore either ponytails or braids. She wasn't sure if she'd grow it long again. Having it short was convenient, especially for summer. Her sister said it framed her face better, and made her eyes look bigger.

"You always swore like a sailor. More quarters in the jar for pizza night from you than anyone."

Erin appreciated them filling in gaps for her, but the stories felt as if they were about someone else. She was just getting to know these people whom she had known for years. Men and women who had trusted her with their lives.

She wanted to have it all back, her history with these people. Her whole life. It wasn't likely; the doctors said the longer she didn't recall anything, the less chance that she would.

She put her beer on the table as her eyes burned.

"Hey, you okay?"

"Yeah, fine," she said, pretending to bend to fix the strap on her shoe while she got hold of her emotions.

Apparently, they did this often, getting together for sports or food. Erin couldn't remember, but it did feel normal. Normal was nice.

When she rose, they were already talking about other things—sports and upcoming vacations. She took a chair near the wall and munched on her wings.

As she licked some of the sauce from her fingers, she stopped and looked up, feeling as if she was being watched. And she was.

Bo Myers sat across the room, alone at his table, his eyes glued to her as if she were the only one there. His eyes rooted her to the spot and sent licks of heat scattering over her skin. She lost track of everything and almost tumbled her plate to the floor, catching it before it fell.

He was the local fire marshal. She'd met with him

a few times since the accident. He'd been there when she'd woken up in the hospital.

He was an intense, somewhat intimidating man in every way—tall, brooding and powerful—with a serious face and eyes that meant business. She wasn't sure she'd ever seen him smile. Irrationally, she always wanted to touch his hair. Bristly on top, but soft, she imagined. As if he had just rolled out of bed or gotten caught in a strong wind.

His magnetic eyes were, right now, focused on the finger she had been sucking some of the wing sauce from. She removed it from between her lips and grabbed a napkin.

The guys told her that Bo had been one of their crew before he'd moved on to being an investigator. It was hard to imagine. He was terse, quiet, and not at all like the rest of the group.

There was no question that he affected her differently than the other guys. They were all handsome, fit, and yet she felt nothing but some vague friendliness toward all of them. As if they were her brothers, or at least friends.

Bo, whom she hardly knew at all, had been taking center stage in her dreams lately—in a mostly naked way. The way he was looking at her now was almost as if he were angry, or as if he were undressing her. She wasn't sure which, or which she wanted it to be.

"I think it's time for me to go," she said too brightly. She stood, pushing her plate to the side.

The guys barely noticed, and after a round of goodbyes, she decided to walk home. Her house was only a mile away and she needed the fresh air. And to get away from Bo Myers. But as she walked to the door, she made the mistake of looking back. His gaze met hers across the room, sending a shiver down her spine.

Then, as she reached for the door, he got up and headed directly toward her.

BO WASN'T SURE why he was following Erin as she left. She didn't want his company. He should definitely keep his distance, as he had been doing. A clear, professional distance that ate away at him a bit each day.

He couldn't remember the last time he'd slept except due to sheer exhaustion. He'd come here tonight to remedy that with a few drinks. Maybe more than a few. He didn't know she'd be here, and if he had, he would have avoided the bar completely. There were plenty more in Syracuse.

He thought he was seeing things when she'd gotten up on that bar—or rather when she'd been hoisted up by a guy with his hands on her ass. Her dancing had nearly killed him. It was so unlike her—except in private. She'd danced for him plenty of times—only for him.

The Erin he'd known would have died before dancing on a bar like that. Dana did it all the time. It was part of her personality, to be wild. Flirtatious. No one took it seriously—if they did, they'd have to deal with Scott.

But Erin, no way. It was all he could do not to drag her down off the bar, but what she did wasn't his business anymore. Unfortunately, his body didn't agree. When she'd started licking the barbecue sauce from her fingers, he'd stiffened and had to wait until he could stand up again.

He'd watched how she laughed and smiled with her

crew, not noticing their covert glances at her curves and movements. She'd been one of them, one of the guys—but not now. They touched her more often than they did before. Casual, supportive touches, but still. Things were already changing.

Bo noticed, because he couldn't touch her at all.

As he caught up with her, she stilled, looking right and left as if seeking an escape. That irritated him. He'd never done anything to hurt her. Quite the opposite.

"Riley," he said, feeling like a teenager who was talking to the beautiful girl he wanted, but he had nothing prepared to say.

He blinked, his head buzzing. Maybe he should have skipped that last Scotch.

"How are you?" he managed to ask.

Erin always had a way of looking at him. Her clear green eyes would darken to a mossy-jade, and she would seem to completely absorb him with that gaze. For a second, he'd caught that look again when their eyes met across the room. Bo felt that connection, strong as ever. He wanted to think what they'd had was too strong for the explosion, or her amnesia, to wipe out.

But now she looked at him like a stranger. There was a gleam of panic in her expression, as well. Why?

"Hello, Marshal. I'm good. Thanks. Actually, um, I was just leaving." Her tone was distant, polite. Eager to go.

She was the woman he knew—in her movements, her expressions—but in many ways she was oddly unfamiliar.

He knew what every inch of her smelled like, tasted

like. He knew everything she liked in bed and out, and the memories of it had haunted him for months. The thought of touching her made his heart slam harder in his chest.

They'd broken up a month before her accident, and in that time, he'd missed her deeply.

What was there to say, really? He'd asked her to make a choice, and she had. It wasn't him. Everything hadn't been right between them, he knew that. They both had secrets, both held back. When he wanted more, she wasn't willing to give it.

That was that.

The day of the explosion was one of the worst moments of his life.

But she was alive. Here in front of him, staring at him as though she very much wanted him to leave her alone.

To her, he was just another jerk in a bar. Or not even that. Anger boiled inside him, not at her, but at the situation. How many times, and in how many ways, could he lose this woman?

"'Night, Marshal." She slipped out the door into the evening without another word.

Bo took a long breath and returned to his table and sat, throwing back the last of the Scotch he'd ordered, cursing under his breath as he tossed a few bills on the table. He told himself to let her walk away.

"Everything okay, Bo?"

It was Hank, one of the crew. Bo had worked with them for five years after leaving the New York State Police, with his eye on the job he had now as an investigator. It was his ultimate goal—the only thing he ever wanted, except for Erin. He had to forget about her, especially when he was investigating her case.

Not that it was getting anywhere. She was the only witness to what had happened, and she couldn't remember a thing. It had been arson, though they had very little evidence to pursue. Whoever had set the fire had known what they were doing. Bo worried that they'd do it again if he couldn't catch them, but he had four other cases waiting on his desk.

"Yeah, everything's fine."

He dismissed Hank, heading for the door. He didn't feel like sitting around making small talk, and he could get drunk in his own living room.

It was a warm June night, and he walked out into the parking lot where the faint smell of cigarette smoke hung in the air. Picnic tables lined a patch of worn grass that ran down the side of the lot, where folks could hang out or smoke. Or find a few minutes alone, away from the crowded bar.

He looked for Erin, hoping she hadn't driven after how much she'd been drinking. He heard a noise, and spotted her at the edge of the lot. She was sitting at one of the tables.

"Erin?"

She turned, startled. "Oh, hi. Again."

"What are you doing?"

He saw her shrug in silhouette. "Just getting some air. Seeing how many constellations I can remember and wondering for the one millionth time why I can tell you exactly where the Big Dipper is but I can't tell you anything really important."

He nodded. "Well, you know the doctors said—"

"I know what they said," she cut him off. "It was more of a rhetorical question."

"Right. Sorry."

"Why are you out here?"

"I was leaving, but I'm glad to catch you before you left. You know, back in the bar…the dancing. That probably wasn't a great idea."

She frowned. "Why not?"

"You might go back to the job, or at least to the department, someday. You don't want to change the way the guys see you, and believe me, they're looking at you differently these days."

She shrugged a second time.

"I don't care. And it's really none of your business."

She'd gotten up from the table, intended to walk past him. He caught her arm gently, stopping her. He left it there for a beat, then dropped his hold.

"There's something else."

"What?"

"Joe's family. They want you investigated. Including any past reports or problems."

"Why?"

"They're grieving, looking for explanations."

"So they think they can pin his death on me?"

"They can't, and their accusations are unfounded, we know that. But it would be advisable to keep, well, a lower profile, I suppose. Until things are settled."

Now he was talking stupid, too. It was the truth about Joe's family, but none of this would impact the investigation. They had no grounds, medical or otherwise, to think that Erin was at fault.

Bo was telling her what he needed to tell her. For his

own reasons. It might not be right, but that was something different altogether.

"Screw that," she said flatly, trying to step around him.

The night air lifted her scent. It surrounded him, mixing with the sweet evening aromas of fresh grass and recent rain. Though distracted, he reached out, stopping her again. He knew he shouldn't.

"So now what? What next?" he asked.

They were close. She looked up at him, and the irritation in her face melted into something else. Bo didn't know if it was his imagination or wishful thinking, but heat arced between them the way it had back in the bar.

The way it always had.

"I don't understand this," she said, stuttering a bit, unsure. Rattled.

"What don't you understand?"

"Why I— What this *thing* is with you."

"What thing would that be, exactly?"

"Why I feel…when we… I don't know you. I don't even think I like you much," she said, shaking her head. "But when I look at you, I…"

She remembered. Or some part of her did.

He took her chin between his forefinger and thumb.

Bo's heartbeat was racing, too. He should walk away, call a cab and leave. He should let this be.

But he wasn't going to.

"I think I know what you mean. I feel it, too," he said, his voice a whisper.

Her eyes widened, and without warning she turned her cheek into his palm. The light rub of her skin on his set his blood on fire, and sense evaporated. Everything was lost to the night except being close to her, finally. Bo wanted to be closer.

He put his hand at the back of her neck, bringing her forward until she bumped up against him. Then they were kissing, and it was the first time he could breathe in months.

He thought it would be a quick, gentle kiss, but need came on so hot and sudden it knocked all the sense out of him. Her arms wrapped around him, and she was pressing into him as she always had, as hungry as he was.

Bo pulled her in tighter, parting her lips and kissing her as passionately as he could. Still it wasn't enough.

She was breathing hard as he slipped his hand along the small of her back, up under the edge of her shirt. Her skin was cool from the night air.

He explored her throat before working his way up to her lips again, but she pulled away, as if suddenly realizing what was happening. At the same time, voices rose in the lot behind them.

Bo couldn't think straight. He reached for her again. "Erin, don't—"

She pushed past him and ran down the sidewalk.

He stared after her, cursed under his breath, some little thread of clarity returning.

What had he just done?

If his place in the investigation had been iffy before, he'd just made it a lot worse. No one knew about his previous relationship with Erin—they'd seen each other in off-hours, never telling anyone. If the department found out now, well, things could get complicated. At best, they'd take him off the case. At worst…well, he didn't want to think about it.

They could think he was covering for her. They could think he was ethically compromised in any number of ways.

As he strode through the lot, reaching for his phone with slightly shaking hands, he couldn't help one thought that kept going around in the back of his head as her scent and taste still lingered. No matter what happened, it had been worth it.

2

ERIN DREW HER hand back quickly as she saw the blood well on her fingertip.

"Stupid thorns."

She was sorting roses for arrangements, making sure only the perfect, healthiest ones made it into the bouquets. Her fingers were freezing, but she couldn't do the work with gloves, so she'd risked the thorns.

Rinsing off the wound, she grabbed a paper towel from the rack and held it until it stopped bleeding. It was only one of about a dozen scrapes and punctures she'd gotten from the flowers that day.

Working for a florist wasn't something she wanted to do, but it was *something* to do. She wasn't a paid employee, but Kit said she could always use the free help, and at least it kept her busy. Erin couldn't hole up in her house all day doing nothing until her memory came back. Then she really would go crazy.

However, even the prickly thorns didn't take her mind off Bo Myers.

Maybe she was fumbling the flowers so much because she hadn't slept all night, and when she did doze off, he was kissing her again. And more.

Much, much more.

She'd dreamed of him before in hazy, undefined ways, but last night... Well, her imagination had had a lot more material to work with. Her fantasies had been very specific. She remembered the whorls of dark hair on his chest as her fingers had touched him. The hard muscles of his thigh and in particular, a mark on the side of his hip that her mind returned to again and again. It was shaped like an almond, dark against his normal skin tone.

She'd pressed her lips to it, hearing him moan as her hands explored elsewhere.

And there had been apples.

Usually, her dreams were smoky and shapeless, everything occurring in jumbles against a blurred background. But last night she'd seen apples. As if she were looking up from the ground, under a tree full of ripe, red fruit.

When he'd kissed her outside the bar, it had been a surprise, but on a deeper, more basic level, it had been familiar and *right*.

Her hands trembled as she returned to the roses, sorting them by variety without further injury and putting them in fresh water and into the coolers. Then she headed out front, where she saw that the closed sign had been flipped and her sister was bent over the computer on the counter.

"Evening already? What time is it?"

"Four-thirty. I closed a bit early."

Kit—short for Kathleen, a name that Erin learned her sister had never liked—looked up from her work, eyeing the front of Erin's shirt with a smirk. "The roses biting again?"

"How could you… Oh," she said, looking down to see blood from various scrapes had gotten on the white blouse she wore.

"I told you to wear one of the aprons," Kit said in true older-sister, know-it-all tone. So what if she had been right?

"I will next time, *Kathleen*," Erin said with appropriate sisterly sarcasm.

Kit's lips twitched with humor.

"Well, it's good that you remember how to be annoying."

Erin stuck her tongue out and they laughed. Joking around was good and helped dispel some of the ghosts she'd been wrestling with—and her thoughts about Bo.

"Do you mind if I take off early, too?"

Kit looked at Erin over the top of her glasses, frowning. "You're going out with the guys from the firehouse again?"

Tension settled between them, as Erin struggled between telling Kit what happened and telling her she wasn't her mother. Erin could go where she wanted, including out with the crew.

Kit had told her outright that she'd never been a fan of Erin's chosen profession. The accident had made her even more set against it. Kit didn't even seem to like her hanging out with the guys, but Erin enjoyed seeing them. She wondered what her sister would think about what happened with Bo.

"I can tell something is bothering you. Spill." Kit was way too perceptive.

Erin chose her words carefully. "Do you know if I

was seeing anyone before the accident? If there was a guy? Someone special?"

Kit's eyebrows rose. "I don't think so. You were all about the job and never mentioned anyone. Did you remember something?"

"I don't know. Maybe. I've been having some dreams, and I can't tell if it's a memory or a figment of my imagination, but I saw someone at the bar last night, and he was…familiar."

"How so?"

"You know. Familiar," Erin said again, with an emphasis that made her sister nod knowingly.

"Well, I suppose you might have hooked up with someone and not said anything. But you never told me about it, not that you would have."

Erin frowned. Apparently, she and Kit had not exactly been close sisters, though Kit had been there for her every minute since the accident. Whatever tension was between them didn't matter when the chips were down.

"Did he know you?"

Erin nodded. "There was definite chemistry. The explosive kind."

Erin couldn't remember anything about sex, not since making out with her senior year boyfriend in high school and letting him get her bra off. That was her last clear memory.

It was disconcerting, not knowing her sexual history. She'd been on birth control at the time of the fire, so she must have had an active sex life, but she couldn't remember any of it.

"Well, what did he say?"

"Um, not much, really. I kind of bolted before we talked."

Kit's expression was sympathetic. "I know this is hard for you, and it has to be frightening to bump into people, especially men, who might know you better than you know yourself, but maybe he could help. Maybe if you talked with him, he could help you remember. Was he a member of the department?"

"Yeah, he was. We talked, and I left. I guess I, well… Last night was weird."

"Talk to him if you get a chance. But make sure there are other people around, you know, the usual safety drill."

Erin had been thinking the same thing. It was clear that there was something between her and the fire marshal, but the only one who could tell her what was Bo. But if they had been an item, why had he kept it secret until now?

"Or maybe it's better if you don't," Kit said, changing gears. "Being with the guys so often at the firehouse could be a bad idea. You should be moving forward, not get stuck in the past."

Erin couldn't help the irritation that her sister's comment spawned. "They're my only friends. And they help. If I can get my memory back—"

"I think you have to face that you're not going back to that job."

"There's a chance, if I can get my memory back—"

Kit shook her head. "I'm sorry, honey, I know you loved it, but it would be like starting from scratch, even if you do remember."

"Then that's what I'll do."

"Being with them gives you false hope. Keeps you

from finding something new. I don't know why you'd want to go back to being a firefighter anyway. It nearly killed you."

Kit's features tightened with fear and grief, and Erin's heart softened. The nurses said that her sister had been by Erin's bedside every day at the hospital. Some nights, too, when things were iffy about her condition. Kit had also taken care of their mother when she was dying, and ran her own business while she was helping Erin.

Erin tried to imagine what it was like for people having to deal with her accident and her amnesia, but she was also tired of feeling responsible for it. She really didn't agree with her sister about hanging out with the guys—it didn't give her false hope. It gave her some sense of stability. But she could understand her sister's fear.

"I'm sorry it was so hard for you. And I'm grateful you've let me be here with you. It's nice to spend time together. I assume we didn't do that so much before?"

Kit sighed, the strain melting away somewhat. "No, we didn't. Sometimes we'd have lunch on your days off, but even then, you were usually at the firehouse. I'd meet you there."

"I'm sorry. The more I hear, the more I know that I gave everything to the job. Maybe too much. But I *do* appreciate it. And I appreciate you. I really do."

Erin closed the distance to hug her sister.

Kit hugged her back. "I'm not trying to be critical. I know they're your friends. But I worry about your future."

"It's only been a few months since I've been out of the hospital. I'm not giving up yet on getting my past back. I don't know what I'll do with my life, and the job, but right now I need to remember. I have to have hope, false or otherwise."

"Okay. But maybe you can find a safer line of work next time?"

Erin held up her scraped fingers. "Like handling flowers? I'm willing to bet I didn't end up this bloody on a daily basis as a firefighter."

Kit couldn't resist a grin, shaking her head. "True, you are not a natural florist."

"What are you doing tonight?" Erin asked, changing the topic.

"Quarterly taxes for the store are almost due. I'm way behind on accounting."

Erin felt a pinch of guilt; her sister was behind, no doubt because of her.

"Another night working? So I take it you're not seeing anyone right now, either?"

Kit rolled her eyes. "The market has been down lately."

Erin chuckled. "Tomorrow night, I'm taking you to dinner."

"That sounds nice."

"Great. It's a date."

Erin left, glad the tension had lifted. With her sister anyway. She was one big knot inside at the thought of seeing Bo again.

Her watch told her that she might already be too late to catch him at his office. There was no way she could get home to change and then head over to the station, but she didn't want to wait until tomorrow.

When she reached her car, the decision was made for her as her cell phone rang. She looked down to see Bo's caller ID. Not his name, just "Fire Investigation," which was how he'd been labeled in her work contact list. If they did have a personal relationship, there was very little evidence of it. Wouldn't there have been emails or phone calls? A cute picture of him on her phone?

"Hello?"

"Erin."

"Marshal Myers."

"Bo, please."

She hadn't used his first name before, but considering she might have ended up having sex with him on the picnic table outside the bar if no one had interrupted the night before, she supposed they were way past formalities.

"I was hoping you might be able to meet me. To talk, if you have time," he said, breaking into her thoughts.

Hearing his voice made her think of his lips. His lips made her think of—

She ruthlessly cut off that line of thought. "I was thinking the same thing, actually. I'm leaving the shop now. I could be at your office in—"

"No, not the office. Your place?"

She paused. Was this smart? Why didn't he want to meet at his office, which was a safe, neutral ground? Did she feel comfortable enough with Bo to invite him to her house?

In a sense, no. She wasn't sure that what they had to talk about was fodder for public ears, either.

"How about that diner by the lake? June's?" she suggested. It had booths in the back, enough privacy to talk, but it was public enough so that they wouldn't, well, whatever.

He was so quiet she thought that he might have hung up.

"Are you there?"

"That works. An hour?"

"Okay, yes. That's good."

They hung up without further discussion.

The hour would give her time to go home, wash up and change her shirt, but as she stood in front of her closet twenty minutes later, she froze, unable to choose what to wear. All of the clothes she'd picked out with Dana now seemed too sexy—too inviting.

But she didn't want to wear any of her department shirts—that felt like a lie.

She growled in frustration, disgusted. She was meeting him at a diner, and it wasn't a date. They were going to talk. That was all. She didn't need to dress to impress.

Taking a blue blouse from the hanger, she put it on with the jeans she was already wearing and didn't bother checking in the mirror lest she change her mind. It would be fine. She lifted her hand to her hair, a reflex making her try to push it behind her ear. She kept forgetting it was short.

Locking the house, she took off and arrived at the diner just in time. The fire department SUV that Bo drove was already parked in the lot. He was early.

Her heartbeat picked up pace, and her hands were actually sweating. Damn.

"Oh, get over yourself, Riley," she muttered under her breath.

Getting out of the car, she slammed the door harder than she meant to. Nerves. She calmed herself, then walked inside.

Bo was at the back—apparently having had the same thought she did about privacy—though June's wasn't too full tonight. All the booths around them were empty, and she stepped forward. He was talking to a server who was putting a drink and menus on the table, and he smiled at the young waitress.

There was no flirtation—it was simply a friendly smile—but it tripped Erin up. He was in his uniform this time and that alone was striking. But that smile. It was killer. And it was for someone else.

A sharp pinch—jealousy?—grabbed at her chest. On the way to the booth, she passed the server who winked at her as she blew her bangs up, as if needing to cool down.

"Nice to see you again, hon. It's been a while."

The waitress had already hurried past by the time Erin could reply. She approached Bo with what she hoped was a casual, friendly smile.

"Hi. I hope you haven't been waiting long. I needed to go home and change. Crazy as it seems, I manage to make more of a mess of myself working with flowers than I probably did when I fought fires."

Oh, cripes, she was babbling.

He looked so good, sitting there in his uniform shirt, those long fingers wrapped around a coffee mug.

"It's only been few minutes. Thanks for agreeing to meet me."

So few words, and yet he managed to make her knees shake. She sat and found that she suddenly had nothing to say. Maybe this wasn't a good idea after all.

How the heck did she tell this man that she'd been having hot and heavy dreams about him, and she needed to know if they'd ever had sex? Jumping right in was the only option that came to mind.

"THE WAITRESS KNEW me. She seemed to know…us. Was there an…us?"

"We used to come here now and then," Bo hedged, taken aback by her sudden question. She was clearly nervous, and he was now doubting the wisdom of meeting again. Especially here.

He was unsure how much to share. Last night he'd shared way too much.

"With other people, like at the bar? Or together?"

Jill, the server, returned with Erin's drink, which he'd ordered on reflex. His error became apparent when she stared at the Coke and lime twist for a second, then met his eyes knowingly.

"How long were we together?"

He blew out a breath and leaned into the table, clasping his hands tighter around the mug as he rested forward on his elbows.

"Almost a year. Maybe I should have told you, but… it didn't seem like it would help. You'd been through enough, and I had a job to do. It didn't seem…relevant."

Her eyebrows flew up, and he saw the pulse fluttering hard in her throat. She reached for her soda and took several long draws.

"Are you okay?"

She put the glass down with a sigh. "I'm fine. After last night, maybe even before, I knew, on some level, but I never thought…a year? I thought it might have been a hookup or something. There's nothing that would have made me think we were dating, not for that long. No pictures, nothing in my home of yours… nothing."

"You weren't sentimental that way, and it was over well before your accident. You probably took me off your email and phone. But you were also paranoid about anyone finding out, so we didn't really text or stuff like that. Anyway, last night is what I wanted to talk to you about. I was out of line. I'd had too much to drink. No excuse, of course. But I wanted to know if you were going to file a report."

She frowned. "What kind of report? I've already given my statement, and I don't know what else—"

"A report on me, Erin. A complaint. About what happened."

"Why? Why would I do that?"

She sounded completely shocked, and he withheld his response as their food arrived. He wasn't really that hungry. He hadn't slept at all the night before, no wonder, and he'd been a growling bear all day. His supervisor wanted Erin's case closed, unsolved. There were others he needed to get to, but he couldn't let this go. Someone had hurt her; Bo was going to find out who it was, if he had to do it on his own free time.

Whatever it took.

"I shouldn't have done what I did. I know I'm all but a stranger to you, no matter what happened in our past. I had no right. I wanted to apologize, but I understand if you want to report it. I wanted to let you know that."

Unlike him, Erin dug into her spaghetti dinner as though it was going to save her from certain death. She'd always been a stress eater. He didn't know where she put it, she was so slim, but she always could eat as much as any of the guys on the crew.

He thought this would be easier. A professional meeting in a public place. He wanted to apologize and reassure her it wouldn't happen again. Still, she had a right to file a formal report. She was a member of the department, and he was investigating an incident in which she was involved. It was his job to let her know she had recourse.

"I don't want to file a report, and you have nothing to apologize for. I wasn't exactly fighting you off."

She said it with a wry grimace, as if more disappointed with herself than him.

"Erin, if I scared you, or hurt you—"

"You did neither." Her eyes met his squarely, but then she looked down, unsure again. "I think though… I need to ask you something."

"Shoot."

"Do you have a mark or a scar on your hip? Almond-shaped?"

Bo's heart skipped a beat. "Yeah, I do. A birthmark. You were always fascinated with it for some reason."

She fumbled her fork and nearly dropped it to the table as she caught her breath, audibly.

"Erin?"

She closed her eyes briefly, as if working up the courage to speak. Her newly short hair sharpened the angles of her cheekbones and her jaw, making her green eyes and her lips look larger and lusher than before. He'd always loved her long brown hair, wrapping it around his fingers and watching it fall over her shoulders, but he liked this new look, too. How it exposed the long lines of her throat and the curve of her neck and collarbone. The soft flesh of her earlobes.

He grabbed for his coffee, his mouth gone dry.

"Tell me what's wrong."

She lifted her gaze to his, and this time, it wasn't veiled or distant, but…there was a spark. She almost smiled.

"I *remembered* that, then. I remembered…after last night. I remembered a lot. It wasn't just dreams."

He straightened, his attention sharpened. "About the fire?"

She shook her head. "No. Not that. Things about you. Like the birthmark. I wasn't sure if I was just fantasizing, but…apparently it was real. I can't believe that I really remembered something!"

Paired with the astonished joy in her expression was the rosy flush of embarrassment. Because she was saying that she had remembered them together—having sex. Naked, since she remembered the birthmark.

"You dreamed about me?"

He didn't mean to ask aloud, but she'd taken him a bit by surprise, too.

Erin nodded. "Before last night, even. And I keep seeing…apples. Like there were apple trees somewhere."

"We made love in a local orchard once."

"Wow. That's…daring."

He smiled, warmth stirring at the memory. "We were alone. Except for some cows in the next field, but they didn't care."

"Where was our first date?"

He couldn't look away from her. "Here."

"Oh."

The significance of her choosing this place tonight seemed to dawn on her.

"So we broke up?"

"We did."

"Amicably?"

"Mostly, I guess."

He said the words tersely, unsure what else to say. He wasn't about to lay himself open for her again, not like this. Not to satisfy her curiosity.

"Why?"

"Why what?"

"Why did we break up? Did we have a fight? Did one of us cheat? Step out?"

He shook his head at the unthinkable, but somewhere in his mind, he wondered. They did have some arguments, because he knew—he sensed—that she was keeping something from him over the month or so before their breakup. He never found out what, but he knew she hadn't been seeing someone else. He was sure of it.

"No, no cheating."

"Then what?"

Everything inside Bo tensed. He really didn't want to peel the scab off this wound, but he could respect her need to know.

"I wanted more, you didn't."

"More of what?"

"More of you, more than we had. More than you were willing to give."

"What does that mean?"

"We were seeing each other in secret. We called it being discreet, since we worked together, but when I wanted people to know, you didn't."

"Why?"

"You were worried the guys would start to treat

you differently. Act differently. That it would affect your work."

She was quiet for a few seconds, her lips turning downward.

"So this was my fault?"

"It wasn't anyone's fault. It just ran its course."

"Wow, okay. Well. So we're…friends?"

"No. Last night should have shown you that we could never be friends. We…avoided each other. It was easier when I moved up to arson."

She nodded, looking uncomfortable again.

"I should go. I wanted to apologize and let you know I know I was wrong, and that you had the right to report what happened. It won't happen again, if that helps." His tone was formal, stiffened by painful memories and desire he couldn't do one damned thing about.

He took out his wallet and paid their check.

"If you do remember anything else, about the fire, that is, please call the office. You can always talk to my assistant if I'm not in."

He slid out of the booth, heading toward the door. Heard her feet on the tile floor behind him.

She caught up with him outside, before he reached his truck.

"Bo, wait. Please."

It was still light out as she followed him down the side of his SUV, between the cars.

He turned on her. "I can't do this, Erin."

He might as well be honest about it.

"Do what?"

"Talk about old times. Tell you all about us. It's over, and I can't see the point in raking back over it."

"I hurt you."

She stated it like a fact, emotionless, studying his face. Bo didn't want her to see, but he supposed that horse was already out of the barn.

"It's fine. Over and done."

She put a hand on his arm. "I'm sorry. For that, and for making you go back over this. From my dreams… from what I can remember, what we had was deep. I can feel it, even if I can't remember it all."

Erin stepped in closer. She didn't look nervous anymore. She was…something else. Bo froze, keys in hand.

"I don't want to play games. Or be played with," he said, his voice almost desperate as he swallowed hard, his breath short.

"I don't want to play games, either. I want to remember," she said softly, and leaned into him, hips first. Her hands drifted up his torso, over his chest to his shoulders as she pressed in closer.

A second later she was kissing him, and everything else fell away. She dropped gentle, easy kisses along his jaw, as if getting to know it again, mapping him with her lips. He swallowed, turning his face away, trying to get control. To resist. So she burrowed into the hollow of his throat, her tongue darting out to taste him.

He groaned her name. She sighed against him.

"If we parted ways, why does this all feel so right?" she asked, nibbling her way back up to his mouth.

Bo dropped his keys as his arms came around her, and his resolve crumbled, reversing their positions and pressing her into the side of the SUV, his mouth hungry for hers.

He slid one hand up under her blouse, his palm settling over her breast. She arched into the touch, an invitation. If this kept happening, they were going to end up naked in the back of his truck as they had the first time they'd left this diner and couldn't keep their hands off each other.

"History repeating itself," he muttered before he sank into another kiss. So much for good intentions.

3

"WE HAVE TO STOP," Bo said against her mouth, his hands on her shoulders, pushing her away.

Erin's entire being protested, and she shook her head.

"No."

Then his big hands were on her face, making her look at him. His cheeks were ruddy, his eyes hot. There was no doubt that he wanted her.

"I'm not going to do this. It's taking advantage, don't you get that? You're not in any state of mind to be making these decisions."

That riled her. She might have lost her memory, but she wasn't so incapacitated that she couldn't decide if she wanted a man or not. Granted, there were a few extra things going on that might influence whether she wanted *this* man, but still.

She dropped a hand, planted it between them as she closed her fingers around the erection that bulged against his slacks.

"Erin, don't," he almost begged, even as he pressed into her.

She took her hand away, shaken by the desperate look on his face. She'd hurt this man, and even if she couldn't remember it, she was doing it again.

Shame welled, and she stopped touching him, dropping her forehead against his chest.

"I'm sorry. I—I really want you, though. It's...crazy, but I do."

"I know. I want you, too."

"I could tell."

He bit out a short laugh, his hands still on her shoulders, squeezing lightly.

Her eyes closed, inhaling his scent, feeling the heat of his body, Erin tried to calm her own need, but her mind had different ideas.

"Oh," she whispered in surprise.

"What?"

"I can almost smell them, the apples. What the heck is it about the apples, Bo?"

Then she knew. As if she'd known it all the time. She pulled back to look up at him. "It was the last time we were together, wasn't it? The last time we made love?"

His jaw tightened, and he nodded before his head dropped back, staring upward at the sky as he answered. "Yeah."

The simple confirmation made another puzzle piece click into place. "So this is June...I was out of commission mid-February through April, and we broke up a month before the explosion, you said. January? So how could we have been in an orchard?"

"It was in October. Our last time. Then I left to train for the new job and came back at Christmas. We officially broke up shortly after that."

Something pulled at the far side of her memory, but she couldn't reach it and groaned in frustration.

"I can feel it's all there, like it's behind a wall, but I can't get to it," she said, closing her fists into his shirt, an expression of frustration more than desire this time.

His arms came around her, holding her close.

But it had happened again. Being close to him loosened up her mind, her reservations, or whatever. Memories, no matter how sketchy, started to form. Whatever he'd been to her, it was strong enough to pull her back in a way nothing else had been.

"It'll be okay, Duck," he said, and she thought he kissed her hair.

Her head came up quickly.

"Duck. You always called me that. Why?"

Blood raced through her veins, excitement coursing through her as she remembered another small thing.

"You were always hitting your head on the bar above the seat in the hook and ladder, and I had to remind you to duck so many times, I started calling you that."

His thumb was rubbing over her jaw, a tender gesture in the wake of the passion that had carried them away a few seconds earlier, though that was still there, too.

She measured her words carefully.

"You said you wanted more from me. I want more, too…from you. Now."

Her eyes met his, and she hoped he knew what she was asking.

Desire flared in the brown depths of his gaze. Of course he knew.

"It's not a good idea."

"Why not? Whatever it is between us, it's the only

thing that's made me remember *anything*. And if I can remember you, and us, maybe I can remember other things."

He smiled slightly, a hint of bitterness there as he dropped his hands from her shoulders and moved away, bending to grab his keys from the ground.

"Erin, as much as I'd like to help, I'm not about to sleep with you to see if it can help jog your memory. Thanks anyway."

She took a step back, giving him some space.

"It's not like that, not exactly," she tried to explain, though she supposed it was exactly like that. She did want to use him, in many delightful ways, and if it got her memory back, even better.

"What is it like, then?"

He caught her gaze, and she grimaced in the face of his challenge.

"Okay, yes, it is about getting my memory back. Can you blame me? I want my life back. My work. My sense of damned purpose," she said in frustration. "But I think there's more to it than that. For both of us. These dreams...they've been with me since the hospital. I didn't know what they were, but they get stronger, more...insistent. And I can see in your face that...you want me."

He pulled up straight, his body tensing. "That doesn't mean I should have you."

"No, but I think all of this might mean that we left things...wrong. Unsettled. There are still issues between us that need to be...addressed."

His eyes narrowed, pinning her. "And you think we should *address* these issues in bed?"

Her cheeks burned, but she didn't let him put her off.

She took a step forward, laid her hand on his chest. "In bed, or wherever else seems right. From what you tell me, and from what I dream about, we weren't exactly... conventional in our choice of places to have sex. Were there others? Other public places? What did I like, Bo? What did I want you to do to me? I don't remember... but I want to find out."

Erin knew she was pushing him, this man she hardly knew, but she also knew it was right. Deep inside, this felt like the right thing to do. She had to get him to see that, to get him past his doubts and uncooperative stance.

"You can't remember anything. How can you know what you want?"

"I know I want you. It's one of the few things I do know. It's not taking advantage, Bo. I'm fully aware of what I'm doing, and what I'm asking for."

"Do you? Really, Erin? Do you know what you're asking from me? After you walked away from us? After you were almost killed? You've looked at me— or rather, looked past me—for months, like a stranger. Do you really know what you're asking?"

His expression was fierce, and Erin was nearly knocked out of her certainty by the frankness of his objections. What he said was true. This wasn't just about her, but she needed to push anyway. She was desperate. He was her only hope to remember anything. To recapture what she once had.

"Maybe it would be different this time. I'm not sure. I only know that I need you, and I think you need me. You said you wanted more from me. I'll give you anything you want, Bo...whatever you need. If you give me...this. Give me a chance to get my life back."

He shook his head at her and got into his truck without another word. Erin's heart, and her hopes, sank. Her eyes burned as he started the engine.

She'd lost. She'd lost Bo and a whole lot more than that.

He sat in the driver's seat with the engine running, not moving.

She didn't move, either. Holding her breath that he'd get back out. Change his mind.

He looked out the window at her.

"I'm sorry, Erin, but I don't think this will work. You'll need to find another way. From now on, please contact my assistant if you need anything."

It was all he said, backing up and driving out of the lot.

Erin didn't realize she was crying until a breeze picked up and made her aware of the cool sting of tears on her cheeks. She got back to her car, sat there until it got dark. She'd taken her last shot and lost. Maybe her memory would come back, and maybe it wouldn't, but Bo clearly wasn't going to be part of it.

Maybe Kit was right. Maybe she had to stop clinging to this foolish hope and the past. It really was time to move on.

BO STARED BLINDLY at the email that filled his computer screen as he sat at his desk the next morning. It was early, and no one was in yet. He hadn't slept again. Not after hours of self-recriminations about backing away from Erin. It had been the right thing to do, but it wasn't what he wanted.

This, the content of the email, was supposed to be what he wanted. An offer he'd been working for his entire life—a job with the FBI's Critical Incident Response Group. He'd helped them a few times as a cop and once recently as an investigator.

He'd use everything he'd ever learned and take it all to the next level. They were asking him back for a final interview, and if it went well, they wanted him to start in August. In Virginia.

He rubbed his hand over his tired eyes, wondering why he didn't feel happier. This was important to him. Since his uncle had been seriously injured in the Pentagon on 9/11, it was all Bo had lived for. Until Erin.

She had made him believe that he lived for something else. For someone else. For a while anyway.

Erin's face, her desperation, her crushing disappointment as he'd left the night before, played in his mind's eye again.

"Damn it." He closed the email, got up and went to get himself another cup of coffee, and went to check out the morning's reports, but he couldn't concentrate.

Could helping Erin remember their past relationship trigger her ability to remember other things, perhaps the fire, or anything she saw that could help them? She'd seemed so sure that being with him would help her remember. Or maybe Bo was finding convenient connections, rationalizations to be with her, when he knew it wasn't ethical.

He felt like a jerk no matter what he decided. If he did as she asked, he was taking advantage of her situation to have sex with her, no matter how much she said that wasn't the case. She was desperate to get her memory back, but just because she'd remembered a few tidbits about him—them—it didn't mean that being with him would fuel any more recollections.

But walking away had been hard. She needed him, and she was right—he needed her, too. He'd tried to pull that need out by the root, but he'd failed. Their last few interactions had proved that.

They'd left things unsaid, and they'd never had any real closure. Maybe that's why she'd been so difficult to get over, even after all this time. And he wanted her so damned badly. It would be too easy to take what she was offering, and what then?

For her, it was only sex. She wanted him—he knew that, he could feel it. But she was just scratching an itch while trying to get her past back—and if that happened, she'd just remember that she hadn't wanted him before. Maybe she'd hate him even more for doing this.

Or maybe something would be different? She'd hinted at that. And she did seem…different. Some things were still the same, but there was no doubt that she'd been through a life-altering experience.

Could it have altered what she wanted from life? What she wanted from him?

The chances of her ever going back to firefighting were slim. She had to know that. Even if her memory came back, her physical status after the brain surgeries and her psychological state would all need to be re-evaluated. Would the crew trust her as they did before? Could she even walk into a fire, or would she freeze?

He put the reports aside and looked at his computer again. He'd done some research on the brain damage that she'd suffered, and more reading on amnesia. It was a highly specialized topic. There were different forms of forgetting and different reasons people lost their memories.

Erin had what was typically called retrograde amnesia—she'd forgotten everything but her childhood memories up until college. But as Bo read through one particularly interesting medical report online, a theory formed in his mind. He found the number of a psychologist he knew who served the police and the fire departments, and called the number, finding himself on the line with Dr. Newcomb minutes later.

"How can I help you, Marshal?"

"I'm investigating the arson case that killed a fireman in February, and left one with serious brain damage and memory loss. I was wondering if you had a second to answer some questions."

"I do. I remember the case. I talked with Erin Riley. That's in the report, so it's not protected information, though I can't share any of what we spoke about, of course."

"Of course. I wanted to ask you about the type of amnesia Erin has. Her neurologist called it retrograde amnesia, caused by the head trauma she suffered, and probably from the brain surgeries, as well."

"Yes, I recall. I've never had a patient with nearly complete amnesia. Is she doing well?"

"I thought you said you were talking to her?"

"Only three times after she left the hospital, and then she opted not to come back."

Bo smirked. Sounded like Erin. She never did like doctors.

"I was reading up on it on the internet, and I wondered if the neurologist could have had it wrong. I was reading about a kind of amnesia called dissociative amnesia, where she could be blocking something traumatic—something stressful that her brain doesn't want to remember. Could it be that instead? Do you think she could have seen something at the fire that was so traumatizing that she doesn't want to remember it?"

"It's possible, though usually dissociative amnesia wouldn't be so encompassing. She might block the event, or things related to it, but not her entire life for over a decade."

"I see. Is it possible to have both? Perhaps the brain damage made what would otherwise just be selective forgetting much worse?"

"Hmm. It's definitely possible. Why do you think this could be the case?"

"I'm not a doctor, of course, but Erin has been remembering a few details regarding a long-term relationship she had—and she thinks that if she could be with the person in that relationship, she might remember more. Is that possible?"

"It's a very good sign that she's remembered anything—that's promising. It could take days or years, there's no telling. The brain is unpredictable. But triggers are a key factor—if there's a strong enough trigger, something so important to her, or so deep in her mind that she's recollecting it, it's certainly wise to pursue that. There's no way to know what or how much she might recall, but it's certainly possible that opening one strong channel of memory could lead to more recollections. And if she is repressing memories that are too frightening to recall, being with someone who makes her feel safe could help that rise to the surface, as well."

"Thank you, Doctor. I'll let her know."

"Marshal Myers, please tell Erin she's welcome in my office anytime, especially if she's going through anything unsettling in this process. I'd love to work with her if she needs more support."

"I'll tell her. Thank you."

Bo hung up, not sure if he should have made an appointment with the doctor. He probably needed his head examined for considering this, but it sounded as though it actually could be possible. That being with Erin could actually bring her memories back.

If that was the case, how could he move on with his life, into his future, and leave her behind without at least trying to help her get her life back, too?

Glancing up as other members of the office arrived, chatter floated in the door, and he smelled fresh coffee brewing. He got up and closed his door, needing to think.

He could potentially help Erin remember—maybe remember everything.

Was he really considering this?

He knew going in this time that there wouldn't be any real reconciliation. They were still "over"—nothing would change that.

He had other plans, too—the job in Virginia, for starters. He'd be here for only a bit more than two months if he got the job. Less than that, since he'd have to give notice and get someone new to take his place here. His assistant was good, but he wasn't ready to move up the ranks yet.

So that meant Bo had a month or so, just a few weeks, to cram in as much of their relationship as he could in hopes it might make her remember everything.

He just had to keep straight on the fact that he wasn't in it this time for the long haul, either. It could be just sex for him, too. A way to get her out of his system?

Closure. A way to leave things better between them than they had before.

It was also a chance to close the case, potentially. Maybe a way to save lives, since they still had an arsonist out there who hadn't been caught. What if Erin had seen something or experienced something that could help them find the person who had set that fire?

He knew he was talking himself into it, but it also made sense. There were more good reasons to take this risk than not to.

He'd already dialed her number, his phone in hand. He was surprised when she picked up.

"I thought you might not answer." He didn't bother with hellos.

"I didn't see who it was first."

She sounded tired. And cranky. For some reason, that made him smile. She was always irritable when she woke up.

"I'm sorry I was hard on you last night. Listen, I want to help if I can. Are you free today?"

"Say when."

Her tone perked up considerably. Bo closed his eyes, steadying his breathing. This felt surreal.

"I'm taking the rest of the day off. I've got a few things to sort out. How about if I come by your place later?"

"Okay. I'll be here."

She sounded nervous now, too. "I just want to talk, Erin. We need to talk about it…first."

"Okay. Sure. Good."

With that, they hung up. Bo packed his stuff and told his assistant to beep him only if there was an emergency. Then he was in his truck, thinking about

Erin, wondering if he wasn't making a huge mistake. It wasn't the first time he'd done that, and probably wouldn't be the last.

KIT STOOD BY the door as she scanned the crowd for Erin's cap of shiny brown hair. It was hard to see anyone in the busy crowd.

This was the place Erin usually went with her firehouse buddies, so it was where Kit figured she'd find her, but as far as she could see, there was no Erin.

She was doubly disappointed, having needed the break from her own worries. The past few months had been a balancing act, largely tilted to the side of addressing Erin's crisis, which was obviously huge. But Kit had her own troubles to deal with. Her flower shop wasn't doing well these days, especially with more people ordering flowers online or getting them at the local grocery stores. She'd been holding it together for a while, but she'd lost one large account last month, and the individual, walk-in business was dropping off, as well. In addition, getting good quality, fair-trade flowers wasn't inexpensive.

Most consumers had no idea that the flowers they bought at many outlets or online at discount prices were often shipped from countries that farmed the blooms and exploited local people, usually women, to keep prices down and their own profits up. Kit supported only fair-trade suppliers, and that meant her flowers were more expensive than most, but she included fair-trade information with all purchases. She found that her customers liked knowing they were buying flowers that truly helped people instead of subjugating them.

But in the troubled economy, being socially conscious was often a luxury.

All Kit had ever wanted to do was run a flower shop. It was her dream, since she was a little girl. She'd worked at one as a teenager, and she used the college money left to her by her parents to open the shop. It had done very well for a while. But times changed, and the internet, recessions and so forth were taking their toll on her dreams.

The shop and her sister were the most important things in her life—they were all she had left. Erin was young when their father had died of a heart attack at the station. He was always at the station. Lived and died there, literally. Their mother was gone eight years later. Erin had been out working on a fire when their mom passed away.

Sometimes Kit felt terribly alone. Feelings weren't always fair, she knew. Sometimes, they were awful, confusing things. Like when the doctors said that Erin had amnesia and very likely wouldn't return to fire-fighting.

Kit had, on some level, been happy about that. It wasn't very supportive, she knew that, but she was so happy to have Erin around again. But Erin seemed drawn to her old crew, even now. It was like an obsession.

As Kit moved farther into the room, she didn't see her sister anywhere, and her heart sank. So much for sister time.

"Hey, you're Riley's sister...the flower lady."

Kit turned toward the voice and found a very, *very* large man standing near a tall table, where he put a beer down and faced her, holding out his hand.

"I'm Hank Aaron."

She raised her eyebrows.

"No joke, that's my name. Dad was a huge baseball fan. Mom couldn't talk him out of it. And you're... Kathy?"

"Kathleen, but everyone calls me Kit." She smiled, looking into his face. "Now I remember. We met at the hospital a few times. I'm sorry. I was not quite coherent back then."

She reached out, shook his hand, which swallowed her own. His skin was rough, but not in an unpleasant way. It scraped on hers and made her wonder how those large hands would feel on the rest of her.

"Understandable. That was hell, waiting to see what would happen, especially for you. Families have it hard in our business. Can I get you a beer?"

She paused, took her hand back. She was going to say no. It was obvious Erin wasn't here, but then Kit changed her mind as her stomach rumbled.

"That would be nice, thanks. I might order something to eat, too. I was hoping to meet Erin here, but I guess she had other things to do."

Hank frowned. "Do you think she's okay?"

"I do. She shut off her phone. She does that when she wants to be left alone. I know what she's going through is so hard...and I don't know how to help most of the time. I try to give her space to figure things out, but I'm never quite sure what to do. Or if she needs me for anything at all."

She failed to keep the slight edge of resentment out of her tone, and Hank noticed.

"I imagine this is difficult for both of you. Riley, um, Erin hasn't been quite the same since she woke up.

We notice it, too. She's…I don't know. Like she's looking for something, I guess. There, and then not there."

"At least I get to see her more these days. I think you guys knew her better than I did before. She certainly spent more time with you all, and I know being around you now is a comfort to her. But I worry she's too caught in the past to move forward. She doesn't like hearing that, as you can imagine."

Hank drew himself up, all six feet who-only-knew-how-many-inches of him, and looked down at her with calm understanding. How did this big bear of a man come off so Zenlike? As he started to speak, she expected him to make excuses and find some means to escape her dumping all her problems on him. She never did that, not as a habit, and wouldn't blame him for wanting to get clear of her.

"Have you had anyone to talk to since this happened?" he asked instead.

A beer came, magically appearing in her hand. Hank said something to the woman that she couldn't hear over the noise.

"I ordered some dinner and got something for you, too."

Kit was taken aback at his presumptuousness, but then she acquiesced as she knew he meant no offense. And he would know what was good to eat here anyway.

"Thank you."

"C'mon, the back is quieter. It can get nuts around here on the weekend."

He led her to a table near the back, pulled out a chair for her and then sat himself. He looked sort of ridiculous at the small tavern table, being lumberjack-sized.

"So you didn't answer my question."

"What question was that?"

Kit started to relax a bit. It had been a long time since she'd been out for an evening, even longer since it had been in a bar with any member of the opposite sex. She'd needed a break more than she thought.

"Have you had a chance to talk to anyone about what's gone on with Erin? The department has counselors for us, and they work with family, too, when it's needed."

She shook her head. "I'm fine. I was just ticked off that she stood me up."

"Yeah, she gets caught up in her head these days. Can't blame her, but it's not easy to live with, either. None of this is. Our schedules, lifestyles...it's hard on loved ones."

"Yours, too?"

"I'm not married, if that's your way of asking. Or involved."

Kit's felt her cheek warm. "I wasn't asking, really, that's none of my—"

"Then it was my way of letting you know."

Kit stopped, flustered. "Oh. Okay."

Luckily, the server arrived with their food. Kit was immediately in love—with the chicken.

"Dig in. Don't be shy." Hank smiled, triggering another warm curl low in her belly that wasn't caused by the spicy aroma of the food.

Kit didn't hesitate, starting in on the chicken and handmade fries without reserve, licking her fingers when she was done. Hank was working his way through his, too, and eyed the remnants left on her plate.

"You and your sister both know how to eat, that's

for sure." He said it appreciatively, and Kit couldn't help but grin.

"Yeah, my parents believed in healthy eaters. Good thing they also passed on their active metabolisms."

"You are in nice shape," he said with a twinkle in his blue eyes.

She couldn't explain her response except that it had been a very long time since she'd been with a man. She was thirty-three, and had always imagined she'd be married with kids by now, but life hadn't made time for romance. It did, however, make time for lust and the occasional fling.

Things were definitely stirring here at the table between her and Hank. She wasn't sure when she stopped thinking about having a long-term relationship—her work, her parents, her sister…it all had consumed the years. Still, she enjoyed a night of hot sex now and then, when it was with the right guy.

But Hank wasn't the right guy. He was a firefighter, for one—definitely not her type—and he had worked with her sister. It was best, when scratching an itch, to have things as anonymous as possible. There was a good chance her path and Hank's could cross again, and that meant it would be a mistake to fan this little ember.

They used the wet wipes at the table to clean their hands, and Kit figured it was time to leave. She didn't want to send false signals by staying too long. She'd catch up with Erin tomorrow. She couldn't imagine where her sister was, but Kit's mood had mellowed on a full stomach.

Some live music started in the main room, though,

drowning out her voice. Hank said something, too, but she couldn't hear him, either.

"What?" she said loudly, her hand to her ear.

He smiled as he stood and reached his hand out to her in the universal invitation to dance.

Kit was momentarily stunned. What she wanted and what she should do were in opposition to each other.

What she wanted won. Just for tonight, she wanted to forget that she had to be at the shop at five in the morning and that she had responsibilities. That she had worries and troubles.

That there was no one to go home to.

She wanted to dance with Hank and enjoy her evening.

So she took his hand and let him lead her out to the floor, where he pulled her up close and proceeded to show her how well a big man could move.

4

ERIN WAS A knot of nerves and anxiety as she got ready for Bo to come over. He'd said they'd talk—and she knew they had to do that, but she wanted to do more.

Maybe.

She wanted to do whatever she needed to do to get this going between them.

"You're such a romantic," she said to herself, smirking in the mirror as she changed her shirt again, unable to decide if she should go with a bra or not.

She'd been with the man for a year. But for her, it was like a first date. A first time.

What had changed his mind?

Was she crazy? Throwing herself at him because it might prompt a few memories? When she was with him, next to him, she felt certain.

Less so right now.

When she heard his truck in the driveway, her hands went cold. She was being ridiculous. So nervous.

She reassured herself that Bo wouldn't do anything she didn't want to do. She knew that. He would leave this up to her. Maybe that was what was so difficult. It would be easier, in many ways, if he would just make the decisions. Take over.

The potential of *that* idea created a flutter in her pulse that got her out of the bedroom and down the stairs to meet him at the door.

She whipped it open before he even had a chance to knock.

"Hi." She was breathless.

He looked so serious; it didn't help with her nerves.

"Hi."

He must have changed out of his uniform, now in a pair of jeans and a faded black T-shirt. He was carrying a box. The way he braced it in his arms made his biceps pop a bit, and Erin found herself staring.

"Can I come in?"

She stood back quickly, feeling foolish. "Certainly. Yes, come in. Sorry. I guess I'm surprised, still. I didn't expect you to call."

He faced her as she closed the door, and suddenly she wished her house was different. More cozy and inviting. When she'd come home from the hospital, even she'd been surprised at how sparse it was. She owned fewer than a dozen pieces of furniture, and the whole house was still painted in the plain beige that it probably was when she bought it. There were only a few pictures and some department awards on the walls, and her kitchen was lightly equipped. As though she barely lived here.

Now, the functional gray sofa in the living room looked cold and boring. Not like something you'd want to curl up on with someone.

Redecorating—and maybe repainting—definitely needed to be done.

"I know. You surprised me, too, last night, when we...talked. I guess I needed some time to cool down and think about...everything."

"Sure. I get that. What's in the box?"

He seemed surprised, as if he'd almost forgotten he was holding it.

"Oh, you mentioned that you didn't have any mementoes of our relationship here. You kept that kind of thing at my place, I guess, so people from the department wouldn't see anything if they came by here."

She frowned. "Was I really that secretive about it?"

"Can I put this down somewhere?"

"Yes, over on the table, please."

"You were concerned about what people would think, and not without reason. Our department has never had any problems, and the guys all think highly of you, the brass, too, but it's not unreasonable to assume they might have seen you differently if they found out we were together. And given our breakup, it was probably for the best that they didn't know. You were just being smart."

"I guess." But it still didn't seem right to her. It wasn't as if they were doing anything *wrong,* after all. Hadn't she proven herself on the job well enough to not worry about that kind of thing? Apparently not. "But anyway, I guess it doesn't matter now."

"No, it doesn't. But I thought maybe...well, that we could talk about this...arrangement we discussed. And that maybe seeing these items could trigger something for you, too."

Erin had to fend off a stab of disappointment. What did she think was going to happen? That he was going to jump her bones and get down to it as soon as he came through the door? Did he bring the box as a way of hoping she might remember without having to have sex with her?

She had a feeling that she wasn't used to feeling insecure. Not normally. It didn't sit well.

"This is weird, isn't it? You're my ex, and for me, this is like a first date. Maybe it was a mistake?"

She folded her arms, rubbing her upper arms, unsure.

He closed the space between them, placing an arm around her shoulders.

"It is strange. Awkward, for sure, which is why we don't have to do anything but talk. You call the shots. You set the pace, you say stop or go, yes or no—and I'll listen. Period. Okay?"

Some of her uneasiness drifted away as she looked at him, and she knew this was going to be okay.

"Yes, thanks. Do you want some coffee? I have some scrambled eggs leftover from breakfast, too, if you want them."

"Sure, that sounds good. I'll help myself if you want to grab the box."

Erin agreed. He probably knew his way around her kitchen as well as she did, given their past. Carrying the box to the sofa, she waited for him to open the box. When he sat down beside her, the box was between their feet on the floor.

She opened it, unsure what to expect. On top were several pictures in cheap but nice frames. She took them out and saw her and Bo, in various settings, and a few of them each alone.

"Wow," she said, swallowing hard as she went through them.

It was like looking at someone else, somebody else's pictures. Her heart clogged her throat at one of them on a beach, pressed up close, face-to-face.

Bo looked at her as if she was his world. She looked at him as if she wanted to be.

"Who took this?"

"I did. Auto-timer. I set it, and then run back to get in the shot before the camera goes off. It was always one of my favorites. Up at Lake Ontario. There's a nature center there with a private beach, and we'd go there now and then. Lots of tall rocks and places to prop the camera."

He reported the details as though they were just... details. Finishing his eggs, he set his plate aside and grabbed his coffee.

"That one," he said as he pointed to the one in her other hand, "was after a fire at a school. When I came around the corner of the truck and saw you there, standing alone, I clicked the picture with my phone. It struck me...how beautiful you looked right then."

She studied the photo—she was standing in a background of dust and smoke, filthy, in her gear, leaning back against the truck with her eyes closed as if she had to escape for just a minute. Or as if she was too tired to move another step.

"Beautiful? I'm dirty and in bulky firefighting gear."

Even so, she examined the picture, intrigued. So this is what she'd done. This is what she'd looked like doing it.

"You helped save twenty-seven kids that day. They were all trapped in a science lab at the back of the school, and one little girl wouldn't come to any of us.

She was too frightened. But she came to you. It was a long, hard day, but a good one. I could see it all in your face, in your posture. How much heart you have. How much you had to hold back to keep a clear head and help them."

Erin swallowed hard, her eyes burning. She put the pictures down, overcome with emotion. If this was everything she'd been, what she'd had—she'd also lost all of it. The pain of it was unbelievable.

"You always liked this," Bo said softly.

He held up a strange turtle with a bobble head that had "I 'Heart' the Bahamas" on its back.

"From the one actual vacation we took together. Some more pictures from the island in there. A few other silly things. A book you bought me for my birthday and a shirt you used to sleep in at my place."

Erin wanted to look, but she also didn't want to. It was almost too much. It had been easier not knowing. Maybe that was a warning—it was a mistake to try to resurrect the past.

"Are you okay?" Bo asked.

She took a breath. "Yes. Sorry. This is a lot. More than I thought it would be."

She picked up the pictures again, sorting through them. The usual array of happy couple photos, always smiling, sometimes romantic and sweet.

It seemed impossible that this couple would have broken up. But they had, apparently.

Bo was quiet as she continued to look, only filling in a detail now and then. Erin kept returning to one picture in particular, of Bo, standing in a room where he stared at the camera very intently. His expression was one of raw hunger, undisguised lust.

"This… I can almost… This is your house. I remember a… I don't know. I can almost see it, but not. Something hanging on the wall behind you, like you are blocking it in the picture?"

She looked at him, expectant.

"There's a small ceramic piece I inherited from my grandmother that you always liked. It was old, antique. From France, I think. You commented on it the first time you came over. That it looked like the garden your father kept when you were a kid."

Erin's eyes widened. "Yes! Yes, it was…oval? And hand-painted?"

Bo nodded, the corner of his gorgeous mouth pulling a slight smile at her excitement. Any doubts or fears that Erin had were washed away in the new memory. She put the pictures down, laughing with glee at yet another part of her past given back to her, and she lunged at Bo, throwing her arms around him.

"Thank you for doing this. For bringing these things over. This is wonderful."

He hugged her back lightly as she squeezed him in her arms, and then realized, as the moment ebbed, that she was almost sprawled completely across him, pressing him back into the cushions.

Her heart raced even faster as she pulled back, but didn't move, looking down into his face.

She dipped down before she could change her mind, kissing him as she wrapped her arms around him again.

He tasted so good. His arms lay at his sides as he let her explore his mouth, let her kiss him. Erin parted his lips, tasted him, went deeper to find more.

This was absolutely the right thing to do.

Angling her body so that she could press her front

to his, she found him hard already and sighed into his mouth.

"This is so good, Bo. How did we ever let this go?"

It was the wrong thing to say.

He stilled beneath her, drawing back to look at her with passion but also...caution. Lifting off him, she sat, unsure what to do with her hands so she picked up the turtle again. Bo sat up, too, taking a minute or two to compose himself, as if he were deciding what to say.

"This will work. I know it. For all the weirdness, I want to do this with you. Please tell me you do, too," she said, hoping against hope that he wasn't going to back away or change his mind again.

His chest expanded as he took a deep breath, released it, and he offered a nod.

"I do. But we need to be clear on what 'this' is. We broke up, Erin, and this isn't a reconciliation. We're not starting again. If this works out the way you want it to, you'll know that. Remember, you wanted out. And at some point, you'll remember why. So let's not fool ourselves or pretend it's anything other than what it is. I care about you or I wouldn't be here—but what happens between us, it's not going anywhere. When it's done, you'll go on with your life, and so will I. You should know, going in, that I'm leaving in August."

That surprised her. "Leaving? Where?"

"I'm taking a job with a federal task force with the FBI. No one knows, so please keep it between us for now. I agree with what you said—I think we need closure. It all ended so fast before. I did some research, and the doctor said it was possible that you could remember if—"

"Wait. What doctor? You told someone about this?"

"Dr. Newcomb. I didn't tell her anything specific. Just in theory, she said being with someone you were in a relationship with could trigger some memories. It might make you feel safe enough to do so. I needed to know that. That this really could help."

"Okay. I guess I can understand that. If that's what you needed to be sure, then okay. And I'm happy for you, about the job. Really. You're right—it's good to get the ground rules out in the open. And I...I like you, too. As much as I know you. I do feel safe with you. I have since I woke up, which was confusing. I thought it was the uniform," she said with a self-effacing chuckle.

Bo smiled, too. "She also said that if you want to see her, she's always happy to make an appointment for you."

Erin shook her head. "I don't need a shrink. I need my life back. I need you." She took a breath, calmed her voice. "I know what we had... Sexually, it had to be good, right?"

"It was mind-bending."

"Wow, okay, no pressure, right?"

"You don't have anything to worry about."

"It's something I haven't talked to anyone about, but Bo, I can't even remember my first time having sex with someone. I don't remember sex with *any-one*. I guess I was a late bloomer. I don't know what I like or don't like, and I can't even remember if I'm any good at it."

His hand came up, touched her cheek lightly. "You're insanely good at it. Believe me."

She smirked. "Well, thanks, except then all of the experience that made me any good is now gone—unless it's like all the other stuff that the doctors said I didn't lose—like driving my car or doing yoga. Maybe sex is like that? I guess being with you is the only way I can know. And when it's over, it's over. When you have to leave, you go. No matter if my memory is back or not. That's a good thing. It gives us a...deadline. But you know, if I'm not any good, and if you don't want to, you have to tell me."

He touched her chin, smiled slightly. "I don't think that will be a problem, but I'll let you know, sure."

It was a strange conversation, this verbal contract they were hammering out, but it was also raising the anticipation. Bo was watching her. Waiting until she was done. He shifted his position, sitting up straighter.

"Likewise, I want you to be very honest with me about what you want or don't want. I'll show you what we liked, what we did...but if you don't want that now, it's okay. Just say so."

Her heart was beating fast in her chest, her mind racing as she wondered what delicious, kinky things they might have done.

"Were there ever...other people?" She wasn't sure why she asked, but something tickled at the back of her brain, that she and Bo might not have been very vanilla in their sex lives.

"No. Never that. Only us. I don't like to share."

She let out a breath of relief. "Good. Me, either. At least, I don't think so. So that means, um, we're exclusive for this time, too, right? You're not seeing anyone else right now?"

"I haven't seen or been with another woman since we broke up."

That surprised her, but she didn't say so.

"So yes, we're exclusive for now. Are you still on birth control?"

"Yes." The conversation was so…calm, so business-like, but all the same, her blood was rushing to every spot that it needed to and a few extra.

She wanted him. As they sat there talking, she could barely hold back from touching him.

"I haven't been with anyone else, but if you want me to use protection, I will. We never did, not after the first month together."

She considered that for a few minutes. If he were a stranger, she'd never go for it, of course. She thought about that photo on the beach. Bo wouldn't lie to her. Not about this.

"I don't know if I was with anyone else."

The flicker of pain in his face made her immediately regret the disclosure. "But I had every test imaginable when I was hospitalized, and I'm completely healthy. Well, except for the memory loss."

He reached over and cupped a hand around her jaw. Bo stared into her eyes so hard, she couldn't say anything else. That was okay; the expression on his face told her that they were done talking.

Bo saw the flush move up Erin's throat. She'd been get-ting aroused simply by talking about their agreement. But this was more than he expected, too. Though he should have considered it, he hadn't considered that Erin had no memory of sex whatsoever. She wasn't a virgin, physically, but if she couldn't remember ever having sex…wasn't that almost the same thing?

This was about more than trying to trigger a few memories. It was about making some new ones for her, whether he'd thought of that or not. But here he was, and he wanted her. Desperately.

"What do you want me to do?" she asked, sitting across from him, her hands in her lap.

He lounged back, throwing one arm over the back of the sofa, open to her.

"What do you want, Erin?"

She scooted closer, her thighs pushing up against his. "I want to kiss you."

Bo was hard again, but he was going to let her set the pace if it killed him.

He remembered his first time, which was also the first time for the girl he had been with, too. They'd kissed a lot, fumbled a lot and had fun. It hadn't mattered that neither of them really knew what they were doing, and he'd been fifteen, so there was no way he could have.

But now it mattered, though he also knew a lot more, and wanted to make this good for her. Memorable.

Erin licked her lower lip, looking slightly unsure, and he shifted so that he could slide his arm behind her, pulling her up close.

"A good old-fashioned make-out session, then?" he said with a smile, looking into her eyes.

He didn't wait for her answer as he looped his arm around the back of her neck and pulled her close, trapping her against him as his lips covered hers.

The previous kisses they'd shared at the bar and the diner had been rushed and hungry. They had time now. Nowhere to be; no need to hurry. So he didn't. Bo took his time, exploring every angle of her mouth, starting with light, teasing kisses that she returned enthusiastically as he gradually deepened his exploration.

She was so damned sweet. He hadn't spent this much time kissing anyone—only kissing—in a very long time. He and Erin had enjoyed kissing, but it was usually an accompaniment to what else they were doing. Only new couples ever sat and kissed like this, and it made him realize they never really had. Their first time had been hot and insane, in the truck outside the diner. They'd skipped this sweet-hot buildup. The slow part. It was intoxicating.

Though he wasn't sure how much he could take when she turned the tables, pushing him back on the sofa and crawling over his lap to straddle him. Still, they continued only to kiss, though the heat was climbing as the kisses became more carnal. Wetter, deeper… their tongues doing what he wanted to do to her elsewhere.

She moaned against him, pressing her breasts to his chest, and shifting to grind herself against the ridge in his jeans.

Erin may have forgotten her sex life, but she remembered how to move her body all too well. He was too hot, too ready for her to keep doing that without him losing it.

She was in the same condition, if the quick little panting sounds she made into his neck as she nipped him there meant anything.

He put his hands on her hips, held her still.

"Two more minutes of that, honey, and this will be all over with," he said hoarsely, wishing he had more control. But it had been a long time, and this was every fantasy that had kept him awake for months coming true.

She leaned her forehead against his. "Sorry, I need... you, Bo. Now."

5

ERIN COULD HAVE cried with joy and relief as Bo met her eyes, his gaze warm.

"I need you, too."

Until now, she thought it might not really happen. She waited, but he didn't do anything. Then she realized he was waiting.

For her.

"I really am ready, Bo."

He relaxed a bit and reached for her. "I think getting these clothes off would be a good start, then."

She smiled as she bent down to drag her lips along his jaw, over to his mouth where she tasted him again for long, starving minutes, as if she hadn't just kissed him for a full half hour straight.

She began to pull her shirt off, but he stood and stopped her.

"Not here. Upstairs."

A part of her didn't want to stop—what if one of them had second thoughts? What if they lost the mood? She left her doubts unspoken as she led him up the stairs.

Her room was as plain and boring as the rest of the house, but he didn't seem to care. She headed to the bed, but he guided her gently to the other side of the room, instead. In front of the large mirror on the wall.

Then he reached around her from behind and started undoing the buttons of her blouse, both of them watching.

Erin thought her knees might give out as the heels of his hands rubbed on her nipples while he undid those buttons. She was so glad she'd opted for no bra.

He left the blouse on, letting it fall open as he slid his hands up over her ribs and then over her breasts as he kissed her neck.

"Bo, please." She sighed. She wasn't even sure what she was begging for as her head fell back against him, the sensations of his kissing and his rough hands massaging her breasts and thrumming her nipples nearly undid her right there.

"Please what?"

She shook her head, reaching back to find his hardness and closing her hand over him the best she could. He moved away, and she bit out a sound of objection.

"More. I need more of you. I need…more."

"Okay," he said agreeably as he continued to tease her. His hands drifted from her breasts to the snap on her jeans, which he undid. She shimmied out of her jeans and kicked them to the side. Bo looked at her over her shoulder.

"See how beautiful you are? You make me crazy. I want to plant your hands on that mirror and watch so that you can see what we do to each other."

Erin could hardly breathe. She wanted that so much.

His being dressed made her feel exposed. Vulnerable. In a good way, though.

He pulled her close, started kissing her forehead, her cheeks, her lips…then her neck, shoulders, and he just kept going.

He stayed awhile at her breasts, kissing her there until she was winding her fingers through his hair to steady herself. Then, down her stomach he went, until he was on his knees in front of her.

She couldn't take her eyes off the sight in the mirror. Bo before her, lifting her knee. He dipped his tongue in to touch her, making her cry out harshly, her hands clinging to his shoulders.

She couldn't say anything but his name, the warm, soft, rhythm of his tongue making her move against him until she was coming apart, sensation making her seek more, beg for more.

He gave it to her. Erin was barely standing now as he wrung every last whimper from her body.

When her cries of pleasure ebbed to shuddering breaths, he moved away, but was careful to make sure she was okay. When he looked up at her, Erin was struck by the raw emotion and passion in his expression, nothing hid from her.

"You're still dressed." Her voice didn't even sound like her own.

He stood, waiting. She reached forward with shaking hands, sliding them up under the T-shirt and reveling in every rippled muscle she felt there. He raised his arms, threw the shirt to the side as she worked his belt, his jeans, until those were gone, too.

Then all she could do was stare.

She was glad she couldn't remember anyone else.

If she never saw another man in her life, she couldn't imagine one that would be more perfect, more masculine, than Bo.

His cock jutted out at her, hard and eager. She closed her hand around him, felt that skin-to-skin contact for the first time.

He cursed under his breath, his body tense as stone, but his expression told her everything she needed to know. She was moved by the need and the honesty in his face. Without him asking, she faced the mirror, placed her hands on it. Met his eyes where he watched from behind her. He joined her, widening her stance gently and pulling her hips up to meet him.

Erin bit her lip as he nudged her, slid forward, rubbing over her sensitized skin, making her gasp.

No way would she have thought she was ready again, but her body felt otherwise.

She arched her back, trembling in anticipation.

"Oh, Erin...." The words ground out of him as he thrust inside, filling her completely. "Sorry...I meant to go slower."

He was breathing so hard, his face tight, eyes burning. She met his gaze in the mirror and shook her head.

"Don't. Don't go slow. Take what you need. Give me what I need."

None of this generated anything in her memory, but her body knew him—knew him well. She also knew how to move to please him. How to plant her feet, how to roll her hips in a manner that made him emit a guttural moan and swell even larger.

She couldn't imagine how she might remember anything, as she couldn't even think—the tightening in her body wiped everything away but the pleasure. Her response sparked his until he called her name out, too, the gut-wrenching tenderness and relief in his tone touching something deep inside her as he rode out his own climax.

As everything slowed and calmed she turned and went into his arms as if it were the most natural thing in the world to do. They stayed wrapped together like that until their breathing settled, the heat easing.

"That was...amazing."

She felt his chest shake as he chuckled and dropped a kiss on her hair.

"Yeah, it was."

"Was it always like that with us?"

"It wasn't always the same, but it was always good, yes. Did anything seem familiar?"

Oddly, she didn't want to go there. Didn't want to interrupt this moment with the past. She shook her head.

"No, though you felt...familiar. Like I knew what to do with you."

"That's a start."

"Do you want a shower?"

"I could use one. You want to go first?"

"There's room for two," she said, not wanting to be separate from him yet.

Remember what this is, she cautioned herself.

She knew. She did. Eyes wide-open.

Erin knew what they were doing, but that didn't mean she wouldn't feel things for him. She might feel quite a lot.

"Why don't you rest up for a while? Maybe we can get some dinner or something later," he suggested.

Hint taken. He needed some distance, and it was the least she could do.

This had to be harder for him, maintaining the emotional boundaries, given their past. She had, after all, left him. Forgotten him. He wasn't packing up and leaving, he simply wanted to shower alone. He'd be there later when she woke up.

She forced a smile. "I could use a nap."

He leaned over, kissed her cheek, then her lips.

"I'll wake you up in a bit."

There was sensual promise in his voice that made it a lot better. She watched him walk out of the bedroom. Her body chilled in the absence of his heat. She pulled the thick quilt up and over her body, still so sensitive from his touch.

Maybe this was going to be more difficult than she thought, she pondered as her eyes slipped shut. She heard the shower come on down the hall, comforting her that Bo was still there as she drifted off and let it all go for a while.

Bo stood in the shower under the scalding water, wondering if he was losing his mind.

The sex had been every bit as powerful as he remembered, and then some. It hadn't affected Erin's memory, but it sure had triggered his. Being with her was dangerous. He had thought he could do this, but now he wasn't sure.

Yet how could he walk away? What kind of man would say, "Sorry, this isn't going to work," after what he'd done with her?

He scrubbed up and got out, grabbing a towel that hung on the back of the door. It smelled like her. That brought back memories, too. They would always shower together under the guise of saving time, but it never did. They ran out of hot water almost every time.

The only way he could manage this was to make it about the sex. He would wear himself out with her, use her, let her use him, in any way they both needed, and then it would be over. Hell, it was over before it started.

He wrapped the towel around himself and went back down to Erin's room. He should have brought his clothes out with him. He didn't want to disturb her.

It would have also made it easier to leave. To get some space. Send a clear message that this was about sex, not a relationship. Nothing more than helping her with her problem, and hopefully getting her out of his system.

Or, he could do what he said he would. Wake her up, roll around with her in that big bed for a while, and then go get some food.

He blew out a breath, unsure what he was going to do, but knowing he couldn't just leave. He'd agreed to help her, and it wasn't her fault if he was feeling jumpy about the whole thing now.

Going past the bed to where he'd thrown his clothes over the back of a chair, he stopped, making the mistake of watching her sleep. He'd done that a lot before, since she could drop off to sleep with no effort at all, and be snoring without him even closing his eyes.

Then her hair would be tangled, spilled all over the pillow. Now it was too short for that, but mussed from his hands nonetheless. She'd pulled the quilt over her, one delicate shoulder exposed, tempting him.

He could crawl in there with her. Wake her up the way he did so often before. Erin always loved sleepy sex.

Once hadn't been near enough to sate the need she'd

rekindled earlier. He dropped the towel, crawled in under the quilt with her.

Her eyes opened as soon as he did, startled at first, drawing back and then relaxing.

"Sorry. I'm not used to anyone being in bed with me."

He smiled, but the words only emphasized that for all of the times together that he could remember, she only remembered what happened today.

"Let me go clean up, too, and then—"

"Not yet," he said, nibbling her shoulder, already hard for her.

"But I'm—"

He cut off their conversation with a kiss, quickly rolling her onto her back and covering her completely. Her arms came around him, and she arched up into him, clearly on the same page.

"Was it always like this? Like we couldn't get enough?" she asked breathlessly, stroking his back.

"Especially at first, yeah. Pretty much all we did was have sex," he said with a laugh, looking down into her face.

"I find that easy to believe."

She pushed on his chest, rolling him onto his back as she came over him and took him deep, as if she couldn't wait. The eagerness and desire in her face satisfied him as nothing else ever had. Erin had always been good in bed, but she'd never been this open with him. She liked to be in control, and he didn't mind that one bit, except that it had always put distance between them.

There was no distance now as she rocked her hips, scraping her nails over his chest and making him share some pretty graphic thoughts with her as she did so.

"Come here." He tugged on her hand until she collapsed over him, seeking his kiss, but he went lower, sucking her nipples, making her frantic as she rode him.

Causing Erin to lose control was the most erotic thing he'd ever experienced, chanting his name and pulling him along with her on the current. When they were done, they showered again, and ran out the hot water.

Bo was exhausted when they made their way back to the bed, falling into it, and he curled around her. He hadn't been sleeping long when he heard his beeper, buzzing on the dresser.

"I have to check that."

He slid from the warm cocoon of her body and grabbed his phone, calling in.

"What's wrong?"

Erin pushed up on one elbow, the blanket slipping down to reveal her breasts. Bo swallowed hard, trying not to look. She was so hot, and all he wanted was to go back to bed and ignore the rest of the world.

"They need me at a fire. I have to go."

"Now?"

"Yes, I'm afraid so."

"Can I come with you?"

"I don't think it's a good idea. I need to close everything else out when I'm there, and I don't think I can do that when you're around. Especially looking like that."

She took a second as if to absorb the information and nodded, blowing him a kiss.

"Okay. Make sure you come back."

Bo stood transfixed for a second as she relaxed into the pillows. It was like going back in time. She might not remember, but that was what they both said when they went to work. Never goodbye. Always "Make sure you come back." Because they knew that in their profession, there was always a chance they wouldn't.

He kissed her quickly and then tore himself from the room, hurrying down to his truck.

Fifteen minutes later, he approached the scene, showing his badge as he made his way past the barricade at the end of the street. His mind clicked over to work.

It was a bad one. Three structures, at least. Several stations were on hand, and a few volunteer units. He counted two ambulances, and then saw the coroner's van just past them.

"Damn," he bit out under his breath, grabbing his stuff and exiting the truck, making notes as soon as he did. They were still putting out the fire. It would be hours, perhaps days, before he could get inside to do a real assessment. But the chief met him out near the street.

"Myers. Glad you're here."

"What can I do? I can't investigate yet."

"Won't be sure until you take a look, but from what we can tell, it started at four to six different points, simultaneously."

"A timer and a fuse, all set to ignite at the same time?"

"Yep. Seems like the same guy who set the fire on Riley and Joe."

"It's been a while. And this one is bigger. Residences, not a warehouse. So that's different. Casualties?"

"One. Three of our guys hurt, but they'll be okay.

Weird accidents again—Mitchell said he fell through the floor when all of it was solid, and then there was a spot where it busted through, but he saw it too late. It's like the place was booby-trapped for them when they went in. Accidents happen, but not this many, not all at once. Something's off."

Bo felt a chill settle at the base of his spine.

Is that what had happened to Erin and Joe? Had it been a trap?

"So we might have some maniac rigging fires to lure us in, and then he sets up traps inside the buildings? Makes it look like an accident."

The chief was grim. "I'll get you in as soon as I can. You can talk to my guys as soon as medical clears them."

"Thanks. Let me know any further developments."

The chief went back to his team, and Bo stayed to watch, studying the fire and the crowd, taking notes. He'd head to the hospital after this, talk to the men who were hurt. See what they could remember.

If they had a serial arsonist on their hands—and one who was targeting firefighters—this was a much bigger problem than he'd anticipated. And Erin's memory of events could be even more important than she knew.

He couldn't leave the scene now; he was going to need to talk to anyone who'd witnessed the event, get pictures gawkers might have taken with their phones, or ones from traffic and security cameras. He'd start amassing information that he'd add to the case file in his office.

Bo focused on his work, and that's all that consumed his attention. It was a relief of sorts.

Here, he knew what he was doing. He was, as much

as he could be, in control of the situation. He knew
what to ask, what to do, and he was very good at it.
Confusion was behind him, with Erin, and for now,
he left it there.

6

Kɪᴛ ᴡᴀs ʜᴀᴠɪɴɢ a bad morning, and that was an understatement.

Erin was remaining tight-lipped and distant, stewing in her own amnesiac juices. She'd been like that for the past few days. She'd come in for the morning and worked on abusing more plants before she lit out with barely a goodbye. Something was going on, but Erin wasn't about to tell Kit what. In addition, her other part-timer hadn't shown up today, having had to go to the hospital because her daughter had their second grandchild.

The bell rang as her next appointment arrived. After spending two hours with an almost-impossible-to-please bride whom Kit had finally managed to quell—while handling the counter—she took a breather. Luckily, that wedding account alone would keep her afloat for another month.

Kit sighed, gathering up the flowers that Erin had savaged earlier in the day. Before she could try to redo the arrangements, her cell rang.

"Hey, Kit."

"Walt. What's up?" It was her delivery guy.

"I'm stranded. Something in the engine blew on the van, and I'm out past Baldwinsville. I called for a tow, but they're not here yet."

"Are you okay?"

"Yeah, I'm fine, but there's no way I'll get all these deliveries done today."

Kit closed her eyes. She had known she needed a new van for some time. Money, of course, was the issue. And there'd be no money if those flowers didn't get delivered.

She heard the bell out front and pulled her shoulders up straight. No one said running a small business was easy. She'd have to try to catch Erin, and if possible, have her pick up the flowers for delivery. That could save the day.

"Thanks, Walt. Go with the van and see what the repairs are—take it to Ike's, and I'm going to try to contact Erin to come by and grab the remaining deliveries. Tell the garage not to make any repairs until I know exactly how much they'll cost."

"Will do, Kit. I'll let you know."

Kit hung up the phone and went out to the front. The first thing she saw was a large, strong male back. The man leaned down to smell a bouquet of Gerbera daisies. As she caught his profile, she knew exactly who it was.

"Hank?"

He spun abruptly, nearly upsetting the vase of flowers, but he was quick and caught it before it fell.

"Hey, Kit. How are ya?"

She swallowed hard, raising a hand to smooth her hair and wishing she wasn't wearing her work apron. She'd had a fantastic time with Hank the other night, dancing the whole evening away. He'd walked her to her car and kissed her until her toes curled before he said good-night.

He hadn't asked or pushed for anything more than the kiss, and she'd been awake for hours, like a teenage girl, thinking about it.

"What are you doing here?"

"I thought you might like to get some dinner. You know, with me. I'm on my three-day-off rotation."

"Oh, I really can't. I'm alone here today, and my driver just called. The van broke down, and I have to try to get a hold of Erin to see if she can be there in time to pick up the remainder and get them delivered, or I have to close and go get them myself."

She hated to close, but the flowers that needed delivering were money in the bank, and she probably wouldn't have much more walk-in traffic today.

Hank stepped up close, reaching out to take one of her curls and rubbing it between his fingers. Then he slid his hand behind her neck before he lowered to capture her lips in a kiss.

For one beautiful second, Kit forgot everything—the flowers, the van, Erin and all her troubles—as Hank's mouth worked some magic on hers. He pulled her up tight against him, and there was no mistaking that the kiss was working on him, too.

When he broke away, they were both breathless.

"Sorry, Kath, but I've been thinking about nothing else but kissing you again since the other night."

Kit was wordless. He was the only one who ever called her anything but Kit and she liked it. But she also didn't have time for it.

"I had a lot of fun the other night, but I don't have time for this right now."

He watched her closely, and his friendly gaze took on a special, masculine warmth as it traveled over her face.

"What can I do to help?"

"Huh?"

"You're having a tough day. How can I help?"

Kit was taken off guard. If she couldn't name the last time someone had made her toes curl, she really couldn't remember when someone had asked to help, and out of the blue.

"Oh, that's not necessary."

"C'mon, Kath," he said softly, turning her around as his strong hands rubbed her neck in a heavenly way that made it hard to think. "You have a lot of fires to put out today, and guess what? That's what I do. I put out fires."

She smiled. "You're good at starting them, too, I'd say."

She was flirting. She couldn't resist.

Hank chuckled. "Where is Erin?"

"She left earlier, but I can try her cell. Hopefully she has it on, though she was in a mood earlier, so probably not."

She grabbed her phone. Hank stopped her.

"Let her be. I'll do it."

"What?"

"Tell me where to go, what to do, and I can get your deliveries done."

She turned back around, facing Hank, and couldn't help but be skeptical. "Are you joking?"

"Nope. I've never delivered flowers, but I did a stint

delivering pizzas in college. How different can it be? Give me the rundown, and I'll go finish your deliveries. I can do tomorrow, too, if you need me to. My SUV should handle whatever you've got."

"You must have better things to do on your days off."

"Not really. I coach peewee baseball, but that's not until tomorrow night."

Kit wasn't sure what to say. She liked Hank, she truly did—and she could fall for him. It would be easy enough. But she didn't want to do that. He might be charming and attentive now, but his heart belonged to his job.

But she also needed her flowers delivered.

"Is this your way of angling for a date?"

"No. I thought that was a given."

When he smiled like that, she lost track of everything. But what he was offering was better than sex—well, almost.

"Okay. Yes, thank you. I'd appreciate it. And it's not complicated. Just a few basic rules."

"Tell me what you need me to do, and I'll do my best to give you exactly what you need."

He had that mischievous look in his eye again, and Kit felt it warm parts of her body that should know better. She blinked, snapping out of her minifantasy.

"Um, here, let me give you copies of the delivery sheets just in case, and you can get the rest from Walt. He'll be at Ike's Garage. You know where that is?"

"I do."

Kit busied herself getting the materials together for Hank, and then called Walt to let him know about the change.

"Okay, he's on his way to Ike's now. You can meet him there."

"Will do."

Hank headed for the door.

"Hank," she called, stopping him. "Thank you. I owe you for this."

The look in his eye set her day right again.

"I'll keep that in mind, honey. See you later."

ERIN HAD EVERY intention of driving home. Instead, she found herself at the home improvement store a few miles from her house, where she was spending too much money and fiercely concentrating on paint colors and new bathroom tile. It kept her from going crazy thinking about Bo.

Two days.

It had been two days since he'd had sex with her and then left her hanging. Maybe he'd gotten everything that he wanted. Maybe she'd not been what he wanted or—her secret fear—maybe she hadn't been any good. His response to her seemed to contradict that, but maybe he'd even been lying about going to a fire. Maybe he'd needed to get out. Maybe he'd just wanted to have sex with her one more time before he left her, evening out the score.

The last part, she knew, was her imagination throwing darts at her. Bo wasn't like that—she didn't think so anyway.

But he hadn't come back and he hadn't called.

She had too much pride to chase him, so instead, she discussed the combination of earth tones and brighter colors for her first-floor rooms, the lighting, and how it would all work together.

Then she carted it all home, spread drop cloths everywhere and started to work. There seemed to be so few things she could control in her life, but the color of her walls was one that she could.

Thankfully, since she'd never really hung anything on the walls, they didn't need any fixing or repair, and they were already painted the dull beige, so she didn't need to prime. She was good to go, and the tension that had been dogging her began to ease as she rolled on a nice cinnamon-brown that reminded her of Bo's eyes.

Cursing, she wrenched the roller away from the wall and ended up splattering paint down the front of herself, including on her face.

Safety glasses hadn't seemed necessary for painting, but good thing she'd worn them anyway.

Sighing, she sat down on the plastic-covered floor, using a rag to wipe some of the splatter off. As she looked at the huge array of paint cans she'd brought home among the other various supplies, her head dropped into her hands.

What had she done?

She wasn't sure the question was about the paint binge—not completely.

Just then, the doorbell rang, and she popped to her feet, peering out the window before she opened it. She wasn't expecting anyone.

Bo.

She seriously considered not answering the door, but he'd seen her look from the window and offered a short wave.

Pulling open the door, she stood in the open space rather than inviting him in.

"Hi." His smile was warm. Sexy.

Sure it was.

"Hi."

Long. Awkward. Pause.

"Um, can I come in?

"Sure."

He stepped inside, moving past her. Normally, a guy might kiss his girl hello when he showed up at her house, but they weren't like that, were they?

"Painting?"

He took in the supplies and drop cloths with a raised eyebrow.

"Yeah. I thought it was time to personalize the place a bit."

He checked out her face and her clothes, visually tracing the cinnamon-brown streak from cheek to thigh.

"The paint fights back?"

She smiled stiffly and crossed her arms in front of her. "Why are you here?"

He blinked, looking slightly taken aback by her abruptness.

"To see you. And also to see if you had time to go somewhere with me."

A date?

"Where?"

"A fire site. I'd like you to look at it with me."

Okay, so not a date.

"Why?"

"I'd rather not get into details, but do you have time?"

He looked at the paint again.

"I have to clean up."

His gaze followed her curiously but he didn't stop

her as she stepped around him, heading for the stairs. She didn't want to acknowledge the disappointment that he hadn't come here to see her. It was only business.

She put it aside and took a quick shower, washing the paint off and putting on clean jeans and a shirt. She didn't worry about what she threw on, as it obviously didn't matter.

When she returned downstairs, not more than a half hour later, the entire wall she'd been working on was painted. A first coat anyway. Bo was sealing up the paint can.

He didn't have a speck of cinnamon-brown on him.

"You finished it."

"There wasn't much left to do on this wall. Nice choice of color. Warms up the room. There are enough windows in here so it doesn't darken it down too much."

"Thanks, I liked it, too." She felt stupidly pleased that he approved of her color of paint. "I'm ready if you are."

"Are you okay?"

He stood in front of her, blocking her route to the door.

"Sure, why?"

"You're not making eye contact, and you're being very...cool. Even for you."

Erin blinked. Even for her? What did *that* mean?

She put her hands on her hips and looked him fully in the face, making sure she made *total* eye contact.

"Yes, as a matter of fact, I was wondering why we had this big talk three days ago, then you slept with me and ignored me ever since. You haven't even picked up the phone." She shook her head, disgusted. "Other than that, nothing's wrong at all."

He actually had the gall to look mildly surprised. Maybe more so at her frankness, but Erin wasn't in the mood to be coy.

"I've been at the office or at the fire site for the past few days and most of the evenings. I... You never would have noticed before. You knew about the work. It was never a question when one of us was working. There were no expectations. And now... I just, well, I didn't even think about it." He shook his head, still seeming perplexed. "I'm sorry about that. I got into the job, and I didn't think."

Erin was unsettled at how quickly her anger dissipated, confusion and anxiety taking its place. She didn't know what to think because he knew the rules, and she didn't. She'd thought they'd fight, but that was what couples did. And they weren't a couple—not really.

"You're right. I have no claim on you that way. You don't have to explain anything to me. It was just... confusing."

He came up behind her, put his hands on her shoulders and pulled her back against him. She still held herself stiffly, though, as much as she wanted to curl into his warmth.

"I'm sorry, Erin. I got to the site, and work took over. It's like that. I have to immerse myself in it to do the job well. But I should have called, at least. Though to be honest, I didn't think you'd care."

"I don't. I mean, I cared, but for all the wrong reasons. I feel so stupid. I thought it was me. That you were avoiding me, or that you changed your mind."

"No way. I'm sorry you thought that," he said as his arms came around her in a tight squeeze.

She was embarrassed that her eyes stung as he held her. His body was solid and safe, and Erin accepted the comfort. Needed it.

That probably wasn't a good thing, but it was what it was.

"This sucks. I hate feeling this way."

"How?"

"I don't even know myself. I think, if I could remember, I'd really be angry at myself for being this needy. I don't think I was like that."

"No, you weren't. Ever."

The way he said it sounded like there was more there.

"I had to have needed *you*."

"I think you did, in some ways."

Again, a note of ambiguity in his response, but Erin didn't know if she had the right to push for more.

"But I would never have called you needy," Bo continued. "And you aren't now. Or, if you are, it's understandable," he said, turning her back around to face him.

As if to prove his point, he dipped down and kissed her. Erin clung to him, letting him in, all of her doubt washed away as he stoked the heat inside her quite effectively.

Then he slowed and stopped. "Anyway, as good as it was the other night, I was thinking that what could be more effective for helping your memory would be revisiting some of the things we did, places we went, that kind of thing."

"Like reliving my past?"

"I guess you could look at it that way. I think you can remember, Erin. You've already had some things come back and the rest has to be there waiting under the surface. I think we really can do this, and I'm willing to do whatever it takes."

Erin stepped back, considering him more closely. She was heartened by his apparent commitment to help her, but her gut told her that there was more going on. Studying him, she started to notice the bleariness in his eyes and the shadows underneath. He looked as if he hadn't shaved for at least a day. He'd obviously been working hard while she was wrapped up in her own self-indulgent worries.

"This fire you were at…it was bad?"

He pulled himself up, looking away as he answered. "Yeah, it was."

"Let me get you a beer, and you can tell me about it."

He hesitated, as if apprehensive.

"What's wrong?"

"It would be easy, Erin, to lose track of what this is between us. To forget that we aren't together. We used to do that a lot, sit down and talk over the day, what happened at a fire or at the station. It's hard to know where to draw the lines."

She paused, trying to understand. This had to be hard for him. She let out a heavy breath.

"I know. But I think we need to be all-in, right? We need to act like we are together, like it was, if this is even going to work. But I also know that's asking a lot, and if you want out, I can see why. I've been selfish, only thinking of myself."

It was difficult for her to say, because she wanted this more than anything—to get her memory back. But some part of her railed at causing him any more pain. She couldn't continue to do that in good conscience. She had to at least offer him an out—though she hoped he wouldn't take it.

"No, I don't want out. This is bigger than either of us, really. I need you to remember, too. And you're right. We do need to be all-in. We'll deal with the end of it when we have to."

Erin frowned as she sat down in the chair near her, at the dining-room table, such as it was. Running her hand over the cheap laminate top, the thought of changing it threaded through her mind as Bo sat, too.

"What do you mean that it's bigger than either of us?"

"Listen, why don't we go somewhere to talk? We can skip going to the fire site—it's getting late anyway. Want to head over to the park?"

"Sure, that sounds good."

As they walked out to the truck, her mind revolved around the emerging image of who she was before. Someone who didn't seem to connect with others very well, it seemed. She clearly hadn't been there for her sister, and she'd even kept her lover at a distance—or at least, she'd kept him a secret. All so that she could save face in her work?

A lot of the guys were married or involved, so why had she needed to keep her personal life a secret? Bo had admitted it could be different for women in the department, but...something didn't ring true.

The idea was an uncomfortable one. It circled around in her mind as they drove. She stared out the window, trying to clear her head. There must have been reasons for her being so emotionally unavailable.

If only she could remember them. It was like seeing only half of a picture, other people's impressions, and not being able to see the whole.

They stopped across the street from Dinosaur Bar-B-Que, a Syracuse landmark. The place was hopping.

"I need something to eat. I'll be right back," Bo said and was out the door before she could get her seat belt off to join him.

The man was definitely antsy. Or maybe he was simply hungry.

She watched him jog to the restaurant and saw several women who stood by a line of parked motorcycles watch him, as well—he was impressive in his uniform. And out of it.

He emerged ten minutes later with a bag under either arm, and Erin wondered exactly how much food he'd ordered. Still, when he opened the backseat and put the bags in, the aromas made her mouth water.

"I hope you're hungry," he said with a grin as his eyes met hers.

Her mind went right to the gutter. She was definitely hungry.

Bo got them back out on the highway and before she knew it, they were pulling into the Green Lakes State Park. They carried their bags over to an available picnic table near the lake. Some families were also eating out, though it was a weeknight, but it wasn't too crowded this early in the season.

"I come here to run sometimes, though it's a bit of a drive from my house. But the lakes are so pretty. I can never get over how still they are, and the green-blue color, though I know it's reflecting sediment in the water," she commented as she helped him get the food out of the bags.

"You say that every time we come here," he said absently with a smile, surveying the table.

"Do I give you the lecture on how they are meromictic, probably formed by plunge waterfalls fifteen thousand years ago when the glaciers came through here?"

"Not if I say it first."

She laughed. "We're such geeks."

The food looked great and she began eating, the fresh air making her hungrier than she expected.

"This is such a treat. Thank you. We did this kind of thing often?"

"Yeah, in the warm weather. It reduced the risk of someone seeing us out together."

Erin's easy mood crashed, and she set the juicy rib down that she'd started munching on.

"Was it always like that? Sneaking around and trying to avoid everyone?"

"I told you why. You had your reasons."

"You didn't like it."

"I understood. Especially when we both worked in the station. When I moved out into investigation, I hoped we could be more open, but—"

"That's when things fell apart," she finished. "I can't remember it, but I feel like I need to apologize for it."

"Don't," he said, leveling a look at her. "Let's just enjoy the evening."

She nodded, though her appetite diminished somewhat. His did not, and she realized he probably hadn't had a decent meal in days, either. Was he always this consumed by his work? In relative quiet, they finished their meal as the sun started lowering behind the trees that surrounded the lake.

"So tell me about the fire. What happened?"

He finally relented. "It was a bad one. Three houses, several families with nowhere to go now, and two dead by the time it was done. One of them a teenage mother who must have gotten trapped. Luckily, the baby was elsewhere with her grandmother. Another older man died of smoke inhalation later at the hospital, and four firefighters were injured, though not critically."

"That's tragic," she said, reaching over to put a hand on his arm. He paused and covered her hand with his.

"There's more. The signatures of the fire resemble the ones from some previous incidents."

"So it wasn't an accident?" Suddenly her hands turned cold.

"No. And the evidence so far very closely resembles the methods used in the fire that hurt you and killed Joe—the location is completely different, but we're beginning to suspect the buildings were booby-trapped to injure firefighters going inside."

Erin covered her mouth in shock, astounded. "Oh, no…someone did this on purpose? To target firefighters? And that could have been what happened to me and Joe, too?"

He was tense again, his face drawn into tight, tired lines. "Maybe. Though your fire completely demolished the building so there's not enough evidence to make sure—this time, we had reports from the guys who were hurt and more evidence of the tampering."

She drew her hand back and closed her eyes for a second, digesting that someone had actually planned this. That they had been targeting firefighters and had killed her colleague while nearly killing her.

"So that's what you meant about my remembering being about more than us. I might know something that could stop this."

"Or that could shed light on it, yes. We don't have much to work with, and there are enough differences between the two fires that perhaps they aren't the result of the same arsonist—and if you know that what happened to you was different, that changes things, too. Or you might know something that could help us catch a serial arsonist. A killer."

Erin reeled, standing up from the table and starting to pace, her hands shaking. If she'd felt pressure to remember before, now it was tenfold. Hundredfold.

She was lost in her own panicked thoughts when Bo interrupted her pacing, stopping her in place.

"What if I can't remember? What if nothing happens and more people are hurt?"

Bo shook his head resolutely. "There's no guarantee your case is connected, or that you could remember anything that would help. It's just a chance. I didn't know if I should tell you—the pressure might hold you back."

"Maybe it will, but it also makes me want to try even harder. I want you to tell me everything. We used to talk about work a lot, right? So we'll do that. Tell me everything about the fire."

Bo's mouth flattened as he looked down into her face. She tipped her chin up, showing him that she was fine—and that she wasn't going to take no for an answer.

He relented. "Okay, but let's go for a walk while we talk. I could use the fresh air."

She agreed, helping him pack up the remains of their meal before they started out on the trail. He was quiet until they got farther along the lake, and then he started telling her all of the awful details. Many that she didn't want to hear, but she listened anyway. Erin was determined to see this through to the end, no matter what. As Bo's hand reached out and clasped hers as they walked, it was good to know she wasn't alone.

Susan Mallery

7

Bo's MOOD IMPROVED by the minute. Though he always teased Erin about her fascination with the area's geologic origins, he always marveled at them, too.

He loved how completely smooth and undisturbed the lakes were. Absolutely mirrorlike on a perfect day, they were very deep. Ancient sediments, never disturbed through the march of time, measured as much as five hundred feet under the two hundred feet of water. Everything changed, but not these lakes, not very much. It was calming to think about, that some things stayed the same.

The fresh air and beautiful views around the lake chased away the nightmares of the past few days. Nightmares that he didn't really want to share with Erin, though he had to.

She'd listened, asking good questions that, to him, provided more evidence that her experience and her knowledge about firefighting were just below the surface—like the ancient sediment at the bottom of the lake, buried, little bits floating up to the surface.

They paused at a spot on the east side of the lake

that had a buildup of solid sediments and minerals in the form of a reef or shelf, unfortunately called Dead Man's Point. Bo shook his head. He wasn't exactly sure why, but he was tired of death. It seemed to be everywhere. He didn't want to be reminded of it in this beautiful place.

"Hey, are you okay?"

Erin was standing before him, her voice reflecting her concern.

"I'm more concerned about you."

She seemed lovelier, if that was even possible, in the soft evening light. She was still physically fit, but he could tell where her face and her shape had softened slightly, away from the rigors of department work. It looked good on her.

"Why?"

"I was afraid knowing about the fire would be too much, that it might actually make your memory harder to reach. Dr. Newcomb said you needed to feel safe, not pressured."

She took his hand, squeezed. "No. I'm glad you told me. I needed to know. And you needed to talk about it."

He blinked, realizing that he really did. He and Erin were always each other's confidants. Friends and work-mates before they were lovers, they could share things at the end of the day with each other that civilians would have a harder time understanding.

He hadn't known how much he'd missed that until right now.

"There's one more thing I have to ask you."

Her tone was apprehensive, and Bo knew she was still thinking about the fire.

"What's that?"

"If this is a serial arsonist, and if he or she did set the fire that Joe and I were caught in, wouldn't I be a potential threat? Do you think I could be in danger?"

Bo frowned. That had been the one thing he'd held back from her—he didn't want to cause more anxiety than he already had, but he should have known she'd reason it out. Or was it that she had other reason to ask?

"Has anything happened? Anything specific?"

She shook her head. "No, not really. I mean, when I first came home, I felt like someone was watching me sometimes, but the doctors said that happened sometimes with amnesia. A level of anxiety or paranoia that usually fades in time, and it did. But what if someone *was* watching me?"

Bo didn't like that possibility at all. He tried to approach the subject objectively, like an investigator, not like a man who wanted to hide her away and keep her safe from anything. It was more difficult than he expected. This was Erin, and he instinctively wanted to protect her.

"Well, the cases may not be related, but if they are, you'd pose a definite threat. However, your amnesia is pretty general knowledge now. It was in the paper and so forth. That would mean our arsonist probably knows, too. Since he or she risked setting another fire, I'm assuming you've been dismissed as a threat. But if you feel that again, like someone's watching, or if anything makes you feel like something is wrong, you have to tell me immediately, okay?"

She nodded, her expression relaxing slightly.

"I guess you should stay as close as possible, then. For a lot of reasons."

"You're probably right about that."

Tugging her forward against him, Bo kept hold of her hand and caught her jaw in his other palm, keeping her still as he took his time kissing her, letting the feel of her mouth under his erase all the dark clouds that had been plaguing his thoughts.

Erin had always been the only one who could do that.

The realization was not a comfort, given their current situation. It was too easy to forget that this was not going anywhere. But as she said, they needed to be "all-in" and deal with the fallout later. Bo wasn't sure he had any choice in the matter, as he'd never really been "all-out."

She slipped her hand free and wrapped both arms around his neck, bringing herself in even closer to him. He did the same, so that they were as tightly fused as two people could be, almost. Erin loved to kiss, and she was so good at it…but the shadows were lengthening. They had to get back before the park closed.

"Hey, let's keep going. I want to show you something," he said against her cheek.

She laughed, a kind of low, soft laugh from her belly that was at once humorous and sexy as hell.

"Yeah, I'm sure you do," she added, pressing her hips forward into the hard evidence his desire.

He laughed, too, thankful for her humor as he grabbed hold of her hand again.

"Not that. Not yet anyway." Bo felt reinvigorated, as though his earlier exhaustion had completely gone. "We have to walk a bit farther."

They ambled down the narrow path toward the main beach and the parking lot, but still out of sight of both.

Then Bo stopped and pulled her aside, off into the woods.

"Over here...."

They climbed up to a higher spot where some sun was still filtering through, and a wide ledge sprawled out from beneath an outcropping of boulders.

"Do you have any recollections? Any sparks of memory about this spot?"

She stood, looking around, and peered out over the trees.

"No, not really. It is a gorgeous view, though. I take it we've been up here before?"

"A few times."

"Why?"

He couldn't repress his smile at his own memories of this private little nook. They'd discovered it one day while hiking and joking around. Erin had taken off into the woods, daring him to find her, and they both found this little bit of magic. He never saw any other foot traffic up here and assumed it was more or less undiscovered.

Her eyebrows rose as she read his expression. "Ah. So this was like our own lovers' lane, I take it?"

"Something like that. A nice private spot, but we also had to be very quiet, just in case any other hikers heard us from below."

He was hard again, and suddenly unworried about the hour. Bo could see the change in her mood as well, as her lips parted, her eyes darkening.

"So what did we do here exactly? Can you show me?"

The desire was plain on her face, reflected in her stance as she leaned toward him, and he was relieved.

The emotional dependence he'd felt while sharing his thoughts about the fire wasn't what he wanted, but this—this he definitely wanted. Thinking about sex focused his muddled mind. And they'd had sex here, in this spot, several times. There was one time in particular that came to mind for him.

She went to him, standing before him with her hands at her sides as he backed her up against the still-warm surface of the rock.

"Caught between a rock and a hard—"

He cut her joke off with a passionate kiss, and she melted into him, moaning as the kiss became hotter and deeper.

He broke the kiss, his own breathing uneven.

"Maybe we should play a game," he said. "You always liked games."

He spun them around so that his back was to the boulder and she stood in front of him. He waited, her eyes darkening with excitement as he watched her closely, wondering if she would remember what happened here.

"What kind of games?"

"Remember with hide-and-seek, how you would be hotter or colder when you were getting close to finding someone?"

She nodded.

"Well, maybe you should try to remember what we did here last time, and I can tell you if you are getting hotter or colder as you do…"

She smiled. "All in the name of assisting my memory, of course."

"Of course."

Erin appeared more than willing to play—she did

like games—and stood back for a minute, looking him up and down as if trying to decide where to start. Bo enjoyed how she took her time, her close study.

"Maybe you should sit down against the base of the rock?"

He shook his head. "Colder."

She stepped forward, pushing up on her toes to nibble his neck, letting her hand drift down to the front of his jeans.

"A little warmer," he whispered.

"Only a little?"

He shrugged, but there was a sparkle in her eyes— Erin was having fun—that he hadn't seen in a long time.

"Hmm...no hands then?" she posited.

He didn't indicate whether she was right or wrong, and waited to see what she'd do next.

Slowly, she pushed up his shirt, flicking her tongue over his chest and then down to his navel. Licks of fire danced under his skin as she did so.

"Definitely warmer," he said, his voice hoarser.

She continued her barrage of light kisses, driving him mad, and then she took the additional liberty of freeing his painfully erect shaft as she did so.

"Hotter," he managed, his body tight with anticipation.

Erin lowered to her knees, her hands on his thighs as she tasted him lightly, rolling her tongue around the tip of him, teasing. Bo's mind blanked.

She looked up at him through her lashes. "Hotter?"

Her tone was all sex kitten, making him even harder. "Very."

He put his hand at the back of her head, applying

gentle but firm pressure until his cock brushed the back of her throat and her lips closed around the root.

Her moan told him that she was okay with his touch. Maybe more than okay. Bo took it the next step, curling his fingers into her hair and pulling back gently, showing her the pace he wanted. The world spun as he watched her move against him, and his hold changed to a light caress of her silky locks. As she lost herself in the act, he let go, needing his hands to brace himself against the boulder as she took the lead, making him tremble from head to toe.

Bo stared out at the lakes in the distance as dusk fell; a guttural moan came from his solar plexus as hot pleasure rose. When he couldn't take it anymore, he reached down and drew her up.

The desire and sheer wanton joy in her expression, her reddened lips and hazy eyes nearly did him in.

She read his mind and shucked her jeans, letting him put her back against the rock. She could barely restrain a gasp of pure bliss as he brought her legs up around him and thrust inside.

"So, so hot," he breathed against her skin.

This he could handle. Erin needy against him, her face a study in sex, her eyes focused only on him.

The boulder was unyielding, and suddenly Erin's moaning became a fervent cry of release—which triggered his own. A sensation of complete and utter satisfaction overwhelmed him. He eased off Erin, but slipped his hand into hers, not wanting to break their contact just yet.

By the time they caught their breath, it was almost dark. As she put her clothes back on, they were quiet.

Then she paused and tilted her head, as if trying to hear something.

"What is it?" Bo asked.

She smiled, taking a deep breath before she spoke.

"Last time, it was in the daylight. I remember looking up, when you were inside me, against the rock, and seeing the sun coming down through the trees."

"That's right. It was." He confirmed her memory with a smile, but behind it, a slight sinking sensation returned.

He should have been as thrilled as she seemed to be. But every memory coming back to her brought them that much closer to what had separated them before. Bo went ahead, making sure they got down the darker hillside safely, though he didn't reach for her hand again as they walked back to the truck.

KIT WAS SO tired by the time she pushed the key into the lock of her back door that night she could just about stand. After Hank had saved the day delivering her flowers, the bad luck had continued. A shipment of flowers came in spoiled, and a customer complained, as well, about their delivery being late that day.

Not to mention Erin was MIA and Kit had kind of hoped she might be there when she got home.

To be honest, she was also disappointed about Hank's not coming back to the store after he was done. She had no right to be—he'd saved her butt finishing the deliveries and following up on the van, which was going to be less expensive than she thought to fix. That was one good thing.

He'd checked in and told her he had something else he had to do that evening, but would see her later. She'd been disappointed—very much so. She'd wondered, if he came back to the shop, where that might lead.

Instead, here she stood, alone as usual. She sat down at the small table by the window that looked out over a very ragged garden—if it could even be called that anymore. How ironic was it that she, a professional florist, had such a messy, unkempt garden?

It had been her mother's pride and joy. For a while after she died, Kit had kept it up, but gardening took time.

There was a message blinking on the machine—Erin? She almost never got calls on her landline anymore, except for telemarketers. She'd been meaning to close out the account for a while and just go to cell. But Erin thought it was important to have as a backup for emergencies, and for 911. Ever the firefighter.

Kit hit the button and listened to the pleasant male voice calling to inform her that a letter would soon arrive informing her that she had been chosen for a personal tax audit from the IRS.

She dropped back into the chair, shaking her head. Chosen? Like she'd won a prize?

Great. This was exactly what she needed. There was nothing amiss in her files, and she kept meticulous records, but it was one more thing to worry about. The call went on with more details, but she wandered away from the room.

Whatever.

Sometimes when she got home, she'd watch some TV or read, but tonight she was just going to bed.

The house was so quiet, though. Until she heard footsteps on the front porch, and then a knock at the door.

Startled, she switched on the porch light. The sheer

white curtain obscured the window, but not so much that she couldn't recognize Hank's huge profile.

She smiled and rushed to the door, then felt silly, slowing down and waiting a beat as she opened it.

"Hank. What are you doing here?"

"Hi, Kath. I hope you don't mind me coming by."

"Um, no, not at all. But how did you know where I live?"

"Miraculous thing, the white pages."

Kit laughed, feeling foolish yet again.

"Now I see the definite value in having kept my landline."

He smiled and looked past her into the house. "I wanted to apologize for not coming back to the shop. I had to go over to my sister's to help her with her kid for a while. She's a single mom, so I sometimes babysit at the drop of a hat, but I'm sorry that I left you hanging."

"We didn't have any definite plans."

"No, but there was that date you owed me, and I said I'd see you later. And this is later."

"That's true."

"Do you want to go out?"

"Not really," she said, and saw him frown. "But I could open a bottle of wine or cook something if you want to come in."

"I'd like that a lot."

He stepped inside and waited in the small entryway as she closed the door.

"Nice house. Where you grew up?"

"Yes, thanks. I love living here, though I haven't been able to keep things up as much as I should. It's a big house."

"Your parents left it to you?"

"Yes, well, Erin and I both inherited it, but I'd been living here taking care of my mom when she was sick, and Erin had already bought her own house, so she signed it over to me. She never was as attached to it as I was. So yeah, it's all mine. Every pipe that needs repair, peeling exterior paint, overgrown garden and all."

"Hey, you're only one person, and you run your own business. I think the house looks fine. It has charm."

"*Charm* is a nice word," she said with a chuckle as she started for the kitchen, but he caught her arm, pulling her back around to face him.

"First things first," Hank said as his arms closed around her and he sought a kiss that she was happy to return.

He felt so good, so big and solid. As if nothing in the world could get through him to her. The kiss deepened, taking on more heat than she expected, and Kit moaned as she pressed against his barrel of a chest.

"You make the sexiest sounds when I kiss you, Kathleen," he said into her neck, his voice rough.

She didn't know what to say to that, and settled for letting him kiss her again, this time taking one of his large, gorgeous hands and settling it over her breast.

"Oh, damn, honey," he muttered, closing his palm over her with more gentleness than she would have expected from such a large, strong man. Kit was learning that everything with Hank was such a nice surprise.

Including his patience. Most guys would have her undressed and against the entry wall by now, but he kept kissing her and moving his thumb over her nipple until she thought she might rip *his* clothes off and push *him* against the wall.

"How hungry are you?" she managed to ask, her breath short as she moved her hands over his broad back.

"Do you have to ask?" he countered with a low chuckle.

She giggled and moved her hand down to slide over him, pleased when he made some nice sounds for her, as well.

"I meant...I was going to cook for you, but, if you wanted to wait for a while—"

It was as far as he let her go, when she felt herself lifted off the floor and swept—for the first time ever in her life—off her feet.

"Hank, what are you doing?"

He held her up in his arms and headed to the stairs at the end of the hall.

"Up?" he asked, desire clear in his expression, his eyes, his voice.

She met his gaze directly. "Yes. Up. Top of the stairs, down the hall, on the left."

He brought her to her room, the one she'd had since she was a girl. She'd never had a man in there, not once. She didn't bring men home, not here.

But Hank was different. As he set her down by the side of her bed and started kissing her again, undressing her as he did so, she knew something with him was very different indeed.

If she wasn't so busy enjoying it, it would have scared the hell out of her. But as he took off his own clothes and joined her on her bed, Kit didn't worry about anything for the rest of the night.

8

Erin was completely exhausted, but from the spot where she sat in the doorway of her sunroom, she could appreciate all of the new changes that surrounded her.

Now, her house was starting to feel like home.

She smiled at her freshly painted ceiling and the summery, soft green walls of her dining room, enjoying how the verdant tone contrasted with the pretty honey color of the room she was in and the rich, cinnamon-brown of the living room.

Hank and Kit were working on the kitchen, which was being redone in sunny yellow and white, and Leroy was retiling her bathroom floor after she had finished painting the room a soft gray with white trim.

Pete was busy on the trim while she'd finished the walls in the entryway—the same honey color as the sunroom—and looked down at her with mock severity.

"No napping on the job, Riley."

"I'm just appreciating the color mixes from a different perspective. I saw it on a design show on TV," she lied, fighting a grin.

All of her blah furniture had been donated, as well.

Someone else might make good use of it, but tomorrow, a new dining and living room set and some decorative pieces would be delivered here.

There were several art shows around the Syracuse area every summer, one in particular downtown in July that was juried, and she couldn't wait to choose colorful, cool stuff to put on her walls and tables. It all made her feel more like herself—or whoever she was becoming. Someone who liked color. Lots of it.

Her smile faded as she thought it would be nice to put up some family photos. Maybe she'd take a photography course and frame some pictures of her own.

The picture of her and Bo on the beach came back to mind, and along with it, a ping of regret that none of those photos could be displayed.

"Hey, no lying down on the job," Leroy said as he came into the room.

Walking up to her, he nudged her with his foot, as if checking to see if she was still alive. She played the game for a second, and then moved fast, grabbing his leg and pulling him down into a wrestling hold that came naturally, though he turned her around and then held her captive in the next second.

"Glad to see you remember some of that jujitsu I showed you, but not enough, lady, not enough," he whispered menacingly in her ear with an evil chuckle. "Loser buys dinner."

She hugged Leroy back, a real hug, not a defensive one this time, and laughed.

"Okay, I planned on treating you all anyway. No need to get violent," she joked as they got up from the floor. "But seriously, you guys do great work. I can't believe how different it looks. And feels. It's a lot more cheerful to be here now."

"It would be even more cheerful with a couple jumbo buckets of fried chicken," Pete said.

"And sides," Leroy added.

"I get it. Food. Okay. I'm going to go upstairs and see how Bo's coming along, and then I'll go."

Bo had joined in when Erin had sent a general invite for a painting party at her place when it became apparent that left to her own devices, she'd never get it all done. With the general invite open to everyone, it didn't make anyone curious about why Bo had joined in.

Dana and Scott had come, and a few other people from the department. It was fun, and the place got done very quickly. She also liked that Bo had chosen to work upstairs. Dana and Scott were with him until they had to leave. Since then, he'd been alone. It had taken all of her willpower to stay downstairs and not go up to see him too often.

Taking the stairs two at a time, she left Pete and Leroy, who were bickering about a sports controversy, and went into her bedroom. The ugly beige was now a soft rose color on one accent wall behind her bed, the others painted in a very pale gray.

"Oh, this is so pretty," she said, making Bo aware of her presence as he put the finishing touches on the trim around her closet. "I can't thank you enough for all of this. It would have taken me forever to do it myself."

She couldn't help but think how he looked at home in her bedroom. He should, she figured, with as much time as he'd spent there in the past two weeks. They'd fallen into a pattern of sorts, much like the one Bo said they had before. They spent evenings and his days off together, sometimes at his place, sometimes at hers. In the meantime, she helped with Kit's store and kept busy.

She had remembered a lot—but it was always from her relationship with Bo, some family memories, or events with friends. Like Leroy teaching her some jujitsu holds and takedowns. Nothing about the fires or the job.

At least there hadn't been another arson in that time, but she couldn't help but wonder if it was only a matter of time.

"No thanks required. This is fun. Relaxing stuff. How are things going downstairs?"

"We're almost there. Still need to do about half the trim and finish the bathroom floor. I don't know where Hank and Kit are on the kitchen. I'll check when I go back down to get dinner orders, which is why I'm here. Fried chicken and sides okay with you?"

Bo looked at her and stepped off the short ladder he was using to reach the upper part of the trim, and crossed to where she stood.

"That's fine, but it isn't really what I'm hungry for."

Then he was kissing her, and Erin didn't mind one bit. In fact, with the door cracked open, and voices from the first floor filtering up as everyone worked and talked, she thought she might have a few minutes to show Bo how appreciative she was for his help.

Sliding her hand down his chest, her fingers made their way to the zipper of his jeans and he pulled back.

"Hey, now, we're not alone."

"I know, so you'll have to be really quiet," she said with a naughty smile.

Bo gave in, bracing one hand against the wall as she

littered kisses over his throat, stroking him in a hard, fast way that she knew he liked.

Someone's voice got louder in the entryway, and they both stilled, but there were no footsteps on the stairs, so she continued. Taking his other hand, she placed it over her breast as she kissed him, and felt him shudder.

His groan was low and deep, and he collapsed against the wall with a resounding *thump* as he climaxed, his breathing harsh, though he made no other sound.

"Hey, everything okay up there?"

Pete must have heard the noise, and Erin smiled as Bo caught his breath.

"Yeah, Bo just dropped a can of paint, but it had the lid on, thank goodness. I'll be back down in a second," she responded.

Bo's chest was still heaving, his eyes hot as he pulled her in for one more kiss.

"You always did like the chance of being caught," he said before he released her, separating so that they could fix themselves up.

She shrugged. "It's fun. The excitement of almost being caught adds a little something."

"Have you ever thought what?"

Erin shook her head. "I don't know. Some adventure, I guess. I do remember the time we had sex under the stands at that concert. That was crazy, with people all over the place, but it was also really, really hot."

Dressed again, he put the lid on the paint can he was finished with.

"That it was," he agreed with a chuckle.

"I guess it's my little bit of kink. You don't have any—or any that I remember?"

Standing, he looked at her speculatively, as if unsure if he wanted to answer. That intrigued her, and she dared him with her smile.

"C'mon, Myers. Confess your naughty secrets to me."

"Nope, not me. I'm kink-free. Straight as an arrow," he said, fighting a smile.

"So you're not going to tell me?"

"There's nothing to tell, Erin."

She took that in, but his tone suggested there was something he wasn't telling her. Why?

"With you, I always thought the sex-in-public thing was maybe because you wanted someone to catch us," he mused, deflecting the topic back to her. "That since we were a secret, it was like tempting fate. Do you think that's what it is now, too?"

"I haven't really given it that much thought, to be honest. It's just a fun thing to do. Does it have to have any deeper meaning?"

"I guess you're right."

What had been a fun bit of sex was suddenly heavy and uncomfortable. Erin didn't want to psychoanalyze her sex life or his, and if she did, she'd see a shrink.

"For what it's worth, if there's anything you want to do that you haven't told me, I'd be willing to try."

She wanted to change the mood between them, and erase the distance that had somehow grown between them.

"That's good to know."

Frustrated and starting to get irritated, she walked to the door, shoving her hands into her pockets.

"Okay, well…I'd better get going before there's a revolt."

She was out the door and down the stairs before he could reply, still annoyed. Whether she wanted to think about it or not, now her mind wouldn't let go of what he'd said.

Was there any merit to Bo's thoughts that she had wanted them to get caught? Why? To make their relationship public or to make it impossible? If they had been caught, would that have pushed them closer or made their breakup even more imminent?

Or was it simply a fun way to have sex that she found particularly exciting?

She headed to the kitchen to grab her purse when another surprise assailed her. Erin couldn't be sure, but as she went into the kitchen, she could have sworn she saw Hank remove his hand from her sister's bottom.

Blinking, she was sure she must be seeing things.

"Erin!" Kit exclaimed, turning pink, though Erin supposed it could have been the exertion of the work she was doing up on the stepladder.

Erin looked at Hank, who was studying the wall he was painting very closely, and she shook her head. Maybe Hank had been steadying Kit on the ladder?

That made more sense. Knowing what she knew about her sister, no way would Kit ever have interest in a firefighter. Though Kit seemed tense lately, too, and worried. Erin had made a few attempts at getting her to talk, but Kit wasn't sharing.

"I'm going for dinner. I'll be back in a bit."

"If you can pick up some cupcakes at Harrison's, that's all I ask," Kit said.

Erin laughed. "I can do that. I love how this is looking," she said, taking in the bright kitchen and white trim. "I'll probably have to have this floor replaced, too. Not right away, though."

"Hardwood is always good," Kit said, and both sisters swung their gazes to Hank as he suddenly was caught by an attack of coughing.

"Sorry, swallowed my soda the wrong way," he said, clearing his throat and turning back to his work.

"Okay, well, I'll return shortly. Thanks for all the help, you guys. This doesn't even look like the same house. Next we'll have to do the outside," she added as she left the kitchen, smiling at their groans of objection.

But as lighthearted as she came off, Bo's comments and her promise to perhaps experiment with him resurfaced as she drove. They were supposed to be reenacting her past, not trying new things, right? But then again, if it was something he really wanted— something she had denied him before—it *was* related to their past. So why wouldn't he tell her? Maybe he was telling the truth, and there wasn't anything. Maybe she was imagining that he wasn't sharing what he really wanted.

Or maybe he'd done that, and she was unreceptive? Or maybe it took a level of trust that they didn't share.

She might never know. Time was getting shorter, and if her memory didn't come back—what then? Bo would be gone, and she would be right where she started, except that now she'd know what a good thing she'd let go.

Bo LOOKED UP as Erin appeared in his office door the next day. He wanted to give her a kiss hello, not worry about anyone finding out about them—what did it matter now? He'd accepted the task-force job, and he was out of here in under a month.

But instead, he said hello and gestured to her to sit down.

"Thanks for coming down here."

"Sure. What's going on?"

"I have some news. They're going to start demo on the arson site—yours—tomorrow."

"Oh. Yes, you mentioned that before."

"I wondered if you'd visit the building with me. Take a look before it's gone. I know you went down once before, and nothing came back to you. You also found it upsetting then. Do you think you're okay to go now?"

She took a second to consider. "Yeah, I think it would be fine. I don't know that it will make any difference, but I think I can handle it. I think the time that's passed has helped. When I went, I was just out of the hospital, and I was pretty raw back then."

"If you're up to it, then, maybe we can stop by the second site, too."

"The second fire?"

"Yes. I want to walk you through a few things. See if anything pops for you. There could be commonalities or something you might notice that we didn't. It's a long shot, but it's worth trying."

"I don't know what I could find. I have no connection to that one."

"You never know. You tagged along with me a few times when I was training for arson investigation, as an interested observer. You showed some skill, too— you have a good eye for investigation. But maybe going over there now that you have some distance will make something pop."

"I can definitely try."

"Great. So, we can take the afternoon to do that, and maybe go somewhere after?"

Erin paused, and then met his gaze. "Sure. We could probably stay around here. I mean, I don't think it's a big deal if anyone sees us. No one seemed to think twice about you coming over to help with the house the other day."

"You invited everyone at the department who wanted to help."

Still, his heart—and his hopes—rose at her notion that it didn't matter if people saw them together. He would have given his left arm to hear her say that six months ago.

"I don't think we have to worry. We're out visiting the sites, so that can be our excuse."

Her words brought him back down to earth. "Yeah, but we'll take my truck and come back for your car later. So it's clear that it's just business. Not personal."

He wasn't sure if he caught a slight flinch as he said that, but she agreed and stood, walking ahead of him out of the office.

Things had been tense between them since their discussion at the house, and Bo hoped this went well. It seemed as if Erin's memories were there, but being with him was only triggering relationship memories. And that was triggering all kinds of other complex emotions.

She'd wanted him to share more about his desires at the house, but he couldn't do it. Not when they didn't have a future. What was the point? In truth, he had expressed a few secret fantasies back when they were together, but Erin had been uncomfortable with it because it meant she had to give up control. She had to trust him completely.

And apparently she didn't. Bo had no desire to tread over that territory again. They had to stay clear on the real reason they were doing this and see if they could rouse memories about the fire. That was the goal.

There'd been no activity for weeks, and for that he was grateful, but the investigation had also hit a dead end. Whoever was setting these fires, they were hard to track.

On their way out to the truck, Bo watched her walk. He liked how her bottom moved. It made him think about other things he wanted to do later.

Maybe he shouldn't have mentioned that bit about her maybe wanting them to get caught. He might have been way off. As she said, it wasn't that, but the idea itself was the thrill. That would be more Erin's style, daring the world to cross her.

She'd been good at firefighting because she knew how to stay calm and keep her cool under pressure— the way she did when she was turning him on with all the guys and her sister a few rooms away.

She liked the challenge. She craved excitement. They were alike in that.

Her offer to try something new—anything he wanted—was tempting. It was also dangerous. Did it mean that Erin had changed? That some of the old rules between them no longer applied? That she trusted him more?

That there could be something new between them?

He shook his head as if trying to cast away the thought.

"What?" she asked, bringing him back to the present.

"What?" he echoed back, taken off guard.

She smiled. "You were shaking your head no at something."

"Oh. Just lost in thought, that's all. Here we are," he announced. "If this is bad and you want to leave, you say so, okay? We're only here to look around— no pressure."

"Got it."

They stopped, and she slid out of her seat to the pavement, taking in the skeletal remains of the burned-out warehouse. Erin seemed to confront it without any particular emotion at all. That was a good start, he supposed.

They approached a small shed, where Bo grabbed hard hats and handed her one. She put it in her head, and he stifled a smile. He'd once told her how cute she was in her firefighting helmet, and she hadn't taken it as a compliment. She'd been cranky with him the rest of the day, until he got her back to her place and did things that made her decidedly uncranky.

"Let's go."

He went ahead. No one else was there, though there was heavy equipment on the other side of the lot. They were obviously prepping to level the place. He couldn't blame the company that owned the property—it lost money the longer it sat here unused, and the investigation had held it up for long enough without yielding much. This was Bo's last chance, literally.

The light was fine as the sun came in through the rafters, and safe passage through the burned-out building was marked with small flags and chalk so that inspectors and others weren't injured.

"Make sure you stay within the marked areas. Other spots are not safe."

Erin nodded, but was otherwise quiet. Bo hoped this wasn't a mistake.

"It's so spooky," she finally said when they paused inside the large entry, looking around. "But also weirdly pretty. The way the sun comes down in between the burned rafters."

"I've thought that, too, though it feels wrong to see something artistic in so much ruin."

She agreed silently and walked ahead of him, her expression mostly curious. He let her lead, but made sure she stayed on the safe route. He wondered what it would be like, to see it all again for the first time. Even with his experience, it was still overwhelming sometimes. The ability to analyze discrete parts of a fire scene as well as the overall picture took discipline and practice because there was so much to look at. It was also easy to see something misleading or something that could fool you.

Eventually, you learned the patterns and the telltale signs of various kinds of fire, how it behaved or how it had started or progressed, but there was still an element of surprise. It paid not to get too bogged down in patterns, since that's when you could miss the most important things.

Maybe it was the same way in relationships? What had he missed that he and Erin had gone so terribly wrong?

He pushed romantic musings from his mind. Though he'd been over the site several times now, some things had changed due to weather exposure and other peo-

ple invading the area, and he tried to see it all with
fresh eyes.

What might he have missed?

Erin started moving faster through the charred
walkway, as if she were moving toward something.
As if she were drawn in a certain direction. Bo followed, fascinated.

She stopped at a spot in the far corner, looking up.

"Something happened up there?"

She turned and looked at him, her face strained—
parts fear, anxiety and pressure.

Bo followed her gaze.

"That was the general quadrant of the building that
you and Joe were sent in to check out. They thought
there could be toxic chemicals stored there. But you
were both found in a completely different area of the
building, which is one of the things we can't account
for."

Her expression was pained as she stared, trying to
remember so hard, and Bo almost couldn't take the
agony on her face.

"I can feel something…like, panic," she said, and
he stepped closer as her breathing quickened. "But
nothing else."

He noticed her hand was shaking as she lifted it to
her face.

"This is enough, I think. Let's get out of here."

"No, I'm okay. I'm just so frustrated. Show me the
spot where we fell."

Bo shook his head. "I don't think that's a good idea."

Erin stared through the rafters at the same spot on
the second level for several more long seconds, and

then, before he could stop her, she took off for the stairs that went up to that floor. Outside the safety zone.

"Erin!" he shouted, but she was fast and halfway up the steps by the time he followed.

"I'm okay."

"It's not safe. Those supports are burned. Come back down slowly."

She looked at him over the rail. "They're knocking this down tomorrow. I need to see."

She continued her progress up the stairs, which seemed to be holding, so Bo muttered a curse under his breath and followed.

Erin was never reckless before, which made her one of the best. She knew that being reckless was what could cost people their lives, and Bo hoped that wasn't the case now.

She was also about sixty-five pounds lighter than he was, and when he stood on the second step, it gave an ominous creak.

She'd ambled up fine, but he could take the whole thing down in seconds, and then she'd be trapped.

Cursing more vehemently, he backed off.

She was up there for a few minutes, quiet, and he started to worry even more.

"Erin? What's going on?" he shouted up the steps, wishing he'd never brought her here.

She came to the edge, peered down at him through jagged, burned-out boards.

"We ran," she said, her complexion as ashen as the walls around her. Then she looked over his head, back toward the east side of the building. "Joe took off and ran that way."

Chills worked down Bo's spine as she pointed in the

direction of the spot where she was nearly killed. He balanced the excitement at her memory with concern for her current safety.

"Okay, good—that's good. Now, come down very slowly, carefully, and show me where."

She looked like a ghost, but she made it back down the rickety steps safely.

Bo grabbed her and hugged her tight to him, relieved, and then held her at arm's length, staring hard into her face.

"Don't *ever* do that again. You could've been hurt or killed. Stay on the damned safety path from here on, or I swear, I'll arrest you and put you in jail for the night."

He wouldn't really—or maybe he would.

He'd replayed the scene of her falling through those stairs about a dozen times while she was up there, and if she couldn't be safe, he was taking her out of here, memory or no memory.

He'd almost lost her once, and he wasn't going to risk it again.

"You're right. Sorry, I know I shouldn't have done that, but I had to get up there. Something made us run. I don't know why, but we took off in this direction."

"Running away from someone?"

She shook her head. "I don't know."

There had been nothing on the second floor that Bo knew of, and it was easy to think you saw something in the room full of smoke and flames. But if she could remember this much, there had to be more there.

Bo slipped his arm around Erin's shoulders as much for support as to make sure she didn't bolt on him again.

"Okay, show me where."

She zeroed in on the exact spot where they had found Joe dead and Erin pinned under a beam.

"What else?" he prompted.

She stared at the spot for a while and then sniffled. When she glanced over at him, fat tears rolled down her cheeks.

Bo was stunned. He had never once seen Erin cry. Ever.

"Nothing. There's nothing else. We came here, but that's all I know. Why can't I remember this? Why can I remember other things but not *this?*"

Sobs took over, shaking her body, and Bo wrapped his arm around her again, walking her out of the warehouse and back into the light and fresh air. Outside, her tears subsided after a few minutes, and he let her lean on him until they did. Another first.

"I'm sorry," she said, sounding miserable.

Bo looked down into her face, wishing he could make every bit of pain he saw there go away.

"You have nothing to be sorry for."

"We don't know that, do we? I remember running and Joe following me, but I don't know why. I led him to his death. It was my fault. Maybe his family is right to blame me."

"No." Bo said the word with absolute conviction. "First, you don't remember enough to know what happened, let alone take responsibility for it. Second, you and Joe were both experienced firefighters. If you knew you had to get out, and he followed, it was a good call, or he wouldn't have gone. What happened next was an accident, or it was someone else's doing. But either way, it is *not your fault*. Don't even go there."

Erin seemed as shocked at his vehemence as he was, but some of her distress cleared.

"Okay. But how can we stop them from demolishing this place? If I can't come back, I may not ever remember the rest."

Bo agreed, but he didn't know if he had enough to reopen the case and stop the demo. A few vague memories wouldn't be much to argue with.

"C'mon. Let's go back to the office and see what we can do to make that happen. It might be too late, but we can try. Then you're going home to relax, dress up in something nice and let me take you out, okay?"

She wiped the tears from her face and frowned. "Okay. Jeez, I hate crying. It makes me feel like such a *girl*."

Bo laughed and hugged her one more time.

"Now there's the Erin I know."

She smiled slightly and Bo smiled back, but it didn't reflect how he felt. Not really. It was good that she was remembering—it seemed like more memories surfaced every day. He couldn't help but wonder how long it would be before she remembered that she hadn't wanted to be with him. Until that happened, he'd be there for her. He'd do his job, and then he'd leave this all behind, as well.

9

ERIN GRIMACED AT the pile of clothes on her bed and made a frustrated growl, looking at the clock. She had four hours before Bo came back to take her for a night out. He'd said to wear something "nice." She wasn't sure what "nice" meant, but she was fairly sure it wasn't anything on her bed. Everything she'd gotten before was casual, flirty, but not necessarily what she needed for a fancier excursion.

She needed to get something appropriate, not that she had much of an idea what that was, and she needed it now. She needed some shoes, too.

Grabbing her bag, she headed for the door. There would definitely be something at the mall, and it couldn't be that hard to find a nice, basic dress and some shoes, right?

Twenty minutes later, she was in one of the larger department stores at the Carousel Center—now also known as Destiny USA. She hoped it was her destiny to find the right dress, and fast.

Spotting the women's department, she approached

a clerk who looked well dressed, and tapped her on the shoulder.

"Yes? May I help you?" The woman was maybe a few years older, but looked like a million bucks.

"Please. I need something nice for a dinner date. A dress, I suppose? Can you find something that would be appropriate?"

The woman stood back and took in Erin from head to toe, making her feel a tad self-conscious, but this was no time to be shy.

"Do you know how nice? Very formal, or less so?"

"I have no idea. He said something nice," she said, rolling her eyes.

The saleswoman laughed. "I think I have a few ideas. Some new styles we just got in from New York."

"Sounds good."

Erin followed the woman, whose name tag said her name was Emily. They arrived at a rack of dresses.

"We'll find something here. I'm Emily, by the way."

"I'm Erin." She stared at the rack, frowning. "They're all black. Don't you think something with more color?"

Emily winked at her. "Trust me. If the key word is 'nice' you can't miss with black. It will fit in any-where. Especially these, with your figure. You don't need much to be stunning."

Erin couldn't be sure, but she thought this could be the first time a woman ever made her blush. Emily chuckled, grabbing a handful of dresses and beckon-ing Erin to follow.

"Here, try these on. This one first," she instructed, and Erin realized the woman hadn't even asked her size, but she probably didn't need to. The woman seemed to know more about dressing her up than she did, so Erin decided to trust her.

Dutifully shucking her jeans and T-shirt to try on the first dress, her trust was well-placed. The slip of fabric fit like a glove.

"Wow," Erin breathed, looking at herself in the mirror.

It had appeared innocent enough on the hanger, but on her body, there was nothing "nice" about this dress. The soft fabric skimmed just above her upper thigh, and Erin had to resist the urge to tug it down. She could feel air-conditioning from the vent at the side of the dressing room wafting up and cooling her...no, this was too short.

And when she saw the price tag in the mirror, she decided it was also far too much money for so little fabric.

"Erin, do you need any help?"

"No, thanks. I, um, I think that first one isn't quite... me." *Or doesn't cover up enough of me to go out in public,* she thought as she flipped through Emily's other choices.

One designer dress was simpler and offered a bit more coverage, as well as being about a quarter of the price of the other dress.

Erin slipped it on, and she liked how the fabric just fell into place. The V-neck was sexy but tasteful, and the hemline was a more reasonable midthigh. She ran her hands over the folds in the skirt—pleats? They made the plain black fancier.

This one was definitely nice.

Confident, she went out to get a second opinion.

"I like this one?" Erin spoke the statement as more of a question as the clerk eyed her critically.

"Gorgeous! That definitely suits you. The satin crepe really softens and accents your shape. Nice choice."

"Good. Thank you. If you can suggest a pair of shoes to match, you will officially be my hero."

Emily laughed. "Oh, shoes, yes. I know just the pair. And you'll need a bag, and perhaps some stockings? Garters?"

Erin stared. "Do I need all that?"

Emily laughed. "It's good to have at least one entire ensemble. And men love garters. Trust me."

"I guess it can't hurt to try it on."

"I'll be right back."

Erin was sure that the saleswoman was more excited about the shopping than she was, but it was going much more easily than she imagined, so that was a blessing. Sitting down on a bench by the entry to the dressing room, she waited and was glad to find she could sit comfortably—and modestly—in the dress.

"Erin?"

Erin saw Dana standing a few feet away.

"Hey, Dana," she said with a smile, and then saw her friend's curious gaze as she took in the dress.

"Whoa. That's a killer dress."

"Thanks. Emily, ah, the saleswoman, picked it. You know me, I know nothing about clothes."

"You suddenly got the urge to shop? Are you feeling okay?"

They laughed, and Erin shrugged. "I had some time and figured I would pick up a few less-casual things. Just in case, you know?"

"Sure. And you hit the nail on the head the first time. That's perfect on you. I love that designer. I have several of her pieces myself, though now I can't wear them after seeing how amazing they look on you."

"Yeah, right." Erin waved her off. "I'd never heard of her before this." Erin had a feeling she'd never heard of any dress designers.

"Here we go! I have some heels I'm sure you'll like, along with the garters and the stockings. I can show you some evening bags on the way out, and I promise your fella is going to have heart palpitations when he sees you tonight."

"Fella? You're seeing a *fella* tonight?" Dana's stare sharpened on Erin like a hawk's on its prey.

"I have to try these on," Erin said hastily and sought refuge in the dressing room, but not before she heard Dana's warning that she could wait.

Oh, crap.

Leaning against the door for her temporary reprieve, Erin knew the jig was up. Whatever a jig was.

She'd have to tell Dana something, and she was a lousy liar. Especially to her friends.

Focusing on the shoes, she checked out the garters and stockings, but decided to pass, simply pulling on a pair of light gold, strappy sandals that ended up being far more comfortable than they looked.

Taking a deep breath, she headed back out, finding Emily and Dana chatting easily, both turning their attention to her with equal approval.

"Perfect." Emily sighed.

"Those shoes make your legs look a million miles long," Dana said with a low whistle.

Erin was pleased with their reactions, and she had to admit, she felt great, too.

"So what will *your* fella think?" Dana asked, blinking innocently.

"I, um, he…" Erin sputtered and cursed under her breath, retreating to the dressing room and closing the door.

Seconds later, Dana's voice came from the other side of the door.

"Hey, Erin. I'm sorry. I didn't mean to make you bolt. I just… I'm surprised if you have a date and you didn't tell me. Are you okay in there?"

Erin's shoulders sagged. Was she okay?

Hours ago, she was climbing up a burned-out ruin trying to remember one of the most critical events of her life—and now she was standing here like Cinderella getting ready for the ball. Maybe talking to someone about all this could help. Maybe it would make everything stop spinning for a second.

Erin opened the door and stood back, inviting her friend inside.

"I'm sorry. I didn't know I had a date until today, so this is kind of last-minute but…the guy thing isn't. It's actually pretty complicated. I'm starting to feel… dizzy. Like I don't know which end is up."

She sat down on the narrow seat on the wall, deflated.

"Want to talk about it?" Dana joined her.

Erin stood up. "Yes. I have some time before I have to get home and get ready."

"Let's get your things, and we can go walk while you tell me about you and Bo. Iced coffee is on me."

Erin gaped in surprise.

Dana rolled her eyes. "I notice things. Like the look on your face when Bo showed up for painting a few weeks ago. C'mon, change, and we'll talk. I've been dying to know about this for, like forever."

"Erin, is there anything else I can help you with?" Emily spoke from the other side of the door.

"I'm good, thanks, Emily. I'm taking the dress and the shoes. I'll be out in just a second."

"Take your time. I'll meet you at the register."

Erin listened as the clerk's heels tapped on the floor as she walked away.

"How long have you known?"

"I didn't know, but I suspected."

Erin was suddenly nervous. "Do you think anyone else knows?"

"No. You kidding? Everyone else we know is male, and they don't notice that stuff. Get dressed, and I'll meet you out there."

Dana slipped out while Erin changed and gathered up her things, coming to terms with the fact that some-one knew—and had known for a while, by the sound of it—about her and Bo. It was…a relief.

They paid for her new dress and shoes and made their way out to the coffee shop, and then walked along the wide aisles of the new mall.

"So you and the marshal," Dana invited. "Tell me."

"Well, like I said, it's kind of…an on-again, off-again thing," she said, for lack of a better way of de-scribing it. "And I don't remember all of it, but that's kind of why we're back together now. For the moment anyway."

"What does that mean?"

Erin wasn't sure how much she should share of Bo's

career plans, as she knew they were waiting until they had a replacement for him before making a general announcement. But after swearing Dana to silence, even with Scott, she told her the whole story—as much as she knew anyway.

"So, let me get this straight. You two were together all last year, you broke up with him, and now he's back with you again, but only so you can remember about the fire?"

"That about sums it up. But he's moving to Virginia soon, so you know…when he goes, that will be that."

Dana leveled a look at her. "And that's okay with you?"

Erin shrugged. "It was the deal."

"That's not what I asked. A woman doesn't dash out to buy special clothes for a guy she's not into—in a big way. I'm worried, Erin. You've been through a lot. Are you falling for Bo, no matter what kind of deal you two had?"

She was about to say no, but stopped. "I don't know. I definitely feel something, I guess. I like him, and we're good together. But without knowing everything, I can't know what's between us. Not really. We broke up for a reason. The idea of him leaving so soon bothers me, but a lot of that is because of what happened today. The building will be wrecked, and I'm remembering some things, but not enough."

"And the fact that he's going means maybe he's not feeling the same things you are?"

Erin shrugged. It pinched to hear the words aloud.

"I can't blame him. I opted out, and this is just… an experiment, I guess. Also, I'm the only one who might be able to help him get more evidence to find this arsonist."

"That's too much pressure for you to put on yourself. It seems to me you have to separate out the fire stuff from the relationship stuff. You're a different person now. Believe me," Dana said with a laugh, looking at her shopping bags. "Maybe what you have with Bo could be different, too."

Erin shook her head. "It's different because I can't remember why I didn't want to stay in the relationship, and he's moving on. He was clear about that. I won't change the rules of the game now. It wouldn't be fair. And you can't tell anyone, Dana, please—even Scott. Okay?"

"I promise. If you promise to talk to me if you need to, when you need someone."

"I will. Thanks. I'd better get going. I still have to shower and get ready."

As they reached the doors that led to the parking garage, Dana put her hand on Erin's arm.

"Erin, please be careful, okay? You've been hurt once, in the fire, but there are a whole lot of different ways you could end up hurt this time. I don't want to see that happen. You've been through enough already."

Erin took a deep breath and smiled brightly. "I'll be okay, Dana. But thanks. I went into this with my eyes wide-open, but it means a lot to know I can talk to you."

After they hugged and parted ways, Dana's parting words lingered. Erin's pace increased across the lot, the anticipation of seeing Bo, and of dressing up for him, giving her an extra zip. Maybe she had changed, and maybe Bo had, too. But she meant what she said.

She wouldn't change the rules of the game now, even if it meant that she was bound to get hurt in the end.

Bo approached Erin's door with a brisk step, hoping he hadn't overdone it as he looked down at the roses in his arms. He hadn't bought roses for a woman in a very long time—the last time was probably for his mother on her birthday. He hadn't ever gotten flowers for Erin, because she never seemed to want that kind of thing.

Maybe she still didn't? He paused on the walk, looking at the roses and his dress shoes, shiny against the concrete, wondering if she might feel pressured, if this was too much.

He wanted to take her away from the ugliness of the fire scene, to take her mind off it completely. But she'd never been much for dress-up.

Well, he had reservations, but he could cancel them if need be. Whatever she wanted, he could go with the flow. That's what he told himself as he continued to the door and rang the bell.

When the door opened, he almost dropped the roses.

"Incredible," he whispered, taking her in as she stood before him, nervously raising her hand to her hair to push it back, and then frowning, as she often did, still forgetting it was short now.

Without saying a word, she invited him in, and Bo accepted, unable to take his eyes off her.

The black dress hugged her curves and fluttered down over her hips in soft folds that made her ultra-feminine, her long, bare legs exposed, the pretty gold sandals she wore making her look like some fairy-tale creature. His gaze drifted up, lingering on the way the deep neckline exposed the swell of her breasts and made his mouth go dry. Her short hair combined with the V-neck made her throat impossibly long and graceful. He swallowed, wanting to taste her there, his cock twitching with interest inside the loose dress pants he wore.

"You are insanely beautiful, do you know that?" he said roughly once he was inside the door, setting the roses down on a nearby table. He needed to touch her to make sure she was real.

"Thank you, I—"

It was as far as he let her go before he kissed her, hands on her shoulders, their bodies not quite touching, but he breathed her in as he touched his tongue to hers.

"You smell like…gardenia."

Nothing strong or overwhelming, but he could pick the scent up on her skin as he came close.

"It's a new soap I bought."

"It's perfect. Like you."

She smiled, her cheeks turning pink in a feminine manner that made him even harder.

If he didn't reroute his thinking, they'd never get out the door. Taking a step back, he picked the roses up again.

"These are for you," he said, presenting them to her.

Her lips parted with pleasure as she brought them to her nose.

"They smell wonderful, thank you. That's the signature of a good flower, you know, the scent."

"Don't they all have scent?"

Bo was again captivated by how the dress swished around her bottom as she crossed the room in front of him.

"Not a lot of the ones you find in grocery stores,

and that kind of thing. I forget why, Kit told me. Some are made that way to not aggravate allergies, but others are just made to be…well, generic, I guess."

"Interesting."

Though, really, all he wanted to do was watch her move in that dress, go to dinner, and then get her alone and take it off her.

"Thank you. They are gorgeous," she said admiringly, putting them in a vase on her new dining room table.

"You're welcome. The place looks great, by the way—you've added new pieces."

She smiled widely then, genuinely pleased as she looked around at her new, renovated surroundings.

"I love it. It feels more personal now, like a home should."

A home—something Erin never seemed to care about much before. Bo cleared his throat.

"We have reservations in a half hour. Are you ready to go?"

"I am," she said brightly, picking up a small black bag with a gold chain. Bo didn't even know she owned clothes like these. She looked elegant and sexy in every possible way as she walked out to the door.

He was glad he'd brought his car instead of the truck.

"Oh, my, that's yours?"

Erin stood by the side of the classic black sports car, looking like every man's fantasy. Bo wanted to put her on the hood and push that dress up—

"Bo?"

He snapped out of his thoughts with a chagrined smile. "Sorry. Yes, that's mine. It was my father's. We worked on it together for years, and he left it to me when he passed on. It's a '67. My pride and joy. I only take it out of the garage for the occasional summer drive and a special occasion."

"It's beautiful," she said admiringly, running her hand over the edge of the roof.

Bo joined her, opening the passenger-side door. "I'm glad you like it."

And he was. Erin had admired the car before, and they had taken a few drives in it, but tonight felt different. He'd wondered if she'd remember. They'd driven the GTO to the apple orchard on their last real date, but apparently none of that was coming back to her as she buckled herself into the luxurious ivory leather seat.

He got in and did the same, heading to the highway, loving the growl of the engine as he did so.

"Where are we going?"

"The inn, in Skaneateles. Do you remember it?"

"Not really. I know the town, but don't have any specific memories of the restaurant. Did we go there often?"

"We went to the pub a few times, but not all dressed up like this."

"Speaking of which, you look great, by the way. I wasn't sure what to wear. I was so relieved when I saw you were dressed up, too."

Bo grinned. "Sorry about that. I wondered the same, on the way to the door, if I had overdone it."

"I'd say we did just fine."

"Agreed."

They drove through the winding roads of the countryside between Syracuse and the small Finger Lakes town to the southwest of the city, enjoying the view. Bo drove slowly along the main street by the lake, enjoying the attention the car always drew, but this time, it was eclipsed by the attention Erin drew after he parked and helped her out.

There wasn't a head that didn't turn as she strolled down the street, and he tucked her arm into his possessively, letting people know she was absolutely taken.

And then he caught himself, realizing he'd forgotten again that this wasn't what it seemed to be.

Erin seemed to pick up on his tension, and put her other hand on his arm, facing him.

"Bo? Everything okay?"

He smiled, leaning in to kiss her cheek. "Yes, sorry. I forgot if I'd locked the car," he lied smoothly.

She relaxed again, too, as they progressed up the stone steps in the inn and were shown to their table.

It was a reminder that this was a fantasy, but he saw no reason not to completely enjoy it anyway. He ordered some wine and watched Erin as she studied the menu, not wanting to look away, as if she might disappear. As if he was imagining it all.

But when she smiled at him over the top of the card, her eyes bright, he knew it was 100 percent real. As were the very dangerous emotions clutching at his chest.

Their waitress arrived and took their orders, and Bo put the worrisome thoughts away for the evening. Right now, he was here with the most beautiful woman he could imagine, and he wanted to embrace it. Live in the moment, that's what they always said, right?

This arrangement with Erin was what it was, but that didn't stop him from having feelings for her—which was why he'd done all of this in the first place.

Because he cared. He'd never stopped caring. It didn't change anything.

"I think I remember walking down by the lake…out on the pier? Something funny happened? We laughed really hard?"

"Yes, that was one day last summer. There was a guy proposing to his girl out there. He wanted to make a big deal, and managed to crawl up on the rail, proposing from there for everyone to hear. When she said yes, he got so excited that he lost his balance and fell in the lake. He was fine, and had to swim the few yards to shore. He was yelling how much he loved her all the way in," Bo said with a grin, remembering, too.

"Yes," she said, staring out the nearby window at the water. "I think I remember some of that. A young man."

"Very. Who was also fined by the local police as soon as he hit the shoreline, but he didn't really care."

They laughed, and it lightened the mood. Their wine arrived, and an appetizer, then their entrées. Bo loosened up as they chatted about this and that, nothing having to do with the fire or anything serious.

But then Erin asked, "So, the new job? Do you have any more news?"

"It's official. I'm heading down the second week of August, and they should have a new investigator ready to take my place here in a week or two. He's experienced, so it won't take long to bring him up to speed. We got lucky in that way. I'll need to go down a week ahead to get an apartment, that kind of thing."

"You're excited," she said with a smile.

"I am. It's what I've been working for all these years. It will be challenging, but I can't wait, really."

Her smile faded, and he wanted to kick himself.

"I mean—"

She reached over, covering his hand with hers. "No, I completely get it. And you should be excited. I'm excited for you. This is incredible."

"Thanks," he said, letting it drop and turning his hand so that he could rub his thumb over the inside of her palm.

The touch made her eyes darken, the mood shifting quickly between them.

"It might have been presumptuous of me, but I reserved a room upstairs for the night. But we could go home, if you want to," he said.

Erin wrapped her fingers around his, squeezing. "A room here is a nice idea."

Bo's heart picked up speed as he paid the check and took her hand, pulling her to his side.

"I couldn't agree more."

10

ERIN EXPLORED THE beautiful room, decorated with antique furniture including a huge, comfortable bed that looked out over the lake. She took the chance to enjoy the view as Bo retrieved their dessert and wine order from the server who brought it to their door.

"I knew you were ordering some wine, but champagne? You're really going all out tonight, Myers," she said with a smile.

Their eyes met, and she took a breath. "That's the first time I've called you by your last name. Like I used to do."

He looked down at the tray, grabbing the bottle of wine, and Erin couldn't tell if he was happy about that memory or not. She also found it disconcerting when old behaviors suddenly appeared, like a name or some bit of knowledge slipping from her lips unbidden.

The pop of the cork made her jump, and when Bo looked up again, he was smiling.

"Grab a glass," he said easily. Erin smiled back, glad he was okay. She was reading too much into everything.

She held both glasses while he filled them and then took one after he put the bottle back in the holder.

"To old memories," he said, raising his glass.

And to making new ones, she wanted to add. Instead, she softly echoed his words instead, and clinked her glass to his.

Bo pulled something from his pocket, setting it on the dresser. Music started to play.

The song... Erin felt it before she could remember anything. It was important. Emotion swamped her, and she felt tears come to her eyes, but she couldn't remember.

"Tell me about that song, Bo. I know it's important, but I don't know why."

"We went to the concert at the fair last year. The band kept doing encores, and we kept trying to leave, as did a bunch of other people. We all made it to the parking lot, but then they started playing this song, and all the people in the lot started dancing. So we did, too. It was the only time we'd ever danced."

"It sounds like magic."

"It was...special."

"There's more. I can see it in your face. What happened?"

Bo took a deep breath. "When we were dancing, I told you I loved you."

Erin felt a flutter in her chest. "Oh."

"And you didn't say it back."

"Oh," she repeated, crossing the room to stand in front of him. "I'm so sorry."

"No need to apologize. It was too soon for you. I didn't mind telling you, and sure, it would have been nice to hear that you felt the same way, but it didn't change how I felt."

"I wish I could remember."

So she hadn't loved him? Even she couldn't believe that, given all of what she did remember and what she felt now. Not that she wanted to think about that, but it was what it was. She couldn't deny it.

Bo's hand cupped her jaw, then fell. "Me, too."

He put his glass down, and Erin stepped in closer, taking his hands in hers. "I don't know what was going on in my head then, or what my reasons were. I don't know why I was…like I was. But if I said I didn't love you…I think I was lying. I don't know why, but I know it's true."

"You don't need to say that."

"I'm not just saying it to make you feel better. I'm saying it because of how I feel now. I know I loved you…I can still feel it. Right here, right now. I still—"

She stopped, aware of what she was about to say, and unsure if she should. It wasn't fair to either of them, was it, to say such things?

"Erin." His voice was so soft she wasn't sure if he'd spoken at first, but when she looked up into his eyes, they were so raw with emotion, so hungry, that she felt it down in her soul. "Say it."

"I don't think—"

"Please."

Erin didn't know what had stopped her from telling him before, but it seemed like the most natural thing in the world now, the words leaving her lips with no effort at all.

"I think I did love you then, Bo, but I know I love you now."

He gathered her in, crushing her against him in his arms, as if she were life itself.

"Erin, I never stopped loving you. Even when it was killing me, I still wanted the pain. And now, to hear you say it…I know this thing we have isn't about love but—"

She pulled back, staring up into his face. "But it can be tonight. I know you have to go, and I don't know what I'm doing next, but we have right now. Tonight."

"Yes," he agreed. "It definitely can be for tonight."

Erin didn't remember anything from her past as Bo kissed her as though he cherished every taste, every touch, but she suddenly didn't care so much about the past. The present was all that mattered.

She loved Bo. She could feel it in her bones, in her blood. Whether she could remember or not, if she had denied it in the past, then she'd been a liar.

The realization made her want to show him how she really felt. Maybe she wanted, to some degree, to make up for how she had hurt him before. She hated that she'd caused him such pain, and placed both hands on either side of his face, showing him the same tenderness he was showing her.

Breaking the kiss, both of their pulses had picked up. The song playing on the iPod he'd left on the dresser ended, and she smiled into his face.

"I think maybe we need a new song."

Leaving him for a second, she went to the device and flipped through the playlist, finally finding one that she loved.

As Nat King Cole's melodic voice, joining his daughter in a duet, and the strains of "Unforgettable" filled the room. Bo laughed softly as she went into his arms.

"Perfect," he said.

They started to sway, dancing in the small space by the window, and Erin knew peace for the first time in months.

But that changed to something hotter as they moved together, and Bo's lips whispered over the skin of her throat, moving up to her lips, and then back down, lower, tracing the vee of her dress. Though he didn't touch her there, her nipples hardened at the proximal contact, and she let out a soft sigh as her head dropped back.

His hands found their way down over her hips, bracing her bare thighs on either side, his skin hot. Pressing his mouth to the inside of her knee, he slid his hands upward, moving her skirt upward, as well.

"I've been dying to know what you're wearing under this dress," he said.

Suddenly, Erin wished she'd bought the garters and stockings, but then took that back as Bo's thumbs grazed a very sensitive spot through the thin silk of the panties she wore, making her gasp. The other accessories would have only been barriers to his touch, and Erin wanted nothing between them.

"Very nice," he said, taking his time as he looked at her in the black bikinis she'd bought on the way out of the store, made of silk and lace, with a tiny bow on the front. Like a gift, which was exactly how Bo treated them.

He pulled them off gently, letting her step out of them without catching them on her shoes, and then worked his way back up her leg in a path of hot kisses that ended right where she needed him.

"Yes, Bo, please," she begged as he widened her stance, the skirt of her beautiful dress crunched in his hands as he knelt before her, and flicked his tongue out to taste her.

He murmured huskily against her sex, using nothing but his mouth to send her into a breathless frenzy of need.

She murmured his name as she felt the tension winding too tight. He looked up curiously, concerned, and she smiled.

"Together" was all she needed to say.

He stood, and she led him over to the bed, taking her time as she undid his tie, then the buttons on his shirt, pushing it off with his jacket. Leaning in, she brushed her lips over the rough hair on his chest, over one nipple, then the other, liking the male groan that followed.

Turning around, she waited for him to unzip her, and let the dress fall to the floor around her feet. He unsnapped the bra as well, and she shrugged that off, turning back to him.

The way he gazed at her, naked before him, made her feel like never wearing clothes again.

Wordlessly, she divested him of the rest of his clothing until they were both completely naked to each other. Her hands trembled slightly as she embraced him, pressing herself against him, his hardness eager against her hip.

The kiss went on forever, as she wanted it to, and when her blood heated even more, she pulled away and lay back on the bed.

"You're too far away," she said, holding out her hand to him.

"I love looking at you."

"There are far better things to do with me than look," she said with a smile that made him smile, too.

In the next second, he was there, next to her, over her, pressing her down into the mattress as the kisses deepened and the need swelled.

They both went as slowly as possible, making every touch last, every kiss linger, until Erin couldn't take it anymore. Wanting to be completely connected to him, she parted her thighs, urging him down in between.

He slipped inside her, slow and easy, planting himself deep as he watched her face, never taking his eyes from her.

"I do love you, Bo. Whatever happens after this, right now I need you to know that."

"Oh, Erin, I love you, too. Always will," he said, coming down for one more kiss as he started to move.

Erin was feeling too much as he pushed her higher, her body wanting everything that his had to give, but also feeling, inevitably, like this was a hello and a goodbye at the same time. It made it all unbearably emotional as the pleasure gripped her, making her shudder under and around him, their arms wrapped around each other so tightly she was surprised they could move at all.

Bo took his time, rocking into her in a steady rhythm as she whispered delicious, naughty words to him. Telling him what she liked best made him lose control in a way that ended in a bone-racking orgasm for both of them, leaving them spent and exhausted, and still twined together as they drifted off to sleep. Erin wasn't anxious to see morning come at all.

KIT PLUCKED PINK-WHITE peony petals from her hair as she let Hank pull her up to standing and straightened her dress. She looked at him with a tender smile. He also had flower parts stuck to him, including one large pink petal that she peeled from his cheek.

Sex in her backyard garden. Amazing. The sex, and the man.

Luckily, Erin had felt guilty for disappearing the day before—and all night, as well—and had come into the shop early, offering to stay for as long as Kit needed her. Her sister didn't say where she'd been, and Kit decided not to ask her. It wouldn't do any good anyway. Still, Erin seemed different—tired, but happy. And smelling like gardenias, which was interesting.

Kit had decided to take the opportunity to come home for lunch only to find Hank weeding and pruning, applying fertilizer like a pro. Of course she did tell him none of it was necessary before she'd seduced him, right there in the yard. They had fences, and the neighbors were at work anyway.

Her knees still had grass stains, and looking down, she was pretty proud of that fact and that she'd ridden Hank into submission right there near the peony patch.

"You surprise me," he said, leaning down to kiss her again, stirring the embers that hadn't quite settled yet.

"You surprised me, too. I didn't expect to find you out here in the garden."

"I know you have your hands full, and I had some extra time. I forgot how much I missed this. I used to have a small garden, but the more the department demands took over, the more I let it go. I think I'll try to get it going again."

"That's a great idea."

They went inside where it was cooler, and Kit washed up at the kitchen sink.

"I took up most of your lunchtime," Hank said, watching her. "Why don't you let me buy you lunch before you head back to work?"

She loved the way he looked at her, how he focused on her. She'd never felt so much the center of someone's attention before, and it was very nice. But it was also a problem.

It made some of the problems in the rest of her life go away, at least for the time that they were naked and sweaty together. Like the fact that she'd hardly seen Erin for most of the week, and that she was nervously waiting on a loan that could give her shop a second chance and save her from taking drastic action to solve her financial worries.

Like selling her mother's home and getting an apartment.

If she had to, she would—it would probably be easier to maintain, and the money would help her keep the business going.

But it broke her heart to think of leaving this house.

"Hey, you okay? Why so sad all of a sudden?"

She'd become completely lost in her thoughts, and forgot Hank was watching. He was too perceptive. She enjoyed his close attention when he was making love to her, but not so much when he tried to read her.

"Nothing, really, I just need to get back. I'll bring a yogurt from the fridge and I'll be fine. Thanks, though."

Kit was shutting him out, she knew it. She had to. She enjoyed Hank's company, and the sex—well, the sex was outstanding. But he was getting too close. She'd enjoyed finding him here when she came home, but he was always doing something for her. Helping at the shop, bringing her food, weeding her garden… making her lose her mind in bed.

But she knew it wouldn't last. Just like the garden she loved but had ignored, this fling, or whatever it was, was doomed to eventually suffer at the demands of his work. He'd been on his off-time rotation, and then had a few vacation days he'd needed to take—as soon as he was back on the job, she would fall to the background. She accepted that and didn't want to make it any harder than it had to be.

"Kit, what's going on?"

"What do you mean?" she asked as she pulled some yogurt and a banana from the fridge, stuffing them in her purse.

"You're hot, and then you're cold. I don't know if I did something wrong. Did I step in something here?"

She took a deep breath, not having the time or the energy for this right now.

"No, you're fine—wonderful, in fact. I would much rather do what we did out in the garden than eat, believe me," she said with a naughty smile in his direction.

Make it about the sex and keep it that way, she told herself.

"Yeah, that was good, but there's more to it, isn't there? You look like you have the weight of the world on your shoulders."

"It's nothing. I really appreciate your help, but I can't

talk about this right now. I have to get back to the shop to meet a bridal party in thirty minutes."

"Sure, whatever you say," he said, turning his back and grabbing his jacket from the chair. It had some grass stains on it as well, where he'd been on his back in her yard, with her lying on top of him.

She'd hurt his feelings. Cursing under her breath, she closed the fridge and faced him.

"Hank," she said, catching him as he was at the door. "It's just… I have a lot going on. That's all."

He nodded slowly. "Sure, Kath. I get it. I wish I could help."

"That's kind of the thing. I appreciate your help, I really do—but I need to handle things on my own. It's just who I am. I appreciate all that you do, but—"

"You'd rather I didn't do it?"

His cool expression and the flat look in his eyes clutched at her chest. She liked Hank, she really did, but it was all too much. Still…

"Yes, kind of. It's hard to explain. I guess that I don't want to be dependent on anyone."

"There's a big difference between letting someone help and being dependent on them," he said reasonably.

"It feels the same to me."

"You don't always have to do things alone, you know."

Kit wasn't convinced. How did she tell him about all the years she watched her mother do exactly that? Handle everything in the house, the finances, her two children, alone? Because her father was at the station most of the time. And after that, how Kit had started her business, cared for her mother, alone, when Erin had been too busy with the job?

Kit was used to relying on herself, and it was safer that way, she finally realized. When you only depended on yourself, no one else could let you down.

"It's how I've lived for so long, I don't know any other way," she said, helpless to explain it to him.

"Maybe it's time you learned. I know you're afraid. And I know why."

She was surprised, and he met her eyes knowingly.

"I know what you must have gone through, with your dad, with Erin... I can't promise that the job won't take me away from you sometimes, but when I can be here, I will. Completely. I want to be here with you, more than just about anything. Do you believe me?"

She wanted him to leave, and she wanted him to stay. It was like being two people: one who needed to focus on her business and protect her heart, and the other who wanted more with this beautiful, generous man. One who yearned for what he could give her. One who wanted to run away from it full tilt.

But both sides believed him.

"I want that, too, though it scares the heck out of me."

The words were out before she could stop them, the part of her that needed him winning. His expression cleared, his eyes warming, and her world felt right again. She couldn't stand to see him hurt, especially when she was the one doing it. She didn't want him to leave and not come back. Fear grabbed at her heart at the same time hope lifted it.

She was a mess. That was so, so bad, but she couldn't deny it.

He leaned in for a gentle kiss. "It's going to be okay, Kathleen. You have to have some faith."

She let him pull her into a hug, unsure exactly what he meant. Faith in what? But she was tired of thinking and enjoyed his strength for a few more minutes before pulling away.

"I actually do have to get back. See you tonight, around seven?"

"I'll be here. Promise."

She took a deep breath, feeling better about the day knowing that Hank would be there at the end of it. She might be foolish, but she couldn't help herself. He was becoming necessary in her life. It was frightening, and it was wonderful.

Only time would tell which side of that contradiction would bear out.

11

Bo sat at his desk, buried in files, making notes that hopefully would make some of his caseload easier for the new guy coming in. They were supposed to meet this morning for an initial discussion about the change-over. They would announce his exit and introduce the new marshal at the end of the week.

It was really happening. In another two weeks, he'd leave Syracuse forever. Leave Erin forever.

It had been four days since he and Erin had spent the night at the inn, and he'd been buried in reports and new information coming in from the FBI. They were getting him up to speed on their new cases as well, so he could hit the ground running when he got there.

"Sir, the court made them delay demolition on the site, but only until the end of the week," Bo's assistant informed him, poking his head around the corner.

"Thanks, Rob."

Three days? That's all he had to try to see if Erin could remember anything more? And a week after that. Then they were done.

The guys around the station knew, of course, that

he was leaving, short of the official announcement, and they were taking him out that evening for a few beers. Strangely, Bo didn't feel like celebrating. He was excited about the new job, but he wasn't excited about leaving.

Not since the inn. Not since Erin confessed her feelings to him and stirred that awful hope that maybe something was still viable between them. She'd changed. She was more open, more willing to share. More loving.

He'd loved her before, even when she was distant, but that distance was dissolving. Still, he wasn't going to pass up this job on the chance that he and Erin might reconcile. He couldn't trust anything they felt or shared right now, since she wasn't herself—not the Erin he'd known. He was a port in a storm, perhaps—of course she'd feel something for him, but whether it was a permanent situation was highly questionable. He couldn't base his future on it.

The heavy workload he'd be taking on with the task force would be a welcome distraction.

To that end, he'd checked into one more possibility to access some of Erin's more-buried memories: a hypnotist. He'd gotten a good recommendation for a guy named Stuart Fox from Dr. Higgins, and had called him that morning. Fox was happy to help if Erin was okay with it. Given her qualms about losing control in any situation, he didn't know if she would be.

Another knock on his door interrupted his thoughts, and he looked up to see Erin smiling at him.

"Hey, you weren't due here for another hour," he said with a smile, standing. He wanted very much to kiss her hello, but couldn't. Not here.

She shrugged. "I was over at the hospital for a checkup and driving home. Decided to stop by early and see what you wanted to talk about."

Erin's hand came forward, touched his lightly, sending heat flashing through him. He stepped back behind the safety of his desk.

"Is everything okay? With your checkup, I mean?" he asked.

"Oh, yes, fine. No problems. They were impressed with my progress, actually."

"That's good news. I have some, too. We got a slight delay on the demo of the warehouse site, so we can go back to see if it jogs any more of your memories, but we only have until the end of the week. Come Monday, it's gone."

Her relaxed expression became tense. "Only a few days? I mean, it's worth trying, but I don't know if I'll remember any more than I did last time."

"I know. Anyway, I had an idea. This is completely up to you—if you say no, it's no, but I spoke about the case with a hypnotist. I thought that if he could come with us to the site, put you under, maybe he could help you remember more. He comes very highly recommended."

She frowned as though she'd eaten something sour. "A hypnotist? You believe in that stuff?"

He had to smile at her sharp skepticism. Sometimes, Erin's old self peeked through the cracks of her new self, and he enjoyed being with both.

"I don't know, but from what I've read it's worked in a lot of cases, helping witnesses remember more details and events. This guy is also a clinical psychologist who specializes in regression therapy. In other words, taking people back to their pasts to see if they can solve current problems. He's worked with the police quite frequently. I don't think he's like the hypnotists who run magic shows and would make you cluck like a chicken," he added with a smile.

She was quiet, and for a few heartbeats Bo thought she might decline. Then she shrugged, though she didn't seem entirely happy about the notion.

"Sure, why not? As long as he doesn't do the chicken trick."

Bo grinned. "Maybe only if I make a personal request."

She stuck her tongue out at him, and he enjoyed the playful exchange.

She eyed the large stack of files on his desk. "I guess I should leave you to your work."

Her tone suggested a reluctance to do that, and her eyes were warm in a way that told him she wanted him.

Here? Now?

The idea got him hot, made his pulse beat faster. Rob was across the hall, but Bo's door shut. He could tell Rob not to disturb him, could close the shades, take her over his desk...

"Yes." She said the word as if reading his mind.

Bo didn't have much time left with her, and he wanted them to indulge every minute they could. Walking to the door, he cleared his throat, calling Rob.

"Yes, sir?"

"Could you run this package over to the courthouse for me? I know it's lunchtime—feel free to take some extra time, if you want. I'll hold down the fort."

His younger counterpart didn't seem to pick up on

any unusual vibe, his eyes lighting up at the prospect
of an extended lunch hour.

"Sure, no problem. See you in an hour or so."

Bo nodded and waited until Rob had cleared the hall
before he closed his door, facing Erin. Her color was
high, her eyes excited.

"Now no one will interrupt."

"Good."

He pulled the shades tightly closed, and then she
was on him, her arms around him, her mouth on his
as if she were as desperate as he was. He didn't waste
time, taking her shirt off and pushing his face into her
breasts, inhaling her soft scent as he pushed them close
together, taking both nipples in his mouth at once, making her moan loudly.

He was ready, almost frantic, and worked the button on her jeans.

"Damn, you make me so hard it hurts," he muttered,
slipping his hand down to stroke her, finding her as
ready as he was.

As if she knew what he wanted, she turned around,
braced herself on the desk, looking back at him with
clear invitation.

There was little finesse for either of them, only
scorching need.

"This is why I came early. I had to have you...I
didn't want to wait," she managed, and then groaned
softly as he traced his lips along her spine.

Bo could only show her how much he appreciated
that decision as he held her hips in his hands, finding a
quick rhythm that pleased them both as their sighs and
moans mingled in a shared climax that nearly made
him black out for a minute. He wasn't even sure if he'd

shouted her name or if anyone could have heard, and he didn't really care.

Still breathless, he pulled her back against him, wrapping his arms around her. "It seems to get better every time, doesn't it?"

"Yes. Very much so."

Her head dropped back against his shoulder. He found her mouth, kissing her tenderly until the heat started building between them again.

It had to be the time frame that was responsible for the urgency he felt. The driving need to have as much of her as he could. She quivered against him as his hands closed over her breasts, kneading gently. He didn't tire of her, wanted her constantly. Looking into her face, he saw the reflection of his own desire. She felt the same as he did.

It had always been good between them, but not like this. Not so…intimate. So *shared*.

"I love you." He couldn't help saying it.

She smiled, and his heart lit up. "I love you, too."

A car door slamming outside his window brought reality back, and he let his hands drop from the warmth of her body. They both took a minute to quickly straighten their clothes.

"Ladies' room?" she asked in a hushed voice, the door outside creaking as whoever was in the lot came into the building.

"Down the hall, to the left."

Footsteps went past his door. They both let out a sigh of relief and laughed.

"Let me know when you want me at the site with the hypnotist," she said on her way out.

"I will. Where are you going now?"

"To help Kit for the afternoon. I've been flaking out on her lately, so I might take her out after she closes the shop."

Bo felt a ping of regret that he wouldn't be able to see her that evening, but offered a smile.

"It's nice that you two are closer. Tell her I said hello."

Was there a flicker of something like disappointment in her eyes, too?

"I will. Um, bye."

As she started to leave, he called out her name.

"Hmm?"

Bo held her gaze, not wanting to let her go. At least, not with this sudden awkwardness that had settled between them.

"Thanks for coming by, Erin, especially coming by early," he said with a wink, enjoying how it made her blush even more deeply. "If you want, give me a call when you get home tonight. Or come by. I'll be up."

Pleasure suffused her expression, and Bo felt immediately better, having reasserted the connection between them.

"I'll talk to you later, then," she said, and then she was gone.

Bo sat down in his chair, dropping his head into his hands. He wasn't making this any easier on himself, but he had a feeling there was no way to do that anyway. He'd let himself fall for her again—as if he'd ever stopped being crazy for her. Not that it mattered. He was leaving, and she hadn't asked him to stay.

He blinked, staring at the wall. Had he really thought she might? Would he if she did?

ERIN DIDN'T IMMEDIATELY get out of her car once she'd arrived at the warehouse as planned. Bo's truck was here, and a silver-gray sedan alongside it. They were waiting for her.

Bo had offered to pick her up, but after the encounter in his office the day before, she'd needed some space. She hadn't been lying—she did go work at the store for the rest of the day, and offered to take Kit out. Or to stay in and watch TV, having some sister time.

An offer that was politely refused as her sister had other plans.

Kit didn't tell Erin what those other plans were, but Erin suspected a man was in the picture, if her sister's sexy new haircut was any indication. Kit had been quieter than usual, but she seemed happier, too.

When Erin tried to tease an answer out of her, Kit had maintained that she was only meeting a friend and had proceeded to hide in the back of the shop with a new shipment of summer flowers.

Erin had felt…slighted. Kit was obviously keeping a secret, and didn't want to talk to her about what was going on in her life. Erin supposed turnabout was fair play—she hadn't told her sister about anything going on in her life, either.

Had it always been this way? She wanted to be closer to Kit, but they felt further apart than ever.

When she'd gotten home, she also hadn't called Bo, even though she'd said she would. He hadn't called her, either.

The sex in his office the day before had been hot—wildly so. If not for the location and possible interruptions, she was sure they would have kept going. It had been difficult not to call as she sat home alone that evening, thinking about him and wanting him fiercely. She'd tried to read, watch TV, but all she could think of was Bo.

Not good. Not when he would be leaving by the end of the next week.

They'd gotten closer. Admitted feelings for each other. That they still cared. It was more than sex, but he was leaving nonetheless. He hadn't asked her for anything more.

Taking a deep breath, she got out of the car and headed toward the entry that they'd used the last time, finding Bo and another man just inside the door. Bo had an extra hard hat in his hand and passed it to her.

"Hi, Erin, thanks for agreeing to try this," he said, sounding very businesslike. He flipped his gaze to the man standing across from him. "This is Dr. Fox, the man I told you about."

Erin studied the man who smiled at her. She didn't know what she was expecting, but the doctor lived up to his name.

Total fox, absolutely. He wasn't tall—not as tall as Bo, and not as built. More like a runner, thin, but still nicely put together. In his late thirties, he had an angular face that accented intense dark gray eyes. A shock of dark blond hair kept falling forward over those eyes, making him absolutely rakish.

"Nice to meet you, Dr. Fox," she said.

"Nice to meet you, too, Erin. I've read up on your case—quite interesting. I've never had a client with complete amnesia before, or at least, as complete as yours has been. I can only imagine how difficult the past months have been."

His voice was unerringly masculine and sympa-

thetic without being overly so. He had a kind face and
a nice smile. His hands were slightly roughened, which
made her wonder what he did to earn the calluses. She
decided that she liked him and relaxed.

"So, Doctor, how does this work?" she asked, smiling brightly at the two men.

Bo, however, wasn't smiling. He looked...strange.
Tense.

"If you'd please show me what happened the last
time, and where—as much as you know—we can
begin. Then, I'll try to put you into a light trance and
take you back to the day of the fire to see if we can
tease any more details out of that brain of yours," Dr.
Foxy—er, Dr. Fox—said with another thousand-watt
smile.

"Sounds good."

"This time, stay on the safety path," Bo cautioned
her sternly. It was all he said before they went in.

Surprised by his abruptness, Erin fell into step with
the handsome doctor, who didn't seem to notice if there
was any tension between her and Bo.

"So, have you ever been put under before?" he
asked.

She shook her head. "Never. They mentioned it
once, early on, in the hospital, but I couldn't do it then.
I was just too freaked out."

"Completely understandable. Most people think
having a clean slate, erasing their pasts, would be
great—but the past is what makes us who we are. And
how we react to it, grow from it, or not. Some people
don't have amnesia, but they push events from their
pasts so far down into their minds that those things sit
there like a thorn, festering. It can be very damaging."

"That's what Bo, um, Marshal Myers, said you specialize in? Getting people to remember their pasts?"

"That is my particular interest, yes. Though hypnotism is a mainstay of my practice, I address a range of mental health issues with my clients. But dealing with past life trauma has been my main interest since college."

"Past life? You mean, like, in reincarnation?" she asked.

"No, I haven't gotten into that, particularly—that's more of a spiritual venue. But certainly childhood events that are forgotten, or milder cases like yours, where a trauma has gotten in the way of a memory surfacing."

Erin noted that they were approaching the spot where she had climbed up on the rafters a few days before. Looking at them now, she realized why Bo had been upset—what had she been thinking?

She hadn't. She'd only been feeling.

"So what do I do?" she asked as they stopped. Bo faced them, still quiet.

"Tell me what you do remember."

Erin did, as best she could. He listened, nodding every now and then as she spoke.

"It's good that you have a tight link between your emotional responses and the memories that are surfacing. Those emotional cues are very important—what would you say is the dominant emotion you remember as you and Joe ran through the building?"

His gray eyes homed in on her as though he could see through her—disconcerting—but Erin reached back to remember.

"Fear."

"Anything else?"

She shook her head. "Maybe…I don't know. Something like urgency, or worry…anxiety, I guess."

"Understandable, given the situation. Okay, so I'm going to put you into a gentle hypnotic trance. You may not feel like anything has happened. You'll feel awake, but very calm. You'll be able to hear us, and be aware of everything that goes on around you—maybe even more so than normal. You are not losing control or being controlled, and no one can make you do anything you don't want to do. We'll be here the whole time, and you will be perfectly safe."

"So how will I know if it's successful?"

Fox's gray eyes sparkled, and he winked. Were doctors supposed to wink?

"Believe me, we'll know."

"Okay then, let's do it."

Erin slid a glance in Bo's direction and felt more reassured when he held her gaze, his own confident and sure.

"It's better if you can sit, so that you don't lose your balance or fall. On the floor is fine, if you're okay with that."

"Sure." Erin dropped into a cross-legged position and looked up.

"Find a spot, something in the building to concentrate on—a small spot of light, or a shadow…whatever your eyes can latch onto, and don't look away…."

Erin did so, finding a glimmer of sun through some broken boards. Dr. Fox continued his patter, and she felt herself relax. She felt calmed as she listened to him, appreciating his voice even more as her eyes drifted shut. He started counting back, back through hours and days. The little sliver of light she'd been staring at began to move, and before she knew it, it wasn't light, but a flame dancing in front of her.

"There's a fire. We have to get out," she said, panicked, worried about Bo and the doctor. How had this place caught on fire again? She started to push up from sitting as the flames got bigger, smoke overcoming the space.

"We're fine, Erin. You're safe, and so are we. That fire is one you are remembering. It's only a memory and is no danger to us right now, okay?"

She had to catch her breath, slowing her heartbeat as he spoke. He was right. She could see the smoke and the flame, there wasn't any heat, no difficulty breathing.

"Okay. This is weird."

She heard the doctor chuckle again.

"You have a sexy laugh," she said, feeling like she shouldn't have said that, but then again, why not?

"Thank you. Now that you know you're safe, let's go through what happened when you came into the building with Joe. Can you walk us through what happened?"

"Joe's dead," she said, tightening up again.

"Yes, he is. But there's no danger to you now, okay? Do you believe me?"

"Yes."

"Fine, so tell us what you see."

Erin tried, peering through the smoke, looking for Joe.

"We were supposed to check the second floor in the back corner and make sure there were no chemicals. Joe went up the steps first. They were fine—the fire hadn't done much damage on this end of the building yet."

"That's great, Erin. You're doing well. What then?"

She saw Joe, in her memory, disappear at the top of the steps, and she walked up behind him.

"There's so much smoke. I can't see."

"Take your time. See if you can clear the smoke. Find Joe. What's he doing?"

Erin tried, but she couldn't see past the smoke, and her heart started to beat fast again, her entire body tensing.

"I can't see him."

"Okay, it's okay. Calm down, take a breath. Think about something happy, a color you love, or a place or person that makes you happy."

Erin's mind went directly to Bo and how she felt when she was close to him. The only time she truly felt safe.

"Okay, that's good. Now, let's skip ahead to you and Joe running from the spot—do you remember what you saw that made you run?"

The smoke thickened again. She could remember running, Joe behind her—she needed to get out. But everything was dense, gray and white, impenetrable.

"I can't find him. I can't see anything," she said loudly. The harder she looked, the less she saw.

"Bring her out of it, now," she heard a voice say, but her mind was lost in the smoke, looking for Joe.

"Erin, listen, I want you to think about a different place, a place that makes you happy. You aren't in the warehouse anymore, and there is no fire." The doctor waited a beat. "Are you there?"

She focused hard, and then apples and blue skies

opened up through the smoke. She was snug in Bo's arms on the ground. Her tense muscles relaxed into his warmth.

"Yes. Yes," she repeated, her breathing coming more easily.

"Good. You did great. I'm going to count back from ten. When I get to one, you'll wake up easily, feeling completely rested. You will remember everything that you saw in your memories, okay?"

"Okay."

The doctor counted down, and Erin opened her eyes, her gaze still fixed on the sliver of light at the end of the building.

Dropping her head into her hands, she said, "That was…disconcerting."

"You were terrific," Dr. Fox said, beaming a smile at her.

"I didn't remember anything." She didn't feel so terrific about that.

"You did, actually. You remembered being at the fire and you will remember more each time, if you want to continue. It's a gradual process, like peeling layers from an onion. Obviously what happened is very difficult for you to pull forward. We might need to talk about that more, those underlying feelings of fear and anxiety, to see if we can get past them to what happened, but you are definitely off to a good start."

Erin tried to be encouraged, but she only felt as though she had failed again. They needed this information *now*.

She pushed up from her spot on the floor and met Bo's eyes. She expected him to be disappointed, let down, but his expression only showed his concern.

"Bo, I—"

"It's all right, Erin. You did your best. Maybe if you can keep working with the doctor, like he said—"

Just then, Bo's beeper and his cell phone went off at once.

He answered and from the look on his face, she could tell it wasn't good news.

"What happened?"

"There was another fire, and some of our guys were hurt. They're being taken to the trauma unit now. Have to go."

He was running toward his truck before she could say another word. Offering a quick goodbye and thanks to the doctor, Erin took off after him.

12

Bo ARRIVED AT the E.R. first, and Erin was right behind him, watching three ambulances pull up and deliver firefighters from their doors. All being raced into the building. It didn't look good.

Her heart was slamming against her chest as she met Leroy and Bo at the entrance. Leroy looked wrecked.

"Leroy, what happened?" Bo asked the firefighter, who was pale even under the grime and soot that covered him.

"Hank, Joanne and a member from one of the volunteer stations were working on the back of the building. It wasn't even that bad. Someone started shouting, and we saw a kid hanging out of a window on the second floor. Hank went in to get him, Joanne went after him. But the guys in the cherry picker got there first, pulled the kid out. The chief radioed Hank and Jo to get out, and then it was like the place just exploded around them."

Leroy's voice choked, and he looked away.

Bo planted a hand on his shoulder.

"C'mon. Let's see what's happening and then I'll go to the site. They're still working the blaze?"

Leroy nodded. "I should be there, but the chief told me to go with Hank, you know, so he wasn't alone, in case… Well, he doesn't look good. Took the worst of it, they said. Joanne and the other guy, Kyle, I think, were conscious when they took them out, but Hank wasn't."

Bo turned his head away for a second, and Erin frowned. Hank was a friend. He was a man that she and Bo had both stood shoulder-to-shoulder with in fires. She couldn't remember it exactly, but she knew it was true. He'd come to the hospital for her almost every day.

He was a good man.

Not *was*. Not yet.

Her chest tightened with fear, her eyes swelling with tears that she choked back. This wasn't about her. She needed to be there for them. Still, she couldn't help but wonder if this had all happened because she couldn't remember enough to stop the person who was doing it.

"Was it the same as the others?" she made herself ask, her voice rubbing across her throat like sandpaper.

Bo shook his head, looking grim. "No way to know for sure yet, but I will find out, and if it is I'm going to track this bastard down if it's the last thing I do. I won't be leaving until I stop this."

Erin stepped back. She agreed and she understood—but part of her cringed. Bo would stay for his job, but not for her.

Again, not important. She needed to focus now on her friends.

"What can I do to help?"

Bo would probably tell her to go home—she was

a civilian. But no doubt he saw the worry in her eyes, her worry and her guilt. Leroy left them for a minute to speak to a nurse, and she welcomed the time alone with Bo.

"Are you okay?" she asked gently.

"No, I won't be okay until this is settled," he snapped, and then shook his head. "I'm sorry. I hate to say it, but this has rattled me."

"It's normal. It's right that it should. I wish I could have helped stop this."

"It wouldn't have mattered, not today. There's nothing we could have done about this," he said.

"I know. Doesn't make it any easier. I need to help, somehow."

"There's nothing you can do, officially," Bo said. "I need to collect as much information as I can here and then get to the fire. I—I may not be around much. Just so you know."

Her heart took a hit, but she nodded as if it didn't matter.

"I know. You have to do this. I get it."

Erin found herself longing to reach out, to touch him, to comfort. But that wasn't possible.

"Joanne's husband will be here soon. I'm not sure about the other firefighter, the volunteer, if his family has gotten notification. You and Leroy should look into that, be here for them," Bo said, his tone masking any emotion, all business now.

"I can do that. You go, don't worry about us," she added, meeting Bo's gaze.

He gave her a short nod and he left. Heading to the nurse's station, he didn't look back, and somehow, Erin knew that this was it. This was the end of what they'd had together.

Leroy came back over to her.

"Joanne and the other injured man, a volunteer, were both conscious and are being treated for some serious but not life-threatening injuries.

"Hank, though, has been taken directly into surgery," he said, chilling Erin's spine.

"He'll pull through. Hank's a bull, he's tough, and he's going to be okay."

She wasn't sure who she was trying to convince.

"You're right," Leroy agreed, pulling her into a hug.

She hugged him back and then saw, over his shoulder, some more of the crew, dirty and still in their gear, crowding in the door, along with police and some distraught people, probably family members.

They broke apart and went to meet the crowd, sharing what they knew, and civilian or not, Erin felt included. Needed.

She thought back to how the trauma nurses and counselors had helped her in the first days of her waking up. How these kind, patient strangers had kept her sane. She echoed some of the things they told her as she comforted Hank's sister, Lily, and helped her make the call to his parents. She listened as some of the crew talked out what happened at the fire, and what they'd seen. Erin held Pete, who couldn't hold back tears.

After several hours, Hank was finally out of surgery, stable but critical, someone finally said. Erin spared a glance at the clock.

"Oh, no, it's so late. Kit is going to be so worried. I completely forgot to call her," she told Leroy, excusing herself.

Dialing the house, no one answered, so she tried Kit's cell. Finally, her sister answered.

"Kit, where are you? I thought you'd be home by now."

"I decided to come back to the store to get some work done."

Her sister sounded strange. Choked up and nasal, like she had a cold.

"Are you okay? You sound odd."

"Yeah, I'm fine. Where are you?"

Erin hesitated. "I'm at Upstate. There was another bad fire today, and several of the guys were hurt, one badly. Hank Aaron? I don't know if you—"

"What did you say?" Kit's voice came out on a hush of disbelief.

"Um, there was a fire. I wasn't there, but a lot of the guys were, and it was bad. I've been here all day, trying to help, and waiting for Hank to get out of surgery, and I lost track of—"

The line went dead.

"Kit?"

Erin looked at her phone, and couldn't believe her sister would hang up on her—even Kit wasn't that resentful—she must have lost the signal, or had a dead battery. Well, at least she knew where Erin was, which was all she wanted to contact her about anyway.

She went back to the group, watching from a distance as Hank's sister talked with a doctor and listened intently, nodding every few seconds.

That was encouraging, Erin thought, hopeful.

"Hey, I didn't think I'd see you here again so soon," someone said from behind her, and Erin saw Tom, one of the trauma counselors who had helped her through her ordeal.

"Hi, Tom. There was a fire, and friends are involved, so here I am. Just trying to help."

"How are things going?" he asked.

"Okay. Good, I guess. I'm remembering some things, and trying to get back to normal."

"Good to hear. I have to get going, but don't be a stranger."

Tom moved on down the hall as Hank's sister turned away from the doctors and rejoined the group. She stood next to Erin, who took her hand and squeezed it as Lily fought through tears.

"He's stable. He has serious head injuries from the explosion, and some internal bleeding, but they think he'll be okay. The next twenty-four hours will tell," she said, choking on the words.

Erin took Lily into a hug, letting her cry it out.

"I'm sorry. It's just so hard… We're so proud of him, and everything he does, but it's always in the back of your head, knowing this can happen. And when it does, it's not like knowing about it makes it any easier."

"It could never be easy. You're doing great. Hank would be proud of you," Erin said easily, but under her comforting exterior, she was realizing exactly how hard it had been on Kit when Erin had been the one coming out of surgery.

And how hard it had been on Kit and her mom when her dad went off to work every night.

It had been hard on Erin, too, but she fought her nightmares about what could happen to her dad a different way—she ran into them. She studied fires—

lived them, even as a kid—and followed her dad where he went rather than staying back.

It hadn't stopped her from losing him, but it made her feel closer to him. But further from everyone else. Something she hadn't quite understood until right now. It was so hard for families, being on the outside, but hurting just as much. Maybe worse.

Talking to Lily in quieting tones, Erin was suddenly surprised by the sound of Kit's voice in the hall, calling her name. Then her sister was there, grabbing her arm, looking frantic—and frightened.

Erin felt sick as she hugged her sister. "Oh, Kit, I'm so sorry—did you think I was hurt? I was trying to tell you, but then the phone cut out—"

"Hank? How is Hank, Erin? Please, tell me."

Erin was blank for a second, caught off guard. "Hank? You mean our Hank? From the crew?"

Kit nodded, swallowing hard. She'd obviously been crying all the way over to the hospital.

"Yes, Hank Aaron. We—we've been seeing each other...."

Erin was blindsided again, and unsure she'd heard right.

"You and Hank? But... For how long?"

"Are you Kathy?" Lily cut in, overhearing them, as they were standing right by her.

"Yes, that's me."

Kathy?

"Hank has told us so much about you. He's over the moon about you, you know. We've never seen him like this with anyone," Lily said, smiling through tears.

Kit was crying now, too, and Erin watched them, trying to catch up.

"I'm crazy about him, too. But is he… How is he?" Kit asked, her voice thinning with fear.

Lily reached out this time, pulled Kit into a hug. "He'll be okay, I think. It's touch and go right now, but I think he'll be okay. Especially knowing he has you waiting for him."

Erin listened, wanting badly to ask about a million questions, but unsure where to start. Her sister had been seeing Hank romantically all this time? And neither one of them had said anything to her?

"I know this is a surprise," Kit said, turning back to Erin. "For me, too."

Her sister involved with a firefighter? It was like someone suddenly saying the sky was orange instead of blue.

"How long?"

"Just over a month."

Erin's eyebrows flew up, and then she closed her gaping mouth and took a deep breath. That was about as long as she'd been with Bo—and it wasn't as if she'd shared that with Kit, either. As sisters, they were pretty much failures, or at least, Erin was. She had so much ground to make up.

"Well, you couldn't have chosen better," Erin said as she hugged her sister again. "If you're going to date a fireman, you might as well accept that you're part of the crew now, too."

Kit wiped her teary eyes and seemed more pleased at that idea than Erin would have imagined as they joined the guys and listened to their conversation. Lily appeared again, touching Erin's elbow.

"They said I could see Hank for a minute. I asked if you and Kathy could as well, and they said yes, but just for a minute or two each. He's sedated, and he looks pretty bad, they warned, but he'll know we're there. They said it might do him good to hear our voices."

"Absolutely," Kit said.

"Why don't you and Kit go first, and if he's up to it, I'll go in then," Erin said, garnering thankful looks from both women.

Her sister was clearly head over heels—one more huge reason Hank had to make it. She was going to be sure to tell him so and paced the hall outside the ICU, waiting for her turn to visit him.

After what seemed like a longer time than it was, Kit and Lily emerged from the ICU, both teary but smiling, looking better. Erin rushed up to them.

"How is he? How are you?"

"He's sleeping, like the doctor said, and hooked up to so many machines, but when Kathy—Kit—touched his hand and spoke to him, his heart rate spiked," Lily said with a smile.

"He knew I was there. I think his fingers moved a little, next to mine. He was really trying," Kit said, starting to cry again.

Erin hugged her sister, repeating how sorry she was that Kit had to go through this—again. Her sister had been through enough—too much. Erin had never realized it before because she'd channeled her emotions differently—or buried them altogether. Thinking back to how she was with Bo, how much she had held back from him, how distant she'd kept herself…regret swamped her and tears flooded her eyes, too, until all three women were weeping and then laughing about it.

"What a sight we make," Kit said, reaching into her purse for a tissue.

"Let me go say good-night to Hank, and I can drive you guys home, if you need me to," Erin said.

"We'll wait here."

Erin entered the ICU, stopping to wash her hands with the antiseptic and covering her mouth with the mask they provided to visitors before she went into Hank's room.

He looked awful, and she had to swallow her reaction before she stepped in closer. He was bruised and cut everywhere. Machines beeped all around him, and Erin found herself standing by his bed, shaking uncontrollably, unable to speak. She was overcome with emotion.

Had she ever told Hank how great she thought he was? Or had she only engaged in the playful banter that they all did, their way of managing the fear and the danger? It was something to keep sane, but when you managed your whole life that way, it didn't work out so well.

At the bottom of that defense mechanism was fear—ugly, snaking fear that threatened to rise up any moment and drag you back down. You could deny it all you wanted, but it was still there. The problem was that you could only avoid it for so long. Sooner or later, it had to be faced.

Erin was facing it right now, more so than she ever had in the past. She'd never really been afraid while entering buildings or dealing with danger, but this— being helpless, being hurt, seeing her friends or family hurt—this scared her.

"Hey, Hank, it's Erin," she said, sounding froggy. "So, you've been dating my sister, huh? We're going to have to have a talk about that when you wake up.

She's special, and she's been through enough. You're
a great guy, the best guy I could imagine for her—so
don't hurt her any more, okay? You make sure you get
through this, because she needs you. So…just get better
fast. Okay? I'll be back to see you tomorrow. Promise."

Erin gasped softly as she thought she felt Hank's
fingers move slightly under hers, though she couldn't
be sure if she imagined it. She hoped not.

Turning to leave the room, Erin paused, feeling
dizzy, so she grabbed Hank's bed rail tightly enough
that her fingers hurt. Light-headed as she closed her
eyes, she could hear the beeps of the machines, the
murmur of the ICU staff working just past the curtain.
Then she was brought back to her own bed, when she'd
been injured, yet now she stood there, listening…re-
membering it all.

She was at the warehouse. She could see the smoke,
and the flames. And Joe.

The smoke eventually cleared, and visions stuttered
behind her eyes as if they were playing on an old pro-
jector that was missing every other frame, but she saw
enough to understand.

And then she remembered some more…and sobs
began to shudder through her body as in one stark,
painful flash, she knew everything again.

BO HAD BEEN working since the night before at the hospital, spending hours at the site, and then at the labs and
with the police. This time, their arsonist had messed
up—this time, setting explosions, he'd left evidence behind. He'd gotten sloppy, thinking the structure would
be vaporized, and the evidence with it.

Not so much.

It was a common error among stupid criminals. They thought they could use fire to hide a murder, for instance, but not anymore. It took a very hot fire and a lot of time for a body to completely incinerate, and with modern methodologies, they could detect all kinds of trace evidence on what was left.

Bo had managed to speed up the processing of the evidence, using his new FBI connections to pull in a favor—it was a bit presumptuous as he wasn't even part of the team yet, but the bureau was more than happy to help. And it had the resources to do it ten times faster.

So for now, Bo had slept at the station, waiting for a call with some news. A name or a place—someone they could close in on.

He didn't want to be in his office. He'd worked in this station for a lot of years. It still felt like home, especially tonight. Truth was, if he was ruthlessly honest with himself, he didn't want to go back to his place without Erin. He was feeling the personal stress of recent events and what had happened the day before—who wouldn't?—but being at his apartment alone was impossible right now.

He wasn't sure what he could do about that. Maybe in Virginia, in a new place, it would be easier. *Yeah, right,* the little devil in his head mocked him.

The guys were out on a call, back to work even after the tragedy of the day before. But someone was moving around down in the kitchen, so he decided to go and see who was there, feeling restless.

Turning the corner, he was surprised when he saw Erin. Bo started to walk into the room, but something made him hold back, watching her from the hidden corner. She seemed to be looking for something, grabbing a chair and climbing up on it, running her hands over the tops of the kitchen cabinets.

He hadn't spoken to her since the hospital, though he heard that Hank had woken up and was off the critical list. He had a long recovery ahead of him, but the signs were promising.

She reached the vent above the cabinets and pulled at the grate—Bo was surprised when it gave way easily, not screwed in completely. How did she know that, and what was she after?

Erin reached into the vent, grabbing something, and then scrambled down, putting the chair back and pulling her phone out of her pocket. She had something in her fingers—an SD card?—and jammed it into her phone, and in the next few seconds, another voice filled the room.

"You don't know what you're missing, girl," a man's voice taunted.

"Leave me alone, Joe, I mean it. This has to stop. I'll report you if you keep harassing me like this."

"Yeah, you think anyone's going to believe you? Especially when you've been screwing Myers for months? Why not share the wealth? No one has to know—it can be our little secret."

Bo's mind reeled as he listened to Joe's voice on the recording playing from Erin's phone. He could see her hands shaking as she held it, even from where he stood ten feet away.

The recording went on, and he could make out the sounds of a slight physical struggle—Joe had touched her. The man had put hands on Erin—not in a good way. He'd known about her and Bo, and he was using that to try to get Erin to sleep with him.

Anger like Bo hadn't known before shot through him, and his hands fisted at his sides. So that was what she'd been keeping from him. He'd been able to sense it back then, especially when she was increasingly cagey. He'd asked, but she never would tell him.

Judging by the tape, she hadn't told anyone. Handling it herself, as always.

Some of his anger and hurt extended to her—why hadn't she come to him? Why had she taken on this guy alone?

And how had she known the recording was there? Had she known all this time? Or had she just remembered? Had she been holding back? It was time to find out.

Finishing off the recording, Bo was relieved to know Erin had come out on top of the struggle. Joe backed off, but Bo knew that probably hadn't been the end of it. Guys like him were predators—they didn't stop until they got what they wanted.

Bo composed himself as well as possible and walked into the kitchen, as if he hadn't been there all along.

"Oh, Erin," he said in false surprise. "What are you doing here?"

She looked up quickly, guiltily, and shoved the phone into her jacket. All of the color had drained from her face, her eyes wide and dark. She swallowed hard, and he wanted to grab her, hold her and let her know no one else would ever hurt her like that again.

But she regrouped quickly, though she didn't meet his gaze. Putting her mask in place.

"Bo. What are you doing here? I didn't think anyone was around. I heard the call come in on my car's radio."

So this was a covert op, he mused. She'd been waiting for the place to empty out.

"I worked late. Didn't want to stay at the office. So I came over here to bunk down and see if there was anything I could do to help. The crew was pretty unsettled by the explosion yesterday."

She looked down at her feet, at the wall, out the window. Anywhere but at him.

Bo had planned on confronting her, but now, he needed to see what she did. Put the ball in her court. What play would she make?

"I came by to grab some things of Hank's—apparently he was seeing my sister all this time, well, for the past month. I had no idea."

Bo was surprised, too, though he was more interested in the fact that Erin clearly wasn't going to tell him what had happened to her and why she was here. She was obviously upset, agitated, but covering it up. Why would she cover for Joe now? Why not tell him? Why lie?

"Kit said Hank had some things here in his locker that he asked her to get, but she had to stay at the store—so I offered to come down. Of course, I forgot the key to his locker," she said, furthering the lie.

Or maybe it was partly true, who knew? Who cared? Her act hollowed Bo out and made what they had together more of a sham than it already had been.

Suddenly, he just wanted her gone.

He also didn't want her to leave.

He wanted to shout at her and make her tell him why she'd kept everything from him, and why she wasn't confiding in him even now. She'd said she loved him, but how was that possible when she couldn't trust him? Be open with him?

"I can let you in, I have a master."

She blinked, her bluff called. "Oh, okay, sure."

Bo was numb as he took out his key and watched her rifle through some of Hank's things, pulling most of them out before closing the locker.

"Great, um, thanks."

"Sure."

They stood there in awkward silence, until she asked, "Any news on who did this?"

"We should have a name soon, I think. We're closing in on a possible suspect. I'm waiting on a call."

No sooner had he said the words than his phone rang.

"Sorry, I have to take this."

"Oh, sure, please. I'll…talk to you later."

He didn't respond as he took the call. The news was good. They were sending in a squad to the suspect's last known address, and Bo was going to be there. The FBI would have a presence as well, since the guy in question was a suspect in several fires spanning multiple states. He had more than one burned building and dead body behind him.

Bo started to tell Erin, but when he turned around, she was gone.

So that was it. They were over. It was just as well, he thought, grabbing his gear and heading out.

13

IN THE HOSPITAL lobby, Erin signed in and got her visitor's badge before taking the elevator up to see Hank. He was awake and talking, and had even called her from his room asking if she could make a lunch run before her visit—he hated the hospital food.

She'd been glad to do it, and the prospect of seeing her old friend—one she could now remember clearly—bolstered her day. And she'd needed the boost.

Bumping into Bo the previous afternoon had been unexpected—and she'd panicked. She hadn't expected anyone to be at the station, which is why she'd offered to go get Hank's things. She remembered hiding the recording in the kitchen, but she didn't know exactly where it was. She needed some time to nose around for it undetected.

She'd almost been detected in a big way. But Bo was distracted by the investigation, which worked in her favor. Everyone had been talking all day about the arrest they made the evening before. The arsonist was a man who'd been tossed out of the volunteer department he'd once joined for drinking on the job, and never let back in. He obviously harbored a dangerous grudge about that.

So he'd been taking it out on innocents and other firefighters in the two years since. His fires had been widespread and unconnected as he moved from place to place, leaving sadness and ruin behind him before he moved on.

But as it ended up, he hadn't set the fire that had hurt Erin and Joe. That had been an arson, but their suspect had been seen fifty miles away that evening. Now the investigation was focusing on the company that owned the building and its employees.

Erin's injuries and Joe's death had nothing to do with the serial arsons. It only made her decision about what *she* should do about what she knew all the more confusing. Now it seemed even less relevant to expose what had happened—Joe was gone, and his family would be the ones to suffer if she revealed what she knew.

Then again, his family deserved answers, and Erin deserved to be cleared of any suspicion in what happened. His family still could bring a civil case against her or the department, though they hadn't. Yet.

She walked into the hospital room and stopped short, seeing her sister draped over Hank like one of his blankets, the two obviously sharing a moment.

"Oh, my eyes! My eyes, they burn," Erin cried dramatically, grinning and turning her head away.

Kit looked up, her hair mussed, her eyes all blurry. Hank still looked bruised and battered, but he was smiling now, somewhat blurry himself. Not from drugs though, Erin thought.

"You could have simply knocked," her sister said drily.

"Eh, what's the fun in that? I can leave if you two aren't done making out."

Hank had recovered sufficiently to be moved from ICU into a regular room—a private one—so they had room to sit and visit. But as Hank and Erin discussed the particularities of the case, Kit became increasingly quiet, eventually excusing herself and leaving the room.

Erin watched after her and sighed.

"Maybe you should go talk to her, since I can't," Hank suggested.

"Let her have some space. We're alike in that—we don't like to be pushed or crowded."

Hank grinned. "Yeah, I noticed that."

"I'll go check on her in a few minutes if she doesn't come back. She's always had a hard time with the job. I can't blame her."

Hank watched Erin closely.

"Why do you think that is?"

"I didn't really understand it myself until you were hurt, and watching what Lily went through, as well as Kit. Me, too. When we were on the crew, we couldn't afford to feel too much of it, in case it got in the way. I think I had to be outside of the job to really get it."

"Get what?"

"That the only way to do the job is to shut everything inside off. To shut off the worry and the guilt. And the fear. But that causes its own problems."

Hank looked at her shrewdly. "So you remember more about the job now?"

Erin bit her lip, and shifted closer to Hank. "I think I

remember almost everything. When I was in here with you, when you were out, that first night... I don't know why, but everything started flooding back."

Hank's eyes went wide. "Seriously? And you've kept this to yourself because...?"

Erin released a long breath. "It's complicated. There's been so much going on, and some other things I need to take care of."

"Like your relationship with Myers?"

Erin sat back in her chair. It was her turn to be surprised.

"What do you mean?"

"What, you think we're all as dumb as we are pretty?" he said, making her laugh. "No one could miss the chemistry with you two, and it's been back in spades. It's obvious when you guys are anywhere within a mile of each other."

"I see. I guess I was the one in the dark, then. I had no idea everyone knew."

"Not everyone, but a few of us who noticed. And I saw you out with him more than once, clearly not wanting to be seen. Why the secrecy?"

Erin frowned. "Back then, I didn't want anyone to know. I thought you would all think less of me, or think I couldn't do the job. You know how it can be for women sometimes."

Hank nodded. "Other places, sure. But you were among friends. None of us would have thought that."

Some did, she thought darkly of Joe. It was one more reason not to tell anyone about what happened— it would be a stain on their station's otherwise honorable reputation.

"I guess. But this time, it wasn't a reconciliation so

much as…a temporary thing, and a conflict with him investigating the case. So we had to be careful. And anyway, there was no point in letting everyone know when it was temporary. And now over, by the way."

"Why does it have to be over? Do you love him?"

Erin thought carefully before answering. "We have too much history. And he's moving on."

"Whose excuse is that, yours or his? Have you even talked about it? Does he know your memory is back?"

"No. You're the only one who knows right now."

She hadn't told Bo because she hadn't been able to face him again until she could figure out what to do about Joe. Or maybe she never wanted him to know. What would he think?

"Erin, if you don't mind me saying so, you and your sister are pretty messed up."

She laughed in shock. "Oh, really?"

"Yes. I love you both, but you need to start relying on and trusting in others—especially the people who love you—including each other. Including me and Bo. Starting there, perhaps. Maybe if you trust in Bo, trust that it can work out, it will. In spite of her fears and what happened, Kathy's put her trust in me. In us. She's not bailing. You shouldn't, either."

"It always sounds so weird to me when you call her that," she said lightly, but only because she needed to be light in response to his words.

"Go talk to your sister, and then go talk to Bo. If nothing else, clear the air before he leaves. You both deserve that."

Erin let her head drop back, closing her eyes as she digested the truth of Hank's words.

"You're going to be such a pain in the ass to have in the family, with all your wisdom and stuff," she said.

"You'll get used to it."

Erin stood, giving him a gentle hug and a kiss before she took off to find her sister. She found her, standing by the window near the end of the hall, staring out.

"Hey. Sorry if the shop talk got out of hand in there. Are you okay?"

Kit gave her a faint smile. "I guess it's something I have to get used to. He's worth it."

"He is. You, too."

"I had doubts, you know. Every day since I've been with him, I'd think, 'I should end this before it goes too far,' or, 'I must be crazy getting involved with this man,' but I just couldn't not see him. He has my whole heart. And last night, when you called, I thought I lost everything, and that he'd never know how much he means to me."

Tears fell freely down her sister's face, and Erin had to choke back her own.

"I think we both learned to avoid pain and fear, to shut it out, growing up. It was how Mom dealt with things—but not how we have to."

"You didn't avoid anything. You don't fear anything," Kit said.

Erin coughed in disbelief. "Are you joking? I think I've been afraid every day of my life. I also worried about Dad, and I grieved when we lost him—but I handled it in a different manner. I needed to be close to him, so I followed in his footsteps. And in doing that, I wasn't as close as I should have been to you because I saw loss all the time, but I couldn't face my own. I didn't want to ever lose anything again."

Kit looked at her in stunned amazement.

"I know," Erin said, shaking her head. "It took literally losing everything to learn this. But…it's all back. Or I think most of it is. The other night, in the room with Hank…I just started remembering. Everything."

Kit flung herself at Erin then, wrapping her in a tight hug, murmuring thanks over and over.

"I'm so glad. So, so glad."

"Thanks," Erin said, feeling connected to her sister for the first time in a long time. "There's something else. I was seeing a man back then, and the reason I wasn't around much lately is because we started up again, but it's been kind of a mess…."

Erin told her sister about Bo, as succinctly as such a tale could be told, and Kit listened, not interrupting until she was done. She also told her about Joe. It was time she confided in someone, certainly in her sister.

"Oh, Erin, what a terrible thing you were living with," Kit said, leading her over to a bench where they could both sit. "I guess we've both been dealing with a lot—and not too well—when we could have been sharing the load."

"Well, I don't know that I would call Hank a load, exactly," Erin said with a grin. "Although he is a big man."

They laughed, but Kit was serious again. "No. It's more than that—Hank has been my joy for the past few weeks or so, but the store… I think I'm going to have to close. Business just isn't great, and unless I mortgage the house or sell it to keep going, I don't think I can stay above water. And I don't want to sell that house or go into debt. I'd kind of like to raise my own kids there, if that ever happens."

And the surprises kept coming. Erin had no idea her sister was dealing with such problems and felt terrible for being so out of touch.

"I'm so sorry, Kit. Is it that bad? There's no other solution?"

"Not that I can think of. I'm competing with all of the places that people can get their flowers less expensively. I could change my inventory, but then I feel like I'm selling out. What I sell makes me different from all the other guys—maybe too different."

"Hank was right. You and I are a mess," Erin said with an unhappy laugh.

"At least we have good men in our corners."

"You do. I mean, Bo is a good man, but we're over. We were over a long time ago. This was just…a mirage."

Kit made a raspberry sound, sticking out her tongue. "Give me a break."

Erin blinked. "Um, way to go with the sisterly sympathy."

Kit shook her head. "There's sisterly sympathy—and believe me, my heart goes out to you about what happened with Joe. I wish he was alive so he could be flayed for what he did to you. But then there's tough love. You and Bo…you're obviously meant for each other. You light up just saying his name. You can work it out, if you both want to. If you don't want to, then maybe it's better this way."

"You didn't hear the part about him leaving? Taking on a new job? I saw him yesterday, when I went to the station to get Hank's things—he was cool. Detached. He hasn't called. Believe me, I know *over* when I see it. The message was loud and clear."

"And you're just going to let it end like that? Again? You said he always sensed you were holding something back, that you didn't trust him, not completely—and that's still the case, isn't it?"

Erin frowned. "No, I do trust him, but—"

"There is no but. Either you do or you don't. All-in or not, Erin. If you trust him, and if you love him, you need to tell him everything and see what happens. That's what trust is. That's when you know you'll have really faced your fears. Believe me, I know. I faced my worst one in the past few days. All I knew was that I wanted Hank to live and to be in my life—regardless of his work. Which reminds me—are you going to be a firefighter now that your memory is back?"

Erin shifted, surprised at the question. Funny, she hadn't even considered that since her memory returned. Weeks before, the job would have been her first thought, not her last.

"I don't think so," she said, realizing it was true. "This whole experience has changed me. I think I might be interested in working in the emergency field, but not fighting fires. That's over for me. It would be tough for me to get cleared to work anyway, but that's not really the point. I want to be involved in another aspect—to be able to use what I've learned to help others who might be in the same spot."

"Well, I would have supported you either way, but I can't say I'm not relieved. What are you thinking about doing?"

Erin acknowledged what she wanted to do in a flash of her future that came to her as quickly as her past had, and her heart told her it was right.

"I'm going to retrain as a trauma counselor. Maybe get a degree and everything."

Kit seemed impressed. "That's terrific. I'm so proud of you—and I always have been, though I might not have acted like it. You'll be a great counselor—once you get your own head on straight, that is."

Erin laughed again, batting her sister's arm lightly. "Hey."

"You know what I mean. You need to resolve your own issues. Go talk to Bo, go face your fear. If he bows out, you'll survive it. You know you will. But at least you will have tried."

The thought of putting herself in a position to be rejected by Bo was a painful one, Erin thought, but her sister was right. And after all, that's what he had suffered from her. Maybe letting him walk away was the closure he needed.

"Okay. I will. I bet Hank's missing you. Maybe you should close and lock the door this time, or take it easy on the man. He's healing."

"And I love playing nurse," Kit said with a waggle of her eyebrows. Erin had to smile.

They hugged again, and Kit went back to Hank's room. Erin sat for a while longer, digesting everything Kit and Hank had said. She got up, left the hospital, and headed to Bo's apartment, where she knew he would be packing.

Getting ready to leave.

But not until they talked, she determined. Talked about everything.

14

Bo had no idea how he had accumulated so much stuff, but he had one day to deal with it, and so it had to be done.

He put things in corners of the room, the same way he would mentally separate evidence or parts of a crime scene. Books in one spot, tech in another, clothes all over the sofa. Pictures, dishes, kitchen implements, things from family and friends, other personal items all strewn in piles everywhere.

He hoped he had enough boxes. A truck rental waited for him the next morning, so he could pack this all up and drive it down to his new apartment in Virginia the day after. Then he'd fly back, get his car and a few last things.

One new life, to go.

There wouldn't be much time to unpack and settle in. He had a week before the task force was throwing him in the deep end, starting with some training on terrorism and biohazards. He had some experience with those things—he'd be getting more.

Welcome to the big leagues.

With a renewed spirit, he started grabbing boxes and stacks of bubble wrap and newspaper and got to work, thinking only about his packing and what was coming. Thinking about what he was leaving behind, well…that wasn't something he could do right now.

They'd solved the arsons, and though Erin's case remained open, he couldn't confront her about it. Maybe he couldn't confront the pain of knowing she would lie to him, keep things from him. His own fault.

He'd let himself believe something was different.

A knock on the door startled him. He didn't get a lot of unannounced visitors. Still, it could be a neighbor, or one of the guys from the station—a few folks had dropped by, hearing about his departure. He had a huge pan of lasagna in the fridge that had come in handy for dinners from the older lady down the hall as a goodbye gift.

"Just a second," he said, making a path to the door.

Erin was the last person he expected to see, making him suddenly feel as scattered as all of his belongings.

"Erin. What can I do for you?" he asked, sounding businesslike.

She pushed a hand through her hair, slightly longer now. She looked nervous, on edge. But she met his gaze steadily.

"Can I come in?"

He paused, and then stepped back to let her in.

"Sure. Don't mind the mess."

"You…you have a lot of stuff."

"Yeah, that's what I was thinking. I put a lot of things in drawers and closets over the years, I guess."

They both stood silently for a minute, hands in pockets.

"Listen, I know things are weird between us right now, but I think it's best if we just let things go. I have to get moving on this—is there a reason you came by?"

She flinched ever so slightly, and he regretted his tone, but then again, he didn't.

"I know you're busy getting ready for your move, but I needed to talk to you. To tell you some things, and…to ask your advice. About something delicate. And to apologize."

She said it all quick together, like trying to fit it all in. Bo blinked, unsure what to say. But his heart picked up rhythm, and he found himself nodding before he had consciously decided to, showing her to the only available chair at the island in the kitchen. He remained standing.

"Advice?" That was what he was most intrigued about, he supposed.

She swallowed visibly and clasped her hands in her lap.

"My memory came back—not one hundred percent, but most of it, I think. Definitely a lot more than before, big chunks, not just flashes."

In spite of the fact that he'd already guessed this, his eyebrows rose anyway. There was no doubt about the excitement in her voice, dim as it was.

He should tell her he knew, but he was curious where this was all going.

"I'm glad. When did this happen?"

"Um, the night of Hank's accident."

"I see."

"Yeah, well, and with it—well, I remember what happened at the fire. I know I should have come to you first, but I had to…take care of a loose end, and it's been tough to reconcile. I needed time to think, but honestly, thinking hasn't helped. The only person I knew who would know the right thing to do is you."

Bo felt as if the air had been knocked out of him.

"I'll do what I can," he offered noncommittally.

"Okay, here's what I know…." She went on, telling him about the tape, the harassment. She was relatively unemotional about it, reporting it like news that had happened to someone else, until she got to the last part.

"So, in the warehouse, we were sent in to check for combustibles that they thought could be stored on the second floor. There weren't any. So that was good. That part of the warehouse wasn't on fire at that point, and when I turned to leave, to go back out and report to the chief, Joe grabbed me."

Her voice tightened, and she took a breath before continuing.

"The day before that fire, I'd told him I had the tape to make him stop bothering me. I thought it was the only way. When he grabbed me, he said that if I didn't tell him where the tape was, he'd make good and sure I never had a chance to use it. To make his point, he hit me. He told me how easy it would be to make sure I had an accident in a fire. That way, I'd never be able to report him."

Bo cursed on a whoosh of breath. Whatever he'd expected, he hadn't expected this. He wanted Joe alive so that he could beat the crap out of him. But she wasn't done yet.

"I hit him back—we fought, and that was why we both had some unusual bruises that the doctors couldn't explain. I ran, he chased me. I was going to tell the chief right then, or whoever would listen, and I had the bruises to prove it. Joe knew he'd made a big mistake, and he tackled me farther down on the first floor. It was unstable there, the fire having burned long enough to start on the supports around us. We struggled, and I managed to get to my feet." She swallowed hard again; this time she couldn't hold back her tears. "He shoved me down, hard. I think I hit my head, I don't know. Things got fuzzy. Then I heard him yell, and I heard the noise, knew something had gone terribly wrong. I looked over, saw the rafters coming down, saw Joe rolling, on fire. Screaming."

Bo reached for her hand, took it, squeezed. She was ice-cold.

"Erin, you don't have to say any more."

She took her hand from his.

"There isn't much more. I guess that's how he died. I only remember something large landing on me, too, pinning me, and the smoke choking me. Then, that's all. Until I woke up in the hospital, and I didn't know anything. I guess being at the hospital with the guys the other night, with Hank, hearing the machines, seeing his injuries… It brought it all rushing back. Or maybe it was the hypnotism, I don't know, but I really do remember now, and I have proof."

Bo's anger dissolved under his concern, and he pulled her against him whether she wanted it or not, wrapping his arms around her.

"I wish I could get a hold of him…" he said under his breath as she wept quietly into his chest.

"What happened was bad enough. But it was an accident, how he died, except for why we ended up there. I have the recording here in my bag," she said, sniffing as she slipped out of his embrace. "But to be honest, I almost destroyed it. I don't know what to do with it. So that's what I thought you could help me with."

"How so?"

"I can't see the point in bringing this to light. It would just hurt his family, be a smear on the department. But…it is the truth. And the truth is important, even if it is painful. Can I look myself in the mirror if I don't come forward with what I know? I keep going round and round, and yes, I should have come to you sooner, but it was… It's been a lot to process."

"And you had to do that alone," Bo said flatly. "As always. I always knew you were keeping something from me, back then—it was Joe. The harassment, wasn't it?"

She looked down, nodded again. "Yes. I know…believe me, it's been keeping me up nights that if I had just told you, if I had not been so prideful, thinking I could handle it, or worrying what everyone would think, then maybe he would be alive, and maybe none of this would have happened if I had acted otherwise."

"Some of that could be true, but what he did in that warehouse—everything he did—it was all on him. He got what he deserved, in my opinion, and the accident—that wasn't your fault. Don't take that on. But yes. You should have come to me. I wish you had."

"I know. I'm so, so sorry. Because it would have

been the smart thing to do, but also because, among everyone, you were the person I could trust. Should have trusted. I just… I don't know. I don't know entirely why it felt so critical that I handle everything myself, that I always had to be completely in control all the time."

The tightness in Bo's chest loosened as he listened as she continued.

"That's what scared me, too, I guess. My feelings for you, they weren't in my control. I loved you so much, and I guess I thought I was losing you when you moved up into investigation—so I pushed you away. I was also ashamed of what was happening with Joe, and he knew about us—he could have hurt your career prospects."

"No, he really couldn't have. That should have been the last of your concerns. And you weren't losing me. If you had only come to me, Erin—"

"I know. I shouldn't have waited until now. Apparently, I still have a few issues to work out, so Kit says," she shared on a short laugh. "This is all too late, but still, I wanted us to have…closure, I guess."

There was a peace in her face that Bo hadn't seen before—ever. As if all the poison had been let out. All the bad stuff she'd been holding in, she'd finally let go. And she'd shared it with him—maybe late, maybe not when he'd wished she had, but she had. She'd come to him, and now it was his turn.

She'd also said "loved"—past tense.

"Listen, you've been through so much. It would be enough to mess anyone up. But I think you're right about the recording. You should come forward. Joe's family has backed off any legal action, but there's always a threat of that. This would protect you. My advice would be to bring it to the new marshal, and I can go with you if you want. The case should be closed, and all the information should be there, including the recording. The physical evidence, the bruising, the progression of events, supports your story. It will be enough, I promise. Like you said, Joe's family deserves the truth, no matter how ugly, and the department can stand it. And this is something the department has to know, in case there were other victims."

"I never thought of that. I thought I was the only one."

He had to stop for a second, look away. The idea of anyone laying a hand on her—hitting her—made him so angry he almost couldn't contain it. But the fact that she'd also felt alone...it killed him to know that. Whatever responsibility she bore, he bore some, too, if she'd felt she couldn't be open with him.

"I'm sorry, Erin," he said, wishing he'd done things differently, too. That he hadn't let her go so easily. That he hadn't pushed or insisted that she share what was bothering her. Maybe he could have changed the outcome for the better—protecting her was part of his job, for crying out loud.

"I'd like it if you could come with me, but I understand if you can't," she said, glancing around at all of his scattered belongings. "I know you have to go."

"Of course I'll come. Whatever will help out."

Loved.

His heart was raw. Erin had admitted why she'd left him, why she'd held herself so distant. She'd apologized. This was what they'd hoped for—that she could remember, and that they could bring this all full circle.

It should have been the closure he was looking for, but nothing felt closed, except for maybe the case.

"While I'm being completely open, then, you know, the new me, and facing my fears and everything…" she said, breaking into his thoughts. Her voice was higher, a little thinner—still nervous.

"And?"

"I'm not going back to the job. I have something new, I think, that I want to do. This…all of what's happened, it changed me. I guess I thought when my memory returned, I would be the old me, with the old job, and old patterns—but I don't even want that."

"Or the old us."

"Yes, not that, either," she said.

"I get it. I'm grateful you're sharing—"

"But the new us…I want the new us. The us we were starting to be. I love you, but not how I loved you before…because that wasn't enough. If you're interested, I wondered…you know, considering that I nearly botched things up again, and that you're leaving, but if you'd want to…keep new us going?"

Bo sat down, his brain stuttering over the words she said, as if not hearing them correctly.

Love?

"You love me?"

"I do. So much. I love what we were becoming… but it was only a start, with me not remembering anything, and all that past behind us, all resolved, so I was hoping…" She paused, taking a breath, clasping her hands together again tightly in front of her, as if she had to hold on to *something*. "Anyway, I just wanted you to know how I felt, but if you—"

"I love you, too, Erin. I never stopped, but I like new us, too…it would be nice to see what we could be."

She beamed, and the shock in her eyes had him hauling her against him again, and this time he didn't want to let go. A fresh batch of tears soaked his shirt and she laughed as she cursed them. New Erin still hated crying—and that made him laugh, too.

Right now, he needed to kiss her and to make sure all of this was real. Finding her lips, he touched softly, then went deeper as her hands curled into his shoulders and she opened, tasting him as desperately as he was her.

Breathing more heavily, they parted, and Bo's mind reeled, his body hard, his heart light. Heady.

"The FBI job will be a challenge," he said, tipping his forehead against hers. "I might not be around even as much as I was with this one, but we'll make this work. I can come here, and we can figure out some kind of travel, stay in touch as much as we can. Something."

"Travel might not be necessary."

"Why's that?"

"I'm applying to Johns Hopkins in Baltimore for the fall. I want to get a psych degree and train as a trauma counselor. They have an amazing program, so I'm selling the house and moving down there. I already talked to a student adviser who knows the trauma counselor, Tom, who helped me. Tom's even giving me a recommendation. Maybe I can use what happened to me to assist other people in the same situation."

Bo grinned, and then he laughed. "That's wonderful."

"We should be able to find a place together, close

to the FBI office and school. I can commute…if you don't think it's too soon for that, I mean?"

"I think it's far past time, actually," he said.

As they talked, he'd worked his hands up under the back of her shirt, stroking the soft skin of her back. *Love. His.*

"I have a few things to finish up here, though— selling the house and helping Kit save the store," she said, filling him in on Kit's financial difficulties. "I talked her into letting me hold some of the firefighter fund-raising events at her store—you know, like buy a bouquet, kiss a fireman kind of thing—to help her raise visibility, draw attention to her business."

"That's a good idea." Bo swooped in and began kissing her lips, her cheek.

"Oh," she said, catching her breath when he kissed her neck. "I thought so, too. She sent some lovely flower arrangements to Hank's room, and to the nurses' stations. The hospital gift shop clerk saw them—she was impressed, and talked to Kit about possibly being the supplier for the hospital florist. It would be a huge account for her."

"That's also a good idea," Bo murmured against her skin, starting to work the snap of her jeans. "I love you," he said against her mouth. "Who you were, who you are…who you're going to be. All of you."

She looked up at him with a sweet-hot gaze so full of emotion that it humbled him. How could he ever have thought he could live without her?

"I love you, too. I'll never hold anything back again. We're in this together. I promise."

"I like the sound of that," he said, caressing her.

"Shouldn't we work on packing up all this stuff? I could help."

"It can wait," he said, his lips raining kisses down from her throat to her breast, making her gasp.

"You're sure?"

Her expression held all the love and promise Bo had ever imagined, and he smiled. He felt his heart expand at the thought of the future they were going to have together.

"Absolutely sure. We have plenty of time. The rest of our lives, in fact."

* * * * *

"It's obvious there's something between us..."

Having sex with Jesse Chisholm would be the worst idea ever.

They were polar opposites. He was wild and exciting and Gracie wasn't. At least, she was doing her damndest to prove that she wasn't.

And that was the problem in a nutshell. Jesse called to the bad girl inside of her.

Not happening. She had an image to uphold. A reputation to protect. She was the mayor, for heaven's sake.

Anxiety rushed through her, because as committed as she was to the path she'd chosen, she couldn't help but feel as if she'd missed out on something.

She wanted one more night with Jesse. One more memory. Then she could stop fantasizing and go back to her nice, conservative life and step up as the town's new mayor without any worries or regrets.

She *would*. But not just yet.

She slammed on the brakes, swung the car around and headed for the motel.

"Okay," she blurted ten minutes later when Jesse opened his motel room door. "Let's do it."

TEXAS OUTLAWS: JESSE

BY
KIMBERLY RAYE

MILLS & BOON

Published in Great Britain 2014
by Mills & Boon, an imprint of Harlequin (UK) Limited,
Eton House, 18-24 Paradise Road, Richmond, Surrey, TW9 1SR

© 2014 Kimberly Groff

ISBN: 978 0 263 91225 8

14-0114

Harlequin (UK) Limited's policy is to use papers that are natural, renewable and recyclable products and made from wood grown in sustainable forests. The logging and manufacturing processes conform to the legal environmental regulations of the country of origin.

Printed and bound in Spain
by Blackprint CPI, Barcelona

This book is dedicated to Curt,
my loving husband and best friend,
You still know how to rock a pair of Wranglers!

1

THIS WAS TURNING into *the* worst ride of his life.

Jesse James Chisholm stared over the back of the meanest bull this side of the Rio Grande at the woman who parked herself just outside the railing of the Lost Gun Training Facility, located on a premium stretch of land a few miles outside the city limits.

His heart stalled and his hand slipped. The bull lurched and he nearly tumbled to the side.

No way was *she* here.

No frickin' *way*.

The bull twisted and Pro Bull Riding's newest champion wrenched to the right. He was seeing things. That had to be it. He'd hit the ground too many times going after that first buckle and now it was coming back to haunt him. His grip tightened and his breath caught. Just a few more seconds.

One thousand three. One thousand four.

"Jesse!" Her voice rang out, filling his ears with the undeniable truth that she was here, all right.

Shit.

The bull jerked and Jesse pitched forward. He flipped and went down. Hard.

Dust filled his mouth and pain gripped every nerve in his already aching body. The buzzer sounded and voices echoed, but he was too fixated on catching his breath to notice the chaos that suddenly surrounded him. He shut his eyes as his heart pounded in his rib cage.

Come on, buddy. You got this. Just breathe.

In and out. In. Out. In—

"Jesse? Ohmigod! Are you all right? Is he all right?"

Her desperate voice slid into his ears and stalled his heart. His eyes snapped open and sure enough, he found himself staring into a gaze as pale and blue as a clear Texas sky at high noon.

And just as scorching.

Heat swamped him and for a split second, he found himself sucked back to the past, to those long, endless days at Lost Gun High School.

He'd been at the bottom of the food chain back then, the son of the town's most notorious criminal, and no one had ever let him forget it. The teachers had stared at him with pity-filled gazes. The other boys had treated him like a leper. And the girls... They'd looked at him as if he were a bona fide rock star. The bad boy who was going to save them from the monotony of their map-dot existence.

Every girl, that is, except for Gracie Stone.

She'd been a rock star in her own right. Buck wild and reckless. Constantly defying her strict adoptive parents and pushing them to the limits. They'd wanted a goody-goody daughter befitting the town's mayor and first lady, and Gracie had wanted to break out of the neat little box she'd been forced into after the tragic death of her real parents.

They'd both been seniors when they'd crossed paths at a party. It had been lust at first sight. They'd had three scorching weeks together before they'd graduated and she'd ditched him via voice mail.

We just don't belong together.

For all her wicked ways, she was still the mayor's daughter, and he was the son of the town's most hated man. Water and oil. And everyone knew the two didn't mix.

Not then, and certainly not now.

He tried to remember that all-important fact as he focused on the sweet-smelling woman leaning over him.

She looked so different compared to the wild and wicked girl who lived and breathed in his memories. She'd traded in too much makeup and too little clothes for a more conservative look. She wore a navy skirt and a white silk shell tucked in at the waist. Her long blond hair had been pulled back into a no-nonsense ponytail. Long thick lashes fringed her pale blue eyes. Her lips were full and pink and luscious.

Different, yet his gut ached just the same.

He stiffened and his mouth pressed into a tight line. "Civilians aren't allowed in the arena." He pushed himself to his feet, desperate to ignore the soft pink-tipped fingers on his arm. "Not without boots." Her touch burned through the material of his Western shirt and sent a fizzle of electricity up his arm. "And jeans," he blurted. "And a long-sleeve shirt, for Chrissake." Damn, but why did she have to keep touching him like that? "You're breaking about a dozen different rules."

"I'm sorry. You just hit the ground so hard and I thought you were hurt and…" Her words trailed off and she let her hand fall away.

He ignored the whisper of disappointment and concentrated on the anger roiling inside him. "You almost got me killed." That was what he said. But the only thing rolling over and over in his mind was that she'd put herself in danger by climbing over the railing with a mean sumbitch bull on the loose.

He pushed away the last thought because no way—no friggin' way—did Jesse care one way or the other when it came to Gracie Stone. He was over her.

Finished.

Done.

He held tight to the notion and focused on the fact that she'd ruined a perfectly good training session. "You don't yell at a man when he's in the middle of a ride. It's distracting. I damn near broke my neck." He dusted off his pants and reached for his hat a few feet away. "If you're looking for City Hall—" he shook off the dirt and parked the worn Stetson on top of his head "—I think you're way off the mark."

"Actually, I was looking for you." Unease flitted across her face as if she wasn't half as sure of herself as she pretended to be. She licked her pink lips and he tried not to follow the motion with his eyes. "I need to talk to you."

He had half a mind to tell her to kick her stilettos into high gear and start walking. He was smack-dab in the middle of a demonstration for a prospective buyer who'd flown in yesterday to purchase the black bull currently snorting in a nearby holding pen.

Because Jesse was selling his livestock and moving on.

Finally.

With the winnings and endorsements from his first championship last year, he'd been able to put in an offer for a three-hundred-acre spread just outside of Austin, complete with a top-notch practice arena. The seller had accepted and now it was just a matter of signing the papers and transferring the money.

"Yo, Jesse." David Burns, the buyer interested in his stock, signaled him from the sidelines and Jesse held up a hand that said hold up a minute.

David wanted to make a deal and Jesse needed to get a move on. He didn't have time for a woman who'd ditched him twelve years ago without so much as a face-to-face.

At the same time, he couldn't help but wonder what could be so almighty important that it had Lost Gun's newly elected mayor slumming it a full ten miles outside the city limits.

He shrugged. "So talk."

Her gaze shifted from the buyer to the group of cowboys working the saddle broncs in the next arena. Several of the men had shifted their attention to the duo standing center stage. "Maybe we could go someplace private."

The words stirred all sorts of possibilities, all treacherous to his peace of mind since they involved a very naked Gracie and a sizable hard-on. But Jesse had never been one to back down from a dangerous situation.

He summoned his infamous slide-off-your-panties drawl that had earned him the coveted title of Rodeo's

Hottest Bachelor and an extra twenty thousand followers on Twitter and eyed her. "Sugar, the only place I'm going after this is straight into a hot shower." He gave her a sly grin he wasn't feeling at the moment and winked. "If you're inclined to follow, then by all means, let's go."

Her eyes darkened and for a crazy instant, he glimpsed the old Gracie. The wild free spirit who'd stripped off her clothes and gone skinny-dipping with him their first night together.

But then the air seemed to chill and her gaze narrowed. "We'll talk here," she said, her voice calm and controlled. A total contradiction to the slight tremble of her bottom lip. She drew a deep breath that lifted her ample chest and wreaked havoc with his self-control. "A fax came in from the production company that filmed *Famous Texas Outlaws*."

The mention of the television documentary that had nearly cost him his livelihood all those years ago was like a douse of ice water. "And?"

"They sold rights to a major affiliate who plans to air the show again and film a live 'Where Are They Now?' segment. They're already running promos for it. Sheriff Hooker had to chase two fortune hunters off your place just yesterday."

His "place" amounted to the burned-down shack and ten overgrown acres on the south end of town that he'd once shared with his father and brothers. As for the fortune hunters, well, they were out of luck. There was nothing to find.

His lawyer had been advising him to sell the property for years now, but Jesse had too many bad memories to want to profit off that sad, miserable place. Ignoring it had been better. Easier.

He eyed her. "When?"

"It's airing next Tuesday." She squared her shoulders, as if trying to gather her courage. "I thought you deserved fair warning after what happened the last time."

His leg throbbed at the memory. "So that's why you're here?" He tamped down the sudden ache. "To give me a heads-up?"

She nodded and something softened inside him.

A crazy reaction since he knew that her sudden visit had nothing to do with any sense of loyalty to him. This was all about the town. She'd traded in her wild and wicked ways to become a model public servant like her uncle. Conservative. Responsible. Loyal.

He knew that, yet the knotted fist in his chest eased just a little anyway.

"I know you just got back yesterday," she went on, "but I really think it would be better to cut your visit short until it's all said and done." She pulled her shoulders back. The motion pressed her delicious breasts against the soft fabric of her blouse. He caught a glimpse of lace beneath the thin material and he knew then that she wasn't as conservative as she wanted everyone to think. "That would make things a lot easier."

"For me?" He eyed her. "Or for you?"

Her gaze narrowed. "I'm not the one they'll be after."

"No, you're just in charge of the town they'll be invading. After all the craziness the last time I think you're anxious to avoid another circus. Getting rid of

me would certainly help." The words came out edged
with challenge, as if he dared her to dispute them.

He did.

She caught her bottom lip as if she wanted to argue,
but then her mouth pulled tight. "If the only eyewitness
to the fire is MIA, the reporters won't have a reason to
stick around. I really think it would be best for everyone." Her gaze caught and held his. "Especially you."

Ditto.

He sure as hell wasn't up to the pain he'd gone
through the first time. The show had originally aired
a few months after he'd graduated high school, five
years to the day of his father's death. He'd been eighteen at the time and a damn sight more reckless.

He'd been ground zero in the middle of a training
session with a young, jittery bull named Diamond Dust.
A group of reporters had shown up, cameras blazing,
and Diamond had gone berserk. More so than usual
for a mean-as-all-get-out bucking bull. Jesse had hit
the ground, and then the bull had hit him. Over and
over, stomping and crushing until Jesse had suffered
five broken ribs, a broken leg, a dislocated shoulder
and a major concussion. Injuries that had landed him
in a rehab facility for six months and nearly cost him
everything.

Not that the same thing wouldn't have happened
eventually. He'd been on a fast road to trouble back
then, ignoring the rules and riding careless and loose.
The reporters had simply sped up the inevitable, because Jesse hadn't been interested in a career back then
so much as an escape.

From the guilt of watching his own father die and
not doing a damned thing to stop it.

It wasn't your fault. The man made his own choice.

That was what Pete Gunner had told him time and time again after the fire. Pete was the pro bull rider who'd taken in thirteen-year-old Jesse and his brothers and saved them from being split up into different foster homes after their father had died. Pete had been little more than a kid himself back then—barely twenty— and had just won his first PBR title. The last thing he'd needed was the weight of three orphans distract- ing him from his career, but he'd taken on the respon- sibility anyway. The man had been orphaned himself as a kid and so he'd known how hard it was to make it in the world. Cowboying had saved him and so he'd taught Jesse and his brothers how to rope and ride and hold their own in a rodeo arena. He'd turned them into tough cowboys. The best in the state, as a matter of fact. Even more, he'd given them a roof over their heads and food in their stomachs, and hope.

And when Diamond had nearly killed Jesse, it had been Pete who'd paid for the best orthopedic surgeons in the state. Pete was family—as much a brother to Jesse as Billy and Cole—and he was about to marry the woman of his dreams this Saturday.

That was the real reason Jesse had come back to this godforsaken town. And the reason he had no in- tention of leaving until the vows were spoken, the cake was cut and the happy couple left for two weeks in the Australian outback.

Then Jesse would pack up what little he had left here and head for Austin to make a real life. Far away from the memories. From her.

He stiffened against a sudden wiggle of regret.

"Trust me, there's nothing I'd like better than to haul ass out of here right now."

"Good. Then we're on the same page—"

"But I won't," he cut in. "I can't."

A knowing light gleamed in her eyes. "I'm sure Pete would understand."

"I'm sure he would, but that's beside the point." Jesse shook his head. "I'm not missing his wedding."

"But—"

"You'll just have to figure out some other way to defuse the situation and keep the peace."

And then he did what she'd done to him on that one night forever burned into his memory—he turned and walked away without so much as a goodbye.

2

WAIT A SECOND.

Wait just a friggin' *second*.

That was what Gracie wanted to say. She'd envisioned this meeting about a zillion times on the way over, and this wasn't the way it had played out. Where was the gratitude? The appreciation? The desperate embrace followed by one whopper of a kiss?

She ditched the last thought and focused on the righteous indignation that came with violating about ten different city ordinances on someone else's behalf. Leaking private city business to civilians was an unforgivable sin and the memo from the production company had been marked strictly confidential.

But this was Jesse, and while she'd made it a point to avoid him for the past twelve years, she couldn't in good conscience sit idly by and let him be broadsided by the news crew currently on its way to Lost Gun.

Not because she cared about him.

Lust. That was all she'd ever felt for him. The breath-stealing, bone-melting, desperate lust of a hormone-driven sixteen-year-old. A girl who'd dreamed of a world beyond her desperately small town, a world filled with bright lights and big cities and a career in photojournalism.

She'd wanted out so bad back then. To the point that she'd been wild and reckless, eager to fill the humdrum days until her eighteenth birthday with whatever excitement she could find.

But then she'd received the special-delivery letter announcing that her older brother had been killed in the line of duty and she'd realized it was time to grow up, step up and start playing it safe right here in Lost Gun.

For her sister.

Charlotte Stone was ten years younger than Gracie. And while she'd been too young—four years old, to be exact—to remember the devastation when their parents had died in a tragic car accident, she'd been plenty old enough at nine to feel the earthquake caused by the death of their older brother. She'd morphed from a happy, outgoing little girl, into a needy, scared introvert who'd been terrified to let her older sister out of her sight.

Gracie had known then that she could never leave Lost Gun. Even more, she'd vowed not only to stay but to settle down, play it safe and make a real home for her sister.

She'd traded her beloved photography lessons for finance classes at the local junior college and ditched everything that was counterproductive to her new safe, settled life—from her favorite fat-filled French fries to Jesse Chisholm himself.

Especially Jesse.

He swiped a hand across his backside to dust off his jeans and her gaze snagged on the push-pull of soft faded denim. Her nerves started to hum and the air stalled in her lungs.

While time usually whittled away at people, making them worn around the edges, it had done the opposite with Jesse. The years had carved out thick muscles and a ripped bod. He looked even harder than she remembered, taller and more commanding. The fitted black-and-gray retro Western shirt framed broad shoulders and a narrow waist. Worn jeans topped with dusty brown leather chaps clung to trim hips and thighs and stretched the length of his long legs. Scuffed brown cowboy boots, the tips worn from one too many run-ins with a bull, completed the look of rodeo's hottest hunk. The title had been held by local legend Pete Gunner up until he'd proposed to the love of his life just two short years ago. Since then Jesse had been burning up the rodeo circuit, determined to take the man's place and gain even more notoriety for the Lost Boys, a local group of cowboy daredevils who were taking the rodeo circuit by storm, winning titles and charming fans all across the country.

Wild. Fearless. Careless.

He was all three and then some.

Her gaze shifted to the face hidden beneath the brim of a worn Stetson. While she couldn't see his eyes thanks to the shadow, she knew they were a deep, mesmerizing violet framed by thick sable lashes. A few days' growth of beard covered his jaw and crept down his neck. Dark brown hair brushed his collar and made her fingers itch to reach out and touch.

"If I were you, I'd stop staring and put my tongue back in my mouth before somebody stomps on it."

The voice startled her, and she turned to see the ancient cowboy who came up beside her.

Eli McGinnis was an old-school wrangler in his late seventies with a head full of snow-white hair that had been slicked back with pomade. His handlebar mustache twitched and she knew he was smiling even though she couldn't actually see the expression beneath the elaborate do on his top lip.

"You'd do well to stop droolin', too," he added. "We got enough mud puddles around here already. A few shit piles, too."

"I wasn't—"

"Drooling?" he cut in. "While I ain't the brightest bulb in the tanning bed, I know drooling when I see it and, lemme tell ya, it ain't attractive on a fine upstanding public servant like yourself. Then again, you ain't actually the mayor yet, so I guess I should be talking to your uncle when it comes to serious public-health issues."

"Uncle E.J. already left for Port Aransas. He and my aunt just bought a house there." Her brow wrinkled as the impact of his words hit. "A public-health issue?" The notion killed the lingering image of Jesse and snagged her complete attention. "What health issue?" A dozen possibilities raced through her mind, from a city-wide epidemic of salmonella to a flesh-eating zombie virus.

Okay, so she spent her evenings watching a little too much cable TV since Charlie had moved into the dorms at the University of Texas last year. A girl had to have *some* fun.

Anxiety raced up her spine. "It's mercury in the water, isn't it?" Fear coiled and tightened in the pit of her stomach. "E. coli in the lettuce crops? Don't tell me Big Earl Jessup is making moonshine in his garage again." At ninety-one, Big Earl was the town's oldest resident, and the most dangerous. He came from a time when the entrepreneurial spirit meant whipping up black diamond whiskey in the backyard and hand-selling it at the annual peach festival. Those days were long gone but that hadn't stopped Big Earl from firing up last year to cook a batch to give away for Christmas. And then again at Easter. And for the Fourth of July.

"You got bigger problems than an old man cooking up moonshine in his deer blind, that's for damn sure."

"Big Earl's cooking in his deer blind?"

Eli frowned. "Stop trying to change the subject. We've got a crisis on our hands."

"Which is?"

"Fake cheese on the nachos. Why, the diner used to put a cup of real whole-milk cheddar on all the nacho platters, but now they're tryin' to cut costs, so they switched to the artificial stuff."

"Fake cheese," she repeated, relief sweeping through her. "That's the major health concern?"

"Damn straight. Why, I was up all night with indigestion. As the leader of this fine community—" he wagged a finger at her "—it's your job to clean it up."

O-kay.

"I'll, um, stop by the diner and see what I can do."

He threw up his hands. "That's all I'm askin', little lady."

Her gaze shifted back to Jesse, who now stood on the other side of the arena talking to two men she didn't recognize. They weren't real working cowboys but rather the slick, wealthy types who flew in every now and then to buy or sell livestock. With their designer boots and high-dollar hats, they probably intimidated most men, but not Jesse. He held his own, a serious look on his face as he motioned to the black bull thrashing around a nearby stall.

"That boy's too damned big for his britches sometimes," Eli muttered.

Her gaze dropped and her breath caught. Actually, he filled out said britches just right.

She watched as he untied his chaps and tossed them over a nearby railing, leaving nothing but a tight pair of faded denims that clung to him like a second skin, outlining his sinewy thighs and trim waist and tight, round butt—

"It's mighty nice of you to come out and warn him." Her gaze snapped up and she glanced at the old man next to her. "Even if he don't realize it."

"It's fine." She shrugged. "It's not like I stop by every day."

Not anymore.

But for those blissful three weeks before they'd graduated, she'd been a permanent fixture on the corral fence, watching him every afternoon after school. Snapping pictures of him. Dreaming of the day when she could leave Lost Gun behind and turn her hobby into a passion.

She'd wanted out of this map dot just as bad as he had. Then.

And now.

She stiffened against the sudden thought. She was happy with her life here. Content.

And even if she wasn't, it didn't matter. She was here. She was staying. End of story.

"Still, you didn't have to go to so much trouble," Eli went on.

"Just looking out for my soon-to-be constituents." No way did Gracie want to admit that she'd come because she still cared about Jesse. Because she still dreamed of him. Because she still *wanted* him.

No, this was about doing the right thing to make up for the wrong she'd done so long ago. She'd had her chance to warn him the first time, and she'd chickened out for fear that seeing him would crumble her resolve and resurrect the wild child she'd been so desperate to bury.

She'd lived with the guilt every day since.

"Tell him to be careful." She took one last look at Jesse, fought against the emotion that churned down deep and walked away.

"THAT MAGAZINE ARTICLE was right about you. You sure put on one helluva show." The words were followed by a steady *clap-clap-clap* as Billy Chisholm, Jesse's youngest brother, walked toward him. Billy was four years younger and eagerly chasing the buckle Jesse had won just last year. "I particularly liked that little twist you did when you flew into the air." He grinned. "Right before you busted your tail."

Jesse glared. "I'm not in the mood."

"I wouldn't be either if I'd just ate it in front of everyone and the horse they rode in on."

But Jesse wasn't concerned about everyone. Just a certain buttoned-up city official with incredible blue eyes.

He barely resisted the urge to steal one last look at her. Not that he hadn't seen her over the years when he'd happened into town—across a crowded main street, through the dingy windows of the local feed store. It was just that those times had been few and far between because Jesse hated Lost Gun as much as the town hated him, and so he'd kept his distance.

But this was different.

She'd been right in front of him. Close enough to touch. To feel. He could still smell her—the warm, luscious scent of vanilla cupcakes topped with a mountain of frosting.

Sweet.

Decadent.

Enough to make him want to cross the dusty arena separating them, pull her into his arms and see if she tasted half as good as he remembered.

Want.

Yep, he still wanted her, all right. The thing was, he didn't *want* to want her, because she sure as hell didn't want him.

He'd thought so at one time. She'd smiled and flirted and rubbed up against him, and he'd foolishly thought she was into him. He'd been a hormone-driven eighteen-year-old back then and he'd fallen hard and fast.

He was a grown-ass man now and a damn sight more experienced. Enough to know that Gracie Stone was nothing special in the big scheme of things. There were dozens of women out there, and Jesse indulged in more than his fair share. And while they all tasted as sweet as could be at first, the sweetness always faded. The sex soon lost its edge. And then Jesse cut ties and moved on to the next.

"...can't remember the last time you bit the bullet

like that," Billy went on. "What the hell happened? Did someone slap you with a ten-pound bag of stupid?"

Okay, maybe Gracie was a little special. She'd been the only woman in his past to break things off with him first, *before* he'd had a chance to lose interest.

He would have, he reminded himself.

Guaran-damn-teed.

From the corner of his eye, he watched her disappear around the holding pens. The air rushed back into his lungs, but his muscles didn't ease.

He was still uptight. Hot. Bothered.

Stupid.

He stiffened and focused on untying the gloves from his hands.

"Alls I can say is thanks, bro," Billy went on. "I bet a wad of cash on your ride just now. My truck payment, as a matter of fact."

Jesse arched an eyebrow. "And you're thanking me for losing your shirt?"

Billy clapped him on the shoulder and sent an ache through his bruised body. "I didn't bet *on* you, bro. I bet *against* you." He winked. "Saw that little gal come round the corner and I knew things were going to get mighty interesting."

Forget stupid. He was pissed.

"She came to warn me," Jesse bit out, his mouth tight. "They're shooting a 'Where Are They Now?' special next week," he told his brother. "A follow-up to *Famous Texas Outlaws.*"

Billy's grin faltered for a split second. "You okay with that?"

Jesse shrugged. "I can handle my fair share of reporters. You know that."

"True enough." Billy nodded before sliding him a sideways glance. "But if you want a little peace and quiet, you can always send them my way." He winked and his grin was back. "I like getting my picture taken."

Billy had been fourteen at the time and excited about being in the limelight. He hadn't been the least bit unnerved by the endless questions about their father's death six years prior, because he'd been too young to really comprehend the gravity of what Silas Chisholm had done. Too young to remember the police and the accusations and the desperate search to recover the money that their father had stolen. Rather, he'd seen the media circus as a welcome distraction from an otherwise shitty life.

"Gracie wants me to lie low," Jesse added. "She thinks it'll help the town."

"And here I thought she came all the way out here because she wanted a piece of PBR's reigning champion."

If only.

Jesse stuffed his gloves into his pocket and fought the longing that coiled inside of him.

Gracie Stone was off-limits.

She'd broken his heart and while it was all water under the bridge now, he had no intention of paddling upstream ever again.

Then again, it wasn't his heart that had stirred the moment he'd come face-to-face with her again. Despite the years that had passed, the chemistry was still as strong as ever.

Stronger, in fact.

And damned if that realization didn't bother him even more than the fact that he'd just landed on his ass in front of an arena full of cowboys. Since Tater Tot had been the ornery bull responsible, he'd just become that much more valuable to the two buyers now waiting inside Jesse's office in a nearby building.

So maybe Gracie's visit wasn't a complete bust after all.

"I've got papers to sign." He motioned to the glass-walled office that overlooked the corral. "Get your gear and get in the chute if you want a turn on Tater Tot before they pack him up and ship him out. And you'd better make it quick because we've got a tuxedo fitting in a half hour and the clock's ticking."

"Sure thing, bro." A grin cut loose from ear to ear. "After that piss-poor display, somebody's gotta show you how it's done."

3

IT TOOK EVERY ounce of willpower Gracie had to bypass the one and only bakery in Lost Gun and head for the town square.

Sure, she eased up on the gas pedal and powered down her window to take in the delicious scent of fresh-baked goodies as she rolled past Sarah's Sweets, but still. She didn't slam on the brakes and make a bee-line for the overflowing counter inside. No red velvet cupcakes or buttercream-frosted sugar cookies for this girl. And no—repeat *no*—Double-Fudge Fantasy Brownies rich in trans fat and high in cholesterol.

Which explained why her hands still trembled and her stomach fluttered when she walked into City Hall.

"How's my favorite mayor-elect?" asked the thirty-something bleached blonde sitting behind the desk in the outer office with a chocolate Danish in front of her.

Longing clawed down deep inside of Gracie, but she tamped it back down. "Fine."

"Methinks you are one terrible liar." Trina Lovett popped a bite of pastry into her mouth and washed it down with a sip of black coffee.

Trina had been working for Gracie's uncle—the current mayor—since she'd graduated high school sixteen years ago—four years before Gracie. Trina had been part of a rise-above-your-environment program that helped young people from impoverished homes—a trailer on the south end of town in Trina's case—find jobs.

He'd hit the jackpot with Trina, who was not only a hard worker but knew everything about everybody. She'd been instrumental in the past few elections—particularly in a too-close-for-comfort runoff with the local sheriff a few years back. E.J. had won, of course, due to his compassionate nature and Trina's connections down at the local honky-tonk. The young woman had bought five rounds of beers the day of the election and earned the forty-two votes needed to win.

Trina had also been instrumental in the most recent campaign, which had seen Gracie take the mayoral race by a landslide.

In exactly two weeks to the day, Gracie Elizabeth Stone would take the sacred oath and step up as the town's first female mayor.

Two weeks, three hours and forty-eight minutes.

Not that she was counting.

"You saw Jesse, didn't you?" When Gracie nodded, Trina's bright red lips parted in a smile. "Tell me *everything*. I caught him on the ESPN channel a few weeks back, but all I could see was a distant view of him straddling a bull for dear life." She wiggled her eyebrows. "What I wouldn't have given to be that bull."

"You work for a public official. You know that, right?"

"Don't get your granny panties in a wad. It's not like

I'm tweeting it or posting to my Facebook status. This is a private conversation." She beamed. "*So?* What's he really like up close? Does he still have those broad shoulders? That great ass?"

Yes and *yes.*

She stiffened and focused on leafing through the stack of mail on Trina's desk. "I'd, um, say he's aged well."

"Seriously? I suppose you look ready to scarf an entire box of cupcakes because of some cowboy who's *aged well?*"

"I suppose he's still hot, if you're into that sort of thing."

"I am." Trina beamed. "I most definitely am."

Gracie frowned. "Not that it makes a difference. I went there strictly in an official capacity. I went. I spoke. He heard. End of story."

Trina regarded her for a long, assessing moment. "He told you to get lost, didn't he?"

"No." The brave face she'd put on faltered. "Yes. I mean, he didn't say it outright—there were no distinct verbs or colorful nouns—but he might as well have."

"Ouch." Her gaze swept Gracie from head to toe and she pursed her bright red lips. "But I can't say as I blame him. You look like you're going to Old Man Winthrow's wake."

"I do black for funerals. This is navy."

"Same thing." She gave Gracie another visual sweep with her assessing blue eyes. "Listen here, girlfriend, men don't take time out of their day to notice navy. It takes a hot color to keep a man from tossing you out on your keister. Red. Neon pink. Even a print—like cheetah or zebra. Something that says you've got a sex drive and you know how to use it. And the skimpier, the better, too. Show a little leg. Some cleavage. Men like cleavage. It gets their full attention every time."

"For the last time—this wasn't a social visit." Gracie eyed Trina's black leather miniskirt. "I'm a public figure. I can't prance around looking like an extra from *Jersey Shore*. Besides, he hates me, and a dress—skimpy or not—isn't going to change that."

"I'm telling you, a good dress is like magic. Slip it on and it'll transform you from a stuffy politician into a major slut. You do remember how much fun being a little slutty can be, don't you?"

As if she could ever forget.

She'd been the baddest girl in high school with the worst reputation, and she'd liked it. She'd liked doing the unexpected and following her gut and having some fun. And she'd *really* liked Jesse James Chisholm.

So much so that she'd been ready to put off attending the University of Texas—her uncle's alma mater—to follow Jesse onto the rodeo circuit. To continue their wild ride together, cheer him on and take enough live-action shots to launch her dream career as a photographer.

But then Jackson had been killed, and Charlie had stopped talking for six months. She'd realized then that she couldn't just turn her back on her little sister and go her own way as her brother had done after their parents had died. Charlie needed her.

And she needed Charlie.

So she'd packed up her camera and her dreams and started playing it safe. She'd followed in her uncle's footsteps, securing a business degree before taking a position as city planner.

Meanwhile, Jesse had ridden every bull from here to Mexico.

They were worlds apart now, and when they did happen to land within a mile radius of each other, the animosity was enough to keep the wall between them thick. Impenetrable.

Animosity because not only had Gracie stood him up on the night they were supposed to leave, but she'd refused to talk to him about it, terrified that if she heard his voice or saw him up close, her determination would crumble. Fearful that the bad girl inside of her would rear her ugly head and lust would get the better of her.

Lust, not love.

She hadn't been able to leave with Jesse, and she'd refused to ask him to give up his life's dream to stay with her in a town that had caused him nothing but pain, and so she'd done the best thing for both of them—she'd broken off all contact.

And her silence had nearly cost him his career.

Not this time.

She'd given him fair warning about the inevitable influx of reporters and now she could get back to work and, more important, forget how good he smelled and how his eyes darkened to a deep, fathomless shade of purple whenever he looked at her.

She fought down the sudden yearning that coiled inside of her. "I don't do slut anymore," she told her assistant.

"Duh." Trina shrugged. "You've been wearing those Spanx so long, you've forgotten how to peel them off and cut loose."

If only.

But that was the trouble in a nutshell. She'd never

really forgotten. Deep in her heart, in the dead of night, she remembered what it felt like to live for the moment, to feel the rush of excitement, to walk on the wild side. It felt good—so freakin' *good*—and she couldn't help but want to feel that way again.

Just once.

Not that she was acting on that want. No way. No how. No sirree. Charlie needed a home and the people of Lost Gun needed a mayor, and Gracie needed to keep her head on straight and her thoughts out of the gutter.

"So what's on the agenda today?" she blurted, eager to get them back onto a safer subject. "City council meeting? Urgent political strategy session? Constituent meet and greet?" She needed something—anything—to get her mind off Jesse James Chisholm and the fact that he'd looked every bit as good as she remembered. And then some. "Surely Uncle E.J. left a big pile of work before he headed for Port Aransas to close on the new house?"

"Let's see." Trina punched a few buttons on her computer. "You're in luck. You've got a meeting with Mildred Jackson from the women's sewing circle—she wants the city to commission a quilt for your new office."

"That's it?"

"That and a trip to the animal shelter." When Gracie arched an eyebrow, Trina added, "I've been reading this article online about politicians and their canine friends. Do you know that a dog ups your favorability rating by five percent?"

"I already have a dog."

"A ball of fluff who humps everything in sight

doesn't count." When Gracie gave her a sharp look, she shrugged. "Not that I have anything against humping, but you've got a reputation to think of. A horny mutt actually takes away poll points."

"Sugar Lips isn't a mutt. She's a maltipom. Half Maltese. Half Pomeranian." Trina gave her a *girlfriend, pu-leeze* look and she added, "I've got papers to prove it."

"Labs and collies polled at the top with voters, and the local shelter just happens to have one of each," Trina pressed. "Just think how awesome it will look when the new mayor-elect waltzes in on Adopt-a-Pet Day and picks out her new Champ or Spot."

"Don't tell me—Champ and Spot were top-polling animal names?"

"Now you're catching on."

Gracie shook her head. "I can't just bring home another dog. Sugar will freak. She has control issues."

"Think of the message it will send to voters. Image is everything."

As if she didn't know that. She'd spent years trying to shake her own bad image, to bury it down deep, to make people forget, and she'd finally succeeded. Twelve long years later, she'd managed to earn the town's loyalty. Their trust.

Now it was just a matter of keeping it.

She shrugged. "Okay, I'll get another dog."

"And a date," Trina added. "That way people can also envision you as the better half of a couple, i.e., family oriented."

"Where do you get this stuff?"

"PerfectPolitician.com. They say if you want to project a stable, reliable image, you need to be in a stable, reliable relationship. I was thinking we should call Chase Carter. He's president of the bank, not to mention a huge campaign contributor. He's also president of the chamber of commerce and vice president of the zoning commission."

And about as exciting as the 215-page car-wash proposition just submitted by the president of the Ladies' Auxiliary for next year's fundraiser.

Gracie eyed her assistant. "Isn't Chase gay?"

"A small technicality." Trina waved a hand. "This is about image, not getting naked on the kitchen table. I know he isn't exactly a panty dropper like Jesse James Chisholm, but—"

"Call him." Chase *wasn't* Jesse, which made him perfect dating material. He wouldn't be interested in getting her naked and she wouldn't be interested in getting him naked. And she certainly wouldn't sit around fantasizing about the way his thigh muscles bunched when he crossed a rodeo arena.

She ignored the faint scent of dust and leather that still lingered on her clothes and shifted her attention to something safe. "Do you know anything about Big Earl Jessup?" She voiced the one thing besides Jesse Chisholm and his scent that had been bothering her since she'd left the training arena.

"I know he's too old to be your date. That and he's got hemorrhoids the size of boulders." Gracie's eyes widened and Trina shrugged. "News travels fast in a small town. Bad news travels even faster."

"I don't want to go out with him. I heard through the grapevine that he might be cooking moonshine in his deer blind."

Trina's eyebrow shot up. "The really good kind he used to make for the annual peach festival?"

"Maybe."

"Hot damn." When Gracie cut her a stare, she added, "I mean, *damn*. What a shame."

"Exactly. He barely got off by the skin of his teeth the last time he was brought up on charges. Judge Ellis is going to throw the book at him if he even thinks that Big Earl is violating his parole."

"Isn't Big Earl like a hundred?"

"He's in his nineties."

"What kind of dipshit would throw a ninetysome-thing in prison?"

"The dipshit whose car got blown up the last time Big Earl was cooking. Judge Ellis had a case of the stuff in his trunk at the annual Fourth of July picnic. A Roman candle got too close and bam, his Cadillac went up in flames."

"Isn't that his own fault for buying the stuff?"

"That's what Uncle E.J. said, which was why Big Earl got off on probation. But Judge Ellis isn't going to be swayed again. He'll nail him to the wall." And stir another whirlwind of publicity when Lost Gun became home to the oldest prison inmate. At least that was what Uncle E.J. had said when he'd done his best to keep the uproar to a minimum.

"I need to find out for sure," Gracie told Trina.

"If you go nosying around Big Earl's place, you're liable to get shot. Tell you what—I'll drop by his place after I get my nails done. My daddy used to buy from him all the time when I was a little girl. I'll tell him I just stopped by for old times' sake. So what do you think?" She held up two-inch talons. "Should I go with wicked red or passionate pink this time?"

"Don't you usually get your nails done on Friday?"

"Hazel over at the motel called and said two reporters from Houston are checking in this afternoon and I want to look my best before the feeding frenzy starts."

"Reporters?" Alarm bells sounded in Gracie's head and a rush of adrenaline shot through her. "Already?"

Trina nodded. "She's got three more checking in tomorrow. And twenty-two members of the Southwest chapter of the Treasure Hunters Alliance. Not to mention, Lyle over at the diner called and said the folks from the Whispering Winds Senior Home stopped by for lunch today. They usually go straight through to Austin for their weekly shopping trip, but one of them read a preview about the documentary in the TV listings and now everybody wants to check out Silas Chisholm's old stomping grounds. A few of them even brought their gardening trowels for a little digging after lunch."

"But there's nothing to find." According to police reports, the wad of cash from Silas Chisholm's bank heist had gone up in flames with the man himself.

"That's what Lyle told them, but you know folks don't listen. They'd rather think there's some big windfall just waiting to be discovered." Which was exactly what the documentary's host had been banking on when he'd brought up the missing money and stirred a whirlwind of doubt all those years ago.

Maybe the money hadn't gone up in flames.

Maybe, just maybe, it was still out there waiting to be discovered. To make someone rich.

"I should head over to the diner and set them all straight."

"Forget it. I saved you a trip and stopped by myself on my way in." Trina waved a hand. "Bought them all a complimentary round of tapioca, and just like that, they forgot all about treasure hunting. Say, why don't you come with me to the salon?"

"I can't. The remodeling crew will be here first thing tomorrow and I promised I'd have everything picked out by then."

It was a lame excuse, but the last thing she needed was to sit in the middle of a nail salon and endure twenty questions about her impromptu visit with Jesse Chisholm and the impending media circus.

"That and I still need to unpack all the boxes from my old office."

"Suit yourself, but I'd take advantage of the light schedule between now and inauguration time. You'll be up to your neck in city business soon enough once you take your oath."

A girl could only hope.

Trina glanced at her watch and pushed up from her desk. "I'm outta here." Her gaze snagged on the phone and she smiled. "Right after I hook you up with Mr. Wrong, that is."

She punched in a number on the phone. "Hey, Sally. It's Trina over at the mayor's office. Is Chase in?…The mayor-elect would like to invite him to be her escort for the inauguration ceremony.…What? He's hosting a pottery class right now?…No, no, don't interrupt him. Just tell him the mayor-elect called and wants to sweep him off his feet.…Yeah, yeah, she loves pottery, too.…"

Gracie balled her fingers to keep from pressing the

disconnect button, turned and headed for the closed door. A date with Chase was just what she needed. He was perfect. Upstanding. Respectable. Boring.

She ignored the last thought and picked up her steps. Hinges creaked and she found herself in the massive office space that would soon be the headquarters of Lost Gun's new mayor.

Under normal circumstances, the new mayor moved into the old mayor's office, but just last week the city had approved budget changes allocating a huge amount to renovate the east wing of City Hall, including the massive space that had once served as a courtroom. Gracie was the first new face they'd elected in years and change was long overdue. She was getting a brand-new office and reception area, as well as her own private bathroom.

Everything had been cleared out and the floors stripped down to the concrete slab. A card table sat off to one side. Her laptop and a spare phone sat on top, along with a stack of paint colors and flooring samples and furniture selections all awaiting her approval. A stack of boxes from her old office filled a nearby corner.

She drew a deep steadying breath and headed for the boxes to decide what to keep and what to toss.

A half hour later she was halfway through the third box when she unearthed a stack of framed pictures. She stared at the first. The last rays of a hot summer's day reflected on the calm water of Lost Gun Lake and a smile tugged at her lips. She could still remember sitting on the riverbank, the grass tickling her toes as she waited for the perfect moment when the lighting would be just right. She'd taken the photograph her freshman year in high school for a local competition. She hadn't won. The prize—a new Minolta camera—had gone to the nephew of one of the judges, who'd done an artsy shot of a rainy day in black-and-white film.

A lesson, she reminded herself. Photography was a crapshoot. Some people made it. Some didn't. And so she'd given it up for something steady. Reliable.

If only her brother had done the same.

But instead, he'd enlisted in the army on his eighteenth birthday, just weeks after their parents had died. He'd gone on to spend four years on the front lines in Iraq while she and Charlie had tried to make a new life in Lost Gun with Uncle E.J. and Aunt Cheryl. But it had never felt quite right.

It had never felt like home.

Her aunt and uncle had been older and set in their ways—acting out of duty rather than love—and so living with them had felt like living in a hotel.

Cold.

Impersonal.

And so Gracie had made up her mind to leave right after graduation, to make her own way and forget the tragedy that had destroyed her family. She'd snapped picture after picture and dreamed of bigger and better things far away from Lost Gun. But then Jackson had died and Charlie had become clingy and fearful. She'd followed Gracie everywhere, even into bed at night, terrified that fate would take her older sister the way it had snatched up their brother.

Gracie couldn't blame her. She'd felt the same crippling fear when their parents had died. She'd reached out for Jackson, but he'd left and so she'd had no one to soothe the uncertainty, to give her hope.

She stuffed the framed picture back inside the box, along with a dozen others that had lined the walls of her city planner's office, and reached for a Sharpie. Once upon a time, she'd hated the idea of tossing them when they could easily serve as cheap decoration, and so she'd kept them.

No more.

With trembling fingers, she scribbled Storage on the outside and moved on to the next box loaded with old files.

She rifled through manila folders for a full thirty minutes before she found herself thinking about Jesse and how good he'd looked and the way he'd smelled and—

Ugh. She needed something to get her mind back on track.

Maybe a brownie or a cupcake or a frosted cookie—

She killed the dangerous thought, grabbed her purse and headed out the door. Forget waiting on Trina. She would head out and check on Big Earl herself, and she wouldn't—repeat, *would not*—stop at the bakery on the way. She'd cleaned up her eating habits right along with everything else when she'd decided to play it safe and stop being so wild and reckless.

And *safe* meant looking both ways when she crossed the street and wearing her seat belt when she climbed behind the wheel and eating right. She had her health to think of and so she followed a strict low-carb, low-sugar, low-fat diet high in protein and fiber. That meant no brownies, no matter how desperate the craving.

No sirree, she wasn't falling off the wagon.

Not even if Jesse himself stripped naked right in front of her and she desperately needed something—

anything—to sate her hunger and keep her hands off of him.

Okay, so maybe if he stripped *naked*.

A very vivid image of Jesse pushed into her thoughts and she saw him standing on the creek bed, the moonlight playing off his naked body. Her lips tingled and her nipples tightened and she picked up her steps.

No *naked* and no brownies.

4

GRACIE PULLED TO a stop in front of the bakery over an hour later and killed the engine.

She wasn't going to blow her diet with a brownie. She was headed straight for the health food store next door and a carob cookie with tofu frosting or a bran muffin with yogurt filling or *something*. A healthy alternative with just a teeny tiny ounce of sweetness to help steady her frantic heartbeat after the visit to Big Earl's place.

She hadn't actually had a face-to-face with the man himself, but she had come this close to being ripped to shreds by his dogs.

Charlie would freak fifty ways till Sunday if she found out. Luckily, she'd moved into the dorms at the University of Texas last year and so Gracie didn't have to worry about explaining the ripped hem of her skirt or the dirt smears on her blouse. At least not until this weekend when her little sis came home for her weekly visit and caught wind of the gossip.

If she came home.

She'd canceled the past three weeks in a row with

one excuse after the other—she was studying; she had a date; she wanted to hit the latest party.

Not that Gracie was counting. She knew Charlie would much rather go out with friends than make homemade pizza with her older sister. Charlie was growing up, pulling away, and that was good. Still, when her little sister finally did make it home, Gracie would be here.

She would always be here.

Because that's what home meant. It was permanent. Steady. Reliable.

Her gaze swiveled to the two old men nursing a game of dominoes in front of the hardware store directly across the street.

At ninety-three, Willard and Jacob Amberjack were the oldest living twins in the county. And the nosiest.

She debated making a quick trip home to change, but that would put her back at the health food store after hours and she needed something now—even something disgustingly healthy.

She drew a deep breath, braced herself for the impending encounter and climbed out of her car.

"Don't you look like something the dog just dragged in," Jacob called out the moment her feet touched pavement. "What in tarnation happened to you?"

"Was it a hit-and-run?" Willard leaned forward in his rocking chair. "Was it a car? A truck? Or maybe you got molested." He pointed a bony finger at his brother. "I been tellin' Jacob here that the world's goin' to hell in a handbasket."

"It wasn't a hit-and-run. And I wasn't molested," she rushed on, eager to set the record straight before their tongues started wagging. "I was just cleaning out my office and I snagged my skirt on a loose nail."

"You sure? 'Cause there's no shame if'n' you was molested. Things happen. Why, old Myrtle Nell over at the VFW hall accosted me just last night on account of I'm the best dancer in the place and she really wanted to waltz. Had to let her down easy and I can tell you, she was none too happy about it. Poor thing headed straight home, into a bottle of Metamucil. Ain't heard from her since."

"That's terrible."

"Damn straight. Everybody knows there ain't no substitute for good ole-fashioned prune juice."

O-kay. "Enjoy your game, fellas." Before they could launch into any more speculation, Gracie put her back to the curious old men and stepped up onto the curb.

"Afternoon, Miss Gracie."

"Hey there, Miss Gracie."

"See you at the church bake sale tomorrow, Miss Gracie."

"I wouldn't miss it for the world," she told the trio of women who exited the bake shop, glossy pink boxes clutched in their manicured hands.

The youngest one, a thirtyish soccer mom by the name of Carleen Harwell, held up two of the boxes that emanated a yummy smell. "Sarah donated ten dozen Rice Krispies Treats."

"Excellent." She waved as the women headed down the street and said hello to a few more people passing by before turning her attention to the display case that filled the massive storefront window. Dozens of pies lined the space, along with a sign that read It's Pick Your Pie Tuesday!

Not that she was going to pick a pie. Or a cake. Or anything else tempting her from the other side of the glass. But looking… There suddenly seemed nothing wrong with that.

"Go for the chocolate meringue."

The deep, familiar voice vibrated along her nerve endings. Heat whispered along her senses. Her stomach hollowed out.

"Or the Fudge Ecstasy. That's one of my personal favorites."

Excitement rippled up her spine, followed by a wave of *oh, no* because Jesse James Chisholm was the last person she needed to see right now.

He was the reason she was so worked up in the first place. So anxious. And desperate. And hungry.

Really, really hungry.

Run! her gut screamed. *Before you do something stupid like turn around and talk to him.*

"If memory serves—" the words slid past her lips as she turned "—you were always partial to cherry." So much for listening to her instincts. "In fact, I seem to recall you wolfing down an entire cherry cobbler at the Travis County Fair and Rodeo." She didn't mean to bring up their first date, but her mouth seemed to have a mind all its own. "With two scoops of ice cream on the side."

"Miss Hazel's prizewinning cobbler," he said, a grin tugging at his lips as the memory surfaced. "That woman sure can bake."

"So can Sarah." Gracie motioned to the display case and the golden lattice-topped cherry pie sitting center stage. Inside gold certificates and blue ribbons lined a nearby wall, along with an autographed picture of

Tom Cruise in his *Risky Business* heyday. "So why the switch to chocolate?"

"When I was laid up after Diamond Dust, Billy thought he'd cheer me up with some fresh-picked cherries from Old Man Winthrow's tree. I ate the entire basket in one sitting and made myself sick. I've been boycotting ever since."

"I don't do chocolate," she announced. She didn't mean to keep the conversation going. She had a strict no-talk policy where Jesse was concerned. And a no-closeness policy, too. Because when she got too close, she couldn't help but talk.

Which explained why she'd avoided him altogether for the past twelve years.

No talking. No touching. No kissing. No—

"I mean, I like chocolate—brownies, in particular," she blurted, eager to do something with her mouth that didn't involve planting a great big one smack-dab on his lips, "but I don't actually eat any."

"What happened to the Hershey's-bar-a-day habit?"

"I kicked it. I'm into healthy eating now. No Hershey's bars or brownies or anything else with processed sugar. I'm headed to the health food store." She motioned to the sign shaped like a giant celery stalk just to her left. "They make an all-natural apple tart. It has a cornflake crust. It's really delicious."

"Cornflakes, huh?" He didn't look convinced.

She couldn't blame him. She remembered the small sample she'd tasted the last time she'd been inside the Green Machine and her throat tightened. "Delicious might be pushing it. But it's decent." She shrugged. "Besides, deprivation is good for the soul. It builds character."

"It also makes you more likely to blow at the first sign of temptation."

And how.

Twelve years and counting.

"Everything all right, Miss Gracie?" Jacob Amberjack's voice carried across the street and drew her attention.

"It's fine." She waved at the old man and his brother.

"'Cause if that there feller's the one what assaulted you, Willard here would be happy to come over there and defend your honor."

"I didn't assault her," Jesse told the two men.

The old man glared. "Tell it to the judge, Chisholm."

"No one's telling anything to anyone, because nothing happened," Gracie said.

"That ain't the way we see it," the two men said in unison.

"I'd give it a rest if I were you," Jesse advised.

"We ain't afraid of you, Chisholm. There might be snow on the roof, but there's plenty of fire in the cookstove. Willard here—" Jacob motioned next to him "—will rip you a new one—"

"How come I'm the one who always has to do the rippin'?" Willard cut in. "Hell's bells, I can barely move as it is. You know I got a bad back."

"Well, I got bunions."

"So? You ain't fightin' with your feet...."

The two men turned their focus to each other and Gracie's gaze shifted back to Jesse. She expected the anger. The hatred. He'd been big on both way back when, particularly when it came to the citizens of Lost Gun. He'd hated them as much as they'd hated him, and he'd never been shy about showing it.

Instead of hard, glittering anger, she saw a flash of pain, a glimmer of regret, and she had the startling thought that while he looked every bit the hard, bulletproof cowboy she remembered so well, there was a softening in his gaze. His heart.

As if Jesse actually cared what the two old men had said to him.

As if.

No, Jesse James Chisholm didn't give two shakes what the fine people of Lost Gun thought about him. He hated the town and he always would.

Meanwhile, she was stuck smack-dab in the middle of it.

She ignored the depressing thought and searched for her voice. "So, um, what are you doing here?"

He motioned to the bridal salon just two doors down. "I have to see a man about a tux. I'm Pete's right hand."

"I didn't mean here as in this location. I meant—" she motioned between them "—*here.* You couldn't wait to get away from me earlier. Now you're standing here having a conversation. Because?"

He frowned, as if he didn't quite understand it any more than she did. "You caught me at a bad time, I suppose."

"I didn't mean to. I just wanted to warn you before the reporters beat me to it."

"You did the right thing."

"I just thought you should know..." Her gaze snapped up. "What did you just say?"

"It's not about what I just said. It's about what I *should* have said earlier." His gaze caught and held hers. "Thanks for giving me the heads-up." Where she'd missed the gratitude that morning, there was no mistaking the sentiment now. "Motives aside, you warned me and I am grateful."

"Me, too." When he gave her a questioning look, she added, "For the flowers that you sent when my brother died. I should have said thank you back then. I didn't."

"I'm really sorry about what happened to him."

"It was his choice." She shrugged. "He enlisted. He knew the risks, but he took them anyway."

"Seems to me," he said after a long moment, "he died doing something he believed in. I can't think of a better way to go myself."

Neither could she at that moment and oddly enough, the tightness in her chest eased just a fraction. "If you're not careful, you'll be following in his footsteps. That was a hard fall you took back at the arena."

A wicked grin tugged at the corner of his lips. "The harder, the better."

"I'm talking about riding."

"So am I, sugar." The grin turned into a full-blown smile. "So am I." The words were like a chisel chipping away at the wall she'd erected between them. Even more, he stared deep into her eyes and for a long moment, she forgot everything.

The nosy men sitting across the street. The endless stream of people walking past. The all-important fact that she needed to get a move on if she meant to get inside the health food store before they closed.

He made her feel like the only woman in the world.

Which was crazy with a big fat *C*.

He was flirting, for heaven's sake. Just the kind of sexy, seductive innuendo she would expect from one of the hottest bachelors on the PBR circuit.

It wasn't as if he wanted to sweep her up and ride off

into the sunset. This wasn't about her personally. She was simply one of many in a long, long line of women who lusted after him, and he was simply living up to his reputation.

Just as she should be living up to hers.

She stiffened. "It was nice to see you, but I really should get going. I've got a ton of work back at City Hall."

"Duty calls, right?"

Her gaze collided with his and she could have sworn she saw a glimmer of disappointment before it disappeared into the vivid violet depths. "Always."

And then she turned and hurried toward the Green Machine before she did the unthinkable—like wrap her arms around him, hop on and ride him for a scorching eight seconds in front of God and the Amberjack twins.

She would have done just that prior to her brother's death, but she was no longer the rebellious teenager desperate to flee the confines of her small town.

She was mature.

Responsible.

Safe.

If only that thought didn't depress her almost as much as the skinny treats that waited for her inside the health food store.

5

"This is just plain wrong." Cole Unger Chisholm frowned as he stood on the raised dais in the middle of the mirrored dressing room of Lost Gun's one and only bridal salon. "Tell me again why I have to wear this."

"For Pete." Jesse ignored the prickly fabric of his own tuxedo and tried to forget the sugary scent of vanilla cupcakes that still teased his nostrils. Of all the people he could possibly run into—the local police chief, the busybodies from the Ladies' Auxiliary, the gossipy Amberjack brothers—it had to be Gracie. Talk about rotten luck.

"Stop your bellyaching," he told Cole. "You're wearing it and that's that."

"Pete don't give two licks about a freakin' tuxedo with a girly purple cummerbund and matching tie, so why should I?"

"Because he's marrying Wendy and she does give two licks." Jesse lifted one arm so Mr. McGinnis, the shop's owner and tailor, could adjust the hem on his sleeve.

Cole eyed his reflection. "But the cummerbund looks almost pink."

"It's actually lavender." The comment came from the petite blonde who appeared in the curtained doorway. Her blue eyes narrowed as she eyed Cole. "And you're right. It's all wrong."

"See?" Cole pushed back a strand of unruly brown hair and stared defiantly at Jesse. "That's what I've been saying all along."

"You've got it hooked in the front," Wendy announced. "It's supposed to hook in the back. Isn't that right, Mr. McGinnis?"

"Sure enough, Miss Wendy." The older man slipped the last pin into Jesse's hem and turned to work on Cole's tux. In a matter of seconds, he readjusted the shiny taffeta material and stepped back. "There. Now it's perfect."

"Perfect?" Cole frowned. "But I look like a—"

"Where's Pete?" Jesse cut in, drawing Wendy's attention before Cole could say something he would later regret.

And Jesse had no doubt his middle brother would do just that. Cole had zero filters when it came to running his mouth, which explained why he ended up in more than his fair share of bar fights.

"He's trying on his tuxedo in the next room," Wendy replied. "He'll be out in a second." She turned a grateful smile on Cole. "Listen, I know you don't feel comfortable all dressed up like this, but I really appreciate it."

"It's our pleasure," Jesse cut in before Cole could open his mouth again.

"Damn straight it is." The comment came from Billy, who waltzed in wearing the same tuxedo.

Wendy turned on the youngest Chisholm and her eyes went misty. "You look wonderful!"

Billy winked. "Anything for you and Pete." He stepped up on the dais next to Cole so that Mr. McGinnis could work on the hem of his pants. "Ain't that right, bro?" He clapped Cole on the shoulder.

The middle Chisholm shrugged free. "I guess so."

"I was hoping you'd feel that way." Another smile touched Wendy's pink lips and Jesse knew she had something up her sleeve even before she added, "I've been meaning to talk to you, Cole. See, one of my friends is flying in from Houston and I need someone to pick her up at the airport. I would get Red to do it, but Hannah—that's her name—comes in smack-dab during his soap opera time, and you know how that goes."

Red owned the only cab in Lost Gun. He was also a die-hard soap opera fan. Since he was as old as dirt, he hadn't yet discovered TiVo or a DVR, which meant he was completely out of commission between the hours of 11:00 a.m. and 2:00 p.m. on any given weekday.

"She tried to get a different flight," Wendy went on, "but it's the only one that will put her here in time for the rehearsal dinner."

"No problem," Jesse said. "Cole here would be happy to pick her up for you." He clapped his brother on the shoulder, his hand lingering. "Isn't that right?"

"But I've got a training session—" the younger Chisholm started. Jesse dug his fingers into muscle and Cole bit out, "All right, already. I'll do it."

"You will?" Excitement lit Wendy's eyes.

Jesse dug his fingers even deeper and the younger

man blurted, "Sure thing. Family's family," he muttered. "We stick together."

"Great, because I told her all about you and she's dying to meet you."

"Who's dying to meet who?" Pete Gunner walked into the fitting area and slid an arm around his wife-to-be.

"Hannah," Wendy told him. "Ever since she moved to Houston from New York, she's been dying to meet a real cowboy. I told her all about Cole and she's super hyped."

"Wait a second." Cole shrugged loose from Jesse's warning grasp. "Picking her up is one thing, but this sounds like a setup."

"Don't be silly. You don't have to be her date for the wedding."

"That's a relief." Cole tugged at the tie around his neck as if he couldn't quite breathe. "For a second there, I thought you wanted me to babysit her the entire night."

"Of course not." Wendy smiled. "Just sit with her during the reception. And maybe ask her to dance once or twice. Oh, and make sure she gets back to the motel that night and—"

"Pretty much babysit her the whole danged night," Cole cut in. His mouth pulled into a tight line. "Hell's bells. I knew it. It *is* a setup."

"Okay, maybe it is." Wendy shrugged. "But it'll be fun. And speaking of fun, I've got to decide on the actual centerpiece so the florist can finalize the order." She planted a kiss on her groom's lips and headed for a nearby doorway and the endless array of floral arrangements spread out on a table in the next room.

Cole opened his mouth, but Pete held up a hand. "Don't fight it, bro. It'll only make things worse."

"But I can get my own date."

"True, but Wendy doesn't want you bringing one of your usual buckle bunnies to the wedding."

"He's talking about the Barbie triplets," Billy chimed in.

"They're not triplets," Cole said. "They're just sisters who are close in age. And I wasn't going to bring all three. Just Crystal. She's the oldest and the prettiest."

"And the wildest," Pete added, "which is why she's off-limits for the wedding. Wendy thinks you need to meet a nice girl."

"I meet plenty of nice girls." Cole unhooked the cummerbund and handed it to Mr. McGinnis.

"Nice and easy," Billy added.

"What's wrong with easy?"

"Nothing if you're sixteen and horny as hell," the youngest Chisholm pointed out. "You're twenty-nine. You should be thinking about your future."

"Like you?"

"Damn straight." Billy nodded. "As a matter of fact, I've got my own date already lined up for the wedding and I can guarantee her last name isn't Barbie."

"Big Earl Jessup's great-granddaughter is not a date," Cole pointed out. "She's a death wish. She's liable to challenge you to an arm-wrestling match."

"So she's a little rough around the edges," Billy admitted. "She's a tomboy, and that just means we've got a shitload in common. She's interesting."

"And safe," Jesse offered.

"Exactly." Billy unhooked his own tie and handed

it to the tailor. "I'm not looking to settle down, which makes Casey Jessup the perfect date for this wedding. I don't have to worry about her sitting around getting bright ideas from all this hoopla. She's as far from wife material as a woman can get."

"Casey's got a cousin." Cole's gaze shifted to Pete. "I could ask her to the wedding."

"Too late. Wendy got the draw on you and now you've got to man up."

"But I hate fix-ups." He shrugged off his jacket.

"Look on the bright side," Billy added, "Wendy's friend *could* turn out to have a smoking-hot body and zero morals."

Cole shook his head. "You know the odds of that are slim to none."

"True, but it can't hurt to fantasize." Jesse motioned to Billy. "Just like this one outriding me in Vegas in a few weeks."

"That buckle is mine," Billy vowed, trying to wrestle free when Jesse grabbed him in a headlock.

"Keep thinking that and maybe one day you'll knock me out of the running." But not this time. Jesse had been working too long and too hard to go down with just one buckle to his credit. He wanted a second. And a third. Hell, maybe even a fourth.

And then?

He let go of his brother and shifted his attention to the next room and a dreamy-eyed Wendy, who moved from arrangement to arrangement eyeing the various flowers.

For a split second, he saw Gracie leaning over a bouquet of lilies, her eyes sparkling, her full, luscious lips curved into a smile. Fast-forward to another vision

of the two of them standing at the altar saying "I do,"
living happily ever after.

Crazy.

Not the "I do" part, mind you. Jesse wasn't opposed
to settling down and having a family. It was the notion
of living happily ever after with Gracie Stone that was
just plumb loco.

She represented everything he wanted desperately
to forget—his past, this town.

He wanted to escape them both. That was why he'd
kept his distance all these years.

Why he needed to keep his distance now.

Jesse stiffened and peeled off the tuxedo jacket. "I
need to head out." The back way this time. No way was
he going to risk another run-in with her out front. She'd
smelled so good and looked even more luscious than
anything in the front window of the bakery.

And damned if he'd been able to think straight with
her right in front of him.

That was why he'd talked to her. Flirted with her.
Crazy.

"Why don't you come back to the house with me
and Wendy?" Pete's voice drew his attention. "Eli's
got the cook working on a big spread for supper. The
twins are visiting from El Paso. We could make it a
family dinner."

The twins were Jimmy and Jake Barber, fast-rising
stars on the team-roping circuit and the last two members of the notorious Lost Boys. They'd lived out at
Pete's ranch with Jesse and his brothers up until Pete
had proposed to Wendy last year. Jesse and the others had gotten together then and decided with Pete
settling down and retiring, it was time for the rest of

them to spread their wings. The twins had moved up to El Paso. Cole was in Houston. Billy had just bought a few hundred acres outside of Lost Gun and was making plans to build a house of his own. And Jesse had finally bought a spread in Austin.

Now it was just a matter of tying up all the loose ends here—namely selling his stock at the training facility—and moving on.

"Come on," Pete prompted. "It's been forever since we've all sat down together. Maybe Eli will pull out his guitar."

"Sounds tempting, but the drive out will put me back at the motel close to midnight and I need to be up early."

"So stay over at the ranch house. Hell, I don't know why you're cooped up at that motel in the first place."

"Because you're this close to tying the knot, bro. You and Wendy deserve a little privacy." Pete arched an eyebrow and Jesse added, "That way if you guys want to get naked in the dining room or the front parlor, there's nobody stopping you."

Pete looked ready to protest, but then he shrugged. "I suppose a man can't argue with getting naked. So what about you?" He eyed Jesse. "You got a date for the wedding? If not, I'm sure Wendy could rustle up a friend."

"I've got a few possibilities."

"Just make sure none of them work down at Luscious Longhorns—otherwise she'll blow a gasket." Pete grinned for a long moment before his look faded into one of serious intent. "Eli mentioned that Gracie came to see you today."

Jesse nodded. "They're going to re-air the television show."

"When?"

"Tuesday a week."

"Maybe you ought to leave early, then. Head up to Austin and get some extra practice time in before your next rodeo."

"I can practice here just fine. Besides, I've got another buyer coming in to look at a few more bulls in the morning. I want to get them all sold off before I leave. That and there's a little something called a wedding I need to be here for."

"You could always miss it."

Jesse shook his head. "Like hell. I'm your best man."

"And I'm the guy who watched you nurse a few dozen broken bones thanks to a she-devil named Diamond Dust. I have no desire to do it again."

"I was eighteen and gun-shy when it came to the press. I can handle it now. You just worry about getting your sorry hide to the church on Saturday." Jesse grinned. "Because I plan to keep you out plenty late the night before for the bachelor party."

"Thanks, man." Pete clapped him on the back. "I owe you one."

But it was Jesse who owed Pete. The man had saved him and his brothers all those years ago, and no way was Jesse jumping ship on the most important day of Pete's life. He was here and he was staying until the festivities were over.

Even more, he wasn't the same kid who'd been blindsided all those years ago. He dealt with reporters all the time now, not to mention overzealous fans and even the occasional critic. It was just a matter of staying one step ahead.

And he was, thanks to Gracie.

Because she wanted to keep the peace in her small town.

That was the only reason she'd gone to the trouble of warning him. He *knew* that. At the same time, he couldn't shake the crazy hope that maybe, just maybe, she'd wanted to see him.

As much as he'd wanted to see her.

There was no denying the chemistry that still sizzled between them. He'd felt the charge in the air, and so had she. There'd been no mistaking the tremble of her full bottom lip or the glimmer in her eyes. He knew the look even after all these years.

Yep, the chemistry was still there.

Not that it meant anything.

She was still determined to keep her distance—her quick retreat into the health food store proved that—and so was he.

He tamped down a sudden rush of disappointment. "I'd better get going. I want to get in another ride or two before I call it a night." He shed the tie and cummerbund and headed back to the dressing room to retrieve his clothes.

And then Jesse snuck out the back way and turned his attention to the one thing that wasn't beyond his reach—another PBR championship.

6

THIS WAS THE last place he needed to be.

The thought struck later that evening as Jesse pulled into the dirt driveway of the three-acre lot that sat just a few blocks over from City Hall.

He was supposed to be back at the motel, eating takeout and icing his shoulder after a hellacious training session. Or nursing a few beers at the local honky-tonk with his brothers. Or playing a few rounds of pool at one of the beer joints out on the interstate.

Anywhere but here, smack-dab in the middle of the town he so desperately hated.

His gaze pushed through the settling darkness and scanned the area. Once upon a time, reporters had walked every inch of this sad, miserable stretch, picking through the burned ruins that had once been the two-room shack that Jesse and his brothers had shared with their dad. The small single-car garage still sat in the far back corner, the paint peeling, the roof rusted out. His dad's broken-down 1970 Buick sat next to the shell of a building, the doors missing, the frame rusted and rotting.

The shame of Lost Gun.

That was how the newspapers had referred to the Chisholm place when *Famous Texas Outlaws* had aired for the first time on the Discovery Channel.

Not that his dad had been a famous Texas outlaw. Far from it. Silas Chisholm had been a wannabe with a lust for easy money and an aversion to hard work, which was why he'd moved his three young boys to Lost Gun in the first place.

The town had originated as a haven to criminals and gamblers back in the early 1800s. Lost Gun, so named because it was rumored to be home to a pearl-handled Colt once belonging to one of Texas's most notorious outlaws—John Wesley Hardin. The man had supposedly hidden the gun while on the run from Texas Rangers, but other than a colorful legend, there'd never been any actual proof of its existence.

Word of mouth had been enough for a recently widowed Silas to uproot his three sons from Beaumont, Texas, and travel across the state in search of the valuable Colt. When the gun hadn't panned out, Silas had started looking for another big-money opportunity.

Now, remember, son, when things look bad and it looks like you're not gonna make it, then you gotta get mean. I mean plumb mad-dog mean. 'Cause if you lose your head and you give up, then you neither live nor win.

His dad's words echoed in his head. As worthless as the man had been, he'd been just as determined when it came to finding an easy payday. After an endless string of dead-end schemes, he'd turned to the Lost Gun Savings & Loan.

Jesse still wasn't sure how he'd pulled it off, but he'd

actually made off with a quarter of a million dollars. All pissed away when he'd drunk himself into a stupor later that same night. He'd passed out with a cigarette in his mouth that had resulted in a deadly blaze.

He'd died in that fire because Jesse, only thirteen at the time, hadn't been strong enough to drag him off the couch. Even more, the fortune Silas had been so anxious to get his hands on had gone up in flames.

Not that everybody believed the money had perished. Curt Calhoun, the reporter who'd aired the story five years later, had posed so many questions that folks had started to wonder if maybe, just maybe, the money might still be out there. Calhoun's speculation had pulled in every two-bit criminal this side of the Rio Grande, not to mention a shitload of fortune hunters. They'd descended on the small town like a pack of hungry coyotes.

Jesse stiffened against the sudden tightening in his chest. He hadn't been out here in a long, long time.

Try never.

No, the closest Jesse came was the rodeo arena that sat ten miles outside the city limits.

But this was it. His last trip to the town itself. He was moving on, settling down, living his dream, and that meant laying the past to rest once and for all.

"Sell it," he'd told his lawyer just yesterday.

The mountain of paperwork would be ready for Jesse's signature by the end of the week, which meant he had all of five days to go through what was left of the garage and the old car and salvage anything he might want to keep.

Of course, he'd have to get out of his truck first.

He would.

He was sure there was nothing of value left to keep. Vandals had made off with nearly everything. Old tools. Car parts. After so many years, there wasn't a single thing left.

Still, he'd promised Mr. Lambert he would do a walk-through, and that was what he intended to do.

Tomorrow.

He eyed the car and a memory pushed its way into his head. Of him and his three brothers sleeping on the backseat so many nights when his dad had been too drunk and too volatile for them to be in the house. That had been before the fire, before Pete Gunner had taken them under his wing.

They would have wound up in foster care if it hadn't been for Pete. They should have, but he'd stepped up and fought for them. Eli, too. It had taken three weeks for Pete to win custody. A speedy process compared to the red tape nowadays. But Pete had had money and fame on his side, and a decent lawyer. That, and the county had been underfunded and severely under-staffed. They hadn't had the resources to worry over three more children.

Still, the threat of foster care had been real for those few weeks and so Jesse had taken his brothers and gone into hiding in the woods. They'd stayed at an old hunting camp until Pete had finally found them and taken them home.

A real home.

But that first night right after the fire, they'd had only the Buick.

He could still feel the cold upholstery seeping through his clothes, the frustration gripping his insides because he hadn't known what to do or where to go. The fear.

For his younger brothers.

Jesse hadn't given a shit about himself. His future. His life. He'd been angry with the world for dealing him such a shitty hand and so he'd spent his young life pushing fate to the limit. Backing her into a corner and daring her to lash out at him. He'd raced his beat-up motorcycle down Main Street every Saturday night and thumbed his nose at authority and climbed onto any and every bull he could find, to hell with rules and buzzers.

Then.

But there was nothing like a severe concussion and thirteen broken bones to make a guy realize that he actually cared if he lived or died. He'd turned his back on his wild and reckless ways and started taking his career seriously after the Diamond Dust incident. He'd trained smarter, harder, and it had paid off.

He'd finally made it to the top.

Even more, he'd made it out of Lost Gun. The purse he'd won at nationals had been more than enough for a down payment on the Austin spread. And the endorsements that came with being a PBR champion gave him an ongoing income that far surpassed his winnings. For the first time in his life, he was financially set.

And so were his brothers.

Billy and Cole were making their own way on the rodeo circuit, pocketing not only their winnings but endorsements, as well. They were the new faces of rodeo. Young. Good-looking. Lucrative.

A far cry from the scared snot-nosed kids they'd been way back when.

He eyed the dismal landscape one last time. It was time to let go. To move forward and stop looking back.

To move, period.

He'd just keyed the engine and revved the motor when he saw the flash of headlights in his rearview mirror. Gravel crunched as a black BMW pulled up behind him.

A car door opened and slammed shut. Heels crunched toward him. The sweet smell of cupcakes drifted through the open window and Jesse's heartbeat kicked up a notch.

He killed the engine, drew a deep breath and climbed out from behind the wheel.

Yep, it was her, all right. Up close and in person. Three times in the same friggin' day.

So much for keeping his distance.

His groin tightened and he stiffened. "Stalk much?" he asked when Gracie walked up to him.

Her carefully arched brows drew together. "I seem to recall, you were the one who snuck up on me outside the bakery. Besides, I'm not here for you. I'm just keeping an eye on things."

He spared a glance at the falling-down stretch of property. "Not much to see."

"Maybe not yet, but with Tuesday looming and the interest picking up, that's sure to change. Besides, it's right on my way home."

"Still living on Carpenter Street?"

She nodded. "Aunt Cheryl and Uncle E.J. bought a place down in Port Aransas and left the house to me and Charlie."

"How's she doing?"

A smile touched her lips and a softness edged her

gaze. "She's in her second year at the University of Texas. She lives on campus, but she drives home on most weekends. Straight As. Beautiful. She's got a ton of boyfriends."

"What about you?"

"I'm too busy for a boyfriend."

Her words stirred a rush of joy followed by a flood of *What the hell are you thinking?* He didn't care if she did or did not have a significant other. He didn't care about her, period.

Ah, but he still wanted her.

There was no denying the heat that rippled through his body or the crazy way his palms tickled, eager to reach out and see if her skin felt as soft as he remembered.

"Running this city is a full-time job," she went on, "especially with the extra notoriety from *Famous Texas Outlaws.* In addition to the out-of-towners coming in to dig for treasure, Sheriff Hooker caught Myrtle Nell's grandsons trying to drive a forklift over the back fence of this place."

"There is no treasure."

"Which makes it all the more aggravating." Her finger hooked a strand of blond hair that had come loose from her ponytail and she tucked it behind the delicate shell of her ear. "At least if there *was* something left, someone would have already dug it up. The press would have broadcast it from here to kingdom come and all the fuss would have died down. Instead, the D.A. is gearing up for a mess of two-bit trespassing charges."

He wasn't going to touch her. That was what he told himself when the silky tendril of hair came loose again and dangled next to her cheek. No reaching out and sweeping the soft strands away from her face. *No.* "Speaking of charges—" he cleared his suddenly dry throat "—shouldn't Sheriff Hooker be the one keeping an eye on things?"

"He had an anniversary dinner with the missus. I had the time, so I figured I might as well do a quick drive-by." She shrugged. "What about you? What are you doing out here?"

"Just looking around." He forced his gaze away from her and studied his surroundings. His gut tightened.

"I wasn't here when it happened," he heard himself say. A crazy thing to say, but it was so quiet that he almost felt as if he were talking to himself. Except that he could hear her soft even breaths and feel the warmth of her body so close.

But not close enough.

"I was over at the rodeo arena helping out with the horses," he went on, the words slipping through the darkness. "Eli used to pay me to rake the stalls. It was enough to buy lunch for me and my brothers, but sometimes it put me home late. The fire was in full force by the time I got here."

"Where were your brothers that night?"

"They were at the rodeo arena with me. They used to hang out until I finished work so that we could go home together. Eli would let them do their homework in the office. He had a few toys in there, too. To keep them busy while I finished up my chores. Eli dropped us off just up the street that night so my dad wouldn't see him. Silas got mean when he drank and he was always itching for a fight. Not that night, though. We saw the blaze clear down the street. We just didn't know what was burning until we got here."

He could still feel the heat licking at his face long after he'd gone in to discover his father passed out on the couch. Immobile. Unmovable. He'd stood outside afterward, his brothers whimpering beside him. There had been no sound from inside. Just the crackle of flames and the popping of wood.

Because his dad had been dead by then.

That was what Jesse told himself. What he wanted so desperately to believe. Because he didn't want to think he'd left the man in there to die.

"It wasn't your fault," she said, concern edging her words.

As if he didn't know that. He did. He *knew.*

So why the hell did he think that maybe, just maybe, he could have done something more? That he would have? It wasn't as if he hadn't tried. He'd rushed in, his shirt covering his mouth and nose. He'd tugged at the man's lifeless body. He'd begged him to get up. He'd even prayed.

But Silas hadn't budged.

The smoke had gotten thicker and Jesse had had no choice but to retreat. To leave him.

So?

His father had been a selfish SOB and Jesse and his brothers had done a hell of a lot better after he'd passed on. No, Jesse wouldn't have done a damned thing to change that night. He wouldn't have stayed a second longer to try to get him out. He couldn't have stayed.

"It's not going to work," he blurted, eager to change the subject. His gaze slid from her face to her modest blouse and plain navy skirt. The getup wasn't the least bit revealing, but it didn't have to be. The soft material clung to her curves, tracing the voluptuous lines. His dick stirred and he stiffened.

"What are you talking about?"

He motioned to her. "The provocative clothing."

"You think this is provocative?" She glanced down. Her brows knitted with concern as her gaze swiveled back to him. "Did you see a doctor today? Because you took a really hard fall earlier—"

"I'm fine," he cut in, determined to ignore the warmth slip-sliding through him. The last thing he wanted was her concern.

No, he wanted something a lot more basic from Gracie Stone.

And that was the problem in a nutshell. He still wanted her. A desire that neither time nor distance had managed to kill.

Because he'd never had the chance to work her out of his system. To grow tired and bored. Rather, she'd given him a taste of something wonderful, and then she'd taken it away before he'd managed to sate his hunger.

Once he did, he would be done with her like every other woman he'd ever been with. Like the cherries. The first few bites had been heaven, but then he'd gotten really sick, really fast.

And although Jesse Chisholm had no intention of letting his emotions get involved where Gracie Stone was concerned, there suddenly seemed nothing wrong with a little physical contact.

One really hot night with her would be enough to give him some closure. At least that was what he was telling himself.

"I really think you should see a doctor." She eyed him. "Maybe you hit your head."

A grin tugged at his mouth and he couldn't help himself. "Darlin', it's not my head that's aching like a sonofabitch." He closed the distance between them. "At least not the one on my shoulders."

And then he kissed her.

7

HE WAS *KISSING* HER.

Here. Now.

Oh, boy.

His strong, purposeful mouth moved over hers. His tongue swept her bottom lip, licking and nibbling and coaxing and—

Earth to Gracie! This shouldn't be happening. Not here. Not with him. Especially not him.

Just as the denial registered in her shocked brain, he deepened the kiss. His tongue pushed inside, to tease and taunt and tangle with hers. All rational thought faded into a whirlwind of hunger that swirled through her, stirring every nerve. It had been so long since she'd kissed anyone. Since she'd kissed him.

She trembled and her stomach hollowed out.

He tasted even better than the most decadent brownie. Sweeter. Richer. More potent. More addictive.

Before she could stop herself, she leaned into him, melting from the sudden rise in body temperature. Her hand slid up his chest and her fingers caught the soft hair at the nape of his neck.

His arms closed around her. Strong hands pressed against the base of her spine, drawing her closer. She met him chest for chest, hip for hip, until she felt every incredible inch of him flush against her body—the hard planes of his chest, the solid muscles of his thighs, the growing erection beneath his zipper.

Uh-oh.

The warning sounded in her head, but damned if it didn't make her that much more excited. Heat spread from her cheeks, creeping south. The slow burn traveled inch by sweet, tantalizing inch until her nipples throbbed and wetness flooded between her thighs.

And all because of a kiss.

Because the man doing the kissing was wild and careless and completely inappropriate. He was all wrong for her, and damned if she didn't want him in spite of it.

Because of it.

Because Gracie Stone wasn't nearly the goody-goody she pretended to be.

The thought struck and she stiffened. Tearing her lips away, she stumbled backward.

Breathe, she told herself. *Just calm down and breathe.* She couldn't do this. She had responsibilities. "I… You…" She shook her head and tried to ignore the way her lips tingled. "You and I…" She shook her head. "We don't even like each other."

"True enough." He said the words, but the strange flicker in his gaze didn't mirror the sentiment. "But it's not about *like,* sugar. It's about *want.* I want you and you want me. The pull between us…" His gaze darkened as it touched her mouth and she felt the overwhelming chemistry that pulsed between them. "It's strong."

"I should get going," she went on, desperate to kill the tiny hope that he would pull her close and kiss her again.

Lust.

That was all this was.

That and deprivation.

Character, she reminded herself. Deprivation built character. It made her stronger. More resilient.

It also makes you more likely to blow at the first sign of temptation.

His words echoed and she knew he was right.

This was temptation. *He* was temptation in his faded jeans and fitted Western shirt. He practically dripped with sex appeal. He always had. It only stood to reason that her starving hormones would shift into overdrive with him so near.

Which was why she'd made it her business to steer clear of him all these years.

And why she needed to get as far away from him as possible right now.

She backed up, eager to put a few safe inches of distance between them. "I should—"

"I told you to bring the shovel!"

The frantic whisper carried on the warm evening breeze and killed Gracie's hasty retreat.

Jesse's head jerked around toward the old garage and Gracie's gaze followed in time to see a pair of shadows disappear behind the edge of the old structure.

"Call the sheriff." Jesse leaned in his open window and plucked a flashlight from the glove box.

"Wait—" she started, but he was already halfway

up the driveway. "Jesse! Stop! You shouldn't be doing this. It's dangerous...."

Her words faded as he darted behind the old car sitting in front of the garage and disappeared into the darkness. Her heart pounded for the next few seconds as the night seemed to close in. Panic bolted through her.

She darted for her car and snatched her cell phone off the dash. With frantic fingers, she punched in 911 and gave the information to Maureen over at the sheriff's station.

She said a few choice words, all of them involving a headstrong cowboy who should have exercised at least a little bit of caution. But no, he'd run off into the darkness and now she was here. Waiting and worrying and— *Hell,* no.

She couldn't just stand here. She stuffed the phone into her pocket and stepped forward.

She was halfway around the falling-down garage when she heard the chilling voice directly behind her.

"Hold it right there, lady."

The air stalled in her chest and she became keenly aware of the barrel pressed between her shoulder blades. Her heartbeat lurched forward and her hands trembled.

"Take it easy." She held up her hands. "No reason to get upset. We should all just stay calm—"

"Quiet," came the deep, oddly familiar voice.

She knew that voice, which killed the hunch that this was an outsider lured into Lost Gun by all the hype. Her brain started rifling through memories, desperate to find a face to go with the distinctive Southern drawl that echoed in her ears. "Just keep your mouth shut and no one will get hurt. I swear it."

I do solemnly swear to uphold the rules of the Lost Gun Ranger Scouts...

The past echoed, rousing a memory of the Ranger Scouts initiation she'd attended on behalf of the city council.

Her brain started fitting the puzzle pieces together and she frowned. "Troy Warren?" Troy was now a fifteen-year-old sophomore at Lost Gun High and a frequent visitor to the sheriff's office, most memorably after spray-painting I Love Sheila Kimber on the back fence of the middle school. "Is that you?"

"Heck, no," came the voice, slightly frazzled this time. "Ain't nobody here by the name of Warren."

"I know it's you." Gracie summoned her most intimidating voice. "I was standing right behind you at the seventh-grade Scout ceremony." She couldn't help but wonder how a once-upon-a-time Scout ended up with a gun in his hands.

The same way a thirteen-year-old ended up being a provider for his two younger brothers. It was rotten luck. A crazy twist of fate. An accident.

Jesse's image rushed into her head and a wave of panic rolled through her. What if this boy had already shot him?

Even as the possibility rolled through her head, she fought it back down. She would have heard a gunshot. A struggle. *Something.* Anything besides the eerie quiet.

"I told you this was a bad idea," came a second voice. Same slow drawl. Same familiar tone. "She knows your name. She knows your friggin' *name.*"

"She does now," Troy growled to his partner. "You were supposed to keep your mouth shut."

"And let you get us locked up and sent all the way to Huntsville? I knew we shouldn't have come here. I *knew* it."

Gracie's memory stirred again. Same Scout meeting. Different boy. "Lonnie? Lonnie Sawyer? Is that you?"

"No, it ain't him," Troy said. "It's somebody you don't know. A stranger. You just shut up if you know what's good for you—" the barrel nudged between her shoulder blades "—or else."

"Or else what?" The words were out before she could stop them. As scared as she was, she was also getting a little angry. She was sick and tired of having circumstances dictated to her. Of being told what to do and when to do it. Of being stuck. And although she couldn't stand up to the world and change the path of her life, she could change this moment. "You really think you have what it takes to pull the trigger?"

"Heck, yeah."

"Heck, no."

The answers echoed simultaneously and Gracie realized that the three of them had company.

"He's not shooting anybody." Gracie heard Jesse's deep, familiar voice a split second before she heard a grunt and a yelp, and suddenly the gun fell away.

She whirled in time to see Jesse standing between the two teenage boys, hands gripping the backs of their collars. The gun lay forgotten on the ground.

Leaning down, she picked up the discarded weapon and her lips pulled into a frown.

"It's just a paintball gun, Miss Gracie," Lonnie

blurted as she inspected the weapon. "Please don't tell my grandma. *Please*."

"Troy Eugene Warren." She turned on the first boy. "You almost gave me a heart attack." She dangled the weapon. "I thought this was an actual gun."

"It *is* a gun." His stubborn gaze met hers. "It can even break the skin."

"Makes a nasty bruise, too," Lonnie offered. "I know 'cause Troy tested it out on me—"

"What are you boys doing out here?" Jesse cut in, giving them a little shake.

"We're after the money."

"There is no money."

"Says you." Lonnie tried to pull away, but Jesse tightened his grip and held the boy close. "The TV says different," Lonnie blurted. "There's sure to be people coming from as far away as Houston looking for that money. Might as well be somebody right here in town who finds it."

"The money was destroyed in the fire," Gracie said.

"Maybe. But maybe Silas Chisholm just did a damn fine job of hiding it."

"Silas Chisholm wasn't that smart," Jesse growled. "There is no money."

"But—"

"If I catch you trespassing out here again, I'll press charges."

"We're only kids." Troy tried to shrink away. "The cops won't do anything but call our parents."

"Maybe," Gracie added. "But maybe the D.A. will be so outraged when I tell her that you led me to believe you were holding a real gun on me that she'll want to try you both as adults."

"They don't do that."

"Heard it happened over in Magnolia just last week," Jesse offered. "You boys should get at least five to ten for armed assault of a city official."

"Five to ten *years?*" Lonnie looked ready to throw up.

"At the very least," Jesse added. "But I'd bet on an even stiffer sentence since there's an eyewitness— yours truly—who saw you threaten the mayor and hold a gun on her."

"I'm not actually the mayor." The words were out before Gracie could stop them. "I mean, I practically am, but it's not official. Not yet."

Jesse gave her a "too much info" look. "She won by a landslide," Jesse growled in Troy's ear. "She's practically the mayor and you boys are both screwed."

"Please, Mr. Chisholm," Lonnie pleaded. "I can't go to prison. My grandma Lou will kill me."

"I know your grandma. She's a sweet lady. What about you?" Jesse eyed Troy. "How do you think your folks will react?"

"They won't." Troy shrugged. "My daddy don't give a shit. He's drunk most of the time since my ma died."

Gracie didn't miss the strange glimmer in Jesse's eyes before his expression hardened into an unreadable mask. He loosened his grip on both boys. "Go. Get on home. Both of you."

Lonnie's eyes widened. "You're letting us off?"

"Hardly." He pointed a finger. "I want you both at the rodeo arena first thing after school tomorrow."

"For what?"

"To work off the cost of repairing that fence you

just cut." Jesse motioned to his left at the barbed wire that hung open.

"Yes, sir," Lonnie said, snatching up the discarded shovel that lay nearby. "I'll be there. We both will. Ain't that right, Troy?"

"What if we don't show?" Troy eyed Jesse as if trying to gauge just what he could get away with.

"Then I'll file an official complaint with the sheriff and he'll arrest you." Sirens stirred in the background and Gracie knew that Deputy Walker was on his way. Both boys stiffened.

"Come on, Troy," Lonnie pressed. "Just take the deal. Please."

"Okay," Troy grumbled. "But I ain't picking up no horse crap."

"Of course you're not." Jesse grinned. "We don't pick it up. We use a shovel." His expression faded into one of serious intent. "And trust me, I've got plenty of shovels." Troy stiffened and Gracie didn't miss the grin that played at Jesse's lips. She watched as he forced a frown and glanced from one boy to the other. "Now get lost before I change my mind."

The two boys scattered toward the cut fence and disappeared on the other side just as a beige squad car pulled up to the curb.

"Are you okay?" Jesse's gaze collided with hers and if she hadn't known better, she would have sworn she saw concern.

But this was Jesse James Chisholm. Wild. Reckless. Carefree. He didn't give a shit about anyone. That was why she'd been so drawn to him all those years ago. He'd been a kindred spirit. Just as wild as she'd been. As reckless. As carefree.

If only she could remember that when he looked at her.

"That was a really nice thing you did," she told him. "Giving those boys a chance."

"Shoveling isn't a chance. It's hard work. Trust me, they'll be begging for me to file charges before I'm through with them." That was what he said, but she didn't miss the softness in his eyes. While he played the same "I don't give a shit" Jesse he'd been way back when, something had changed. He'd changed.

Even if he didn't seem as if he wanted to admit it.

A rush of warmth went through her that had nothing to do with the fierce attraction between them and everything to do with the fact that she admired him almost as much as she lusted after him.

Before she could dwell on the unsettling thought, she turned her attention to the deputy who rushed up, gun drawn, gaze scouring the landscape.

"I came as soon as I got the call," he said in between huge gulps of air. "I was right in the middle of Wednesday-night bowling. Just threw a strike." He drank in a few more drafts of air. "So where are they? Where are the perpetrators?"

"False alarm, Dan."

"But I ran two blocks just to get to the squad car on account of mine is in the shop and my wife dropped me off at the bowling alley."

"Sorry."

"But you said we had trespassers. Two of them."

"They turned out to be just a couple of kids taking a shortcut on their way home," Jesse added. "No harm, no foul."

Dan glanced around a few more seconds before

shoving his gun back in his holster. "Doggone it. I shoulda known it was too early for any real excitement. That TV show doesn't air until next week. It'll be the usual snoozefest until then."

"Not true. It's bingo night at the Ladies' Auxiliary tomorrow night. That should mean at least three cat-fights and maybe even an incarceration," Gracie reminded him.

"Stop trying to cheer me up. You need a ride home?"

"I've got my car but thanks."

"You folks take care, then." The deputy turned. "If I hurry, I should be able to get back before the game is over. Not that I'll win now, on account of I missed my turn...."

"So?" Jesse eyed her when Dan walked away. His gaze darkened and the temperature seemed to kick up a few degrees.

Every nerve in her body went on high alert because she knew something was about to happen between them. She knew and she couldn't make herself walk away. "So what?" she managed, her lips trembling.

"Are you going to finish what you started with that kiss or not?"

8

"I DISTINCTLY REMEMBER *you* kissed *me*."

A grin tugged at his lips, but the expression didn't quite touch the depths of his eyes, which were a deep, mesmerizing violet. "Then are you going to finish what I started?"

Yes. No. Maybe.

The answers raced through her mind and her heartbeat kicked up a notch. "I don't know what you mean," she said, despite the fact that she knew. She knew because she knew him. The wicked gleam in his eyes. The heat rolling off his body.

Even more, she knew herself. The bad girl buried deep inside who urged her to take the initiative and make the first move. And the second. And the third.

She swallowed against the sudden lump in her throat and tried to get a grip. "I think you're misreading the situation."

"You want me and I want you." He stared deep into her eyes. "We should do something about it."

"Not happening," she blurted, despite the *yeah, baby* echoing through her. "I'm the mayor."

"Soon-to-be mayor."

"I can't just go around hopping into bed with every cowboy who propositions me. I mean, yes, I liked the kiss, but that's beside the point. We're all wrong for each other."

"You say that like it matters."

"It does."

Pure sin teased the corner of his sensual lips. "I don't want to date you, Gracie." His gaze collided with hers. "I want to have sex with you."

She wasn't sure why his words sent a wave of disappointment through her. It wasn't as if she *wanted* to date him. Sure, he'd changed from the wild, careless boy he'd once been, but he was still Jesse James Chisholm. Still off-limits. Still temporary.

And Gracie had sworn off temporary when she'd turned her life around.

"It's obvious there's something between us," he murmured, his deep voice vibrating along her nerve endings. "Something fierce."

"I think—"

"That's the problem," he cut in. "You do too much thinking. You ought to start feeling again. You might like it."

Before she could respond, he pressed a key card into her hand, kissed her roughly on the lips and walked to his truck.

The engine grumbled, the taillights flashed and just like that, he was gone.

She stared at the plastic card burning into her hand. The Lost Gun Motel. It was the only one in town. Right on Main Street, next to the diner, the parking lot in full view of anyone who happened by.

Not that she was thinking about taking him up on his offer. Having sex with Jesse Chisholm would be the worst idea ever.

Because?

Because they were polar opposites. He was wild and exciting and she wasn't. At least she was doing her damnedest to prove that she wasn't.

And that was the problem in a nutshell. Jesse called to the bad girl inside of her. He made her want to forget the past twelve years of walking the straight and narrow. Forget the pain of losing her brother. Forget the promise she'd made to Charlie.

To herself.

Not happening. She had an image to uphold. A reputation to protect. She was the mayor, for heaven's sake.

Sort of.

She hadn't actually taken the oath.

Anxiety rushed through her as she climbed into her car and started for home. As committed as she was to the path she'd chosen, she couldn't help but feel as if she'd missed out on something.

On life.

On lust.

Forget the slutty college years. She'd spent hers taking extra classes at the university so that she could graduate early and earn an apprenticeship with the city planner's office. She'd missed out on so much. That was why she was feeling so much anxiety about the upcoming inauguration. Once she took her oath, her life would be set, the commitment made, her chance lost.

She wanted one more night with Jesse. One more memory. Then she could stop fantasizing and go back to her nice conservative life and step up as the town's new mayor without any worries or regrets.

She *would*.

But not just yet.

She slammed on the brakes, swung the car around and headed for the motel.

"Okay," she blurted ten minutes later when Jesse opened the motel door to find her standing on his doorstep. "Let's do it."

And then *she* reached out and kissed *him*.

THE MOMENT GRACIE touched her lips to his, Jesse felt a wave of heat roll through him. The real thing was even better than he remembered. She felt warmer. Smelled sweeter. Tasted even more decadent.

Her tongue tangled with his and she slid her arms around his neck. Her small fingers played in his hair. Heat shimmered down his spine from the point of contact.

His gut tightened and his body throbbed. He steered her around, backed her up into the hotel room and kicked the door shut with his boot. Pulling her blouse free of her skirt, he shoved his hands beneath the soft material. She was warm and soft and oh so addictive against the rough pads of his fingertips. His body trembled with need and he urged her toward the bed.

He shoved aside the duffel bag sitting on top and guided her down. He pulled back, his hands going to the button on his jeans. He made quick work of them, shoving the denim down his legs so fast that it was a wonder he didn't fall and bust his ass. He'd spent so many nights fantasizing about her and now she was real.

Warm.

Soft.

A passing spray of headlights spilled through the windows and she seemed to stiffen. As if she feared someone would bust through the door any moment and see them together. Because as much as she wanted him, she still had her doubts. Her fears.

Jesse fought for his control and steeled himself against the delicious heat coming off her body. He could wipe away the doubt if he wanted to. All he had to do was speed up and push things along as fast and as furious as the heat that zipped up and down his spine. She would be so mindless that she wouldn't care if they were standing on the fifty-yard line of the local football stadium at half-time.

But he didn't want her mindless. He wanted her on the offensive. He wanted her to want this despite the consequences.

He wanted her to want him with the same passion she'd felt so long ago.

That meant slowing down and giving her the chance to think about what was happening, to feel each and every moment, to forget her fear and give in to the heat that raged between them.

He closed his hands over her shoulders and steered her down onto the mattress. His fingers caressed the soft material of her blouse, molding the silk to her full breasts.

Easy, slick. Just take it easy.

The warning echoed in his head and he managed to move his hands away before he could stroke her perfectly outlined nipples.

He would. But not just yet.

He scooted down to pull off her heels and toss them

to the floor. One hand lingered at her ankle and he couldn't help himself. He traced the curve of her calf up to her knee and smiled as he heard her breath catch. Then his fingers went to the button on her skirt. His heart pounded and his pulse raced and an ache gripped him from the inside out. He stiffened, fighting the lust that roared inside of him.

Easy...

He grabbed the waistband and helped her ease the navy material down her hips, her legs, revealing a pair of black lace panties that betrayed the prim-and-proper image she fought so hard to maintain.

He knew then that there was still a little of the old Gracie deep inside and his heartbeat kicked up a notch.

His fingertips brushed her bare skin, grazing and stirring the length of her legs as he worked the skirt free. The friction ripped through him, testing his control with each delicious inch.

Finally he reached her ankles. He stood near the foot of the bed and pulled the skirt completely off.

His gaze traveled from her calves up her lush thighs to the wispy lace barely covering the soft strip of silk between her legs. He grew harder, hotter, and anticipation zipped up and down his spine.

He swallowed, his mouth suddenly dry. With a sweep of his tongue he licked his lips. The urge to feel her pressed against his mouth nearly sent him over the edge. He wanted to part her with his tongue and taste her sweetness.

Need pounded, steady and demanding through his body, and sent the blood jolting through his veins at an alarming rate.

He dropped to the bed beside her and reached out.

His fingers brushed the velvet of one hip and that was all it took. Suddenly his hands seemed to move of their own accord, skimming the length of her body to explore every curve, every dip. He lingered at the lace covering her moist heat and traced the pattern with his fingertip. He moved lower, feeling the pouty slit between her legs.

She gasped and her legs fell open.

He followed the scrap of lace, his fingertip brushing the sensitive flesh on either side. The urge to dip his finger beneath the scant covering and plunge deep into her lush body almost undid him.

Almost.

But he wouldn't.

Because it wasn't about what he wanted. It was all about her at that particular moment. About convincing her that this was right. That *he* was right.

About making sure that this moment exceeded her expectations and made it impossible for her to turn her back on him again.

Jesse forced his hand up over her flat belly. Her soft flesh quivered beneath his palm as he moved higher, pushing her blouse aside until he uncovered one creamy breast.

His fingertips circled the rose-colored nipple, and he inhaled sharply when the already turgid peak ripened ever more. Leaning over, he touched his lips to her navel, dipped his tongue inside and swirled. She whimpered, the sound urging him on. He licked a path up her fragrant skin, teased and nibbled, until he reached one full breast. He drew the swollen tip deep into his mouth and suckled her.

He swept his hands downward, cupping her heat

through the scanty V of her panties. Wisps of silky hair brushed his palm like licks of fire and his groin throbbed.

She gasped and then it was as if the floodgates opened. She grabbed his hand and guided him closer. Her pelvis lifted, coming up off the bed, searching, begging for his touch.

The sound of a car door outside pushed past the frantic beat of his heart and he noted the flash of head-lights that spilled around the edges of the blinds.

"The door's unlocked," he pointed out.

"So?" she breathed and he knew she was beyond caring at the moment.

Satisfaction rolled through him, followed by a punch of lust as he slid a finger deep inside her warm, sweet body. And then he started to pleasure her.

9

GRACIE STARED UP at the man looming over her. His finger plunged deep and she closed her eyes for a long moment before he withdrew. Her eyelids fluttered open in time to feel him part her just a fraction before tracing her moist slit. He knew just how to turn her on.

He knew her.

Her heart.

Her soul.

Her.

Hardly.

If he'd been the least bit clued in to the real Gracie Stone, the one who wore sweats and ate healthy snacks and watched late-night reality TV, he would have dropped her just like that. That was who she was now. She was nothing like the wild and wicked girl who'd climbed into the bed of his pickup truck way back when.

Even if she had done something only a bona fide bad girl would do—she'd chased him down and now they were going at it.

Still…he'd been the one to issue the proposition, to make the first move.

She held tight to the notion. But then he pushed a finger deep inside and all thought fled.

She gasped, her lips parting, her eyes drifting closed at the intimate caress.

"Open your eyes," Jesse demanded, his voice raw with lust. "Look at me."

Gracie obeyed and he caught her gaze. He slipped another finger inside her.

Her legs turned to butter. Her knees fell open, giving him better access. But he didn't go deeper and give her more of what she wanted. Instead, he stared down at her, his gaze so compelling that she couldn't help herself. She arched her hips shamelessly, rising up to meet him, drawing him in.

The more she moved, the deeper he went. The pressure built.

"That's it, sugar. Just go with it."

She continued to move from side to side, creating the most delicious friction, her insides slick, sweltering from his invasion. She tried to breathe, to pull oxygen into her lungs, but she couldn't seem to get enough. Pleasure rippled from her head to her toes, and the room seemed to spin around her. Her hips rotated. Her nerves buzzed.

Incredible.

That was what this was.

What *he* was.

Her head fell back. Her lips parted. A low moan rumbled up her throat and spilled past her lips.

He leaned down and caught the sound with his mouth. His hand fell away from her as he thrust his tongue deep, mimicking the careful attention his purposeful fingers had given her only seconds before.

Straddling her, his knees trapped her thighs. He leaned back to gaze down at her.

She touched his bare chest, felt the wisps of dark silky hair beneath her palm, the ripple of hard, lean muscle as he sucked in a deep breath. Her attention shifted lower and she grasped him, trailing her hand up and down his hard, throbbing shaft. His flesh pulsed in her palm and a shiver danced up her spine. She wanted to feel him. She wanted it more than she'd ever wanted anything.

He thrust into her grip as she worked him for several long moments before he caught her wrist and forced her hand away.

And then he touched her.

His hands started on her rib cage, sliding over her skin, learning every nuance. He touched her anywhere, everywhere, as if he couldn't get enough of her. As if he wanted to burn the memory of her into his head because he knew they would have only this one night.

That was it. She knew it and so did he.

If only the truth didn't bother her so much.

Before she could dwell on that fact, he lowered his head and drew her nipple into the moist heat of his mouth. Suddenly the only thing on her mind was touching him. She slid her hands over his shoulders, feeling his warm skin and hard muscle, memorizing every bulge, every ripple.

He suckled her breast, his teeth grazing the soft skin, nipping and biting with just enough pressure to make her gasp. Her breast swelled and throbbed.

Jesse licked a path across her skin to coax the other

breast in the same torturous manner. A decadent heat spiraled through her and she rubbed her pelvis against him.

"Please." She wanted him, surrounding her, inside of her.

"Not yet," he murmured. He slid down her slick body and left a blazing path with the teasing tip of his tongue. Strong, purposeful hands parted her thighs. Almost reverently, he stroked her quivering sex. "I've thought about doing this so many times. I never had the chance that first night."

Their only night.

They'd both been so crazy with excitement that it had been fast and furious, and pretty fantastic.

But this… This went way beyond that night.

The breath rushed from her lungs when she felt his damp mouth against the inside of one thigh. Then his lips danced across her skin to the part of her that burned the fiercest.

She gasped as his tongue parted her. He eased his hands under her buttocks, tilting her to fit more firmly against his mouth. His shoulders urged her legs apart until she lay completely open. He nuzzled her, drinking in her scent before he devoured her with his mouth. Every thrust of his tongue, every caress of his lips, felt like a raw act of possession. Complete. Powerful.

Mine.

As soon as the thought pushed its way into her head, she pushed it right back out. There was no hidden meaning behind his actions. It was all about pleasure. About instant gratification. Sex.

His fingers parted her slick folds and his tongue swept her. Up and down. Back and forth. This way and that.

Heat drenched her. She bucked and her body convulsed. A rush of moisture flooded between her thighs, and he lapped at her as if he'd never tasted anything so sweet.

When she calmed to a slight shudder, he left her on the bed to rummage in his pocket for a condom. A few seconds later he slid the latex down his rigid penis and followed her down onto the mattress. Pulling her close, he kissed her long and slow and deep. She tasted her own essence—wild and ripe, bitter and sweet—on his lips. Desire spurted through her. Her blood pounded. Her insides tensed and she clutched at his shoulders.

He wedged a thigh between her legs and positioned himself. Thrusting, he joined them in one swift complete motion. The air rushed from her lungs and she gasped.

He pulsed deep inside of her for a long decadent moment before he started to move. He withdrew, only to push back inside, burying himself deep.

Over and over and over.

She skimmed her hands along his back, wanting him harder and faster, racing toward the bubbling heat of another climax. She clutched at his shoulders. She cried out his name.

He buried himself one last time deep in her body and went rigid. A groan rumbled from his throat as he gave in to his own release. He stiffened, bucking once, twice, before collapsing atop her. He nuzzled her neck, his lips warm against her frantic pulse beat.

She cupped his cheek and felt the roughness of his skin. The faint hint of stubble tickled her palm and she had the sudden thought that this—this closeness—felt almost as good as everything leading up to it.

The notion sent a rush of panic through her because tonight wasn't about getting close to Jesse. She'd had that once before and it had been even more addictive than the most decadent brownie. No, this was all about sex. About hooking up with him this one last time and building another sweet memory to add to her store before she took the oath and said goodbye to her past once and for all.

Mission accomplished.

She barely resisted the urge to wrap her arms around his neck and kiss him again. Instead, she slid out from under him and started snatching up her clothes.

He leaned up on one elbow and eyed her. "What the hell are you doing?"

"Leaving. I need to be up early in the morning. Really early."

"Gracie—"

"That was nice." Nice? "I mean, great. Really great. Thanks," she blurted for lack of anything better to say.

And then she headed for the door before she gave in to the wild woman inside who urged her to turn around and jump his bones again.

And again.

And *again.*

She wanted to. She wanted it so bad that it scared her and so she moved faster, shrugging on her skirt and blouse in record time and stepping into her shoes.

It wasn't until she heard the voices from the walkway outside that she slowed down. Her hand stalled on the doorknob.

"This has to be the room. The maid said so."

"Knock, then, and we'll find out."

The wood rattled against her grip and Gracie

jumped. Jesse was on his feet in that next instant. He peered past the edge of the drapes, a tight expression etching his face.

"Who is it?" Her voice was a breathless whisper.

"A couple of guys I've never seen before," he told her. "One of them has a camera."

"Reporters," she murmured. "Trina said there were a few checking in today." Her gaze locked with his. "What am I going to do?"

A dark look carved his face for a long moment, but then his expression softened. "Wait a sec." He grabbed his jeans and pulled them on just as another knock sounded. A third knock and he reached for the doorknob. "I'll distract them and you can slip out." He pressed his lips roughly to hers, urged her back behind the door and then hauled it open.

"What the hell, dude?" He glared at the two men before stepping outside. "I'm trying to sleep." The door closed behind him.

"We just have a few questions—"

"That you can damned well ask at a decent hour. I'm filing a complaint with management."

She peeked past the edge of the drapes in time to see Jesse start down the walkway and disappear inside the motel lobby a few doors down. The reporters trailed after him, snapping a few pictures along the way. In a matter of seconds, they'd piled inside after him, their attention fixated on Silas Chisholm's oldest son, and the coast was clear.

Gracie drew a deep, calming breath, but it didn't help. Her heart still pounded, her blood rushed and her nerves buzzed, and none of it had anything to do with the fact that she'd almost been caught red-handed by the press. She was worked up because, despite the damage it might do to her reputation, she wanted to rip off her clothes and hop back into bed to wait for another round of hot, mind-blowing sex.

Jesse was dangerous to her peace of mind because he made her forget all about what she *should* do and reminded her of what she *wanted* to do.

Of the girl she'd been so long ago and how she'd lusted after him with a passion she hadn't felt in the twelve years since.

A passion she would never feel again after tonight.

She ignored the depressing thought and held tight to the fact that she'd yet to start her acceptance speech and she still needed to come up with a strategy to get past Big Earl's dogs.

She drew a deep breath, pulled open the door and did a quick check to make sure the coast was still clear. And then she made a beeline for her car parked several spaces down.

Climbing behind the wheel, she gave one last look at the main lobby, hoping to catch a glimpse of Jesse through the glass doors. Instead, she saw Hazel Trevino, the motel's manager, gesturing wildly while on the phone and she knew the woman was calling the police to report the disruptive reporters.

Which meant Deputy Walker would be responding any second and the last thing Gracie needed was to be seen sitting outside the local motel, her hair mussed, her lips swollen, her cheeks pink.

Talk about fuel for gossip.

She fought down a wave of regret, shoved the key into the ignition and headed home.

"Show's over, folks." Deputy Walker waved a hand at the small crowd gathered in front of the check-in desk in the motel lobby. "You two, get out." He motioned to the reporters.

"But we're staying here."

"Then get back to your rooms and leave everyone alone."

"But we just have a few questions—"

"Which you'll be asking from jail if you don't get going right now." Deputy Walker pulled open the door and motioned the two men outside. "I'll see you back to your rooms myself."

"Sorry about that, Mr. Chisholm." Hazel Trevino was in her late forties with black eyes to match her dark hair. "Hope you won't hold the disturbance against us. We usually run a nice quiet place here. But with all the hoopla about this whole *Famous Texas Outlaws* episode, I guess it's to be expected."

"It's not your fault."

"It's not yours, either." Hazel smiled. "I know how folks treat you around here, but you ain't your pa. Some of us are smart enough to know that."

"Thanks, Miss Hazel."

"None necessary. You'd think folks could just let sleeping dogs lie."

"Not when they think money is involved."

Her eyes took on an eager light. "You really think all that money went up in flames?"

Jesse shrugged. "If not, someone would have surely found it by now."

"Probably. We had more than our share of treasure hunters the first time it aired. Why, I remember watching it on TV. Wilbur and I had just got married. Even thought about looking for the cash ourselves. Would have made a nice little nest egg to raise our boys, but then his daddy passed and left us this place and just like that, we had our hands full."

"It's a nice place."

"Lord knows we try to run a tight ship." She reached into a drawer. "I hope you won't let tonight spoil your visit. Here's a free voucher for the Rusty Pig. Your next plate of barbecue ribs is on us."

He nodded at the motel manager and headed back to his room. A wave of disappointment swept through him when he walked inside to find the room empty. Not that he'd expected Gracie to wait for him. The whole point of throwing himself to the wolves had been to give her a chance to escape.

Still, a part of him had held out a tiny sliver of hope. The part of him that had longed to fit in all those years ago. To belong to a town that had never given him the time of day, to befriend the very people who'd turned their backs on him.

Which was most people.

There were a few, like Pete and Hazel, who'd refused to hold him accountable for someone else's sins. They'd always treated him decent.

But Jesse had wanted more.

He'd wanted to walk into church every Sunday without half the congregation staring at him as if he'd forgotten to wipe his boots. He'd wanted to walk down Main Street without people whispering behind his back. He'd wanted to spread out a blanket at the town picnic and share a slice of apple pie with Gracie Stone in front of God and the Ladies' Auxiliary.

He'd wanted to fit in.

Like hell. Fitting in was just a pipe dream he'd come to terms with a long, long time ago. He never would and that was okay. *He* was okay. Healthy. Successful. Happy.

He didn't give a shit what anyone thought.

But she did, and damned if that didn't bother him even more than when he'd been the one eager to fit into a town that had long ago locked him out.

He fought down the feelings and debated climbing back into bed and trying for some shut-eye. That was what he would have done after a pretty incredible sexual encounter. What he needed to do right now. He had a busy day tomorrow. He had two more bulls to sell and then he needed to get the rest of his stock shipped off to Austin, and he needed to make plans for the bachelor party.

He didn't need to feel so on edge, his muscles tight, his mind racing. As if he still sat poised at the starting gate rather than at the top of the scoreboard after a wildly successful ride.

Crazy.

The whole point of sleeping with Gracie was to give him some relief. So that he could stop thinking about her. Stop wanting her. Stop fantasizing.

Stop!

He snatched up his keys and his gaze snagged on a scrap of black lace peeking from between the sheets. He leaned down and scooped up the forgotten lingerie. His fingers tightened as a detailed memory of the past few hours washed over him. Her body pressed to his, her hands touching him, her voice whispering through his head, each syllable softened with that honey-sweet drawl that had haunted his dreams too many times to count. She tried so hard to hide her passionate nature, but it was there, bubbling just below the surface, waiting for the chance to fire up and boil over.

She hadn't even come close tonight.

Sure, she'd exploded in his arms, but he couldn't shake the feeling that she'd still been holding back.

Below the surface, she'd still been controlled. Restrained. Caged.

Shoving the undies in his pocket, he grabbed a shirt and his keys. A few minutes later he left the motel behind and headed out to the rodeo arena for the kind of ride that could actually tire him out.

Otherwise it was going to be one hell of a long night.

It was the longest night of Gracie Stone's life.

She came to that conclusion several hours later as she tossed and turned and tried to forget Jesse and the all-important fact that she'd had *the* best orgasm of her life.

She'd known it would be great. That had been the point of going to his motel room in the first place. To experience a little greatness before she doomed herself to the monotony of small-town politics.

At the same time, she'd sort of secretly hoped that it might be disastrous so that maybe, just maybe, she would want to forget it. Him. The two of them.

Fat chance.

Instead of putting tonight behind her, she kept thinking how great it would be to head back over to the motel and do it again. And again.

Not that she would ever do such a thing. Instead, she was doing anything—everything—to keep her mind off of him and her hands away from the car keys.

She answered email and cleaned out her refrigerator and watched three back-to-back *Bridezillas* reruns on cable and even checked her voice mail. Three messages from Trina detailing tomorrow's schedule and one from her sister.

"I just wanted to give you a heads-up." Charlie's voice carried over the line. "I've got study sessions on Friday and Saturday for my economics test on Monday. So I won't be able to make it down this weekend. Call you later." *Beep.*

"So much for homemade pizzas," she told Sugar Lips, who wagged her tail frantically before racing for the back door. That made four weeks in a row that Charlie hadn't been able to make it home.

Not that Gracie was counting.

In the two years since her sister had gone away to school, she'd seen her less and less. Which was a good thing. It meant Charlie was growing up, becoming independent, relying on herself instead of clinging to Gracie.

At the same time, she couldn't help but feel a little lonely because Charlie was the one making the break, pulling away, getting out of Lost Gun. Meanwhile, Gracie was stuck here. That was the promise she'd made to her sister and she intended to keep it regardless of what direction Charlie took with her life. She wanted her sister to have a home base. A place to come back to when life kicked her a little too hard.

She wanted Charlie to have the home Gracie herself had never had.

She finished listening to one more message from Trina reminding her about a meeting with the local library committee and then headed to the kitchen for a chocolate cupcake.

Okay, so it wasn't a cupcake.

If only she'd had a cupcake or a cookie or a candy bar, then maybe, just maybe, she wouldn't feel so deprived.

Instead, she scarfed a handful of Wheat Thins and then went after a glass of ice water. Her hands trembled as she turned on the faucet and her gaze shifted to Sugar, who sat nearby, her ragged stuffed animal beneath her. The maltipom wrestled for a few seconds with the worn toy before whimpering when she couldn't seem to get it beneath her for a little humping action.

"I know the feeling." She downed half the glass, but it did nothing to ease the heat swamping her from the inside out.

She still felt nervous.

Frazzled.

Disappointed.

She ignored the last thought and took another drink. Disappointed? Because Jesse hadn't come running after her? Begging her for round two?

A one-night stand, she reminded herself. That was all tonight had been. All it could ever be, because Gracie had an image to protect. She was a leader now. A role model.

She'd made a promise to the town.

Just as she'd made a promise to her sister to be there when Charlie needed her.

Even if Charlie didn't seem to need her all that much anymore.

She ditched the thought along with the glass of water

and headed back upstairs. She bypassed the bedroom and headed straight for the bathroom. Since a glass of ice water had failed to cool her down, maybe a cold shower would do the trick.

Hopefully.

Because the last thing, the very last thing, Gracie intended to do was to climb back into her car and head back over to Jesse's motel room.

No matter how much she suddenly wanted to.

10

"I KNEW YOU still had it in you," Trina declared when Gracie walked into City Hall a half hour late the next morning.

After an endless night spent tossing and turning and trying to forget all about Jesse Chisholm. "What are you talking about?"

"You and a certain PBR champion."

"How did you find out?" She had the sudden vision of her and Jesse spread across the front page of *Lost Gun Weekly*, all the important body parts blacked out to preserve the newspaper's reputation.

But still...

She fought down a sliver of excitement and held tight to the fear coiling inside her. "The newspaper?"

"I admit that you gallivanting with anyone is definitely worthy of front-page treatment, but no. Kathy Mulcany heard it from Laura Lou Spencer, who heard it from Mitchell Presley, who said he was just hanging out watching the domino game with the Amberjack twins when he saw you and Jesse in front of Sarah's Sweets."

"The bakery? That's what the 'attagirl' was all about?"

"I'll admit I would rather hear that you were getting a little action instead of talking, but a girl has to start somewhere, I s'pose."

"We weren't talking. I mean, we were, but not in a social capacity. Trespassers," Gracie blurted. "He was worried about trespassers and I told him I would have the sheriff keep an eye on his place."

"So he didn't invite you out?"

"Of course not."

"And you didn't invite him out?"

"No." Technically she'd invited him *in*. A wave of heat swept through her and she cleared her suddenly dry throat. "Are the, um, painters here yet?"

"They're taping up edges right now." She eyed the cupcake sitting on her desk. "Look what the church ladies dropped off. There were six, but I didn't have time for breakfast so I scarfed down a few and gave the receptionist next door some. I guess I'll just save this one for later since you're always on a diet—"

"I'll take it." She snatched the vanilla goody out of Trina's hand.

"Really?"

Yeah, really?

"Picking out paint colors can be taxing work." That and she'd worked up an appetite last night that she'd yet to satisfy, particularly after two pieces of whole wheat toast and a grapefruit for breakfast.

She needed carbs in the worst way.

That or another night with Jesse.

Since option number two was out of the question,

she would have to settle for second best. Besides, it was just one teeny tiny cupcake.

"I'd be happy to get you a bran muffin." Trina eyed her. "I know how you hate to cheat."

"That's okay, I don't mind cheating a little. Besides, maybe they're sugar-free. With whole wheat flour and egg substitute. I heard Myrtle Nell is experimenting with some new Weight Watchers recipes. This is probably the result."

"It's not," Trina said, snatching the cake out of her hand. "Trust me, I've had three. There's nothing weight conscious about it." She set the vanilla confection on the far side of her desk. "I'll get you a bran muffin."

Gracie thought about arguing, but Trina was already looking at her as if she'd grown a third eye. She swallowed against the rising hunger and focused on the stack of papers on the edge of her assistant's desk. "So what's on the agenda for today?" She rifled through the papers. "A city council meeting? A water commission hearing?"

Trina plucked the papers from her hands and returned them to their spot. "The Senior Ladies expect you for their weekly breakfast in the morning, and then there's the middle school car wash. Then there's the Daughters of the Republic of Texas bake sale. It's at three o'clock on Thursday. The local kindergarten is also having their fundraiser on Thursday afternoon. I've also got you scheduled to lead the Pledge of Allegiance at the quilting circle on Friday morning. In the meantime, when you're not playing the goodwill ambassador—" Trina smiled and motioned to the open doorway "—you get to redecorate your new office."

Forget getting out and about today to distract herself. She was going to be cooped up all afternoon in her shell of an office. With nothing but flooring samples and furniture catalogs and her own damnable thoughts. Gracie swallowed again. "Now I *really* need a cupcake."

"YOUR CONCENTRATION'S for shit," Eli told Jesse when he finally managed to catch his breath after taking a nosedive off the back of an ornery bull.

"Stop giving me grief and help me back up, old man." It was early in the afternoon and his fifth time in the dust in as many hours.

Eli held out a hand. "I think you've had your butt beat enough for one day. Yesterday I could understand. You had that pretty young thing to catch your eye. But today?"

Today was worse. Yesterday Gracie had just snagged his eye. Today she was under his skin, in his head.

Why, he couldn't rightly say.

Last night had gone just like any other night with any other woman. They'd gotten down to business and then bam, she'd walked away. No talking or cuddling or sleeping over.

That fact bothered him a helluva lot more than it should have considering he'd gone into last night knowing full well where he stood.

Sex.

That was all he'd been interested in. That was all she'd been interested in.

At the same time, he couldn't forget the way she'd pressed her lips against the side of his throat and hesitated. As if leaving wasn't as easy as she'd thought.

The possibility had eased the throbbing in his shoulders enough so he could close his eyes. Or maybe it had been the swig of whiskey he'd downed the minute he'd walked back into the empty room after causing enough of a distraction for her to slip out unnoticed.

To preserve his own reputation.

That was what he told himself. The last thing he needed was the two of them all over the local paper. The *Weekly* would have them committed and married within a few paragraphs and his image as rodeo's hottest bad boy would be blown to hell and back.

He surely hadn't done it because she'd looked so petrified that he'd wanted—no, *needed*—to do something to ease the fear.

So he'd waltzed out of the room for a run-in with a duo from a local news network out of Austin and given her a way out.

"...if you don't start paying attention, you're going to split your head open."

He ignored the disappointment churning inside him and focused on Eli and the brand-new bull kicking and spitting across the arena.

Shitkicker had been delivered first thing that morning from a breeder out of California. He would have had the bull shipped straight to Austin, but the breeder had been ahead of schedule and so he'd arrived in Lost Gun instead. A descendant of two of the most notorious rodeo bulls to ever buck a rider, Kicker was two thousand pounds of pure whup-ass and had cost him a load of money. Well spent, of course. Jesse hadn't gotten to be the best by training halfway. He went all out in the practice arena, just the way he went all out during any ride.

Because every ride meant something.

Every time he climbed onto the back of a bull, he was one step closer to the next championship.

Another step away from the scared, angry kid he'd been way back when.

He focused on dusting off and heading back to the bull pen, where Troy and Lonnie, the trespassing duo from the night before, were busy shoveling manure. And complaining every step of the way.

"Let me use the shovel and you hold the bucket."

"I'm on shovel duty for at least fifteen minutes. Stop bellyaching and just hold the bucket steady."

Shit plopped over the side and both boys cursed.

Jesse would have smiled, except he didn't feel much like smiling. He drank in a deep draft of hay and manure, but instead of smelling either, he smelled Gracie. The clean scent of her skin. The strawberry sweetness of her hair. The ripe, decadent aroma of her sex.

Gracie had been there for so long in his memories, taunting and teasing and tempting him. One brief encounter wouldn't be nearly enough to get her out of his system. He needed to overindulge, to satisfy himself over and over until he was sick of her. Gracie was like that overflowing basket of cherries. One night with her wouldn't be enough to make him swear off her completely.

He needed more.

A lot more.

He bypassed the boys and pushed open the corral gate.

"Where you going?" Eli called after him.

"I've got business in town."

Eli chuckled. "I'll just bet."

Jesse was going after Gracie Stone, all right, and

they were going to put out this fire that burned between them once and for all.

But first…

First it was going to get hot.

Very hot.

"I CAN HARDLY BREATHE," Gracie told Trina as she stood in the middle of the mess that would soon be her new office. The painters had finished two of the walls, but the rest they'd left until tomorrow. She fanned herself with a circle of paint swatches and eyed her assistant. "Is it hot in here or is it just me?"

"The electrician had to kill the power to the air conditioner unit supplying this room in order to replace the old ducts."

"That explains it."

"That and him." Trina stared past Gracie. "He definitely kicks up the body temp a few degrees."

Gracie turned to see the man who filled her open doorway. Faded jeans clung to his muscular legs. A crisp white T-shirt stretched over his hard, broad chest. Stubble shadowed his strong jaw. Her gaze collided with a pair of violet eyes, as rich and lush as crushed velvet. The air stalled in her lungs.

"If it isn't the infamous Jesse James Chisholm," Trina said. "To what do we owe the honor of this visit?"

"I've got some unfinished business with our new mayor." Jesse closed the distance between them and stopped just scant inches away.

"I'm not the mayor," Gracie heard herself say. "Not yet." Trina gave her a knowing look and she shrugged. "So, um, what can I do for you?"

"Actually, it's about what I can do for you." He

grinned and pulled her black undies from his pocket. The scrap of dark lace dangled from one tanned finger. "You forgot these."

Gracie's heart stopped beating.

Trina cleared her throat. "I, um, really should get going. It's ladies' night over at the saloon and I've got to pick up my dry cleaning and get my eyebrows waxed. I always knew you had it in you," Trina murmured a split second before she hightailed it for the door. "I'll be leaving now. For good. So you'll have plenty of privacy to, um, talk, or whatever." The click of a door punctuated the sentence and then she was gone.

"We've been painting," Gracie blurted, eager to drown out the thunder of her own traitorous heart. "Sahara Tan." She eyed one of the finished walls.

"Tan, huh?" Jesse rubbed the silky material of her underwear between his two fingers in a sensual caress she felt from her head clear to the tips of her toes.

Crazy. He wasn't even close to touching her.

Not now. But last night? He'd touched. And teased. And seduced. And damned if she didn't want him to do it all over again.

Heat uncoiled in her stomach, followed by a slow burning embarrassment that washed through her. She came so close to snatching the panties from his hand, but she wasn't about to give him the satisfaction of knowing that he was right about her. That she was different now. Stiff and uptight and *good*.

"I like tan."

"Seems to me like you've got a hankering for black." He eyed the panties. "Me, too." He stuffed them into his shirt pocket and glanced around. "Tan's a little boring. I'd go with something a little bolder. Maybe yellow. Brighten the place up."

"I don't need brighter. I need reliable." Her gaze narrowed. "Is that why you stopped by? To offer decorating advice?"

"Actually—" his voice took on a softer note "—I wanted to talk to you about last night."

"There's nothing to talk about. It's over and done with."

"That's the point." His mouth crooked in the faintest grin. "It's not."

"What makes you say that?"

"Because I want you and you still want me."

"Speak for yourself."

His gaze caught and held hers. "So you haven't been thinking about me kissing you or you touching me or me sliding deep, *deep* inside?" His eyes darkened as he reached out to finger the collar of her charcoal blouse. "One night isn't enough." His fingertip dipped beneath the neck and traced her collar bone. "We need to do it again. And again. However many times it takes."

"For what?"

"For me to stop thinking about me kissing you and you touching me and me sliding deep, *deep* inside. For you to forget, too."

"What makes you think I haven't already?"

"Because your cheeks are flushed and your pulse is erratic." He pressed a fingertip to the side of her neck in a slow sweeping gesture that sent goose bumps chasing up and down her arms. "And you look a little faint."

She felt a little faint. And flushed. And completely erratic.

"You're turned on."

He was right. Despite the fact that she'd cut loose last night, she was no closer to being free of the fantasies that haunted her night after night. If anything, she was even more worked up. Desperate. Hungry.

Still…she couldn't just hop back into bed with Jesse. She was the mayor, for heaven's sake. She had a town to run. Commitments. Car washes and bake sales and quilting circles.

Okay, so she wasn't actually running anything at the moment. Not until the day of the inauguration. Then her life would officially become a series of city council meetings, park dedications and press conferences.

Ugh.

She swallowed the sudden bitterness in her mouth and focused on the man standing in front of her. For now, the only thing she *had* to do was put in a few personal appearances, which meant she had a few precious days to forget about what she needed to do and simply do what she *wanted* to do—play out the bad-girl fantasies that had been driving her crazy for the past twelve years and store enough memories to last her the rest of her boring, predictable life as mayor.

"Okay." The word was out before she could stop it. Not that she would have. She was doing this. She *wanted* to do this. Her gaze met his and a ripple of excitement went through her. "Let's do it again."

A grin played at his lips. "And again." His expression faded and there was nothing teasing about his next words. "I've got until Sunday. Pete gets hitched Saturday night and I head for Austin on Sunday morning."

And she would take her oath of office a full week after that.

She licked her lips and trembled at the anticipation

that rippled through her. "So, um, when should we start? I could meet you tonight after the Little League game. I'm throwing out the opening pitch—"

"Let's go," he cut in.

"Now?"

"Unless you need to practice for that pitch?" He arched an eyebrow, a grin playing at his lips.

"It's just ceremony. Accuracy isn't a big factor."

He motioned to the window and the jacked-up black pickup that sat out front. "Then what do you say we take a little ride?"

Meaning dripped from his words and for a split second, she hesitated. There was just something about the way he looked at her—as if he'd been waiting for this moment even longer than she had—that sent a spiral of fear through her. Because the last thing she wanted was to unlock any of her old feelings for Jesse.

This wasn't about the past. It was about this moment. He wanted her and she wanted him and once they'd satisfied that want completely, it would all be over. It was Tuesday and he was leaving Sunday. That meant they had five days.

The realization stirred a wave of anxiety as she felt the precious seconds ticking away. "Let's go."

11

THEY ENDED UP on a dusty back road that wound its way up to a steep cliff overlooking the lake. Lucky's Point had once been the hottest make-out spot back in the day. The spot, in fact, where she'd made out with Jesse James Chisholm for the very first time. Times had changed and the kids now hung out down below on the banks of Lost Gun River, and so the Point was deserted when they rolled to a stop a few feet away from the edge.

Still…this wasn't what she'd signed up for.

"I thought we were going to the motel," she said as he swung the truck around and backed up to the edge of the cliff.

"And fight our way past the reporters camped out on my doorstep?" He spared her a glance before killing the engine. "I thought you wanted to keep this low-key."

"I do. That's why I thought we'd go someplace a little more private to do the deed."

"Sugar, there's not a soul up here." He climbed out and went to lower the tailgate.

"That's not altogether true," she said as she followed him around to the back of the truck.

The sharp drop-off overlooked a spectacular view of the canyon and the rippling water. A huge bonfire blazed on the riverbank below. Ice chests were scattered here and there and dozens of teenagers milled about. Trucks lined the edge of the dirt road leading up to the gathering. Jason Aldean blasted from one of the truck radios, his rich, deep voice telling the tale of a dirt road just like the one that wound its way to the river.

"They won't bother you if you don't bother them." He winked and patted the spot on the tailgate next to him. "Climb up."

She hesitated, but then he touched her hand and she couldn't help herself. She climbed up and settled next to him.

He shifted his attention to the scene spread out before them. "It's still just as pretty as ever up here."

Her gaze followed the direction of his and she drank in the scene. A strange sense of longing went through her. It really was beautiful. Picturesque.

She dodged the thought and focused on the frantic beat of her own heart and the six feet plus of warm, hard male camped out next to her. "I'm surprised you remember." She slid him a sideways glance. "If memory serves, you didn't spend much time enjoying the view."

A grin tugged at his lips. "Oh, I enjoyed it plenty. It just didn't have much to do with the canyon."

"You were pretty fixated on one thing back then."

"Yeah." His gaze caught and held hers. "You." The word hung between them for a long moment and she had the crazy thought that he wasn't just talking about the past.

That he still felt something for her despite the fact that she'd walked away from him and ruined all their plans.

Crazy.

This was about lust and nothing else. Sex.

Thankfully.

"Thirsty?" His deep voice distracted her from the dangerous path her thoughts were taking.

She nodded. The truck rocked as he slid off the tailgate to retrieve a cooler from the cab.

She drew several deep breaths and damned herself for not insisting he take her to a motel. At the same time, she couldn't deny that he had a point. Last night had been fast and furious and much too fleeting. Maybe they did need to take their time and ease into things. Enjoy the moment.

The notion sent a burst of excitement through her almost as fierce as what she felt when he actually touched her. Her body tingled and her nipples pebbled and heat rippled along her nerve endings.

"It's awful hot." His deep voice drew her attention as he walked back, beers in hand.

And how.

She took the bottle he offered her and held tight to the ice-cold brew. The glass was hard and cold beneath her fingertips, a welcome relief against her blazing-hot skin.

He hefted himself back onto the tailgate. Metal shifted and rocked and his thigh brushed hers. A wave of heat sizzled through her. The urge to lean over and press her lips to his hit her hard and heavy and she leaned forward. Laughter drifted from below and her blood rushed that much faster before she caught herself.

She couldn't do this in front of an audience. She wouldn't. Even if the notion didn't bother her half as much as it should have.

Because it didn't bother her.

The old Gracie would have jumped at it.

She shifted her attention away from Jesse and focused straight ahead. The sun was just setting and the sky was a spray of oranges and reds. "The view really is something. I can see why they call it Lucky's Point. I'm sure many a girl gave it up just because of the ambiance."

"Actually, this spot was named for Lucky Wellsbee. He was an outlaw back in the late 1800s. He was on the run from Texas marshals after a stagecoach robbery when they cornered him right here. Legend says he took a nosedive off the edge of this cliff and was never seen or heard from again."

"Did he drown in the river?"

"Probably. Still, they never recovered a body and so no one really knows." He shrugged and twisted the cap off his own beer. "Anyhow, that's where the name really came from." He took a swig. "Though your version is a damned sight more fun." He grinned and the expression was infectious.

She felt a smile tug at her own lips. She took a pull on her beer and stared at the scene before her, her mind completely aware of the man sitting only inches away. As anxious as she was to get down to business, there was something oddly comforting about the silence that stretched between them, around them, twining tighter, pulling them closer. As if they were old friends who'd shared this exact moment time and time again.

They had.

The thought struck and she pushed it back out. Jesse wasn't her friend. Not now. Not ever again.

Even so, a strange sense of camaraderie settled between them as they sat there for the next few moments. She sipped her beer while he downed the rest of his. One last swig and he sat the bottle between them. It toppled onto its side with a clink, and suddenly a memory made her smile.

"Remember that time we played Truth or Dare?" The question was out before she could remind herself that the past was better left alone. "It was back before we started dating. Back when we were sophomores and you barely noticed me."

"Honey, any man with eyes noticed you. You didn't exactly go out of your way *not* to get noticed."

"I *did* wear my shirts a little too tight, didn't I? And my shorts a little too short." A smile tugged at her lips. "It used to drive my aunt and uncle nuts."

"Which is exactly why you did it."

"A fat lot of good it did." She shrugged. "I did my damnedest to fight destiny, but I guess in the end, she won anyway."

"Or you let her."

"What's that supposed to mean?"

"That sometimes it's a lot less work living up to people's expectations than it is changing their minds." He gave her a pointed look. "Nothing's written in stone. Take me for instance. I could have followed in my old man's footsteps, but I didn't. I made my own destiny. You gave in to yours."

"I didn't have a choice." The words were out before she could stop them. "When my brother passed away…" Her throat tightened. "I couldn't just run off and leave my sister when she needed me most." She blinked back the sudden stinging behind her eyes. "I couldn't."

She could still remember the funeral and her brother's closed casket. Charlie had held tight, clinging to Gracie, desperate for some stability.

And that was what Gracie had given her.

"I should have told you that instead of just cutting things off between us." She wasn't sure why she said the words, except that they'd been burning inside of her for so long that she couldn't help herself. "I'm sorry about that." The memories of those first few weeks after the funeral raced through her and her heart ached at the loss. Of her brother. Her freedom. Jesse. "You deserved an explanation when I bailed on you, not the cold shoulder." She stopped there because she couldn't tell him she'd been afraid to face him, to talk to him, so fearful she would change her mind the moment she saw him because she'd been hopelessly, madly in love with him.

Then.

Because they'd had so much in common. They'd shared the same hopes and dreams. The same desperation to escape the labels of a small town.

But now? She was different, even if she did feel the same flutter in the pit of her stomach when his deep voice slid into her ears.

"It was at one of Marilyn Marshall's parties, right? That time we played Truth or Dare?"

She nodded. "The one right after the homecoming

dance." A smile played at her lips as she remembered the short red Lycra dress she'd worn that night. She'd been crazy for that dress even though her aunt and uncle had hated it, just as she'd been crazy for a certain tall, sexy boy in faded jeans, scuffed boots and a T-shirt that said Save a Horse, Ride a Cowboy. "I can still remember her making us all sit in a circle. Kevin Baxter kept landing on me and daring me to play Seven Minutes in Heaven in Marilyn's closet."

"But you didn't."

"I didn't want to go into that closet with him. I wanted to go inside with you." She shrugged. "But when it was my turn, it kept landing on the wrong person."

He eyed the bottle and his eyes gleamed with challenge. "Maybe you'll have better luck now."

Reason told her to turn him down. Cutting loose behind closed doors was one thing, but this... This was different. This was talking and reminiscing and... *No.*

She didn't need a walk down memory lane with Jesse Chisholm.

But, oh, how she wanted one.

She met his gaze and reached for the bottle. A loud *thunk, thunk, thunk* echoed as she sent the glass spinning across the tailgate. Slowly it came to a stop, the mouth pointing directly at Jesse.

"Truth or dare?" she asked him.

His eyes twinkled. "Dare."

"I dare you to kiss me."

"Whatever happened to Seven Minutes in Heaven?"

"There's no closet, so I thought I'd adjust accordingly."

"We don't need a closet for heaven, sugar. We can

do it right here." No sooner had the words slipped past his lips than the truck dipped and he pushed to his feet. "Right now."

Before she could take her next breath, he stood directly in front of her, pure sin twinkling in his violet eyes.

He nudged her knees apart and stepped between her legs. Anticipation rippled through her as he leaned close. His warm breath tickled her bottom lip and her mouth opened.

"Relax," he murmured a split second before he touched her shoulders and urged her back down. The cold metal of the truck bed met her back and reality zapped her. There was no stifling darkness to hide her excitement. No closet walls to shield her from the rest of the world.

They were outside, in full view of God and at least a dozen teenagers partying on the riverbank below.

He reached for the waistband of her skirt. He tugged her zipper down, his gaze locked with hers.

"I think a kiss would be better," Gracie blurted, her anxiety getting the best of her. Jason Aldean had faded and Luke Bryan took his place, crooning about love and lust and leaving, and her heart beat that much faster.

"Oh, I'm going to kiss you, all right." He unfastened the skirt and pushed the material up around her waist, his fingers grazing the supersensitive skin of her stomach. "Just not on the lips. Not yet."

The sultry promise chased the oxygen from her lungs as he urged her legs apart and wedged himself between her knees. His fingertips swept her calves, up the outside of her knees until his hands came to rest on her thighs.

He touched his mouth to the inside of her thigh just a few inches shy of her panties. White cotton this time with tiny pink flowers. Sensible, or so she'd thought when she'd tugged them on that morning. But damned if she didn't feel just as sexy as when she'd worn the black lace the night before.

He nibbled and licked and worked his way slowly toward the heart of her. She found herself opening her legs even wider, begging him closer.

He trailed his tongue over the thin fabric covering her wet heat and pushed the material into her slit until her flesh plumped on either side. He licked and nibbled at her until her entire body wound so tight she thought she would shatter at any moment.

She didn't.

She couldn't.

Not until she felt him, skin to skin, flush against her body. No barriers between them. That was what she really wanted despite their location.

Because of it.

Being outside filled her with a sense of freedom she hadn't felt in a long, long time.

She ignored the thought as soon as it struck and focused on the large hands gripping her panties.

She lifted her hips to accommodate him. The cotton eased down her legs and landed on the truck bed next to her.

He caught her thighs and pulled her toward the end of the tailgate until her bottom was just shy of the edge. Grabbing her ankles, he urged her knees over his shoulders.

He slid his large hands beneath her buttocks and tilted her just enough. Dipping his head, he flicked his tongue along the seam between her slick folds in a long slow lick that sucked the air from her lungs.

His tongue parted her and he lapped at her sensitive clit. He tasted and savored, his tongue stroking, plunging, driving her mindless until she came apart beneath him. A cry vibrated from her throat and mingled with the sounds drifting from below.

Her heart beat a frantic pace for the next few moments as she tried to come to terms with what had just happened.

She'd had the mother of all orgasms. An orgasm worthy of the most erotic dream.

But as satisfied as she felt, it still wasn't enough.

She opened her eyes to find him staring down at her. A fierce look gleamed in his bright violet eyes, one that said he wanted to toss her over his shoulder, tote her home and never, ever let her go.

A spurt of warmth went through her.

Followed by a rush of panic because it was all just the heat of the moment.

He *would* let her go, and then he would leave. That was why she'd agreed to this in the first place. A few days of lust and then they both walked away. She headed for City Hall and he headed for Austin.

My turn.

That was what she wanted to say, but she wouldn't. While she'd agreed to indulge her lust for him, she had no intention of unleashing the bad girl that she'd locked down deep all those years ago. Giving in to him was one thing, but turning the tables and taking charge?

Not happening.

"Stand up," he murmured, killing the push-pull of

emotion inside of her and taking the decision out of her hands, and she quickly obliged.

She slid to her feet to stand in front of him. Her skirt fell back down her thighs, covering the fact that her panties still hung on the edge of his tailgate.

A fact he was all too aware of, if the tense set to his jaw was any indication.

He stood in front of her, his eyes gleaming in the growing shadows that surrounded them. His muscles bunched beneath his T-shirt. Taut lines carved his face, making him seem harsh, fierce, *hungry.*

She knew the feeling.

She swallowed against the sudden hollowness in her throat and fought to keep from reaching for the top button on her blouse. But then he murmured "Undress," and she quickly obliged.

She slid the first button free, then the next and the next, until the silky material parted. A quick shrug and the blouse slid down her shoulders, her arms, to glide from her fingertips and pool at her feet.

Her fingers went to the clasp of her bra. A quick flick and the cups sagged. The lace fell away and his breath hitched. His gaze darkened and his nostrils flared as if he couldn't get enough oxygen.

Her lips parted as she tried to drag some much-needed air into her own lungs. Her breasts heaved and his eyes sparkled, reflecting the last few rays of sunlight.

She touched the waistband of her skirt. Trembling fingers worked at the catch until the edges finally parted. She pushed the fabric down her legs and suddenly she was completely naked. Warm summer air slithered over her skin, amping up the heat already swamping her from the inside out.

"Damn, but you're beautiful, Gracie." The words were reverent and her heart beat that much faster, drowning out the sounds coming from below until the only thing she focused on was him and the way he was looking at her and the way it made her feel.

Sexy.

Alive.

Free.

"You're not done." His deep voice sent excitement rippling down her spine.

"I don't have any clothes left."

"I do. Take them off."

She stepped forward to grasp the hem of his T-shirt. Flesh grazed flesh as she obliged him, pushing the material up his ripped abdomen, over his shoulders and head, until it fell away and joined her discarded clothes. A brief hesitation and she reached for the waistband of his jeans.

A groan rumbled from his throat as her fingertips trailed over the denim-covered bulge. She worked the zipper down, tugging and pulling until the teeth finally parted. The jeans sagged on his hips, and his erection sprang hot and pulsing into her hands.

She traced the ripe purple head before sliding her hand down his length, stroking, exploring. His dark flesh throbbed against her palm and her own body shuddered in response. She licked her lips and fought the urge to drop to her knees and taste him.

Luckily, he wasn't nearly as restrained.

He drew her to him and kissed her roughly, his tongue delving deep into her mouth over and over until the ground seemed to tilt. And then he swept her up, laid her on the tailgate of his truck and plunged deep, deep inside.

12

SHE STILL HAD her panties.

Gracie held tight to the knowledge as she slipped inside her house later that night. The steady hum of a motor out front reminded her that Jesse still hadn't pulled away yet.

Which meant she could easily forget the fact that she had to crawl out of bed before the crack of dawn in order to make it to Wednesday Waffles, the Senior Ladies' weekly gathering. She was scheduled to recite the opening Pledge of Allegiance and serve the first waffle. Not a bad gig except half the group was diabetic and the other half had intestinal trouble. Forget stacks of fluffy golden squares topped with whipped cream and chocolate chips. The waffles were all-bran, served with sugar-free syrup and Myrtle Nell's infamous prune compote.

Which meant instead of counting down the hours until tomorrow morning, Gracie would much rather haul open the door, throw herself at the cowboy idling in her driveway and beg for round two.

And three.

An all-nighter, as a matter of fact.

The urge gripped her and her hands trembled, but then Sugar Lips scrambled from the kitchen. Her claws slid across the hardwood floor in a frantic scrape as she rushed for the door.

Bran was good. Healthy.

Gracie latched onto that all-important fact and scooped up the white ball of fluff. The dog licked at her frantically for a few seconds before her high-pitched barks filled the air. Gracie set her on the floor and she danced in place for a few seconds before leading the way to the kitchen and the treat jar.

Gathering her control, Gracie forced herself away from the front door and followed Sugar Lips into the kitchen. She unearthed Sugar's favorite powdered donuts from the cabinet and fed one to the frantic animal.

The dog wolfed down the goody and barked and danced for another.

"One a day. You know the rule."

Rules. That was what life was all about. About respecting boundaries and walking the straight and narrow and playing it safe. That was who she was now, even if Jesse had made her forget that all-important fact for those few blissful moments at the river.

She was still the Gracie who ate granola for breakfast every morning and wore conservative shoes and spent her Saturday nights in front of the TV. She wasn't wild and wicked.

Even if she had worn a black lace thong to the office yesterday. Sexy lingerie was her one indulgence. Pretty undies and lacy bras. Even the white cotton bikini panties she'd worn tonight were on the risqué side.

Which explained her thoughts at the moment.

The underwear. She needed to tame it down in a major way, which meant that first thing tomorrow she was going to do some online shopping for some sensible lingerie. Some Spanx and granny panties and boxy bras.

You're still as out of control as ever.

He was wrong and he would see that soon enough.

She intended to make him see that, to keep the emotional wall as strong as ever between them so that when Sunday rolled around, it would be that much easier to say goodbye.

Because Gracie Stone didn't want a forever with Jesse Chisholm. She wanted to get him out of her head. Her fantasies.

Once and for all.

That meant keeping her guard up, holding back and showing him she'd turned into a bona fide good girl.

He would gladly call it quits then and run the other way once he realized she truly had changed.

She just wished that fact didn't suddenly bother her so much.

HE WANTED MORE.

The thought echoed in Jesse's head as he sat outside the modest brick home a few blocks over from City Hall, his engine idling, his blood racing.

While they'd just gotten down and dirty in the bed of his pickup, they hadn't come close to burning up the lust that blazed between them. He still felt every bit as restless. As hungry.

Not that he intended to do anything more about it tonight. He had to be up early tomorrow morning for a training session and he had no intention of letting their agreement get in the way of his next championship.

His heartbeat kicked up a notch as the lights flipped on inside and he watched her shadow move across the first-floor window. A vision played in his head and he saw her pushed up against a nearby wall, her legs wrapped around his waist. Her hands clawed at his shoulders and her tits bounced as he pumped into her and—

Awww, *hell.*

His gut tensed and his dick throbbed. He tightened one hand on the steering wheel and shoved the truck into Reverse with his other. With a squeal of tires, he pulled out of her driveway and headed for the motel.

Five minutes later, he sat idling in the parking lot, his attention fixed on the photographer camped out on the doorstep of his room. He'd expected the two from last night, but this guy was new. And probably just another in a long line he was sure to encounter over the next few days.

He thought of calling the front desk but then changed his mind. He could have this guy escorted off the property, but there would just be another to take his place. Better to give them what they wanted, answer a few questions and let them have their photo op, which was what he fully intended to do.

Just not tonight.

He turned his pickup around and headed for the training facility that sat outside of town. Ten minutes later he pulled into the gravel parking lot and killed the engine. He headed for the exterior staircase that led to a small apartment over the main office. During rodeo time, the competing cowboys used the spot to unwind or catch a nap in between rides. With a window that overlooked the main arena, they could enjoy the other events while kicking back and conserving their strength.

The place sat dark and quiet now.

Jesse flipped on a switch and the overhead light chased away the dark shadows, revealing a large living space complete with a living room, a fully equipped kitchen and a bathroom. Jesse was just about to head for the bathroom and a nice cold shower when he saw a flicker of light beyond the wall of windows overlooking the dark arena.

He closed the distance to the glass and sure enough, a light bobbed in the far distance near the animal pens.

A few minutes later he rounded the first bull pen to find Troy spread out on a blanket, an iPod in one hand and a magazine in the other. The minute he saw Jesse, he snatched the headphones out of his ears. The magazine slapped together as he scrambled to his feet.

"What are you doing?"

"W-working late," Troy blurted. "Eli wants us to clean out the pens first thing tomorrow. I thought I'd get a jump on it tonight."

"So you're here this late to clean pens?"

"Actually, I thought I'd just crash here and get an early start."

"And your folks are okay with you sleeping here?"

"My mom is dead. A car wreck about eight years ago." He shrugged. "My dad doesn't care what I do. The only thing he cares about is getting drunk. He's on a bender right now." His gaze met Jesse's. "If you let me stay here tonight, I promise I'll be up before anyone gets here. I'll even shovel all the stalls myself."

"A car wreck, huh?"

Troy nodded. "She was on her way home from work."

"My mom died when I was four," Jesse murmured. "She had complications when she had my youngest brother. My dad was never much of a dad, either."

"A drunk?"

"Among other things." He eyed the blanket. "But you can't sleep here."

Troy's head snapped up and his gaze collided with Jesse's. "Please, Mr. Chisholm. I won't get in the way. I promise."

Jesse shook his head. "As much as I'd like to let you sleep right here, I'm afraid I can't. If you start snoring, you might spook the bulls." The kid actually looked ready to cry until Jesse added, "I'm bunking out in the small apartment upstairs, but there's a pullout couch in the main office. Clean sheets in the cabinet. You can sleep there."

"Really?"

Jesse nodded. "But only if you promise to get up five minutes early and put on a pot of coffee. If you're camping out in the office, you're in charge of the coffee machine."

"I promise."

"Get some sleep, then." Jesse motioned toward the office. "I'll see you tomorrow."

Troy snatched up his blanket and magazine and made a beeline for the office. A smile played at his lips and Jesse's chest tightened.

He knew exactly what Troy was feeling at the moment. He'd felt it himself every night when his dad had been three sheets to the wind and he and his brothers had bedded down in the old Buick just to get away from the chaos.

Relief.

Bone-deep, soothing relief because he didn't have to worry about waking to a drunken rant or picking his dad up off the bathroom floor or winding up on the opposite end of his fist. For tonight, Troy was safe.

If only Jesse felt the same at the moment.

Instead, he was on edge. Wired. Desperate.

And all because of Gracie.

Yep, he wanted more, all right. And he had only four days to get it, because he was leaving first thing Sunday morning.

That meant he was going to have to spend a lot of time with her between now and then, more than just the proposed sneaking around after hours, that was for damned sure. No, Jesse needed to *overindulge* if he meant to get Gracie out of his system and lay the past to rest once and for all.

He had to.

Because Jesse was finally moving on with his life. But in order to move on, he needed to let go of the past.

Of Gracie.

He would.

But first he was going to haul her close and hold on tight.

13

WHEN GRACIE WALKED into City Hall on Wednesday morning, she was more than happy to find Trina ready and waiting with a full day's itinerary. After a sleepless night spent reliving her encounter with Jesse, she needed something—anything—to get her mind off what had happened and how much she'd liked it.

And how she couldn't wait until it happened again.

But she would wait because she had responsibilities. Places to go. People to see. Waffles to eat.

High-fiber bran waffles that looked like cardboard and tasted even more bland.

"These are interesting," she said to the blue-haired woman sitting across from her.

"Don't be silly, child. They taste terrible like that." Myrtle Nell, president of the Senior Ladies' Auxiliary and chairperson for the brunch, handed Gracie a bowl filled with a dark brown jellylike substance. "You need the prune compote on top to really bring out the flavor."

"Wow. This looks yummy." *Not.* Gracie watched as

the woman heaped a few spoonfuls onto her plate and tried not to make a face.

"It's homemade." Myrtle motioned her to take another bite and Gracie had the sudden urge to run. Away from the waffles and the gossip.

Straight to Jesse.

She ditched the thought, forced herself to take a bite and tuned in to the conversation flying back and forth across the table.

She learned all about Carl Simon's new hair plugs and Janet Green's collagen injections and Helen Culpepper's latest affair with some rancher from nearby Rusk County.

Carl had developed a massive infection from the plugs that no amount of antibiotic cream could touch. Janet had overdone the treatment and now looked like a blowfish. And Helen's latest fling was a huge *Brokeback Mountain* fan.

The only thing she didn't hear about was any mention of her run-in with Jesse in front of the bakery. Not that the entire town wasn't privy to the information. They were, but they'd obviously written it off as a friendly exchange between politician and constituent.

That should have been enough to ease Gracie's nerves. She was still worked up after a sleepless night spent replaying her evening with Jesse. Want gripped her, but she tamped it back down. She had obligations first. Responsibilities.

Which was why she forced down not one but two waffles before she headed over to the seventh-grade car wash.

"I'm ready to work," she told Shirley Buckner, the fortysomething English teacher and supervisor for the fundraising event. Shirley wore blue-jean capris, a Lost Gun Middle School T-shirt and a haggard expression that said she needed a giant margarita a lot more than a helping hand.

She handed Gracie a bucket and directed her over to a dust-covered Chevy four-door pickup truck with the familiar Cartwright Ranch logo on the side. "You can start on Lloyd Cartwright's truck. He brought in all six of them." She indicated the row of matching vehicles that spanned the length of the middle school parking lot.

"Oh, and smile." Shirley lifted the camera that hung around her neck as an afterthought and clicked a picture. "Great. Now get moving."

"Shouldn't you take off the lens cap first?" Gracie pointed to the covering on the high-dollar camera similar to the one she'd had back in the day.

"A cap?" Shirley eyed the contraption as if seeing it for the first time. Her eyebrows drew together into a frown as she twisted the covering. The cap popped off into her hands. "Great. Just friggin' great. I've shot over forty pictures in the past hour. All for nothing." She grabbed the walkie-talkie from her belt. "Charlene? Is June still in the bathroom?"

"I sent her home. She's *really* sick."

"Great. Just friggin' *great*."

"June?" Gracie eyed the teacher. "June Silsbee? The reporter from the newspaper?"

Shirley nodded. "She was here covering the event for the paper, but then she upchucked in the parking lot on account of she's pregnant with triplets. She and Martin did that in vitro thing. Anyhow, she handed me her camera and made a beeline for the restroom.

I haven't seen her since." She eyed the camera. "The kids are so excited. The paper promised us front-page coverage, which we're counting on because the car wash itself never brings in quite enough money. But then the paper comes out and we get a rush of donations from local businesses." She shook her head. "But none of that's going to happen, since I can't even work this blasted thing."

"I can." The words were out before Gracie could stop them. Not that she would have. Her gaze shifted to the dozens of kids piled around a nearby car. They worked diligently, scrubbing and laughing. She ignored the doubt that rippled deep inside and gave in to the grin tugging at her lips. "Hand it over and I'll see what I can do."

She spent the next hour taking picture after picture while the kids sprayed and washed and got each other wet. She was just about to snap a pic of the girls choir group serenading one of the customers when she caught sight of a familiar pair of Wranglers in her peripheral vision.

She turned in time to see Jesse slam the door shut on his jacked-up pickup truck. He wore a fitted white T-shirt and faded jeans that hugged his muscles to perfection and tugged at the seams as he started toward her.

What the hell?

He wasn't supposed to be here. Not now. They'd made arrangements to meet tonight at his motel room. He wasn't supposed to be here in full view of everyone. Especially not looking so downright sexy. Her stomach hollowed out and she had the sudden urge to throw herself into his arms and kiss him for all she was worth. In front of God and the entire Lost Gun seventh grade.

"Excuse me." She snatched the water hose out of a nearby girl's hand and before she could think better of it, she let loose a stream of water directly in Jesse's direction. He sputtered and frowned, and she put her back to him, giving herself a silent high five for marksmanship.

Now he would turn and head the other way.

That was what she told herself, but then she heard his deep voice directly behind her.

"What the hell are you doing?"

She whirled and tried to look surprised. "Oh, my. Did I get you wet? You must have walked into my line of fire."

"I didn't do any such thing. I was your line of fire."

"Don't be silly." She tried to laugh off the coincidence, but he wasn't buying it. She finally shrugged. "So I got you a little wet. Stop making such a big fuss."

"A little wet?" He arched an eyebrow at her, amusement dancing in his violet eyes before they darkened and the air stalled in her lungs. "I'm soaked to the bone, in case you haven't noticed."

She'd noticed, all right. His white T-shirt, now practically transparent, stuck to him like a second skin, showing off every bulge and ripple of his broad shoulders and sinewy chest. She could even see the shadow of hair that circled his nipples and funneled down his abdomen. "At least I'm in good company." He nodded at her.

She became acutely aware of the glide of water down her own neck, the sticky wetness of her silk blouse plastered against her chest. A glance down and she realized her aim hadn't been that great. Her own clothing was in no better shape than his, her shirt practically transparent, revealing the lacy bra she wore and the puckered tips of her breasts. Her only consolation? The high-dollar camera hanging around her neck, the strap plunging between her perky nipples, was waterproof.

"It's a car wash." She bristled. "People get wet. It's a hazard of the job." She grasped for a change of subject. "What are you doing here?"

"I thought I'd pick you up and we could have lunch."

"Here? In town?"

"Why not?"

"Because you hate this town."

He shrugged. "A man's gotta eat. So what do you say?"

"I'd say your timing sucks. As you can see, I'm busy."

"Oh, I see, all right." He eyed her wet blouse and his smile widened. "You look good wet." His deep voice stirred something even worse than the sudden panic beating at her senses. "But then I already knew that." Excitement flowered inside her, making her heart pound and her blood rush.

She felt herself melting beneath the warmth in his eyes, his smile, and so she did what any freedom-loving woman would have done. She squirted him again for good measure, ignored the urge to snatch a picture of him soaked to his skin, turned on her heel and walked away.

Walked being the key word when all she really wanted to do was run. Because as much as Jesse excited her, he scared the crap out of her, too. The way he smiled. The way he made her feel when he smiled.

This feeling was not part of her plan. Working him

out of her system to gain some much-needed closure—
definitely tops on her agenda. But this warm, achy feeling? The urge to shirk her duties, climb into the cab of
his pickup truck and drive off into the sunset?

No.

No matter how hot the temperature, how hot his
gaze or how hot the heat that burned between them.
This was strictly sex.

Closure sex.

Unfortunately, she wasn't used to any kind of sex,
which explained why she couldn't forget Jesse James
Chisholm or his damnable grin the rest of the afternoon after she dropped off the camera to the newspaper office and headed back to City Hall.

She turned her attention to unpacking the boxes
of books back at her office and sliding them onto
the newly delivered shelves. Unfortunately, it wasn't
enough to make her forget Jesse or the upcoming evening.

He was there in her head, teasing and tempting and
reminding her of last night. Of how much she still
wanted him.

She found herself counting down the seconds until
she could see him again.

Because he'd awakened her long-deprived hormones
and so, of course, he was starring in a few crazy fantasies. But that was all they were. No way did Gracie
actually want to ride off into the sunset with Jesse. She
wasn't riding anywhere. She was here in Lost Gun to
stay.

And Jesse wasn't.

Sunday.

The word echoed in her head, fueling her resolve

as she picked up the phone and dialed his number. His voice mail picked up.

"I'm afraid I've got a late meeting. I'll have to take a rain check tonight. Talk to you tomorrow."

There. No matter how much she might want him, she didn't need him.

That was what she told herself as she slid the books into place, one after the other, until the shelf was full.

Like her life. Full. Content. She didn't want for anything.

OKAY, SO MAYBE she wanted for one thing. A way past Big Earl's trio of pit bulls.

"I need the biggest steak you've got," she told the butcher the next morning after a night of tossing and turning and surfing late-night cable TV.

She'd ended up on Animal Planet watching a *K9 Cops* marathon. After twelve back-to-back episodes and four packs of Life Savers, she'd hit on an idea.

"Rib eye? New York strip? Filet?" asked Merle Higgam, the head butcher at the local Piggly Wiggly.

"Yes."

"Yes to which one?"

"All three." She wasn't sure which cut would go over best with the vicious trio, so she didn't want to take any chances. "Just make sure they're all really thick."

Ten minutes later she climbed into her car with the freezer-wrapped package and headed over to Big Earl's. Trina had reported back that Big Earl was even older and more decrepit than they remembered. No way could he actually be making moonshine again.

At the same time, Gracie needed to see for herself. To warn him what would happen if he violated his probation.

"Lookie here, big boy," Gracie said, summoning her sultriest "come and get me" voice as she held one of her purchases over the fence and did her best to entice the first animal that poked his head out of an oversize doghouse. "I've got something *really* special for you."

He barked once, twice, before making a mad dash for her. She tossed the steak to her far left and waited while the other two dogs joined the first. Summoning her courage, she climbed over the fence and made a beeline for the house. She hit the front steps two at a time and did a fast knock on the door.

"Big Earl? It's me. Mayor Stone. I need to talk to you."

"Who is it?"

"Mayor Stone."

"Mayor who?"

"Stone."

"Sorry, I ain't got no phone."

"I didn't say phone. I said Stone."

"The mayor?"

"That's me."

"Ain't got no key, either. 'Sides, you don't need a key. The door's unlocked."

Gracie's fingers closed over the doorknob just as she heard the barking behind her. She chanced a glance over her shoulder to see one of the dogs catch sight of her. She pushed open the door and slammed it shut behind her just as Ferocious Number One raced for the porch, his jaws wagging, his teeth flashing.

Heart pounding, she turned to drink in the interior of the double-wide trailer. Wood paneling covered the walls. An old movie poster from *The Outlaw Josey Wales* hung over an old lumpy beige couch piled high with old lumpy pillows. A scarred mahogany coffee table sat stacked with crossword puzzles. In the far corner sat an old lumpy recliner with an old lumpy man parked on top.

The last time she had seen Big Earl had been at a Fourth of July picnic six years ago. He'd been in attendance with his great-granddaughter, Casey, who'd been helping Frank Higgins, the owner of the local gas station, set off the fireworks. Casey had just graduated high school. She'd been working for Frank at the time, pumping gas and cleaning windshields, and so he'd brought her along to help tote the fourteen boxes of sparklers and Roman candles he'd donated. That had been the night that Judge Ellis had bought a case of moonshine off of Big Earl and stashed it in the trunk of his Lexus, which had turned out to be the finale of the fireworks show.

Big Earl had been wearing the same red-and-white-checked shirt he had on now. Except the colors had been a lot more vibrant and the fabric a lot less wrinkled.

The old man had a head full of snow-white hair that was slicked back with pomade. His eyes were pale blue and enormous behind a pair of thick round glasses.

"Well, I'll be." Big Earl peered at her. "Don't just stand there, come on in." He waved a hand for her to sit down next to him, only the nearest chair was a good five feet away.

She eased onto the edge of the sofa across from him. "So?" Her gaze skittered around the room, from an old cuckoo clock that ticked away in the kitchen to the ancient movie poster. "How have you been?"

"Fair to midland, I s'pose. Why, back in the day I was as spry as a young spring chicken. I was into everything back then. Knew everybody's business. Had plenty of business of my own, if you know what I mean."

"About that…" she started, but Big Earl wasn't quite finished yet.

"But time sure has a way of slowin' a man down. Why, my back's been achin' somethin' fierce and I got these bunions. I've been doin' Epsom salts in my bath and that helps some."

"That's good to hear. Speaking of hearing, I was just wondering…" Her words faded off as she noticed the way his eyes fixed on the spot just over her left shoulder. As if he couldn't quite focus on her. She noticed the magnifying glass on the tray table next to him. And the extra batteries for his hearing aid. And a tube of arthritis cream.

She realized then that the only thing Big Earl could possibly cook up in his condition was a piece of burnt toast. The man could hardly see. Or hear. Or walk, judging by the cane propped next to him and the nearby walker parked in the corner. He certainly wasn't in any condition to measure out ingredients or tiptoe around and keep one eye out for the cops while maintaining watch over a highly combustible still.

He wagged a bent finger in her general vicinity. "So what is it you needed to talk to me about?"

Gracie shrugged. "Just checking in to see how you're doing."

He grinned a toothless grin. "Mighty nice of you.

Why, I ain't had visitors in years. Used to head into town once a week for bingo, but I cain't even do that anymore. Thank the good Lord for cable—otherwise I'd be bored out of my mind."

"You watch a lot of TV?"

"I mainly listen to it. Turn the volume up real loud on account of my hearin' ain't what it used to be. But I get by. Still catch my favorite shows. Never miss an episode of *The Rifleman* or *Bonanza*. I love those old Westerns."

Her gaze shifted to the movie poster. "You a Clint Eastwood fan?"

"I'm a Josey Wales fan. Eastwood ain't never done anything since that's worth a hill of beans."

"Now, remember, when things look bad and it looks like you're not gonna make it, then you gotta get mean." Gracie read the movie quote at the bottom of the poster. "Plumb mad-dog mean." There was something oddly familiar about the saying, but she couldn't quite place it.

"Words to live by." Big Earl grinned. "'Course, I ain't in much condition to get mean anymore, either. I leave that to my Casey. Girl's got a fiery streak that would make her mama proud. Why, she don't let no-body push her around. She ought to be back in a few minutes. Ran into town to pick up my foot cream."

"I'm sorry I missed her." Gracie pushed to her feet. "Maybe we can catch up next time."

"You sure you don't want to wait and say hello?"

"I really should get going." Her hand closed on the doorknob and she heard the growls coming from the other side. "On second thought—" she summoned a smile and sank back down onto the sofa "—I wouldn't want to be rude."

14

WHAT THE HELL was he doing here?

Gracie's hand faltered on the brownie she was stuffing into a plastic baggie. She stood behind one of the handful of tables set up on the lawn in front of City Hall. She set the treat aside, next to the dozen or so she'd just bagged for the annual Daughters of the Republic of Texas bake sale and did her best to calm her pounding heart.

Pounding, of all things. When she'd promised herself just last night after she'd cancelled on him that she wasn't going to get nervous. Or excited. Or turned on when she finally saw him again.

Especially turned on. She had a reputation to protect and salivating at the first sign of the town's hottest bad boy, particularly in front of the biggest busybodies in said town, was not in keeping with the conservative image of Lost Gun's newly elected mayor.

Tongues were already wagging about the car wash incident. Of course, they all focused on the fact that Jesse James Chisholm had been wet and practically half-naked in front of every female teacher at the middle school rather than Gracie, who'd been the cause of it.

It was all Jesse's fault. He was too bold and much too sexy for his own good.

She forced an indifferent expression and tried to ignore the way his tight jeans hugged his muscular thighs as he approached her table. He wore a black T-shirt and a dusty cowboy hat that said he'd been in the middle of a training session not too long ago.

Yet here he was in the heart of Lost Gun.

"Brownie, cupcake or cheesecake bar?" she croaked when he reached her table.

"I'll take all three."

"Wow. Somebody's hungry."

"You have no idea."

She knew by the way his eyes darkened that he wasn't talking about the scrumptious goodies spread out on the table between them. She tamped down on her own growling stomach and reached for a white bakery bag. With trembling hands, she loaded his goodies inside and handed them over. "That'll be three dollars."

He pulled out his wallet and unfolded a ten. "Keep the change." Their hands brushed as she took the money and a jolt of electricity shot through her.

"Why did you cancel last night?"

"I was busy."

"Busy or scared?"

"Scared of what? Of you?" She shook her head. "I'm not scared of you."

"No." He eyed her for a silent moment. "You're scared of us," he finally said.

"There is no us. This isn't a long-term arrangement. You're leaving on Sunday." She didn't mean to sound so accusing. "Which is a good thing," she blurted. "A really good thing. Enjoy." She pushed the goodies in his direction and turned her attention to the next customer in line.

She glimpsed his handsome face in her peripheral vision, his eyes trained on her, his lips set in a grim line. As if he was thinking real hard about some question and he wasn't too pleased with the answer.

As if he wasn't any more happy to be here than she was to see him here.

She pondered the notion for a few seconds as she served up several more baggies of goodies and tried to pretend for all she was worth that his presence didn't affect her.

Fat chance.

Every nerve in her body was keenly aware of him. She felt his warm gaze on her profile and a slow heat swept over her, from the tips of her toes clear to the top of her head, until she all but burned in the midday heat. She shifted her stance, her thighs pressing together, and an ache shot through her. Her nipples pebbled, rubbing against her bra, and her fingers faltered on the pie she was about to slice.

The pie splattered to the ground at her feet and her heart slammed against her rib cage. She shoveled the gooey mess back into the pie plate and headed for the building and the small kitchen situated at the rear of City Hall, next to a large conference room being used for the monthly Daughters of the Texas Republic meeting immediately following the bake sale.

Inside the kitchen, the ladies had stored all of their extra sweets. There were rows of pies and cakes and cookies.

She dumped the peach mess into a nearby trash can and went to the sink to wash her hands. Her fingers trembled and the soap slipped from her grasp. "Damn it," she muttered.

"Careful, sugar. You'll have the ladies dropping to their knees for an impromptu prayer meeting."

The deep voice froze her hands.

Worse, Jesse leaned in, his arms coming around her on either side, his hands closing over hers to steady her as she reached for the bar of soap.

His large tanned hands were a stark contrast against her white fingers. His warm palms cradled the tops of her hands. The rough pads of his fingertips rasped against her soft flesh and heat spiraled through her body. His nearness was like a fuzzy blanket smothering the cold panic that had rolled through her the moment she'd realized that he'd followed her inside.

"Easy, now." His voice rumbled over her bare shoulder and warm breath brushed her skin. Goose bumps chased up and down her arms and she came close to leaning back into him, closing her eyes and enjoying the delicious sensation. Just for a little while.

She stiffened and fought for her precious control. Twelve years of cloaking herself in it should have made it easy to find, but not with Jesse so close. Too close for her to breathe, much less think, much less pretend.

"You have to cradle the bar of soap and slide it through your fingers like this." He slid his fingers over the slick bar and suds lathered between their fingers. "You have to go easy and slow." As he said the words, she got the distinct impression that he was talking about more than just washing her hands.

"Thanks for the advice, but no thanks. I do not need

to go slow and easy." To prove her point, she focused every ounce of energy she had on ignoring the delicious feelings assaulting her body. She held her breath and rolled the bar between her palms before shoving her hands under the spraying faucet.

His arms fell away as she turned off the water and reached for a dish towel. She scooted past him and headed for the large storage room that sat just behind the kitchen, eager to put as much distance as possible between them.

"What are you doing here?" she demanded when he followed her into the back room. She forced her face into the tightest frown she could manage, considering she wanted to kiss him more than she wanted her next breath.

"We made a deal. Sex," he murmured, the word rumbling up her spine.

"Not now. Not here." While she wanted Jesse, she wasn't supposed to want him. That meant no blushing or trembling or kissing. "There are too many people here."

"Why, there isn't a soul in sight." He glanced around to prove his point. A bare bulb hung overhead, illuminating the small room that housed everything from gallon cans of chili and beans to five-gallon jars of tomato sauce for the Senior Ladies weekly spaghetti night. The place stocked all of the supplies for any of the functions held in the main conference room next to the kitchen. Boxes of paper goods, from plates to napkin packets to disposable cups, lined a metal shelf that ran the length of one wall.

"This isn't a good idea." She turned her back on him, determined to forget his presence and keep her mind on the task at hand. She made her way to a six-foot table that held the rest of the goodies that the Ladies' Auxiliary had donated for today's luncheon. There were dozens of pies and platters of brownies and a few cakes. She was busy reading the masking tape labels on the tops of the plastic-wrapped goodies when she heard Jesse step up behind her again.

"This really isn't a good idea." She snatched up a carrot cake and turned, the confection smack-dab between them.

"Actually, I think it's a pretty fine idea." Jesse's deep voice sent a jolt of adrenaline through her. His eyes glittered with a hungry light that sucked the oxygen from her lungs and made her hands tremble. He caught the edge of the door that adjoined the kitchen and shut it behind him, closing them off from the rest of the world.

The cake slid from her grasp, landing in a pile of smashed frosting and plastic wrap at her feet. Ugh. That made not one but two desserts she'd killed on account of Jesse James Chisholm.

"You'd better get your checkbook ready to make a nice big fat donation." She knelt to retrieve the mess, but he was right beside her, his hands bumping hers as they both reached for the cardboard base at the same time.

"I'm not the one that keeps dropping everything."

"Because of you."

"Because you like what I do to you. You just don't want to admit it."

His hand stalled on hers and heat whispered up her arm. "I can't do this here."

"You don't have to *do* a thing." He reached for her

hands, which were now covered with frosting. Before she could draw her next breath, his tongue flicked out and he licked one finger. Once, twice, before sliding it deep in his mouth and suckling for a breath-stealing moment. "Just feel."

"I…" She swallowed and tried to think of something to say, but with his lips so firm and purposeful around her finger, his tongue rasping her skin, she couldn't seem to find any words. "Somebody might come looking for me," she managed to say several moments later after he'd licked her finger clean.

"You'll be back with more desserts in no time." He licked his lips, and she had the sudden image of him licking other parts of her body. Lapping at her neck and her nipples and her belly button and the wet heat between her legs. "But first I want my dessert."

Chatter drifted through the open doorway. The PA system crackled as it switched on and Myrtle's voice came over the loudspeaker as she tested the mic for the upcoming meeting. Even closer, the hum of the coffee machine drifted from inside the kitchen, along with the rush of water as someone flipped on a faucet. There were people just beyond the thin walls of the storage room. People starting to prep for the upcoming meeting. People who could walk in at any moment and find their mayor having dessert with the town's baddest bad boy.

She stiffened and forced aside the stirring images. "I really think we should wait until this evening. I'll meet you at the motel."

"You cancelled on me once. I won't take that chance again. Besides, I don't like to wait." He kissed her then, his lips wet and hungry, his tongue greedy as he devoured her.

"I don't think—" But then he fingered her nipple through the soft cotton of her shirt and she stopped thinking altogether.

He dropped to his knees in front of her, his hands going to her hips. He paused to knead her bottom through the fitted material of her skirt. Fabric brushed her legs as he slid it down over her thighs, her knees, until the skirt pooled on the floor.

He stood, then slid his hands around to her bottom and lifted her onto the counter. He paused only to grab one of the large wire racks filled with boxes and shove it in front of the door. It wasn't enough to keep anyone out should they really want to get in, but it was enough to buy them some time to grab their clothes should they be discovered.

Walking back to her, he wedged himself between her parted thighs. He urged her backward until her back met the countertop and then he slowly unbuttoned her shirt and unhooked the front clasp of her bra.

He fingered a dollop of frosting from the cake plate. "I really do like cream cheese," he murmured before touching the filling to one ripe nipple. He circled the tip, spreading the glaze until it covered her entire areola.

His gaze drilled into hers for a heart-stopping moment before he lowered his dark head. His tongue lapped at the side of her breast.

The licking grew stronger, more purposeful, as he gobbled up the white confection, starting at the outside and working his way toward the center. Sensation rippled up her spine.

The first leisurely rasp of his tongue against her ripe nipple wrung a cry from her throat. Her fingers threaded through his hair as he drew the quivering tip deep into his hot, hungry mouth. He suckled her long and hard and she barely caught the moan that tried to escape her throat.

She bit her lip as he licked and suckled and nipped. Her skin grew itchy and tight. Pressure started between her legs, heightened by the way he leaned into her, the hard ridge of his erection prominent beneath his jeans. She spread her legs wider and he settled more deeply between them. Grasping her hips, he rocked her.

Rubbed her.

Up and down and side to side and—

The shrill whistle of a tea kettle filled the air, penetrating the haze of pleasure that gripped her senses. Panic bolted through her and she went still.

"Wait." She grasped his muscled biceps to still his movements. "I need to go check the tea. If I don't, someone else will."

He leaned back, his gaze so deep and searching, as if he were doing his damnedest to see inside of her. "No," he finally murmured, his fingertip tracing the edge of her panties where elastic met the tender inside of her thigh. "You're not going anywhere. This isn't about going, sugar." His finger dipped into the steamy heat beneath. "It's about coming."

One touch of his callused fingertip against her swollen flesh and she arched up off the counter. She caught her bottom lip again and stifled a cry.

With a growl, he spread her wide with his thumb and forefinger and touched and rubbed as he dipped his head and drew on her nipple.

It was too much and not enough. She clamped her lips shut and forced her eyes open. But he was there, filling her line of vision, his fierce gaze drilling into hers. Searching and stirring and—

"Is somebody back there?" Lora Tremayne's voice echoed in the background, followed by the rattle of the doorknob as the president of the Daughters of the Republic of Texas tried to open the door to the storage room.

Gracie stiffened, her hands diving between them to stop the delicious stroke of his fingers.

As if he sensed her sudden resistance, his movements stilled. His chest heaved and his hair tickled her palms. Damp fingertips trailed over her cheek in a tender gesture that warmed her heart almost as much as her body.

"Come for me." His gaze was hot and bright and feverish as he stared down at her, into her. But there was something else, as well. A desperation that eased the panic beating at her senses and sent a rush of determination through her.

"Hello? Who's in there?"

It was Lora again, but it didn't matter. Gracie no longer cared if the entire Ladies' Auxiliary stood on the outside of the door, waiting and listening.

It wasn't about what everyone else thought about her. It was about him. What he thought about her. What he felt for her. What he wanted from her. What he *needed* from her.

And what she needed from him.

Her fingers dove into his front pocket and retrieved the small foil packet tucked there.

He answered her unspoken invitation by tugging

at the button on his jeans, pulling his zipper down and freeing his hard length. He opened the condom and spread it on his throbbing penis before leaning in closer, until the head pushed just a fraction of an inch inside of her.

Pleasure pierced her brain for a split second, quickly shattering into a swell of sensation as he filled her with one deep, probing thrust.

Her muscles convulsed around him, clutching him as he gripped her bare bottom. He pumped into her, the pressure and the friction so sweet that it took her breath away.

She was vaguely aware of the voices on the other side of the door. But then he touched her nipple and trailed a hand down her stomach, his fingertips making contact with the place where they joined, and all thought faded in a rush of sweet desire. She met his thrusts in a wild rhythm that urged him faster and deeper and…there. Right. *There!*

Her lips parted and she screamed at the blinding force of the climax that picked her up and turned her inside out. He caught the sound with his mouth and buried himself deep inside her one last time. A shudder went through him as he followed her over the edge.

She wrapped her arms around him and held him. Oddly enough, the fact that she would have to walk out of here with Jesse, past whoever had knocked on the door, didn't bother her nearly as much as it should have.

The heat, she told herself. It was so hot outside that she'd obviously suffered a minor heatstroke and so she wasn't thinking clearly. Because no way would she want anyone to know that their respectable leader had hooked up with the most disrespectable man in town.

The very last thing she needed was to tarnish her image. Unfortunately, what she needed and what she wanted were two very different things, and at that moment, the only thing she really wanted was Jesse.

In her bed and her life.

Temporarily, of course.

She knew full well that he was leaving in a few days, and she was staying, and that was that.

There would be no long-distance texts, no late-night phone calls, no keeping in touch. Jesse meant to let go of the past, to erase it, and she meant to let him.

Cold turkey.

It worked.

She knew firsthand and where she'd turned her back once before, she intended to let him turn his now. He needed to forget this place.

He deserved to forget.

Which meant she would let him go. She had to.

But not yet. Not just yet.

"I'M TELLING YOU, James Lee, the door is locked from the inside." Lora Tremayne's voice penetrated the frantic beat of Jesse's heart.

"But this door ain't got no lock on the inside, Miss Lora," came the deep voice of City Hall's lead maintenance man. "Maybe you aren't pushing it hard enough."

Jesse felt Gracie's body go tense and he knew she'd heard the speculation outside the door. He leaned back and saw the worry that leapt into her bright blue eyes.

"I pushed on it plenty hard," James Lee went on. "It's not locked, but it might be barricaded. Someone's definitely in there."

"Maybe it's Mabel Green," said another female

voice and Jesse knew the situation had attracted the attention of more than one of the women on hand for the monthly meeting and bake sale. "She's been on a no-carb diet for the past six months and it's made her batty. She probably saw all those goodies and went on a binge."

"Sarah Eckles is doing the same diet," another voice said. "It could be her."

"Maybe it's an animal. I get possums in my trash all the time. One of 'em could have crawled in a window."

"Maybe it's a raccoon."

"Maybe it's a zombie."

The voices joined in a loud back and forth as the doorknob jiggled and James Lee did his best to push open the door.

"We have to get out of here," Gracie started, but Jesse touched a finger to her lips.

"Wait here and don't come out until the coast is clear." He worked at the buttons on his jeans and then pulled on his shirt. A split second later, he kissed her quickly on the lips before turning toward the door.

He pulled open the door just as James Lee pushed. The man would have tumbled him backward, but Jesse was much younger and stronger. James Lee stumbled backward instead as Jesse stepped forward, slipped out the door and shut it firmly behind him.

"Afternoon, ladies," he said, giving Lora and the half dozen women that surrounded her a wink and a tip of his hat.

"Jesse Chisholm," Lora said, her face puckering up as if she'd just sucked on a lemon. "What in land's sake are you doing here?"

"I must have got lost on my way to the clerk's office."

"You mistook the kitchen for the clerk's office?" She didn't look convinced.

Meanwhile the whispers floated around the room.

"The clerk's office? Fat chance on that."

"Why, that man cain't be up to no good."

"The Chisholms don't know the meaning of the word *good*."

"Somebody better count the brownies and pies."

"I'm selling some property," Jesse announced, as if that would kill the speculation. It wouldn't. His last name was Chisholm and nothing would ever change that. He knew as much and he'd come to terms with it, but he explained anyway because this wasn't about him. It was about Gracie. She was stuck in the room behind him and he wanted to give her a way out that didn't involve waltzing past these gossips. "I must have taken a wrong turn."

"Likely story," Lora snorted in the condescending way that had earned her the reputation as the most stuck-up bitch in the county.

He ignored the urge to tell her which way to go and how fast to get there. Instead, his ears perked to the sound of footsteps behind him. So soft that no one else would have heard unless they were listening.

A slide and a faint thud and then all was quiet.

No jiggle of the knob behind him. No creak of hinges.

Nothing because Gracie was heeding his words and not coming out until the coast was clear.

He ignored the crazy disappointment that twisted at his insides. It wasn't as if he wanted her to waltz out in front of God and everybody and tarnish the image she'd fought so hard to build.

At the same time, he couldn't shake the sudden urge to feel her hand on his arm, her warmth beside him, as she stepped up and declared to the world that she was here with him. For him.

"I'll just be on my way."

"I'll show you to the clerk's office," James Lee offered. "It's just down the hall." The man started forward, but Jesse wasn't budging until he had the entire entourage behind him.

"You sure you don't want to escort me out yourself?" He eyed Lora. "Just to make sure I don't overpower James, here, and come back to steal a peach cobbler."

"A smart-ass just like your father," she muttered, but she started after him anyway. As expected, the women followed and soon they were moving down the hallway toward the county clerk's office. When they reached the doorway, James turned.

"Show's over, ladies. There's a bake sale still going on out on the lawn that could use all of you, not to mention y'all got your meeting to get to." He motioned back down the hall. "Just get on about your business. I'll take care of things here."

"Make sure you do," Lora said, giving Jesse one last scathing look. He grinned and her frown deepened before she turned on the women. She rattled off new duties to them and they all disappeared through a nearby door that led to the front lawn.

"Sorry about that, Mr. Chisholm," James said once the women had disappeared. "Those busybodies don't think before they start running their mouths."

He winked. "Saw you ride in Houston last year. You were something."

"Thanks, James Lee."

"Had my granddaughters with me. Bought 'em each a shirt with your name on it. Tickled 'em pink, it did."

"That's mighty nice of you."

"Ain't nothing nice about it. I was hoping you might sign those shirts for me. It sure would mean a lot to the girls."

"Bring them by the training facility and I'd be happy to. In fact, bring the girls with you. They could watch a few sessions. I might have some rodeo passes sitting around, too, for the next event if you think they might like that."

The maintenance man grinned from ear to ear. "Boy, would they ever."

THE COAST WAS CLEAR.

Gracie gathered her courage, slipped out of the storage room, hurried through the kitchen and moved down the hallway toward the ladies' room at the far end.

She needed a few minutes to herself before she headed back out to the bake sale and the curious faces and the hot gossip that Jesse James Chisholm had been shoplifting brownies and cakes.

As if.

Jesse would never do such a thing, even if he had destroyed a few goodies in the name of some really hot sex.

Heat swamped her as she remembered the frosting on her nipple, followed by his lips. And his tongue. And...

Sheesh, it was hot in here.

She pushed inside the restroom, hit the lock button on the door and made her way to the sink. A second later, she splashed cold water on her face and tried to understand what had just happened.

She'd hopped up onto the table and had sex with Jesse James Chisholm just inches away from a very nosy group of constituents.

Even more, she'd liked it.

She liked him.

She ditched the last thought and focused on grabbing a wad of paper towels to blot at her face.

She didn't *like* him. *Like* involved a connection that went beyond the physical. It involved shared interests and mutual respect and admiration. It meant understanding someone's hopes and dreams and—

Okay, so she liked him. A little.

He was a strong, compassionate man. A man who put family first. Who went after what he wanted. A man with hopes and dreams and determination.

A man with a future that did not involve Lost Gun or her or what they'd just shared.

Before she could dwell on the suddenly depressing thought, her cell phone rang. She fished it out of her pocket and hit the Talk button.

"Hey, sis," Charlie's voice floated over the line. "What's up?"

"My sugar level." She reached for another paper towel and dabbed at the water running down her neck. "I'm up to my elbows in brownies and cookies."

"A bake sale?"

"Unfortunately."

"Sounds like a blast. Listen, I just wanted to make

sure you got my message about this weekend. I hate to cancel on you, but I've got a lot going right now and—"

"Sure." Why the hell was it still so hot in here?

"—I really don't have time to drive all the way to Lost Gun just to make homemade pizzas, even though they're like *the* best pizzas in the world and you're the best and—what did you just say?"

"We can do it some other time." Gracie blew out a deep breath and made a mental note to ask Trina to have James Lee check the main air conditioning unit. "Don't worry about it." She tossed the used paper towels and tried to ignore the rush of heat as she stared into the mirror and noticed that she'd missed one of the buttons on her shirt.

"You're not mad, are you?"

"Of course not."

"Yes, you are," Charlie insisted, obviously startled when Gracie didn't launch into a ten-minute lecture about how she'd bought all the pizza ingredients and pulled out the Monopoly board.

She would have. She would have reminded her sister about all the details and how much fun they would have being together, but suddenly the only thing she could think of was how hot it was and how she desperately needed to calm down and how she really needed to forget Jesse Chisholm.

And the fact that she liked him.

"You're mad and worried," Charlie went on, "but I'm not a little girl anymore. I know how to take care of myself. I won't be out late and I'll be super careful and—"

"I know you will. Call me later." She killed the connection before her sister could ask another question.

And then she concentrated on redoing her shirt and returning to the real world without thinking about Jesse Chisholm and the all-important fact that she couldn't wait to see him again.

15

He was friggin' crazy.

That was the only explanation for the fact that the more Jesse James Chisholm touched Gracie Stone, the more he kissed her and slid deep, deep inside, the more he wanted to do it again and again and again.

Crazy, all right.

While he managed to get himself up and out of bed the morning after, it wasn't getting easier the way he'd expected. The way he'd hoped.

He stood beside the bed early Friday morning—four days after he'd first gotten her into his bed—and stared down at her luscious body spread out on his plain cotton sheets. Instead of the motel, they'd been keeping company in his apartment at the training facility. Away from prying eyes and the horde of reporters camped out at the motel.

He left the tack room and headed for the main corral. He had to give her up. He told himself that as he checked the feeding troughs. He had to give her up and forget about their time together and start thinking about the future. About Austin and his next ride and—

"Jesse!"

The name rang out and scattered his thoughts the minute he spotted the woman on the opposite side of the railing.

"Hey there, Wendy." He climbed over the railing and headed around to where she stood. "Pete's not here. I dropped him off on your doorstep myself last night after the bachelor party."

"I know, and thanks for not getting too wild and crazy. He said you kept it low-key."

He hadn't meant to. He'd meant to take Pete over to Luscious Longhorns and get them both as drunk as skunks. But Pete had been more interested in texting Wendy and Jesse had been more interested in getting back to Gracie, and so they'd left Cole and Billy and Jimmy and Jake to tie one on and close the place down.

"I'm not looking for Pete," she went on. "I'm looking for you. I need a favor."

"I really need to get going. I promised Eli I'd—"

"It's my cousin. She's flying in for the wedding this afternoon and I need someone to pick her up."

"I'll get one of the boys to drive out—"

"And take her to the wedding. And keep her company."

"I'm sure Joe or Sam or—"

"I need you, Jesse. I was thinking you could be her date for the wedding."

"But I already have a date."

"You do?"

That's right, buddy. You do?

Okay, so he didn't actually have a date, but he wanted one. He wanted to ask Gracie to be his date. The thing was, he wasn't one hundred percent positive she would say yes. When it came to sex, he knew she couldn't resist him. But this was different. This wasn't about being lovers. It was about being companions. Friends. And to a man who'd been judged and shunned most of his life, those were much harder to come by. Gracie had called it quits and turned her back on him once before. He wasn't going to be blindsided again.

"It's not one of the Barbies, is it?" Wendy went on. "I know they're a lot of fun, but I thought you might want to meet someone with a little substance. Someone more long term—"

"Okay, I'll do it." He planted a kiss on her cheek. "Text me the flight information and I'll see to it she gets to the motel in one piece. And the wedding." And then he turned and walked away before he did something really stupid—like change his mind.

Gracie wasn't dating material. What they had was purely physical and very, very temporary. She'd made that clear from the get-go. Not that he wanted anything more permanent. Hell, he was leaving in two days. No strings. No regrets.

That meant ignoring the feelings churning deep in his gut and laying the past to rest once and for all.

He wasn't falling for her all over again.

Not this time.

Never, ever again.

THE WOMAN WAS driving him to drink.

Jesse finished off the last of his second beer and reached for number three as he watched Gracie two-step around the dance floor with one of Pete's ranch hands. Even dressed in a plain beige skirt and a matching jacket that did nothing to accent the luscious curves hidden beneath, she looked good enough to eat. With every turn, the skirt pulled and tugged across her round ass. With every dip, the bodice of her jacket shifted and he glimpsed the full swells of her breasts. A thin line of perspiration dotted her forehead, making her face glow. Her lips were full and pink and parted in a smile—

Hell's bells, she was smiling at the two-bit cowboy. She wasn't supposed to be doing that. She wasn't even supposed to be here. Her name hadn't been anywhere near the guest list and so he'd been more than a little shocked when she'd waltzed up to him, flashed a press pass, snapped a picture and said, "June Silsbee, the about-town photographer for the newspaper, is sick. I'm filling in for her."

Only she wasn't standing around on the fringes, snapping pictures for the world to see. No, she was having fun. Dancing. Laughing. *Smiling.*

Jesse latched onto beer number four as the song played down and Gracie traded Pete's ranch hand and the two-step for Eli and a popular line dance.

She twirled and wiggled her ass and smiled—holy crap, there she was smiling again. And winking. And at a man old enough to be her father.

Not that Jesse had any room to talk. He'd let Wendy fix him up with the brunette sitting next to him. A mistake if he'd ever made one. While she was nice enough, she wasn't Gracie.

And the problem is?

No problem, he told himself for the umpteenth time, shifting his attention to the woman and trying to focus on whatever she was saying. Something about the bridesmaids' dresses and how pretty everything had been and what a great time she was having.

"Would you excuse me for just a second?" A few seconds later, he left Lisa or Lynette or whatever her name was staring after him as he headed for the bar and did his damnedest to ignore the sexy blonde who floated around the dance floor.

"Beer?" the bartender asked, but Jesse shook his head.

"I need something stronger." A split second later the man pulled a jar of clear liquid from behind the bar and held it up. Jesse nodded and reached for the homemade moonshine.

He was on swig number three when Billy cut in for a waltz with Gracie. Jesse's hands tightened on the jar and he fought the urge to rush over, pull Gracie into his arms and make her smile and wink at him. An urge he managed to resist until Billy closed the few inches that separated them. Jesse forgot all about his moonshine.

"Don't you have your own date?" He tapped his brother on the shoulder. "Shouldn't you be dancing with her?"

"Are you kidding?" He motioned to Casey Jessup, who sat near the bar, her elbow planted on top, her entire focus on the man she was currently arm-wrestling. "She hates to dance."

"So go referee the match for her." He elbowed his way in between them, his gaze fixed on the surprised woman who stared back at him.

"Don't you have your own date?" Gracie arched an eyebrow as he pulled her close.

"It's not an official date. I'm just keeping her company for Wendy."

"You're doing a piss-poor job considering you're here with me."

"I want to dance." He slid a possessive arm around her waist and pulled her close.

"What's gotten into you?"

"A special batch of white lightning."

She pulled back. "Big Earl's white lightning?"

"Something like that." His gaze caught and held hers. "You look really nice."

"You're drunk."

"Not drunk enough. I don't like it when you dance with other men."

"Then you should have asked me to be your date instead of bringing someone else."

"It's not a date."

"It sure looks like a date."

"You're right. I'm sorry." He stared deep into her eyes. "I should have asked you to come with me, but I didn't. I thought I needed some distance. But it doesn't matter if you're clear across the room or right next to me, I still want you the same." He saw the flash of surprise in her gaze. "I need you." He pressed a kiss to her soft lips before pulling her close. She seemed stiff at first, as if she didn't believe him. But then just like that, her body seemed to relax. She inched closer. And the rest of the world faded and they started to dance.

GRACIE HAD WON the battle, but not the war, she realized later that night when she rolled over after several hours of Jesse's fast and furious lovemaking to find the bed next to her warm but empty. As usual. Instead of the motel, he'd taken her to the training facility and the comfy full-size bed that filled up the bedroom of the small apartment that sat over his office. She heard him moving around in the next room—the creak of the chair as he yanked on his boots, the slide of change as he loaded his pockets, the clink of a coffee cup as he finished his last swallow. He was leaving her again. It was still dark, still a long way until sunrise, and Jesse was heading out to practice the way he had last night and the night before.

Admiration crept through her, along with a surge of anxiety. This was it. It was well past midnight, which meant that Saturday had come and gone and it was officially Sunday morning. The wedding was over and there was nothing keeping Jesse in Lost Gun. He would pick up and head for Austin first thing tomorrow morning. Even more, she would take her oath of office and assume the role of mayor.

It was now or never. Otherwise, she would never really know if she'd meant more to him than just a casual fling. If after today he would at least think about her every now and then. Remember her. And she would remember him. She pulled on his tuxedo shirt, snatched up the camera she'd been using at the wedding and started for the adjoining room. She wanted, needed, a place in Jesse Chisholm's memory since she couldn't claim a place in his heart.

JESSE HAD JUST retrieved a blanket from the tack room and walked back to the corral when the gate creaked open and he heard the camera click.

His entire body went on high alert when he caught sight of her—her long blond hair tousled, her face soft and flushed from sleep, her lips swollen from his kisses. She clasped her camera in one hand and a pang of nostalgia went through him. She wore only his white tuxedo shirt and an old worn pair of his boots. The shirt stopped mid-thigh, revealing long, sexy-as-hell legs. He felt a stir in his groin despite the fact that he should have had his fill of her by now.

He was full. Sated. Sick.

That was what he told himself, but damned if he felt it as she walked into the barn. The tuxedo shirt, unbuttoned to reveal the swell of her luscious breasts, teased him with each step. She snapped a few more pictures of him, the *click, click, click* keeping time with the sudden beat of his heart.

Work, he told himself, forcing his gaze away, determined to get back to work. He headed for the mechanical bull sitting off to the side of the rodeo arena where he'd been adjusting the settings. He leaned down and reached up under the backside of the bull to change the speed and friction. Harder. Faster. That's what he needed right now.

Unfortunately, *harder* and *faster* weren't the two words to be thinking of at the moment. Not with her so close.

He felt her gaze and every nerve in his body cracked to attention. He frowned. He was in the homestretch. No more wanting what he couldn't have. No more Gracie.

As relieved as the thought should have made him, the only thing he felt at that moment was desperation. To get back to work, he reminded himself. He was desperate to get the hell out of Lost Gun and head to Austin. End of story.

"What are you doing out here?" he asked gruffly.

"Same as you." She hooked her camera over a nearby corral post. Boots crunched as she neared the mechanical bull. "I thought I'd take a ride."

The words drew his gaze and he found her standing on the opposite side of the bull. "I hate to break it to you, sugar, but you can't ride."

"Maybe not at this moment, but practice makes perfect." Her eyes glittered. Her full lips curved into a half smile that did funny things to his heartbeat. "This is a training facility, right?"

"Last time I looked."

"So train me." She gripped the saddle horn, swung a sexy leg over and mounted up. "I'm all yours."

If only.

He shook away the thought and swallowed against the sudden tightness in his throat. "You're serious?"

"As serious as Old Lady Mitchell's last heart attack."

He eyed her for a moment more before he shrugged. "All right, then." He motioned to the side. "Put your right hand in the grip."

She slid her fingers under the leather strap. "What next?"

"Put your left up in the air."

"Okay."

"Now arch your back."

She thrust her breasts forward and an invisible fist punched in right in the sternum. "What now?"

He drew in some much needed air and tried to keep his voice calm. "Hold on tight."

He flipped the switch and the bull started to rock back and forth, this way and that.

"Mmm..." She closed her eyes at the subtle motion and a smile touched her lips. "Now I know why you cowboys spend so much time doing this."

"I don't think it's the same for us cowboys. Different parts."

Her eyes snapped open then and her passion-filled gaze met his. "I know." The bull kept moving and her eyelids drifted shut again. She threw her head back, her eyes closed, her lips parted as she leaned back and rocked her lower body, following the motion of the bull.

A sight that shouldn't affect him. After a week together, she was out of his system. His head was on straight, his mind back on business, his future crystal clear.

A soft, familiar sigh quivered in the air and the sound sent a bolt of need through him. A wave of possessiveness rolled through him and burned away reason. He flipped the switch and the bull slowed to a halt. He closed the distance between them in a few quick steps.

At the first touch of his fingertips on her thigh, her eyes fluttered open.

She stared down at him, her eyes bright and feverish. "Is it over already?"

"It's just getting started." He reached across her lap and urged her other leg over the bull until she sat sideways, facing him, her lap level with his shoulders. "*I'm* just getting started." He shoved the shirt up and spread her legs wide, wedging his shoulders between her knees. "Ah, baby, you're a natural." Her slick folds were pink and swollen after her recent ride, and he knew she was close. "You've got perfect form." He touched her, trailed a fingertip over the hot, moist flesh and relished the moan that vibrated from her lips. "So damned perfect."

There were no more words after that. He hooked her booted ankles over his shoulders, tilted her body a fraction just to give him better access, dipped his head and tasted her sweetness.

She cried out at the first lap of his tongue and threaded her fingers through his hair to hold him close. But he wasn't going anywhere. This was her first time on the back of a mechanical bull and Jesse intended to make it the wildest, most memorable ride of her life.

He devoured her, licking and sucking and nibbling, pushing her higher and higher and, oddly enough, climbing right along with her. He took his own pleasure by pleasuring her and when she screamed his name and came apart in his arms, the feelings that rushed through him—the triumph and the satisfaction and the warmth—felt as good as any orgasm he'd ever had.

Chemistry, a voice whispered. They were simply good together. That explained her effect on him.

It wasn't because she was different.

Because she was his one and only.

That's what he wanted to think. But truthfully, he didn't just want to hoist her over his shoulder, take her back to the bed and drive deep, deep inside her deliciously hot body until he reached his own climax.

He wanted to curl up with her afterward, talk to her, laugh with her, hold her. He wanted to walk down Main Street, her hand in his, and let the world know that she was his. She always had been.

She always would be.

Need gripped him, fierce and demanding and intense. He gathered her in his arms and started for the office.

"What about your training?" she murmured against his neck.

"It'll wait."

THE MINUTE JESSE pressed her down on the bed, Gracie knew something had changed. There was an urgency, a fierceness about him that she'd never seen before. Tension held his body tight, every muscle taut. His hands felt strong and purposeful and desperate as he ripped off his clothes, spread her legs wide and slid home in one fierce thrust.

"You are the wildest woman," he growled, resting his forehead against hers for several fast, furious heartbeats. "My woman."

She didn't expect the declaration any more than the determination that glittered in his eyes as he stared down at her, into her. And she certainly didn't anticipate the pure joy that rushed through her.

Before she could dwell on the feeling, large hands gripped her buttocks and tilted. He slid a fraction deeper and all rational thought fled.

The next few moments passed in a frenzy of need as Jesse pumped into her over and over, as if his life depended on every deep, penetrating thrust. His mouth ate at hers, and his touch was greedy and hungry, as if he could no longer control his need for her. As if he'd stopped trying. They joined together on a basic, primitive level unlike anything she'd ever experienced before, and as she stared up into his face at his fierce, wild expression, she knew she'd driven him over the edge. Way, way over.

The realization sent a thrill coursing through her, followed by warning bells. But before she could worry over what the change meant, he slid his hand between them and touched her where they joined, and she went wild with him.

Seconds later she screamed his name for the second time that morning as her climax slammed into her and she shattered in his arms. Another fierce pounding thrust, and Jesse followed her into oblivion, her name bursting from his lips as he spilled himself deep.

"I love you," he groaned as he collapsed atop her, his arms solid and warm, his body pressing her into the mattress.

I love you.

The words echoed through her head and sent a swell of happiness through her for a full moment before Gracie remembered the last thing, the very last thing, she wanted from Jesse James Chisholm was his love.

Love? He couldn't… He wouldn't… No! This wasn't happening. Not him and her and *love*.

"I really have to go." She scrambled from the bed, her heart pounding furiously as she snatched up her clothes in record time. She retrieved her camera from the corral and then Gracie did what any responsible, dedicated community leader would do with a totally inappropriate, sexy cowboy who loved her right at her fingertips.

She ran for her life.

JESSE LISTENED TO Gracie's footsteps as she left the training facility and barely resisted the urge to go after her. He wanted to. He wanted to haul ass, toss her over his shoulder and keep her here forever. *She was his.*

Now and always.

But the thing was, she wasn't his. Not now. And, judging by the panicked expression on her face when he'd declared his feelings, *always* seemed pretty far out of the question, too.

Not that she didn't have feelings for him. She did.

She felt the same chemistry. The undeniable attraction. Even the companionship that came with being friends at one time and sharing a history. But love?

Maybe.

But if she did, it wasn't going to matter. She'd learned to put her feelings second, behind everything and everyone else in her life. She had too many people depending on her, watching her, judging her.

He knew the feeling.

He'd spent a lifetime being the object of everyone's scrutiny. Hell, he still was. Being escorted out of a bake sale, of all things, proved as much. It testified to the fact that there were folks in town who had no intention of forgetting who he was or what his father had done.

And James Lee and his granddaughters proved there were a few who couldn't care less about Jesse's past. A few who accepted him for who he was and what he'd done with his own life. Like Wanda Loftis who worked at the local pizza parlor. Wanda always gave him extra cheese on his pepperoni. A celebrity perk, she'd told him time and time again when he'd offered to pay, only she'd always given him extra cheese even way back when he'd been barely able to scrape together enough money to pay for a small to share with his brothers. And there was Mason Connor, the local pharmacist who'd given him free antibiotic samples that one time when Billy had caught strep back in kindergarten. And Miss Laura, the head waitress at the diner, who had his coffee and a great big smile waiting for him the minute he walked in on Saturday mornings. She'd given him leftovers too many times to count back when his daddy had been alive and food had been scarce. She'd helped him then, and she still had a smile for him when she spotted him now.

The realization sent a rush of warmth through him even though he'd learned a long time ago that the only opinion that really mattered at the end of the day was his own. It was nice to know he had a few supporters in Lost Gun. Friends even.

Which explains why you're still running away.

The minute the thought struck, he tried to push it back out. He wasn't running from anything. He was burying the past. Making peace. Moving on.

Running.

The truth struck, sticking in his head as he pulled on his clothes, parked his hat on top of his head, and headed outside to his pickup truck.

It was just this side of seven a.m. and he needed to get a move on. He had a meeting with Eli to tie up all the loose ends at the training facility—he'd sold all of his stock except for his one new bull and he needed to make arrangements for the old cowboy to look after it until he made arrangements for transport. That, and he needed to pick up the last few boxes of his stuff still stashed at Pete's ranch. Afterwards, he was going to head back into Lost Gun and swing by the motel to say goodbye to his brothers. Then it was just a matter of pointing his truck toward the city limits, pressing on the gas and getting the hell out of Dodge.

Once and for all.

He climbed behind the wheel and gunned the engine. It was the first morning of the rest of his life free and clear of his past. His lawyer had several prospective buyers on the list for his dad's run-down property. Hell, one of them had even made an offer. A damned nice one. Plenty for him to take his share and invest in his very own training facility closer to his spread in Austin. Maybe even buy one clear and outright for himself. Then when his heyday ended as PBR's number one, he could stop riding and start coaching the up-and-comers. That, or breed his own bucking bulls. He'd entertained that possibility, as well.

Either way, he had a solid plan.

One that had kept him up thinking and planning and dreaming on so many lonely nights.

It just didn't fill him with the same sense of hope that it once had. There was no rush of excitement. No sense of accomplishment. No flash of impatience to haul ass and never look back.

Instead, Jesse spent the next half hour driving out to the Gunner spread at a slow crawl that had even Martin Keyhole—the ninety-five-year-old owner of a nearby turtle farm—lying on his horn. Sure, Jesse tried to oblige and pick up his speed, but damned if his boot would stay down. There was just too much going on his head.

Because as much as he wanted to, he couldn't stop thinking about Gracie and the town, and the undeniable truth that whether he went after his own training facility or started breeding his own bucking bulls, he could do either of them right here. Even more, he couldn't shake the feeling that if he did leave, he would be running away from the best thing that had ever happened to him.

16

GRACIE PULLED OUT onto Main Street and took a whopping bite of the extra large fudge brownie she'd just picked up at the local bakery. Her second in less than fifteen minutes. She'd scarfed number one after three cups of coffee and a carob-covered scone from The Green Machine which had done nothing to touch the hunger that ate away inside of her. So she'd caved and walked into the bakery where she'd spent fifteen minutes listening to the clerk, Marjorie Wilbur, complain yet again about the pothole on the corner of Main and Hill Country before taking the rest of her order to go.

She hung a left at the first corner and waited for the rush of satisfaction that always came with even the smallest nibble of her favorite dessert, and the guilt. Especially the guilt. Anything to escape the feelings still pushing and pulling inside of her thanks to Jesse and his declaration.

The heat of the moment.

That's all it had been. Guys were notorious for it and so it should have come as no surprise. Hell, it was a wonder he hadn't proposed after the way she'd rocked his world.

That's what she told herself as she stuffed another bite into her mouth and tried to lose herself in the rich taste of chocolate and the all-important fact that she'd fallen off the wagon in a major way. Not one, but two brownies. She was a loser. A slug. She should feel terrible.

Not excited.

Or happy.

Or anxious to head back to the training facility, throw herself into Jesse's arms and beg him to take her away with him.

Yeah, right.

She hung a left at the second stop sign and eased onto her street. She had a life here with potholes to fix and a town that depended on her and a sister who needed her.

The minute the thought struck, she noted the familiar red Prius parked in her driveway. Charlie was home.

And Gracie wasn't.

She stifled a wave of guilt and pulled into the driveway. Stuffing the bakery bag under her seat, she snagged the camera and her purse and climbed out of the car.

"I thought you weren't coming home this weekend," she said when she walked into the living room to find her younger sister sitting cross-legged on the couch, her laptop balanced on her knees. The petite blonde, hair pulled back in a loose ponytail, wore a Texas Longhorns T-shirt, a pair of sweats and an expression that said *you are so busted.* "I would have had the blueberry pancakes ready and waiting had I known—"

"I'm not eating pancakes anymore," Charlie cut

in. "Too much processed flour. And I wasn't coming home this weekend. But you sounded funny when I last talked to you, so I got worried." She shrugged. "I drove in last night."

"*You* were worried about *me?*"

"You didn't sound like your usual neurotic self when I told you I wasn't coming home. No twenty questions about where I was going or what I was doing. No blasting me about being careful. I figured you were sick, but I'm starting to think it might be something else. Or someone else." A knowing light gleamed in her gaze. "You've been out all night."

"I was working late."

"I drove by City Hall. I didn't see your car."

"I wasn't at City Hall. I was at the Gunner ranch. I was helping out with the local newspaper. Their photographer is out, so I offered to take pictures at Pete's wedding for the About Town section."

Charlie didn't look convinced. "That would put you home at midnight."

"I wasn't tired so I drove over to the all-night movie festival in Milburn county."

"All-night movies, huh?" Charlie's fingers moved across the laptop keyboard for a few frantic heartbeats before her gaze narrowed. "The only all-night movie festival in Milburn is Kung Fu Movie Madness at the Palladium." She eyed Gracie. "Since when did you become a Bruce Lee fan?"

"Are you kidding? I love Bruce Lee." Gracie sat her purse aside and headed for the kitchen. "He's super athletic. Listen, I've got some fresh fruit if you're hungry…." Her words trailed off as she headed straight for the refrigerator and tried to ignore the rush of guilt.

"And since when do you take pictures?" Charlie shifted the subject back to the wedding as she followed Gracie into the kitchen. "You don't even own a camera anymore."

"Yes, I do. I just don't use it."

Charlie gave her a knowing look. "Something's up with you."

"Nothing's up." Gracie ignored the gleam in her sister's eyes and busied herself pulling several peaches and a crate of strawberries from the refrigerator. "I was just helping out. It's my job. I'm trying to beef up my public service presence before the inauguration. Speaking of which, I was planning on getting a new dress, so maybe we can go shopping next weekend—"

"It's okay, you know." Charlie leaned on the granite countertop and plucked a ripe strawberry from the container. "It's high time you got a life."

"I have a life, thank you very much." Gracie retrieved a container of yogurt.

"No, you don't." Charlie nibbled on the ripe red fruit. "You facilitate everyone else's life."

"I'm the mayor." Gracie set the yogurt on the counter and reached for two bowls in a nearby cabinet. "That's what I do."

"No, you're you." Charlie pointed the strawberry at her. "That's what *you* do. You make sure everyone else is happy and healthy, but you don't waste five minutes worrying over yourself." The words hung between them for a long moment before her sister added, "You deserve to be happy and healthy, too, you know."

"I am happy." And healthy. Or she had been before Jesse's impromptu declaration and the double dose of brownies. "I'm happy if you're happy."

"That's the thing." Charlie abandoned the half-eaten strawberry. "I have enough stress. Do you know how much pressure I deal with knowing that your well-being rests on my shoulders?"

Gracie thought of the past twelve years since her brother's death. "Actually, I do."

"Then you know it's not that much fun." A pleading note crept into her voice. "I was supposed to go with Aubry and Sue to Dallas to go club-hopping, but I bailed on them to drive here because I was worried about you."

"I wish you wouldn't have done that."

"I did it because I know you would do the same for me. I know you love me, Gracie. You don't have to keep trying to prove it."

"I just want you to feel it. Every second of every day. I want to be there for you—"

"That's the thing," she cut in, "you can't. Not all the time. Not because you don't love me, but because that's the way life is. It's a bitch sometimes and there are moments when things don't always pan out. I'm going to have to stand on my own two feet eventually. All by myself. Alone. That doesn't mean I'm lonely, but you are. Which is why I was thinking that we could sign you up for one of those online dating sites. A friend of mine's mother did it and she has a date every Saturday night—"

"Charlie, I'm not lonely."

"You went to an all-night Bruce Lee festival," Charlie pointed out. "You're beyond lonely. You're just this side of depraved. You need a man."

"Just because I don't have a man doesn't mean I'm lonely or depraved. I've got an entire town to keep me company." She eyed the dog wagging at her feet. "And Sugar, too."

Charlie bent down and picked up the ball of fluff. She gave the animal an affectionate scratch behind the ears. "You really think Sugar Lips, here, is a fitting substitute for a *man?*"

She thought of Jesse and the past few nights they'd spent together. She remembered the way he'd touched her and kissed her and laughed when she'd said something really funny. The way he'd looked at her when she'd talked about her past, as if he understood what she felt. As if he felt it, too.

And then she thought of the nights that lay ahead with Sugar curled up on her lap and the remote control in her hand and the latest reality show blaring on the TV.

"Which dating site was that?" she heard herself ask.

GRACIE SPENT SUNDAY morning trying not to think about Jesse. Or the all-important fact that he loved her and she loved him and he was still leaving. He hadn't said a word otherwise. No phone call. No text. Nothing but silence.

Not that it would have made a difference. She'd made her choice. Her life was here.

Which was why she'd dragged herself into City Hall to get a jump-start on her week. She had dozens of things to do before the inauguration in one week. Today alone she had to put in an appearance at the local tractor races, recite the Pledge of Allegiance at the weekly softball games and then dish up potato salad for the afternoon picnic at the Lost Gun Presbyterian Church. Even if she wasn't too keen on facing an entire town

full of people at the moment. She would do it anyway—
all of it—because it was her duty. Gracie had made a
promise, and she always kept her promises. *Always.*

But first...

She focused on the lime-green Hula-Hoop in her
hands and started to swirl her hips. A quick twist of
the hoop and for the next few seconds, she moved in
perfect synchronization with the plastic circle swirling
around her waist. But then it fell and she found herself
back at square one.

"Why are you doing this?" Trina asked when she
walked into Gracie's office to find her huffing and
puffing and sweating up a storm.

"Because I promised Sue Ann Miller that I would do
the Hula-Hoop for Hope with the rest of her Brownie
troop tomorrow afternoon. I won't buy much hope if
I can't Hula-Hoop for more than ten seconds a pop.
People pledge by the minute."

"I'm not talking about the Hula-Hoop. I'm talking about this." She motioned at the office surrounding them. "All of this. It's Sunday. A day of rest. You
should be sitting in your backyard, sipping a mai tai
and reading a romance novel or a glamour mag. Or
traipsing through the woods with that camera you love
so much."

"I don't use my camera anymore."

"Sure, you don't." Her eyes twinkled. "I saw you
last night at the wedding. The entire town saw you."

"That's different." She remembered all of the pics
of Jesse she'd snapped at the training facility after the
festivities. Pics that had nothing to do with what was
happening about town and everything to do with the
fact that she'd wanted to keep him with her. Not that

she was admitting as much to Trina. "I was filling in for June."

"You were enjoying yourself, which is what you should be doing right now. Instead, you're working. You're cooped up when you hate being cooped up. You hate going to city council meetings and old-lady breakfasts and monthly VFW luncheons."

"I don't hate it."

"You don't like it."

"I'm good at it."

"That's not the point. Aren't you tired of faking it?" Trina echoed the one question that had been nagging at her all morning.

She *did* hate playing the part of little Miss Perfect. Sure, she was good at it. She'd learned to be good at it, but she didn't actually *like* it.

She never had and she never would.

"It doesn't matter what I like or what I don't like. I'm still the mayor-elect."

"And as mayor-elect, you are more than capable of picking a replacement should you decide to retire early."

The meaning of Trina's words sank in and for the first time in a very long time, Gracie felt a flutter of excitement deep inside.

"I can't just give it all up." That was what she said, but where that statement had been true twelve years ago, it was no longer true now. Times had changed. *She'd* changed. She didn't have to keep playing the martyr. She knew that.

At the same time, she'd been doing it for so long that she wasn't so sure she could stop. Even if she desperately wanted to.

An image of Jesse pushed into her head and she remembered the possessive look on his face when he'd cut in to dance with her last night. He'd taken her into his arms and held her as if he never meant to let her go.

He'd also been tipsy thanks to the primo moonshine that had been circulating at last night's wedding.

She ignored the ache in her chest and focused on doing something—anything—to keep her mind off Jesse and the fact that he was leaving and she was letting him go. Without putting up a fight. Or telling him how she felt.

"Where are you going?" Trina asked when Gracie abandoned the Hula-Hoop and reached for her purse.

"I need to see a man about some moonshine."

"You really think Big Earl is cooking again?"

Gracie thought of the pint of white lightning she'd seen at the wedding the night before and then she thought of the way Casey Jessup had helped her great-grandfather into his chair. "I think it's his recipe, but I don't think he's the one doing the cooking."

Gracie's instincts were jumping and buzzing because she knew Casey had something to do with the case of white lightning at the wedding the night before. It was just a matter of proving it.

"MY GREAT-GRANDPA'S taking a nap. You'll have to come back later," Casey said when Gracie knocked on the door a half hour later, after another visit to the butcher.

"I'm not here to talk to him." She glanced behind her at the dogs busy devouring the raw meat before turning a pleading look on Casey. "I want to talk to you and I'd like to do it with all of my limbs intact."

Casey looked undecided for a split second before she shrugged and stepped aside.

Gracie retreated into the safety of the double-wide trailer. A faint snore drifted from a nearby bedroom, confirming that Casey, at least, wasn't lying about Big Earl's nap.

"I know you made the moonshine for him," Gracie said, turning on the young woman. "I also know that you aren't going to do it again—otherwise I'll be obliged to report you to the sheriff."

Casey looked as if she wanted to deny the accusation, but then she shrugged. "It's no big deal. It was just one batch."

"It's still illegal."

The girl glanced toward the open bedroom door. "But cooking makes him happy, and not much else does these days. He used to love his crosswords, but now he can't see the puzzle. And he used to love to watch his old Western flicks, but now he can't even do that because of his glaucoma. And he cain't cook either and enjoy a glass every night like he used to on account of he can't see or move around or do anything else like he used to. So I took his recipe and I did it myself so he wouldn't miss out on the one thing he can do, and that's drink. I just want him to be happy."

Enough to sacrifice her own freedom should she gt caught.

Gracie knew the feeling.

"I understand you did it for a good reason, but it's still highly illegal. You can't cook out here. He'll have to switch to beer or whiskey or something they actually sell in a store."

"And if he doesn't?"

"Then I'll have the sheriff arrest the both of you. Consider this your warning. No more cooking."

Casey nodded and Gracie knew she'd won this battle. But Big Earl was well over ninety years old and had acquired a taste for moonshine a long, long time ago. Even more, Casey was too devoted to deny the old man much of anything. And so Gracie wasn't so sure she was going to win this war.

Still, she intended to try.

"No cooking," she said again, and then she held her breath, darted out the door and raced for her car.

A HALF HOUR later Trina was on her fourth drink while Gracie worked on her second. They sat at a small table at a local sports bar that was all but deserted thanks to the softball game going on down at the ball field. Still, a few die-hard football fans sat in the far corner, as well as the entire ladies' sewing circle who were drinking peach schnapps and watching a rerun of *Bridezillas* on one of the monstrous TV screens.

Gracie's gaze swiveled away from a bitchy bride named Soleil just in time to see a pair of worn jeans moving toward her. Her gaze slid higher, over trim thighs and a lean waist, to a faded denim shirt covering a broad chest... Jesse. A straw Resistol sat atop his dark head, slanted at just the angle she remembered and making him look every bit the cowboy who'd stolen her heart.

"Shouldn't you be on the interstate by now?" she asked as he stopped next to her table.

"I forgot something." Jesse's gaze caught and held hers and his words echoed in her head.

"What?"

"You."

Joy erupted inside her, stirring a wave of panic that made her heart pound faster.

"I don't know what you mean."

"I want you to come with me." His gaze darkened. "Be with me. You don't belong here, Gracie. You and I both know that."

"You don't know anything. Sorry, Trina," she told her assistant as she pushed to her feet. "I need to get out of here." Before Jesse could reach for her, she started past him toward the nearest exit. Fear pushed her faster when she heard Jesse's voice behind her.

"Gracie, wait!"

But she couldn't. Not because he wanted her to go but because she wanted it. She wanted to chuck it all, throw herself into his arms, walk away and never look back. The knowledge sent a rush of anxiety through her and she picked up her steps. She slammed her palms against the exit door and stumbled out into the parking lot. Gravel crunched as her legs ate up the distance to the car.

"Gracie!" The name rang out a second before he caught her arm in a firm jerk that brought her whirling around to face him. "Gracie, I—"

"Don't say it!" She shook her head, blinking back the tears that suddenly threatened to overwhelm her. "Please don't say it again."

"I love you."

The tears spilled over and she shook her head, fighting the truth of his words and the emotion in her heart. "Let me go. I—I need to get back to the office. I've got work to do."

"Gracie?" Strong, warm hands cradled her face, his

thumbs smoothing her tears. "What is it, baby? Didn't you hear me? You know I love—"

"Don't!" Pleasure rushed through her, so fierce it stirred the fear and the panic and made her fight harder. She pushed at his hands. "Don't say those things to me. Don't make this situation any harder. You have to leave and I have to let you."

"If saying I love you makes it harder for you to let me go, then I love you, I love you, I will *always* love you." His eyes took on a determined light. "That's why I want you to come with me. I thought you'd be happy. I thought you wanted out of this town."

"You thought wrong."

"Did I?" His fierce violet gaze held hers, coaxing and tempting, and she came so close to throwing herself into his arms—to hell with Lost Gun.

Instead, she shook her head, clinging to her anger and her fear and the pain of hearing her sister cry herself to sleep every night after their brother passed away. Charlie had been so uncertain for so long, but Gracie had changed all of that. *She'd* changed.

While she wasn't the goody-goody she pretended to be and she was far from content, she still liked it here. She liked the people and the town and her house.

Her home.

"I'm not going with you. I made a commitment to the people of this town. I have a responsibility. I can't drop everything just because you say you love me."

"How about because *you* love *me?*"

She shook her head. "I don't. I can't."

No matter how much she wanted to.

She fought against the emotion that gripped her heart and made her want to throw all pride aside, wrap her arms around him and confess the feelings welling inside of her.

"It doesn't matter how we feel. It doesn't change the fact that you have to go and I have to stay. I *have* to." She yanked free and started for her car, steps echoing in her head like a death knell. Inside, she gunned the engine and took a deep, shaking breath.

Heaven help her, she'd done it. She'd done the right thing by giving Jesse the freedom he so desperately needed.

So why did it suddenly feel as if Gracie had turned her back on the one thing that mattered most?

Wiping frantically at a flood of hot tears, she chanced a glance in her mirror to see Jesse standing where she'd left him, staring after her, fists clenched, his body taut, as if it took all his strength not to go after her.

It was an image that haunted her all through the night and the rest of the week as Gracie wrote her acceptance speech and picked out a dress for the inauguration and prepared for the rest of her life.

Without Jesse Chisholm.

"LET HER LOOSE!" Jesse yelled, stuffing his hand beneath the rope and holding on for all he was worth. The two cowboys monitoring the chute threw open the doors. The bull reared and darted forward, nearly throwing Jesse, who held tight, riding the fledgling for the very first time.

He held on, his grip determined as the bull kicked and stomped and snorted against the feel of the weight on his back. Seconds ticked by as he bucked and twisted and made Jesse the proud papa of a brand-new bucking bull.

Cheers went up a few minutes later as he climbed off after a brief but exhilarating ride.

"You did good, boy," he murmured, wishing Pete could have been there. But he was off on his honeymoon with Wendy, making memories and babies.

A pang of envy shot through Jesse. While he'd achieved so much in his life, he was just getting started. He had years left on the circuit. Too long to be thinking about a future beyond.

A home. Kids. Gracie.

It was three days since he'd last seen her. Instead of hauling ass to Austin on Sunday, he'd gone back to the Gunner ranch to pick up some boxes and ended up staying the night. To think on things and try to get his head on straight. Then Monday had rolled around and his lawyer had called with two more buyers and Jesse had stayed to meet with the man and go over things later that day. And then Tuesday had rolled around and he'd had papers to sign. And Wednesday he'd had to accept delivery of the fledgling bull since Eli had made an appointment to get new glasses.

But tomorrow… Tomorrow was the day.

Jesse helped the hands get Ranger back into his chute. He'd just flipped the latch when he caught sight of a familiar car pulling into the parking lot.

He pulled off his gloves, exited the corral and started toward her. Gracie climbed out of the car and met him near the front entrance.

"You're here," he said, his heart pitching and shaking faster than a bull busting out of the chute.

"I heard you got delayed with the offers on your

place and so I thought I'd stop by before you finally do hit the road." She handed him a box. "I made it for you. Something to remember me by."

As if he could forget her.

She'd lived and breathed in his memories for so long and now she'd taken up permanent residence in his heart, and there wasn't a damn thing he could do about it.

There was, a nagging voice whispered. He could hitch her over his shoulder, load her into his pickup truck and haul ass for Austin. And when he got there, he could love her until she changed her mind and stayed. The heat burned so fierce between them it would be hot enough to change her mind. For a little while, anyway.

But then she would leave. He knew it. She belonged here and he didn't, and there wasn't a damned thing he could do about it.

His fingers itched and he touched her hand. Her gaze met his and he read the fear in her eyes, the uncertainty. As much as she wanted him to stay, she wanted to go. But she was afraid. Afraid to follow, to abandon the town that had embraced her when she'd needed them.

The same town that had shunned him.

He pulled his hand away even though every fiber of his being wanted to say to hell with Austin, to crush her in his arms and never let go.

He concentrated on opening the box.

A navy blue photo album lay inside, nestled in tissue paper. Jesse pulled the album free and turned to the first page to see several landscape shots of Lost Gun. The surrounding trees, the lush pasture, the historic buildings lining Main Street. He flipped through several more pages, saw more pictures of the town, including James Lee and the kids at the car wash and even one of each of his brothers. Billy two-stepped his way around the dance floor down at the local honky-tonk and Cole held tight to an ornery bronc.

"It's a memory book. I know you don't have good memories of your childhood, but these are new memories. Good ones to replace the old ones."

Jesse simply stared and flipped until he reached the last page, which held a full glossy of himself astride one of his training bulls. He swallowed the baseball-size lump in his throat. With stiff fingers he managed to close the book. "It's missing something."

She looked genuinely puzzled. "What?"

His gaze captured hers. "You."

"I don't think this is the right time—"

"Do you love me? Because if you do, I need to hear it."

Fear brightened her eyes, made her hands tremble, and for a split second, he thought she was going to turn and run without ever admitting the truth to him. To herself.

"Yes."

The word sang through his head, echoed through his heart. He wanted to hear her say it again and again, to feel the one syllable against his lips. "Then come with me. You don't have to stay here for your sister. She's all grown up now, living her own life. She doesn't need you here. The town doesn't need you."

"But I need it." Tears filled her voice, betraying the calm she always tried so hard to maintain. "All I could think about for so long was getting out. It's all I dreamed of. I wanted to hit the road, to find someplace where I felt at home. But once I stopped trying to run, I realized that I felt it here. This is home for me, Jesse. It'll always be home."

He stepped toward her and touched his mouth to hers. The photo album thudded to the ground. Jesse wrapped his arms around Gracie and held tight, as if he never meant to let go. He gave her a gentle, searing kiss that intensified the ache deep inside him and made him want to hold her forever.

She loved him, he loved her. This was crazy. They could have a life together starting now. Today. In Austin. Or here.

It didn't matter to him.

The realization hit just as she pulled away.

This was home. Gracie was home.

Her warmth. Her smile. Her love.

It was all right here, and that was why he'd been stalling. This was where he needed to be.

He needed to stay.

And she needed him to go.

Because he knew she would never forgive him if she thought that he'd changed his plans just for her. She would never forgive herself.

Maybe she would. Maybe she'd be happy he'd changed his mind and they'd live happily ever after.

It wasn't a chance he could take. He didn't want her feeling as though she'd destroyed his dreams. Trapped him.

He knew what it felt like to live with guilt. He wouldn't doom her to the hell he'd faced for so long. The doubt. The uncertainty.

"You know where to find me," he murmured against

her soft, sweet lips. "If you change your mind." While he knew with dead certainty that they were meant to be together, Gracie had to discover it for herself.

And if she didn't?

Jesse shoved his greatest fear aside and did the hardest thing he'd ever had to do in his life. He walked away from Gracie Stone.

And then he left Lost Gun for good.

"FORGET THE PICS at the bouncy house!" Trina motioned Gracie toward the large tent set up at the far end of the fairgrounds. It was the first day of the town's infamous three-week-long rodeo and barbecue cook-off, a huge event that drew tourists and fans from all over the state. "Cletus Walker is this close to breaking the record for eating the most bread-and-butter pickles. He's already eaten four hundred and twenty. He'll either blow or land himself in the *Guinness Book of World Records.* Either way, you're going to want firsthand shots."

Gracie clicked off two more shots of three-year-old Sally Wheeler sitting midbounce with her big toe in her mouth and rushed after the town's new mayor.

Rushed. That described her life over the past three weeks since she'd resigned as mayor, handed over the office to the new mayor-elect—Trina—and bought out June Silsbee's photography studio. June was now awaiting the birth of her triplets in peace. Meanwhile, Gracie was up to her armpits in work.

Between babies and youth sports and local chili cook-offs, she barely had time to look through her viewfinder before she was hustling off to the next assignment.

Not that she minded the whirlwind. She welcomed it

because it kept her busy. Too busy to think about Jesse and the all-important fact that she missed him terribly.

"Are you okay?" Trina asked as Gracie caught up to her at the entrance to the pickle-eating tent.

"Fine."

"Uh-huh." Trina gave her a quick once-over. "I'm the mayor, sugar. You can't put anything over on me."

"I think I might be coming down with something."

"Yeah, a bad case of the gimmes."

"What?"

"You know. The gimmes. It's when a woman's been getting some and then all of a sudden she's not getting any. She goes into withdrawal and her body is like, 'Gimme, gimme, gimme.'"

"That's ridiculous."

And all too true.

"I just need a little vitamin C and I'll be fine."

That was what she said, but she wasn't placing any bets. While she'd done the right thing and let him go, a part of her still wished that she had begged him to stay.

Not that it would have made any difference. He would have left anyway. He'd had to leave.

She understood that.

She just wished it didn't hurt so much.

She forced aside the depressing thought, made her way up to the front of the tent and focused on a red-faced Cletus, who eyed pickle number 421 as if it were a snake about to bite him.

She documented the momentous occasion as he devoured the last bite and lifted his arms in victory before making her way toward the corral set up at the far end of the fairgrounds. Dozens of rookie bull riders lined the metal fence, cheering on the wrangler atop the angry bull twisting and turning center stage. The preliminaries hadn't actually started, but the cowboys were giving it their all in a practice round that would pick the lineup for the main event.

She maneuvered between two button-down Western shirts and started snapping pictures.

She aimed for another picture and a strange awareness skittered over her skin, as if someone watched her. As if...

She glanced around, her gaze searching the dozens of faces.

It was just her imagination, she finally concluded, turning her attention back to her camera. Because no way in heaven, hell or even Texas could Jesse Chisholm be here—

The thought scattered the minute she sighted the familiar face in her viewfinder.

He'd stepped from behind a group of wranglers. The crowd milled around him and the noise rose up, but her full attention fixated on him. She watched as he talked to some cowboy who stood next to him, obviously oblivious to his surroundings, and her hope took a nosedive. For a split second, she thought that he'd come for her, that he was going to sweep her up into his arms and whisk her away.

Right.

He was obviously here for the rodeo. To ride his way straight to another buckle.

Without her.

The thought sent a burst of panic through her because as happy as she was here in Lost Gun, she could never be truly happy without him. She loved him. She always had and she always would, and it was time she owned up to it.

She'd made the last move and ended things with him, and now it was time to make the first move and set things right.

She pushed her way through the crowd, working her way around the corral until she came up behind him. A tap on the shoulder and he turned to face her.

Where she'd expected surprise, she saw only relief. As if he'd been waiting for her for a very long time.

He had, she realized as he stared deep into her eyes and she saw the insecurity, the doubt, the guilt. He'd been waiting for twelve years for her to admit her feelings, to tell the world, and now it was time.

Her gaze snagged on the weariness in his eyes and her heart hitched. "You look like hell," she said as she noted the tight lines around his mouth, the shadows beneath his eyes, as if he hadn't slept in days. Weeks.

"Nice to see you, too."

"You here to compete?"

"That, and I thought you might want these back." Two fingers wiggled into his jeans pocket and he pulled a familiar scrap of black lace from inside. He grinned his infamous rodeo-bad-boy grin that made her insides jump as he dangled her undies from one tanned finger. "These do belong to you, don't they?"

A few weeks ago she would have snatched the undies from his hand and stuffed them in her purse, desperate to keep up appearances and avoid any scandal that would disappoint the good folks of Lost Gun. But things were different now. She was different. She loved Jesse and she didn't care who knew it. She gave in to the smile that tugged at her lips. "They are, but I don't see that I need them at the moment. I'm wearing new ones."

"I know. I thought maybe we could make a trade."

"So you're collecting women's lingerie?"

"Just yours, Gracie. Only yours. I was hoping to add every damn pair you possess to my stash." Determination lit his eyes. "Just so you know, I might have retreated, but I'm not giving up. I would never try to force you to do anything. I've been staying away to let you know that I respect your decisions, and I'll keep staying away if I have to. If that's what you want." His fingertips trailed along her cheek as if he couldn't quite believe she was real. "Because you're what I want and I don't care who knows it."

"What about Austin? It's your home."

"You're home." His hands cradled her face, his thumbs smoothing across her trembling bottom lip. "Wherever you are, that's where I'll hang my hat."

"You hate it here."

He glanced around at the multitude of faces surrounding them. "I hate my past and the people who refuse to let me forget it. But not everyone here is like that. Miss Hazel is the sweetest woman who ever walked the planet, and she's here." He shrugged. "This place isn't so bad."

"But Austin is your dream. I can't ask you to give up your dream. I won't ask it."

Anger flared deep in his eyes as his mouth tightened into a grim line. "So you don't love me. Is that what you're trying to say?"

"No! I do love you. With all my heart. It's just…I don't want you making all the sacrifices." She shook her head and turned to stare at the bull kicking up dust in a nearby chute. "That's not what love is all about. It's about give-and-take. An equal amount of both."

"Meaning?" He came up behind her, so close she could feel the heat from his body, hear his heart beating in her ears.

"I'm pretty good with this camera," she told him. "I was thinking I could take some time off and follow you out onto the road. If you could use a good action photographer, that is." Her gaze met his. "I do want to live here, but I know you have a job that you love, one that takes you away for weeks on end. I don't want to be away from you that long." She caught his arms when he started to reach for her and held him off, determined to resolve the unanswered questions between them. "I'm willing to follow you—I want to follow you—if you're willing to follow me right back here when it's all said and done. Give-and-take. Fifty-fifty. You and me."

"What about your sister?"

"She's a big girl. She doesn't need me."

"I'd be willing to bet she still needs you."

She shrugged. "True, but I'm just a text away. So that's it. That's my offer. You let me go with you and I'll let you come back here with me."

He grinned, the sight easing the anxiety that had been coiling inside her. "I could use a new head shot or two," he declared as he drew her into his arms and hugged her fiercely. "To keep the fans happy."

"Not too happy," she said, her heart swelling with the certainty that he loved her as much as she loved him. "I don't share very well."

"Neither do I." His expression went from sheer happiness to serious desperation. "Marry me, Gracie, and we'll make a home for ourselves right here in Lost Gun.

You can take pictures to your heart's content and do anything that makes you happy, as long as we're together. I want you in my bed." He touched one nipple and brought the tip to throbbing awareness. "In my heart." His hand slid higher, over the pounding between her breasts. "In my life." His thumb came to rest over the frantic jump of her pulse. "Everywhere."

She smiled through a blurry haze of tears and pulled away from him to grab the hem of her sundress and run her hands up her bare legs.

His expression went from puzzled to hungry. "What are you doing?"

She smiled wider. "Giving you a deposit."

She shimmied and wiggled until her hot pink panties pooled at her ankles. Stepping free, she dangled the scrap of silk in front of him before stuffing the undies into his pocket along with the other pair already in his possession.

"Just so you know, there's more where those came from. A future of them. Forever." And then she kissed him, surrendering her body to his roaming hands, her heart to his and her soul to whatever the future held.

Right here in Lost Gun.

Epilogue

"You sure you want to do this?" Jesse asked Gracie as he braked to a stop near the fence that surrounded Big Earl Jessup's property. He killed the engine on the pickup and flicked off the headlights.

"No." Gracie tamped down on her anxiety when she heard the dogs start to bark and held tight to the hand of the man sitting next to her. "But Jackie Sue Patterson told Martin Skolnik who told Laura Lynn McKinney who just so happened to mention when she brought her twins into the studio for pics that she saw Casey Jessup at the hardware store yesterday. She bought two propane lanterns, some rope, a tarp and some tie-down stakes. That means she's cooking moonshine again and I'm the one responsible since I let her off with just a warning instead of turning her over to Sheriff Hooker."

He squeezed her hand reassuringly. "It could just mean she's going camping."

"Maybe, but maybe not. Either way, I need to find out. If something's up, we'll head back to town and I'll notify the sheriff." For Casey's own good.

While Gracie knew the girl was just helping out

her grandfather the only way she knew how, cooking moonshine was still illegal. And dangerous. And Gracie wouldn't be able to live with herself if something bad happened and someone got hurt.

She eyed the small house that sat several yards away. A television flickered just beyond one of the windows, but otherwise everything seemed quiet.

She whipped out her binoculars and scoured the area, from the old toilet that had been turned into a planter near the front porch, to the stretch of pasture that extended beyond the house. Her heart stalled when she noted the small light that flickered in the far distance.

"See?" She pointed and handed Jesse the binoculars. "It's her."

"It's definitely someone." He gazed at the horizon before handing the binoculars back to her. "I don't know that it's Casey."

"Who else would it be?" Gracie watched as the figure lifted the pinpoint of light and suddenly Casey Jessup's face came into view. "It's her." The young woman turned and walked toward the tree line, lantern in one hand and what looked like a shovel in the other. "I told you she was up to something."

"She's walking."

"Exactly."

"And carrying a light."

"Even more incriminating."

"Babe, she could just be going for a walk."

"At half past midnight?"

"Maybe she's meeting someone."

"To sell a few cases."

"Or to hook up." He shrugged. "It *is* one hell of a nice night."

She abandoned the binoculars to slide him a glance. Her heart hitched as her gaze collided with his and she felt the familiar warmth that told her she was sitting next to her soul mate. A man who loved her as much as she loved him. A man who always would.

She noted the gleam in his rich, violet eyes. "Since when did you turn into the eternal optimist?"

A grin tugged at his lips. "Since a certain buttoned-up city official whipped off her panties in the middle of town and handed them to me in front of God and the Amberjack twins."

Her own lips twitched at the memory. "I did give them something to talk about, didn't I?"

"Enough fuel to keep things interesting for at least another year." He winked. "It was definitely one of my most favorite moments."

"Glad I could renew your hope in mankind."

"Sugar, you *are* my hope." He leaned across the seat and touched her lips with his own in a fierce kiss that made her stomach quiver.

It had been a week since she'd handed her panties to him in front of an arena full of people and declared her love. A busy week since Jesse had changed his mind about selling his dad's old place and decided to clear the spot and build a brand-new house smack-dab in the middle of Lost Gun.

Not that he'd made complete peace with his past.

We're talking a week.

The recent airing of *Famous Texas Outlaws* had, as expected, lured a ton of tourists to town and stirred a wave of fortune hunting. And speculation. About the money. About Jesse and his brothers and their integrity. According to the latest round of gossip, they not only knew what had happened to the money, but they'd gone on a spending spree that included everything from new cowboy boots to a private island in South America.

Crazy, but that was the rumor mill in a small town. And part of the reason Jesse had been so desperate to get out of Lost Gun for good.

But while he'd yet to forgive the townspeople who'd made his life a living hell while growing up—the same people who were wagging their tongues and feeding the frenzy right now—he had managed to acknowledge those people who did accept him. Even more, he'd found the strength to forgive himself.

And so even though it had only been a week, the past didn't hurt quite so much. And when it eventually did, Gracie would be right there to soothe the ache.

She loved him and he loved her and they were now focused on the future. Lost Gun's infamous three-week-long rodeo extravaganza was in full swing. Jesse had swept the preliminaries and landed at the top of the leader board. Meanwhile Gracie had been named the official photographer by the board of directors of the Lost Gun Livestock Show and Rodeo. Her pictures had been featured on the front page of the weekly newspaper just yesterday and her photography studio was booked solid for the weeks to come.

Speaking of which, she had an early shoot tomorrow morning and the last thing she needed was to be traipsing around in the middle of the night.

At the same time, she would never forgive herself if something bad happened to Casey or Big Earl.

While she'd given up carrying the weight of the world, old habits were still hard to break.

Before she could pull back and tell Jesse as much, he ended the kiss, pulled his keys from the ignition and reached for the door. "Let's get this over with so that we can get on with our own hookup."

"Such a romantic."

"It will be, darlin'." He winked. "That much I can guarantee."

She tamped down the excitement the blatant promise stirred in her and reached for the door handle. A few minutes and a full stretch of pasture later, they reached a cluster of trees. They picked their way through the thick foliage, following the small light that glowed in the distance until they reached the line of trees that gave way to yet another pasture. The light grew brighter, illuminating Casey Jessup and the shovel in her hands.

Gracie watched as the young woman shoved the sharp edge into the ground, pushed it down with her foot and scooped a mound of dirt to the side.

"That doesn't look like a still to me," Jesse whispered against her ear.

"Maybe she's burying the evidence. People bury everything from money to time capsules. Why not moonshine?"

"Because the goal is to sell it, not bury it," he pointed out under his breath. "Something else is up."

He was right, Gracie realized as she watched Casey dig not one, but two holes. Then three. Four.

Forget burying something. The woman was looking. Desperately looking, her movements frantic, anxious, determined.

She finished another hole and let loose a loud cuss as she hit another dead end.

Still, she didn't give up. She went for yet another spot, her expression mad. *Mean.*

The minute the thought struck, something niggled at Gracie's subconscious. Her mind rifled back and she remembered the meeting with Big Earl and the Josey Wales poster on the wall. The quote echoed in her head, so familiar, as if she'd heard it somewhere before.

She had, she realized as she held Jesse's hand and watched Casey Jessup break ground at another spot.

When things look bad and it looks like you're not gonna make it, then you gotta get mean. I mean plumb, mad-dog mean. 'Cause if you lose your head and you give up then you neither live nor win.

It was the quote engraved on Silas Chisholm's headstone. It had been his favorite saying or so Jesse had told her when they'd visited his grave just a few short days ago.

He'd been a die-hard Josey Wales fan, just like Big Earl.

"They knew each other," she murmured, the words louder than she intended.

Casey's head snapped up and she turned. Her gaze locked with Gracie's and a dozen emotions rolled across her face. Surprise. Aggravation. Relief.

"He knew Silas, didn't he?" The words were out before Gracie could stop them.

Casey didn't look as if she meant to answer.

No, she looked ready to come at them, shovel swinging. But the anger quickly subsided as her gaze shifted to Jesse and something close to defeat filled her expression. She shook her head. "He didn't just know him. They were friends. Partners." She slung the shovel down and stuck a hand on her hip. "You said we couldn't cook anymore and we need that money." Her gaze met Gracie's. "I can't take care of Big Earl like I need to. He's got heart problems and he needs that money."

"What money?" Gracie asked, but she already knew.

And so did Jesse. "It wasn't lost in the fire," Jesse murmured after a long, drawn-out moment. "It's here."

Casey nodded. "Silas gave it to Great-granddaddy and he buried it out here for safekeeping."

"That's great." Gracie's heart pumped with the realization of what such a discovery meant. Recovering the money would put an end to the treasure hunting and the speculation. The money would mean real closure.

For the town, and for Jesse.

"Actually, it's not so great." Casey blew out a deep, exasperated breath and stared around her at the multitude of holes. "Great-granddaddy's memory isn't what it used to be. He buried the money out here, but the thing is, he can't remember exactly where." She glanced behind her at the endless expanse of land that seemed to stretch endlessly. "We've got fifty acres and the only thing he can remember for sure is that he buried it in some tall grass."

Gracie stared around, at the endless stretch of tall grass and trees and enough possibilities to keep Casey Jessup digging night after night for the rest of eternity.

"It could be anywhere," Jesse's deep voice echoed in the dark night, confirming what Gracie was already thinking.

That there would be no quick fix. No digging it up

and giving it back, and laying the past to rest for Jesse and his brothers.

Not just yet, that is.

* * * * *

A sneaky peek at next month...

Blaze®

SCORCHING HOT, SEXY READS

My wish list for next month's titles...

In stores from 17th January 2014:

❏ A SEAL's Salvation — Tawny Weber

& Texas Outlaws: Billy — Kimberly Raye

❏ Hard to Hold — Karen Foley

& Game On — Nancy Warren

Available at WHSmith, Tesco, Asda, Eason, Amazon and Apple

Just can't wait?

Don't miss your

Blaze®

March books

From 1st March 2014, Blaze stories will be available as eBooks only.

Blaze fans SAVE 20%

Don't miss our special eBook offer—enter promotion code **Blaze20** to save 20% on all Blaze titles.

Find out more at www.millsandboon.co.uk/Blaze

PLUS, don't miss our special Blaze website hub for your favourite authors, new reads and the latest news at

www.millsandboon.co.uk/Blaze

Tall, Dark and...Yours!

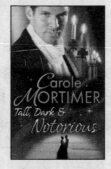

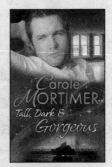

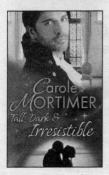

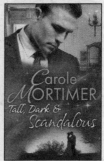

Get your hands on Carole Mortimer's fabulous
Tall, Dark and... collection.

Six stories, six delicious alpha males. Now all you
need to do is try and pick your favourite...

To buy the collection visit:
www.millsandboon.co.uk

The World of Mills & Boon®

There's a Mills & Boon® series that's perfect for you. We publish ten series and, with new titles every month, you never have to wait long for your favourite to come along.

Blaze.

Scorching hot, sexy reads
4 new stories every month

By Request

Relive the romance with the best of the best
9 new stories every month

Cherish™

Romance to melt the heart every time
12 new stories every month

Desire™

Passionate and dramatic love stories
8 new stories every month

Visit us Online

Try something new with our Book Club offer
www.millsandboon.co.uk/freebookoffer

M&B/WORLD3

Discover more romance at

www.millsandboon.co.uk

- ❤ WIN great prizes in our exclusive competitions

- ❤ BUY new titles before they hit the shops

- ❤ BROWSE new books and REVIEW your favourites

- ❤ SAVE on new books with the Mills & Boon® Bookclub™

- ❤ DISCOVER new authors

PLUS, to chat about your favourite reads, get the latest news and find special offers:

- 📘 Find us on facebook.com/millsandboon
- 🐦 Follow us on twitter.com/millsandboonuk
- ❤ Sign up to our newsletter at millsandboon.co.uk